RACHI
E\

RACHEL ETHELREDA FERGUSON (1892-1957) was born in Hampton Wick, the youngest of three children. She was educated at home and then sent to a finishing school in Florence, Italy. By the age of 16 she was a fierce campaigner for women's rights and considered herself a suffragette. She went on to become a leading member of the Women's Social and Political Union.

In 1911 she became a student at the Royal Academy of Dramatic Art. She began a career on the stage, which was cut short by the advent of World War 1, whereupon Ferguson joined the Women's Volunteer Reserve. She wrote for *Punch*, and was the drama critic for the *Sunday Chronicle,* writing under the name 'Columbine'. In 1923 she published her first novel, *False Goddesses*, which was followed by eleven further novels including *A Harp in Lowndes Square* (1936), *A Footman for the Peacock* (1940) and *Evenfield* (1942), all three of which are now available as Furrowed Middlebrow books.

Rachel Ferguson died in Kensington, where she had lived most of her life.

BY RACHEL FERGUSON

RACHEL FERGUSON

EVENFIELD

With an introduction by
Elizabeth Crawford

DEAN STREET PRESS
A Furrowed Middlebrow Book

A Furrowed Middlebrow Book
FM2

Published by Dean Street Press 2016

Cover by DSP
Cover illustration a detail from *Interior at Furlongs* (1939)
by Eric Ravilious

First published in 1942 by Jonathan Cape

ISBN 978 1 911413 75 2

www.deanstreetpress.co.uk

INTRODUCTION

A FAMILY – a House – and – Time. These are the ingredients whipped by Rachel Ferguson (1892-1957) into three confections – *A Harp in Lowndes Square* (1936), *A Footman for the Peacock* (1940), and *Evenfield* (1942) – now all republished as Furrowed Middlebrow books. Her casts of individuals, many outrageous, and families, some wildly dysfunctional, dance the reader through the pages, revealing worlds now vanished and ones that even in their own time were the product of a very particular imagination. Equally important in each novel is the character of the House – the oppressive family home of Lady Vallant in *A Harp in Lowndes Square*, comfortable, suburban Evenfield, and Delaye, the seat of the Roundelays, a stately home but 'not officially a show place' (*A Footman for the Peacock*). Rachel Ferguson then mixes in Time – past, present, and future – to deliver three socially observant, nostalgic, mordant, yet deliciously amusing novels.

In an aside, the *Punch* reviewer (1 April 1936) of *A Harp in Lowndes Square* remarked that 'Miss Ferguson has evidently read her Dunne', an assumption confirmed by the author in a throwaway line in *We Were Amused* (1958), her posthumously-published autobiography. J.W. Dunne's *Experiment with Time* (1927) helped shape the imaginative climate in the inter-war years, influencing Rachel Ferguson no less than J.B. Priestley (*An Inspector Calls*), John Buchan (*The Gap in the Curtain*), C.S. Lewis, and J.R.R. Tolkien. In *A Harp in Lowndes Square* the heroine's mother ('half-educated herself by quarter-educated and impoverished gentlewomen') explains the theory to her children: '... all time is one, past, present and future. It's simultaneous ... There's a star I've heard of whose light takes so many thousands of years to reach our earth that it's still only got as far along history as shining over the Legions of Julius Caesar. Yet that star which is seeing chariot races is outside our window now. You say Caesar is dead. The star says No, because the star's seen him. It's your word against his! Which of you is right? Both of you. It's only a question of how long you take to see things.' The concept of 'simultaneous time' explains why the young first-person narrator,

Vere Buchan, and her twin brother James, possessing as they do 'the sight', are able to feel the evil that haunts their grandmother's Lowndes Square house and uncover the full enormity of her wickedness. In *A Footman for the Peacock* a reincarnation, one of Time's tricks, permits a story of past cruelty to be told (and expiated), while *Evenfield*'s heroine, Barbara Morant, grieving for her mother, takes matters into her own hands and moves back to the home of her childhood, the only place, she feels, 'where she [her mother] was likely to be recovered.'

For 21st-century readers another layer of Time is superimposed on the text of the novels, now that nearly 80 years separates us from the words as they flowed from the author's pen. However, thanks to *We Were Amused*, we know far more about Rachel Ferguson, her family, and her preoccupations than did her readers in the 1930s and early 1940s and can recognise that what seem whimsical drolleries in the novels are in fact real-life characters, places, and incidents transformed by the author's eye for the comic or satirical.

Like Barbara Morant, Rachel Ferguson was the youngest of three children. Her mother, Rose Cumberbatch (probably a distant relation to 'Benedict', the name 'Carlton' appearing in both families as a middle name) was 20 years old when she married Robert Ferguson, considerably older and a civil servant. She was warm, rather theatrical, and frivolous; he was not. They had a son, Ronald Torquil [Tor] and a daughter, Roma, and then, in 1892, after a gap of seven years, were surprised by Rachel's arrival. When she was born the family was living in Hampton Wick but soon moved to 10 Cromwell Road, Teddington, a house renamed by Mrs Ferguson 'Westover'. There they remained until Rose Ferguson was released from the suburban life she disliked by the sudden death of her husband, who was felled by a stroke or heart attack on Strawberry Hill golf course. Fathers in Rachel Ferguson's novels are dispensable; it is mothers who are the centres of the universe. Rose Ferguson and her daughters escaped first to Italy and on their return settled in Kensington where Rachel spent the rest of her life.

Of this trio of books, *Evenfield*, although the last published, is the novel that recreates Rachel Ferguson's earliest years. Written as the Blitz rained down on London (although set in the inter-war years) the novel plays with the idea of an escape back into the security of childhood, For, after the death of her parents, Barbara, the first-person narrator, hopes that by returning to the Thameside suburb of 'Addison' and the house of her childhood, long since given up, she can regain this land of lost content. The main section of the novel describes the Victorian childhood she had enjoyed while living in 'Evenfield', the idiosyncrasies of family and neighbours lovingly recalled. Incidentally, Barbara is able to finance this rather self-indulgent move because she has made a small fortune from writing lyrics for successful musical comedies, a very Rachel Ferguson touch. What might not have been clear to the novelist's contemporaries but is to us, is that 'Addison' is Rachel Ferguson's Teddington and that 'Evenfield', the Morant family home, is the Fergusons' 'Westover'. In *We Were Amused* Rachel Ferguson commented that since leaving Teddington 'homesickness has nagged me with nostalgia ever since. I've even had wild thoughts of leasing or buying Westover until time showed me what a hideous mistake it would prove'. In writing *Evenfield* Rachel Ferguson laid that ghost to rest.

But what of the ghost in *A Harp in Lowndes Square*? Vere senses the chill on the stairs. What is the family mystery? Once again Rachel Ferguson takes a fragment of her family story and spins from it what the reviewer in *Punch* referred to as 'an intellectual ghost story'. The opening scene, in which a young girl up in the nursery hears happy voices downstairs, is rendered pathetically vivid by the description of her frock, cut down from one of her mother's. 'On her small chest, the overtrimming of jetted beads clashed …' This humiliation, endured not because the family lacked funds, but because the child's mother cared nothing for her, was, Rachel Ferguson casually mentions in *We Were Amused*, the very one that her own grandmother, Annie Cumberbatch, inflicted on her daughter Rose. 'The picture which my Mother drew for me over my most impressionable years of her wretched youth is indelible and will smoulder in me till I die.' Rachel

Ferguson raised the bar by allotting Sarah Vallant a wickedness far greater than anything for which her grandmother was responsible, but it is clear that she drew her inspiration from stories heard at her own mother's knee and that many of the fictional old lady's petty nastinesses – and her peculiarly disturbing plangent tones – were ones that Rachel Ferguson had herself experienced when visiting 53 Cadogan Square.

The *Punch* reviewer noted that in *A Harp in Lowndes Square* Rachel Ferguson demonstrated her 'exceptional ability to interpret the humour of families and to make vivid the little intimate reactions of near relations. Children, old people, the personalities of houses, and the past glories of London, particularly of theatrical London, fascinate her.' Rachel Ferguson's delight in theatrical London is very much a feature of *A Harp in Lowndes Square*, in the course of which Vere Buchan finds solace in a chaste love for an elderly actor (and his wife) which proves an antidote to the wickedness lurking in Lowndes Square. As the reviewer mentioned, old people, too, were among Rachel Ferguson's specialities, especially such impecunious gentlewomen as the Roundelay great-aunts in *A Footman for the Peacock*, who, as marriage, their only hope of escape, has passed them by have become marooned in the family home. Each wrapped in her own treasured foible, they live at Delaye, the house inherited by their nephew, Sir Edmund Roundelay. The family has standing, but little money. Now, in the early days of the Second World War, the old order is under attack. Housemaids are thinking of leaving to work in the factories and the Evacuation Officer is making demands. 'You are down for fifteen children accompanied by two teachers, or ten mothers with babies, or twenty boys or girls.' This is not a world for which the Roundelays are prepared. Moreover other forces are at work. Angela, the sensitive daughter of the family, watches as, on the night of a full moon, Delaye's solitary peacock puts on a full display, tail feathers aglow, and has an overpowering feeling he is signalling to the German planes. What is the reason for the peacock's malevolence? What is the meaning of the inscription written on the window of one of the rooms at the top of the house: 'Heryn I dye, Thomas Picocke?' In *We Were*

Amused Rachel Ferguson revealed that while staying with friends at Bell Hall outside York 'on the adjoining estate there really was a peacock that came over constantly and spent the day. He wasn't an endearing creature and ... sometimes had to be taken home under the arm of a footman, and to me the combination was irresistible.' That was enough: out of this she conjured the Roundelays, a family whom the *Punch* reviewer (28 August 1940) assures us 'are people to live with and laugh at and love' and whom Margery Allingham, in a rather po-faced review (24 August 1940) in *Time and Tide* (an altogether more serious journal than *Punch*), describes as 'singularly unattractive'. Well, of course, they are; that is the point.

Incidentally Margery Allingham identified Delaye 'in my mind with the Victoria and Albert', whereas the 21st-century reader can look on the internet and see that Bell Hall is a neat 18th-century doll's house, perhaps little changed since Rachel Ferguson stayed there. Teddington, however, is a different matter. The changes in Cromwell Road have been dramatic. But Time, while altering the landscape, has its benefits; thanks to Street View, we can follow Rachel Ferguson as, like Barbara Morant, she pays one of her nostalgic visits to 'Evenfield'/'Westover'. It takes only a click of a mouse and a little imagination to see her coming down the steps of the bridge over the railway line and walking along Cromwell Road, wondering if changes will have been made since her previous visit and remembering when, as a child returning from the London pantomime, she followed this path. As Rachel Ferguson wrote in *We Are Amused*, 'I often wonder what houses think of the chances and changes inflicted on them, since there is life, in some degree, in everything. Does the country-quiet road from the station, with its one lamp-post, still contain [my mother's] hurrying figure as she returned in the dark from London? ... Oh yes, we're all there. I'm certain of it. Nothing is lost.'

Elizabeth Crawford

AUTHOR'S NOTE

IF THE READER's taste lies in the direction of battle, murder, horrors and Hitler, or alternatively of cocktails, bedrooms and The Eternal Triangle, this is not the book for him, and I can only trust it may prove as much of a release to those who long for normal life to return and who despise not the day of small things as it has been to me to write.

It may well be objected that a family which, like the Morants, existed from the nineteen-hundreds to the nineteen-forties could not have evaded the Great War, especially with a son of military age. That evasion is deliberate. Too many of us are so sick of war in fiction that violent measures have to be taken to overcome what to all writers of chronicle stories is and will remain a very real dilemma.

R. F.

PART ONE

CHAPTER I

I

OF ALL OF US Morants I was to be the one who fell in love with our house: lived with it, was separated from it, re-united to it and finally parted from it by mutual consent. There was no legal separation, let alone a public divorce; we just discovered mutual incompatibility and it was, I see now, my fault from beginning to end. Certainly the house as my senior by over fifty years should have had sense for the two of us; on the other hand I, as the woman in the case, was the mental senior by probably as many years more as women so persistently are where wisdom is in question, and my affair with Evenfield was a boy-and-girl one, a childhood affection that should have turned out well since we knew the best and the worst of each other by the time that matters reached their climax.

My grievance against Evenfield was that it failed, at the last, to give me what I expected of it; its grievance against me was that I was too clinging, too romantic-idealist (which I knew already and spend my life fighting against in vain) and too fond of the sentimental scene for its own sake, when all that Evenfield probably wanted was to get on to the next change, to take things and families as they came and not to be confused with a castle in Spain when it made no pretensions to anything but mid-Victorian brick and slates and a reasonable amount of comfort.

Mother, in a burst of sub-acid facetiousness, once exclaimed to Mrs. Stortford, "'Evenfield'! *I* call it an uncommonly hard row to hoe!'; Marcus, my brother, apostrophized it as a 'dog-hole' when fresh from a wigging from father, while the servants complained that it was haunted and that their ankles were gripped when they filed up to the top floor to bed.

We made use of the house, and were robust with it, and it was left to me to enmesh it later in a net of nostalgic aspiration, pestering it with my solicitude and reminiscence which led in time to disillusion and discords and the end. I must have been aggravating to a decent house which only asked to settle at leisure on its foundations.

We shall, I think, never forget each other, but I feel at last, instead of merely considering, that we are better apart.

2

If Doctor James, who knows his bogeys so well, had written this book he would have called it *A Warning To Nostalgics*, and if it should prove a deterrent to even one human being's making the mistake that I did it will probably be a good thing, except that where that twilit condition of the mind, nostalgia, is concerned people *won't* be 'said' and prefer to die of it in their own way than to be cured by common sense. There ought to be a Nostalgics Club. The condition of entry would be a capacity for retrospective hankering, for your true nostalgic (fated wretch!) can be steeped in melancholia at a moment's notice for the price of a spray of lilac. Does not hot asphalt conjure up the whole of Ramsgate? And there is a turret staircase in Carisbrooke Castle smelling roughly of soapsuds, pipeclay and cold stone, yet climbing it I am back at one blow at school; once more I am twelve years old and drilling to battered operatic airs jingled out by a mistress at the piano.

If it comes to that, I was to discover, on first becoming a Londoner, that a box-room at Evenfield smelt of the Albert Hall, with the result that when I returned, grown-up, to the box-room I was irresistibly impelled to hum airs from *The Messiah* all the time I remained in it, while at the Albert Hall I missed whole tracts of the Oratorio through a sharp sensation of old trunks, and mentally tallying up their contents.

And nostalgia doesn't even stop there, for the person who suffers from it in its acutest forms can with the greatest ease be homesick for places he has never seen, suffer awareness of reigns he has never lived through, their pace and flavour, their slowness, colour and tediums, and know to his undoing the feel of life as it was lived in more spacious, gracious days in certain of London's streets and squares.

There is in Lowndes Square at least one mansion whose daily life, if I may put it so, I can imaginatively remember, both, oddly enough, as mistress and servant. I have certainly sensed some service in Bruton Street, and driven *home* down Arlington Street to a house which is now a club, while I cannot walk along Wilton Street without being instantly afflicted by a sensation of children's Christmas parties, knowing to the last detail that lapping warmth and safety which was the Victorian epoch – did not those very trees, chained and glittering with goodness and the lavish, emanate from the sentiment of the lonely Royal widow?

And for every party I have known and never seen, for every great house in which I have been ageing grande dame and cook (I hope I satisfied here!) one pays: pays for goods one has never handled nor owned, suffers vicarious longings for the unpossessed and unpossessable, and comes close to tears that are dismayingly of the present century.

And I am pretty sure all this is not re-incarnation, or second sight, but nothing more complicated than some mental affinity, a facet of universal memory, perhaps, of which we, of the company so sadly, delightfully doomed, are heirs.

But it is futile to continue. Those who know will eternally know and those who don't will continue not to understand. Their minds are like a pavement under a noonday sun, heedless of the shadow that is past and the shadow that is to come.

3

I have usually found that to get a thing down on paper robs it of its force at once, and all my life I have made a list of present worries or pleasures to come and crossed them off as they settled themselves, as one does the card or calendar people on one's Christmas list. When system comes in at the door depression flies out of the window, or so I have found. Sometimes I come across an old overlooked worry-list. The items on one ran:

1   Row with A.
2   No letter from C.
3   Tooth.
4   Look for green overall again.
5   No ideas for magazine story.
6   What D said last week (Wed: 7th).
7   People I ought to be dining.

And I am harassed this time by occasional total failure to remember who the 'C' of the missing letter was or what the deuce 'D' had 'said', which only shows that if you sit tight long enough nothing matters at all, while I know that this particular brand of philosophy is no good and never will be to people like myself. One must live. And worrying is probably a part of the business and a sign that one is still in the swim! It is rather the same thing with old letters that you re-read. Like a rude, whispering couple who exclude you from the conversation, they indulge in allusions you can't trace, hint at emotions you can't recall, and make infuriating plans of the outcome of which your mind is a complete blank. 'Who is this stranger hissing in a corner?' one despairingly thinks, and it is oneself, as little as five years ago. And as for the letters dating further back, you get well-nigh to the stage of begging the correspondence to let you in on the conversation, to give you at that moment a little of the love expressed for you in the letter of which you are dimly jealous! You almost whimper, 'It's Barbara asking my best friend, in those days', and it's no good at all. The Barbara of the note excludes the Barbara who holds it in her hand (though you feel she would be miserably remorseful, eagerly, tenderly explanatory, if you did meet again). Meanwhile, you are left hiding a secret from yourself, and a most extraordinary and forlorn sensation it is.

CHAPTER II

I SOMETIMES wondered at what time of year we first moved in to Evenfield. Was it when crocuses appeared sparsely round the rose-trees that bordered the lawn of the gravel drive and even cropped up (more sparsely) at the foot of that contraption like a small pillar-box with a grille'd glass window whose purpose baffles me to this hour and about which I refuse to enquire on the grounds that as I didn't know in my peak-time of happiness I will not know at all lest I am disillusioned? Or did we move in in high summer when dust begins to settle on the pollarded limes in the avenue facing a turnip-field opposite which Evenfield is set? Somehow, this hardly seems likely because of the seaside holidays. Autumn, then? The time of dripping dahlias in that border by the greenhouse, and of green 'cookers' that thumped overnight from the apple-trees aligned at the bottom of the garden, of tipsy swathes of michaelmas daisies, of the premonitory smell of fireworks, and of hot toast rising to the nursery from the drawing-room where mother sat with Mrs. Field, fortifying herself, bless her, against an approaching assault upon the classics lest she become as static as the turnips over the road.

When I was seven they were, I remember, 'doing' *The Inferno*, and I remember that I was seven because our current cat died two days later and so remained my senior by what sounded like a year by the skin of his teeth. On the other hand, the purport of the murmurings from the two women side by side on the sofa did not reach me for quite twenty years, by which time I had acquired a smattering of Italian myself, and fluked quite unintentionally upon the spoken line quoted in a modern novel, and realized with a shock what they *had* been at, and wondered if they liked it and felt quite certain they didn't, but were simply using Dante as a stick with which to beat the mongrel dog that was suburban existence.

If we moved in in the winter, it could have been in one of those pea-soup fogs that crept up the Thames Valley and with which I shall eternally associate the real (dried) pea soup that appeared under the light of incandescents upon the dining-room luncheon table – a generous brew, redolent of bacon bones, studded with sippets and sprinkled with mint, and followed invariably on Mondays by the cold sirloin and a rather clammy, morbid combination of beetroot salad and hot baked potatoes in their jackets.

And, on the day we moved in, what were those people doing whom we came to know so well? That again (like the old letters) is a for ever hidden secret. Was old Stiles, the jobbing gardener, going off to his midday dinner? Did he wonder as he stumped along what the Morants were going to be like as employers, if there were children, and if so whether they would trample his onion beds and pull his radishes untimely? Was dear Mrs. Field of the Dante readings returning to her house, Cumptons, from a morning's shopping? What, if it came to that, was *our* cook preparing for us, and what her comments upon kitchen, larder, scullery and pantry? What her reactions to a coal-cellar the size of a room that opened off her sink, to her outside w.c. or to that appalling open wooden dustbin into which the men had to climb to remove the rubbish, which could never be cleaned out properly, and in the summer smelt to heaven? For not only can I never glean from family or friend the hour of our arrival, but not a soul could vouch for the time of year that the house became ours. This has always struck me as quite incredible of my family. The only consolation is that I could not possibly have appreciated the wet dahlias or the yellow fogs, the dusty lime-trees and the red suns (or red currants) whenever it was that the front gate opened for the very first time to admit us all, because I was a baby in arms – in whose arms I can't discover. But I wonder if that house, viewing the procession advancing up the drive or (surely?) being conveyed in station flys, glanced with prophetic interest upon the probably angry bundle that was myself, sensing in the very mortar of its bricks that here, in point of fact, Came The Bride ...

Two facts about the settling-in process are on record (two! out of thousands now lost for ever!). Item: (1) that the furniture vans were all behind schedule and the men still about the rooms when we got there and had to be regaled with tea out of mantelpiece vases, since the cups were still unwashed and largely unpacked, and (2) that Mrs. Stortford, another dear who was to be auntie S to us for the rest of her life, said to mother, 'Let's get baby's chair into the nursery, then it'll begin to look like home'.

My poor little mother! To her, neither that river-town of Addison nor Evenfield ever became anything but a prolonged and abominable phase. For she was born to the life of the fashionable London square, the dinner party and the striped awning, the before-dinner pageant of Hyde Park, the chiffon sunshade and the house-party. And she sold out for a voice, a turn of phrase, a different mental outlook.

The *wreckage* that attraction can achieve! She could have married an archbishop, an ambassador, a doctor who was Physician Extraordinary to Queen Victoria, and I often wonder, if she had, what difference it would have made to us. Should I have become a Deaconess in what Louisa Alcott described as 'a mortified bonnet', or a hospital Matron, a Continental vamp, or merely a successful London hostess who furthered the careers of promising young attachés? Or should I have, somehow, contrived to remain myself through all the hazard of maternal mating? For of course mother was the dominant partner in the final Morant marriage as women so often are, without being remotely aggressive in the process. And in living for our happiness at Evenfield, out of inverted apology for it, I think, now, that she lost touch with her own contempts and, in my case, succeeded so well in endearing the house and garden to me that she let me in unwittingly for all I was to endure later.

2

One begins to catch up with the life of a house at about nine years old; from then on, memory becomes roughly consecutive. I can't mentally bridge the gap between complete illiteracy and being, overnight as it seemed, able to read: on the other hand I can capture two impressions of being in my perambulator and a fantastic one of being in a two-foot-by-one bath before the fire. And there was the afternoon on which one tied one's first bow and struck one's first match (both in mother's room by the dress-

ing-table), and the adventure that was taking one's first bath alone
– self-soaped, without the nurse!–while father, mother and sister
dined a flight below. And an envious curiosity as to what they ate
and did, and a hiding beneath the table while the gong (of brass,
cheese-plate size, which, I was to discover later when cocktailing
a musician friend, was in E above the treble clef) tintinnabulated
the feasters from their bedrooms: and of how I lost the courage
of my mild naughtiness at the very start and crawled out to be
discovered and embraced and sent upstairs.

CHAPTER III

I

MOST PLACES go through cycles. What Addison had been before
we knew it I don't know. Even as it stood, my mother rejected
half of it, primed as she was with London standards; for some
people remain inexorably suburban wherever they settle. It is a
state of mind, not geographic entirely, as the snobs believe. And
then, too, the era was against her. We had, for instance, only just
got round to trams by the time we left Addison: the motor-bus
which bundles you comfortably to town in forty-five minutes
was in the future, and so the Addison residents stewed in their
own placid juice.

It threw them upon their social resources and the place fairly
burst with Progressive Whist for prizes of repoussé objects featuring The Angelic Choir, with badminton clubs in the Parish
Room, with Shakespeare readings in drawing-rooms, Book Teas
and The Afternoon Call. Tennis was still a game and not a dog-
fight but was definitely left to the young women who had come
out and who played on the grass courts of their own gardens.
Golf was for the elderly and the business week-end, and the children bowled hoops in contentment in the Park, shaded in summer by the horse-chestnut avenue, nudged in autumn by the deer
who ate the nuts from their hands when they weren't locked in

battle with each other and having to have their antlers sawn off by keepers.

The ages of my brother, sister and me were all over the place. Marcus was ten years older than I, two years the senior of Melisande, which meant that Marcus was always at Winchester when I was in the nursery and that one met him mainly on the stairs or in seaside lodgings. I never thought of school terms and accepted his intermittent appearances among us as I did the atrocious pattern of the hall wall-paper which looked like a bad thunderstorm in a forest of fir-trees which grew pineapples.

Poor Marcus hated his name and said it was like the sound that would be made by a crocodile eating sugar almonds, and father, turning purist as he so often did, took him up on this in a twinkling and said it was a far-fetched simile and that all similes should have a basis of probability, which so annoyed Marcus that he went out into the garden and broke the kitchen window playing golf with a walking-stick and a windfall pear. He was very morose, at sixteen, because he was in love with Ada Reeve, and in the Christmas holidays he climbed out of a back window to go up to town to see her in a musical comedy and came back in a fog and was sermonized and Old Testamented by father.

My sister Melisande wasn't too pleased with her own name, either, and it didn't appease her in the least to know that she was named after one of those swoony and probably fated lovers that mother lapped up and enjoyed, and even went to the Coronet Theatre, Notting Hill Gate, to see portrayed by Sarah Bernhardt and Mrs. Patrick Campbell. So quite soon the family called my sister Mell and my brother Cuss, because he objected to Mark as being noble and Biblical and pi-jaw. I only wonder that I didn't get called Beatrice in compliment to the Dante readings, which is a name that should be reserved for cooks and oil-stoves, but luckily I escaped with Barbara after a great friend of mother's, and as nicknames rained on me from the start, I only realized in my 'teens that I was Barbara at all, and even to-day certain people retain the old names, so that whereas I am always Ara to the Fields, I am Babby to my old nurse, Babs to the relations, and Bunt or

Buggins to the family. The gardener for some unearthly reason called me Miss Bobbin from the beginning, and stuck to it.

Father, poor wretch, never achieved a nickname from any of us, and mother was somehow above all that kind of thing for very different reasons. We all found it quite impossible to take father seriously because he did all the taking there was, in advance, and I cannot express the prevalent feeling better than by mentioning that when I was about nine I went to mother and asked, 'Is father your husband?' and was quite unnerved to find that this indeed was the case as it seemed to put some barrier between her and ourselves that in all other matters was non-existent. She had, as we should say now, let down the side!

In time, Cuss and Mell and I discovered that the only possible way to take father was to pretend he was somebody else, when sent for by him, or at table, or during the hazard of selection of a son or daughter for the Sunday walk after church. Whom he should figure as depended upon your general knowledge, tastes and reading, and the latter depended upon age. Thus, to Marcus, father was Lord Chesterfield and (when father's homily had been unduly prolonged, or the bad temper induced by love-pangs for Ada Reeve or Ellaline Terriss unusually sharp) Charles Peace, and once, when father had boxed his ears, Jack The Ripper. To Mell, father was in turn Napoleon, Nero, Mr. d'Arcy and the Reverend Patrick Bronte. To me, he was 'The Procession', from Lord Mayor's Day once seen by me on a jaunt to London, for father contrived to suggest pomp and circumstance no less in his conversation than in walk and manner, and our meal times were apt as a result of these conflicting creations to be a perfect maelstrom of cross-purposes, with all three of us acting our relative parts to the head of the house; Marcus being excessively polite and formal if father was at the moment Lord Chesterfield, and even calling him Sir, Mell being exaggeratedly gentle and solicitous about the salt and pepper when he was old Mr. Brontë, or bright and playful (Mr. d'Arcy), or anxious and browbeaten (Nero), while I stared, fascinated, every time father opened his mouth, seeing behind his chair two gorgeous flunkeys in aguillettes and plush, while mother, who knew our game, sat torn between apprehension and giggles at the foot of the table. Father sensed nothing, beyond the fact that we seemed to be behaving unusually well. Of course it was, between giggles, anxious work for mother, for we three *were* on thin ice with father and, as she said in going over old times in after years, she never knew when or if the thaw of paternal perception would set in, and father, so to speak, be rendered unfit for skating!

Father believed he was fond of us. Actually, in common with so many men of the period, he was merely cowed by the weight of that mid-Victorian sentimentality in which he himself had been reared, and had children for the look of the thing as he wore a top-hat and ate sausages for breakfast and roast beef for luncheon on Sunday, voted Conservative and paid a yearly visit to the Royal Academy before a month at the seaside. After all, what man in his senses could honestly want a schoolboy, a nurse and a baby as housemates, particularly the bookish kind of man that father was? But having been landed with them, he did the only possible thing, and got round a nasty corner by sheer self-deception. It's no use deliberately setting to work to have people who will slam doors and give notice and cry in the night and be sick on your waistcoat if you're going to waste half the rest of your life resenting them. But what a relief these fathers would have found in doing so! As it was; they were uniformly kind and misunderstanding and misunderstood, and deferred to and avoided and imposed on and indulged and managed. To their children they were Look Out! and Cavé! and Oh Lor! and to their wives If Only, Oh Dear Me, Why Can't He *See*, They Didn't Mean To, Henry, and Well, I'll Speak To Cook About It.

Father wrote essays and biographies, but as leaven to this regrettable eccentricity, this mental frivolity and high-kicking over the traces of convention, his real work was in the City, where he was a senior partner in the firm of Halliday, Morant and Fusting, solicitors. Of this occupation, all we knew was that he was suddenly not in Evenfield after breakfast and was as suddenly in the billiard room after tea, while the perquisites of office that came our way were foolscap sheets of a satisfying gloss eminently suited to noughts and crosses, the writing of plays and novels, the drawing of dragons and caricatures of nurse and cook and house-parlourmaid, plus bunches of pink tape, paper-clips and nibs. They really *did* understand waste in 1900! Beside them, our modern efforts pale and dim.

What father did in his office it never even occurred to us to enquire. To us, it existed only for London's pageantry, seen from his windows, with a lavish luncheon laid out in the room at our back and the clerks' quarters converted into cloakrooms for my frilled organdie sun-hat or Mell's gaiters and sealskin cap, and mother's odds and ends and fur, shoulder-length cape with its cauliflower collar which dished up her little face as a *pâté* in its terrine, or for the sailor hats and mufflers of our contemporary Addison cronies, according to the time of year. Father always did the thing well. Sometimes there was an invited sprinkling of the come-out young women, those, by us, seldom glimpsed persons who by rumour played tennis on their own lawns. Others lingered in my mind for an isolated sentence quoted in my family, as did Johnnie Lawnford, the Doctor's son, who, questioned by father in the homegoing train from Waterloo about the eminents he had picked out in the procession, eagerly stuttered, 'I saw Sir Michael Pig's-Speech!'; and his elder brother, Chetwyn, who exists for me to this day by a rumour that he had once pelted the errand boys with manure from the top of his garden wall, and who, as a result, through all the years will be astride that wall, pelting. Or there was 'Baby' Irmine who lived at the end of our road, whose alleged ringworm penetrated our nursery from below stairs and who, for me, and because I heard about it at seven years old, will go through life with that complaint ... other children existed, largely, through the shape of their front doors or the tested goodness or badness of their schoolroom teas and toys.

Once, in father's office, a male appeared whom father addressed as 'Ha, Clifford!', as we gazed down upon the teeming street, its good-natured hucksters selling red, white and blue souvenir handkerchiefs and coloured paper tiddlers. Ha-Clifford was comparatively stricken in years (he must have been quite nineteen), and turned out to be the elder brother of freckled Jacky Barstowe, at whom I once threw a stone in the Park because I was disgusted with the shape of his hat, which was a large, white, three-cornered felt with a rosette. We Morant children knew vaguely that the creature had brothers but they had for us no existence at all. And it wasn't for nearly thirty years that I assimilated the fact that Ha-Clifford and I had once shared a Royal Progress.

2

In that large, scattered riverside town-village, with its roomy houses, comfortable gardens, its failures to be entirely sophisticated or completely rural, and its intermittent London accessibility, we in a way knew everybody without being intimate with the majority. Mother saw to that: hoping, as I now believe her always to have been, eternally for a final escape with us that we might not stagnate. Her social picksomeness together with an inevitable nodding-acquaintance put the whole place for us in our pockets.

Sociably inclined and always interested in people of all ages, whether in children of sixty or adults of sixteen, I strayed to many a door marked Lord Have Mercy Upon Us, a habit which mother made no attempt to check, knowing that children, particularly in the summer, are licensed bandits, guessing no doubt that her cool smiles and dreadful politeness to detrimentals would act as deterrent to any attempts on the part of the naow-and-haow brigade to press to intimacy, as indeed proved to be the case. And as for the accent question, there was never any danger of any of us parroting a twang in a house like ours where father was ever in lurk, from the literary point of view, to put our sentences twice through the mincer before they were passed as fit for table.

Woe to the daughter who stated that she had cut her bun in 'Half'; curs't be the son who asked 'Can' he go to the cricket match?; while the very sideboard groaned at a split infinitive, and once when Mell said, 'What do you mean to infer?' father's lecture upon the misuse of the word, together with his astoundment at an illiteracy of such magnitude emanating from a member of his family, concluded, 'As soon should I expect a daughter of mine to spit into the butter-dish', at which Marcus unfortunately burst out laughing and was sent from the dining-room.

Yet when father set out on a progress of facetiousness, we, like Queen Victoria, were unable to be amused. In the cold months he would ask one of us to 'put a semi-coal-on', and would sometimes pace the dining-room, declaiming:

> I would if I could
> If I couldn't, how could I?
> I wouldn't, unless I could,
> Could I? Could you?

which for a period Mell and I thought was Shakespeare, and discarded in advance. On the other hand, his non-comprehension of children was so complete that he rounded the circle by treating us at times as if we were his own age, and would enter into details of the most harrowing illnesses of his friends, garnished with medical terms and revolting symptoms, or favour us with his vigorous views upon the decadence of French Courts and kings' mistresses according to the biography he was in labour with at the time and during which he became positively Biblical in his outspokenness, giving me, at ten, the present of the word Strumpet, which for a long time I confused with muffins, by which I came to believe that King Louis consistently over-ate and knew I was right when father dismissed him as being 'a fellow of gross appetites'. I liked food as well, and. went to find mother (who was in the pantry, washing some porcelain tea-cups that she never would trust to the servants, as the cups were sprinkled with hand-painted flowers and banded with English gold) and asked, 'Would you say that I am a Strumpet?'

She stopped and considered and looked slightly harassed, and was, if I know her, weighing the question of blame and the direction in which to cast it, upon kitchen or my too catholic visiting list? But the query enlarged upon, it was her turn to go out into the garden and yell, and the episode comfortably closed with the caution, '– but don't say it at parties'.

The words one must not say at parties included, according to one nurse, Stomach and Flea, and (the same mentor), No child must ever make open request for the lavatory but must ask 'May I sit down?' As one was frequently sitting down at table, conjuror, or Punch and Judy show or even musical chairs, the request too often ended in a hopeless impasse bred of misguided gentility and hospitable bewilderment. About the forbidden words, Mell made a verse which we recited in duet, marching round the nursery, fingertips on shoulders, and dipping deeply at the end of each alternate line:

> Strumpet and Stomach and Flea
> Went for a walk on Salisbury Plain
> Walking by three and by three
> And they never were seen again:
> Oh never, oh never again.

When we quarrelled, we would hurl phrases at each other of no known origin but of a quality quite admirably enraging. We knew! Not for us the popular epithets of abuse; to be termed a duffer, fool, ass, pig, left us unmoved. But if Mell wanted to make me cry with impotent fury she would recite abstractedly,

> Drink in a Bournemouth cup
> With a hat like a bon-bon block!

while Mell could be rendered purple in a moment if I retaliated in a quick-time march,

> They called her *Thun*der Of The Lord!

or, with a rhythmic stamping of one foot upon the floor or any likely surface,

> Sweets, tea and *su*gar
> And *large* hunks of *bread*,
> *Along* came *Meli*sande *expect*ing to be *fed*!

3

But, allied again, we pooled our resources against the residents, by prose and verse.

There was a certain Miss Dove, often seen by us in church, of a quite spectacular piety, who curtsyed when the congregation rose at the entry of the vicar and choir. Miss Dove lived heaven knows where and I don't know now and she was to us a Sunday figure alone. Because she was so good and looked so plain with primness, we named her Lucilla, and Mell, at seventeen, committed her to paper.

> Who the world's lusts has quite resigned
> And tulle round last year's hat doth wind
> With starfish dead clapped on behind,
>   Lucilla.

Or there was Sheppard, a verger, who, father, horrified, confided to us had 'too great a liking for the bottle', and of whom we made a carol based on *When Shepherds Watched Their Flocks By Night*, and which began,

> When Sheppard scoffed his Scotch by night
> Depleted was his pound,
> The angel of the rye came down
> And laid him on the ground.

There must, in that large and High Church assembly, have been quite a number of those whose social cause the vicar professionally canvassed among the established residents on the grounds that they were 'sweet little women', a description which ruled them out from the start with a lot of us, the feeling being that clergymen, bound in charity to everybody, must broadly speaking lose sight of what was what, which was recognized and countered by the obdurate who saw that vicars, being out of their homes three-quarters of the time themselves, left the hospitable donkey-work to their females, and that, being a clergyman's household, they had to recognize any caller in any case. For Lucilla, I hear, wasn't the only adorant and remorseless penitential: there was something about the vicar's direct ugliness which set a dozen of irretrievably respectable women to combing their scanty histories for some remembered sin that might be of interest to him, and the road wound uphill all the way, yes, to the very end, poor wretches. As well play tiddleywinks with Savonarola! Mell and I, having no emotional fish to fry, secured his friendship and attention from the start.

But to offset his personal rigours, the services at St. Anselm's were of a pageantry which had once caused me to whisper to mother as he toddled, stiff with brocade and embossments in gold thread, to the altar, 'Is he the Fairy Prince?' And I really believe that if a demon had sprung in red limelight and sequins from the pulpit we should not have been surprised. For on high days and festivals and saints' days there were processions and banners and pairings-off and bowings and censers and red lamps and thunderous marches from the organ and even a string orchestra from among the personnel of the senior girls from the High School, among which, later on, Mell, concealed behind a pillar, played second violin with a stocking tied round her eye because her strings were always bursting. The choirboys were as well drilled as ballet girls and were forbidden to march in step round the church as foot rhythm was considered irreverent, or inartistic or secular, so they wavered and stumped and teetered behind a huge silver crucifix borne by the verger, which old Mr. Grimstone (who lived at The Moorings by the river) had presented, together with a bottle of Jordan water from a tour of the Holy Land. In Holy Week the church was steeped in purple and swathed in black like a *rusée* widow, and concluded with Tenebrae, about which I questioned mother, who answered, 'Oh, they turn all the lights out one by one and you trip over your umbrella'.

At Easter, the scent of the lilies made people faint in rows, especially those *devotes* who, like Lucilla, arrived on a systematically empty stomach. The banners when not in use were propped all down the church against the pillars, and I can see the needlework faces and robes of every single saint upon them to this day, far more clearly, indeed, than I can see the face of my mother as she was at that time. The clarity of the mind's eye has apparently nothing to do with degree of affection, and it is the extraordinary and grievous truth that the faces of dozens of comparative strangers can rise up photographically before me while the best-loved heads are lost for ever.

I've never understood this. On the other hand, more inexplicable still, I can pick up here and there, and over large gaps of time, objective glimpses of myself, seeing myself as a stranger would, even to the clothes and hat I was wearing and when no looking-glass was within miles. In *Peter Ibbetson*, du Maurier writes of the same thing, calling it 'double sight' and describing it as a mystery that Ibbetson discovered by slow degrees, as he developed the faculty of re-living the past.

To re-live the past and one's part in it was never to come my way though I believe it to be an absolute possibility. I set about the business in the wrong way, but at least I hurt no one in the process, and it is all over now. It is, indeed, just credible that the past is meant to be left behind you, in spite of what the time-experts say, and that I didn't realize this fact. This must be why people who live in the present are so uniformly contented and easygoing. I see their point. Living is *now*, not turning your mind back, or impatiently straining forward into the future of mere ambition or boredom. Yet … I feel in my bones that I shall never be of that sane company.

CHAPTER IV

I

AND SO, at about seven years old, I, as it were, woke up for the second time in Evenfield and began to take my place in its life, to mingle with the persons and doings of Addison.

The night-nursery that I shared with Mell and the nurse, until the latter's more hygienic banishment to one of the four large box-rooms at the top of the house, faced the drive and the road and the turnip field over which mists hung in the autumn.

It was one of the meaningless, do-little rooms of Evenfield, and didn't attach itself to any of us, much, even then. Its light was partly taken away by the dressing-table, the wall-paper I have striven to remember and can't, but the pictures on the walls were a caution, and all religious, bad art of a rather bad period that veered, for juvenile consumption, at any rate, from brightly coloured Bavarian Nativities and The Light Of The World to the photographic horrors of good-looking young men being larded like capons with arrows, and grisly Crucifixions. What sum-total of religious conclusion children were supposed to derive from these morbidities and placidities I can't imagine. But parents in those days seemed to need a lot of educational properties' to atone, perhaps, for their own inarticulateness and reticences upon matters Divine.

Actually, the *doyen*, the Matron, guardian, familiar and friend of the room was not a saint or martyr, virgin, angel or admission-seeking Saviour, but a stove. It was portable, stood a yard high, had a shutter of ruby glass and cast through its elaborate ironwork reflections upon the ceiling which we called 'skulls'; it smelt slightly of magic-lanterns, so that, as Mell and I agreed as we were undressed and groomed and reclad in festal silks and satins at improbable hours of dusky winter afternoons, one was almost at the party before starting to it.

The night-nursery was essentially a winter room, and even then one missed odd weeks in it through bouts of chicken-pox and measles, which were convalesced through in the day-nursery across the landing or in the spare room next door: I don't quite know why, unless the night-nursery fireplace was defective or –far more likely – the servants grumbled at too many grates to clean. There were only two gas fires in the whole house. Therefore we lay in ruby-glowing darkness or watching candle flickering upon those pious pictures when the nurse came up from her supper at ten and undressed with elephantine caution that could be heard as far away as the bathroom. She wore, I remember, the kind of stays for which, nowadays, actresses appearing in revivals of early Shavian plays and *Trelawney of the Wells* comb London in despair, for the corsets were black or slate-grey, with unexplained arrowheads in white stitching, moulded to the figure and giving the wearer a stomach and a bust and hips whether she had them by nature or not. One watched her, stupid with interest, – and the next second it was morning.

When winter had really come and wrapped itself all round us we were brought up pre-breakfast tots of hot rum and milk, which we both hated, in willow-pattern cups. Poor Mell as the elder got the largest jorum, and once whoever mixed it mixed it

too strong, and when she tried to say her prayers, got her peti-
tions handsomely mixed up with an old tune on my musical-box
and began, 'Oh Lord, God bless the man who broke the bank at
Monte Carlo'. The nurse tumbled to the situation first (she had
brothers of her own) and looked incredulous and then scandal-
ized, and poddled off to inform, as she warned Mell, 'y'mother
or father', and Mell shouted, 'Publish and be damned!', from one
of father's biographies, and the nurse exclaimed, 'Well, there's a
sauce! Whatever next?' Mother was rather reprehensibly entertained, and it was father who emerged with superbness from the
incident, for he quite sincerely took the line that no daughter of
his could conceivably be in such a monstrous dilemma, and that
that being the case, the behaviour of Melisande was due to some
other cause which was patently the business of the women of his
house to deal with. And left the room, razor in hand.

For the rest, the night-nursery is memorable for the pre- and
post-dinner visits that mother paid me, for by that time Mell
was dining below, eating the good smells that were sometimes
wafted to me in bed, she being too old for nursery tray. I never
even thought of asking her to bring me up tit-bits when she
came to bed herself at nine o'clock. It was mother who 'when a
dinner-party was expected', as I put it, could be counted upon
to arrive, a silhouette against the landing gaslight, in cord-laced
Liberty velvet gown of her own design, with a handful of those
dessert sweets which, in silver baskets, centred the table and quite
deliciously consisted of sugar almonds, nougatines, chocolate
creams and a certain square jujube, rose-flavoured and of ravish-
ing colour and hardness. I can smell the assortment now.

Sitting on the bed, she would keep me posted on what was
going on downstairs, describing dresses, imitating their wearers,
always well and with the loving malice of Lady Teazle, or criti-
cizing the courses as one housekeeper to another. (Had we not
bought their ingredients that morning? Had I not, elbow on billiard table, pored with her over the list of the more rare delica-
cies ordered from 'The Stores', as Harrods was persistently called?
These lists possibly included the sweets and indisputably the small

tubs of anchovies which were constantly served and that I never could be induced to taste – nor can I now.)

'That saddle of mutton –' I would begin from the open doorway, and mother with a sigh of relief pronounced, 'A bit overdone. Clara got flustered because the jelly wouldn't set'.

'Was it all of a dither?'

'No. The Lord was with us – very much at the eleventh hour, bless him! And everyone went chiefly for the cabinet pudding.'

'What've they got on?'

'The vicar's in green silk and Auntie S's trousers have a beautiful crease down the middle.'

'No, but *really*?'

'Auntie S is really looking awfully nice in golden-brown and sent her love to you: Mrs. Grimstone's in purple (moiré I *think*) with a foetid little V neck.'

'And Molly?' I asked, referring to the daughter of what I called 'the other doctor', as he wasn't ours.

'Can't remember for m'life so it must be something rather stumatic. Oh, if I had the dressing of her!'

Together in the warm dark with the circle of little black skulls on the ceiling we dressed Molly Voles; I was for pale blue satin of the shade which was called 'electric', and then it was over time for mother to leave me.

Or sometimes the vacuums at her own table caused her to rush upstairs for what she called 'a refresher', actually between courses. At these times the news was equally comforting but far more telegraphic.

'Dear Mrs. Field sends you a kiss and Daisy's got a chill and won't be at school to-morrow, she says.' Or,

'New pudding quite a success and the Ackworth-Meads asked for the recipe which I thought such bad manners that they won't get it out of me, and Mrs. Markham wants our Shakespeare readings in costume!'

This item meant a lot to me. For Mrs. Markham was not only a near neighbour in an avenue over the road, but for one who was to remain a non-intimate of us Morants, a complete specimen, i.e. a known face, house and definite address, also several listed

characteristics, among which were a high colour and hard looking hair, a horsey and doggy and doeskin-glove'd atmosphere,
and had once been rumoured, amid much laughter and cries
of 'She *would!*' to have smoked one of her husband's cigarettes.
The Markham joke was allowed quite cheerfully to be shared by
Mell and myself and ran concurrently with a policy which still
sent children and maidens from the room if the word Divorce
was going to have to be mentioned or the belief circulated that
somebody dyed her hair, and elaborately burst into French at
the children's midday dinner-table at the slightest provocation,
thus putting us all on the alert at once where an open discussion
in English would probably have left us completely unheeding.
Many books (including *Trilby*) and the reading of all newspa-
pers were forbidden us until we were well on in our 'teens, and
we never dreamed of surreptitious peeps and abstractions from
bookshelves.

Perhaps we grew up a little backward according to the standards of to-day – no forced pleasures or premature ennuis – but
at least normally and at our own pace which, in my case at least,
was to be a slow one.

For the rest, I can pin down three glimpses of the night-nursery: A Christmas dawn, very grey, and waking after a night broken by anticipation, and feeling at the rails above my head for
the woollen stocking, and squeezing it to hear the rustle of tissue
paper packets. Duty-sleep accomplished! The Day is here! that
disorganized delight darkened only by thoughts of church, or if
one escaped the service itself, of losing mother and members of
the family for what seemed to be endless tracts of time.

An Easter morning, and displaying the incredible quantity of
advance eggs given to me upon the top of our chest of drawers
– it looked like a confectioner's window: of seeing all the year
round upon the other chest of drawers the personal treasures of
Aggie Drumhead, the nurse, which included a certain cabinet
photograph framed in green plush with gilt tin corners, of her
mother, in shawl, busk'd and bodice'd and a central parting, and
a bulky, opulent family album with gilt clasps and a key, which I
thought quite beautiful.

2

I thought then, and I think still, that even in an era when toys were toys and not hideous models or imitations in miniature of world-belligerence, mother gave me the best presents in the world. Owing to her seniority, at an age when every year makes such a huge disparity, Mell's gifts and my own were never in the same group, so that she had moved on to new dresses and those chunky handkerchief sachets of satin piped with cord and ornamented with a dry looking spray of 'hand-painted' flowers while I was still in the immeasurably preferable stage of objects which caught the eye and imagination.

One year, my present-in-chief was a large Christmas tree all to myself, fully decorated, and dangled and tinselled and candled and hung on its lower boughs with paper packets of more presents; or there was the year of the dolls' dinner-table, complete with tiny cutlery and glass, siphons, épergne and damask cloth, next it the dolls' draper's shop which mother, contemptuously bundling the original contents to oblivion, stocked herself, and spent hours blocking four-inch bolts of material, rolling ribbon on to reels, contriving stands for hats trimmed and untrimmed, and filling the cash-drawer with dolls' money – she even rigged up an overhead change system from cash-desk to counter, where a marble rolled in a groove conveying bills. Or there was the year of the Bavarian village, a wooden, three-sided oblong depicting a pleasant vista of peasants standing up and sitting down and driving cows up the hill behind a red-roofed church; you turned a handle, and instantly from two slits in the street rose an unending chain of more villagers who passed across the stage and disappeared to a tinkling melody down the other slit.

Mother would come in, cheek chill to one's kiss, as she pushed up her veil of spotted net, from one of her day-trips to London; six o'clock was therefore a lurking-time in the hall, waiting for the special series of raps upon the knocker that she kept for my ears alone.

How I should like to be able to relate in Dickensian detail and heartiness, with perhaps a tear of domestic sentiment to wind up with, the feasts which celebrated our Christmas. But it is heaven's truth that I can't recall one single meal that we all ate at Evenfield in the whole eleven years that we lived in the house, except the repellent souvenir that, feed she the servants never so madly, orange-and-nut she them never so generously, the servants nearly always pilfered our oranges when they had exhausted their own. And once, Marcus and Mell had a passage concerning a small box of glacé fruit; Mell, invited to take one, with great moral courage made for the centre-piece of resistance, the apricot, and Cuss, unable of decency to protest aloud, was so riled that he silently rushed out into the snow and posted the whole lot into the pillar-box, which I have always considered a magnificent gesture.

We had, I imagine, no family games on Christmas Night: it may have been owing to our conflicting ages and bedtimes and the necessitous inclusion of father, who as we all agreed was passable at active games but no good at all on paper, because he became far above everybody's head at once, even at that admittedly difficult pastime 'word and question', in which you are faced with a noun and a query and have to make a verse against time in which you bring in the word and answer the question. It is a splendid game, but needs, like pastry, a light hand, and father's contributions were so scholarly (they included palindromes and Latin puns and mythologic references and historic incidents) that he morally broke up the party in no time. Also, in those days, everybody in the place was growing up, and that meant strictly family parties of their own. I don't, now I come to think of it, recollect one tangibly lonely person in Addison. And so, as with so many dozens of other households if we had only known it, our Christmas Day made the mistake of starting crescendo and finishing diminuendo.

CHAPTER V

I

I LOVED winter mornings in the day-nursery, with its contrast of sky-blue wall-paper sprayed with fat pink apple-blossom, the rime on the lawn, and the red sun behind the silver birch-tree that separated our garden from the house next door.

Sitting in my high chair that I stuck to long after I was old enough for an ordinary one (could it have been that self-same chair that auntie S wished installed first thing in the house?), with my back comfortably to the fire, head beneath the elaborate oil lamp suspended from the ceiling from which the paper chains of Christmas had been removed, I watched poor Mell shrugging into coat and tam-o'-shanter, slinging satchel round her shoulders and taking a last demented look at her German Grammar over the preparation of which she would sometimes cry with bewilderment at night in the dining-room. She invented, finally, a scheme to help her, which consisted of illustrating the margins of the book with vegetables and dressing them in trousers or skirts according to their sex. From nine o'clock to tea-time the nursery saw her no more, and she would pick up Janet Martin, who lived at 'Stamboul', that large weather-cock'd house over the wall at the bottom of our garden, to accompany her the two miles to the High School.

In the nursery, I was left to please myself until the morning walk or shopping with mother, the heaven-sent rumour conveyed by gardener or errand boy via Aggie that the ice was 'holding', which delightfully upset the morning, or until it was time to go downstairs for lessons with mother. Of these lessons I remember that as a punishment I was made to read the stodgier of the letter-press at the end of *Lays Of Ancient Rome* instead of *How Horatio Kept The Bridge*, which also bored me greatly in any case, and the woodcuts of which, depicting young men in curly *toupés*, knee-length skirts and repulsively muscular calves, seemed to me to be so unreal as not to be worth my attention. Anyway, that session ended in tears and mutual disappointment, and the day closed with a visit to the toyshop and the bestowal of a box of dolls' notepaper with gilt edges and a spray of forget-me-nots in the corner of each tiny sheet. On another occasion, mother concluded the lessons with the present of a copy of *Sesame and Lilies*. I was pleased, regarding the book as a piece of property, but I never read it and haven't got round to it yet! I feel certain that something instinctive whispers in one's ear that certain literature is not and never will be one's cup of tea. Why Sesame, and wherefore Lilies? I don't even want to know. It's all very shocking, and I may have missed something, after all, but don't think I have!

Over geography I made the same grandiose errors in location at eight years old as I make now, and mother once said, very reasonably, 'No, *that* island belongs to *us*. You wouldn't want the French to pull down our flag and set up theirs on it!' Scripture she very wisely left alone, for I defy anybody in the world to make that subject interesting until the time that they shall be old enough to read such books as *Ur of The Chaldees* and *The Bible As Literature*, which weren't published or thought of then, because neither society nor public opinion had faced the fact that if the Bible is worth study it is worth research and checks-up that would redeem it from the pit into which it had fallen and align it with the vital things of life. And so in the most happy and comfortable manner I learnt to read, and very little else. Mother probably knew that learning only begins when the textbooks close and that the ultimate point of reading is not so much the retention of facts as the knowledge of where to put your hand on them when wanted.

I cheated, once, in a spelling lesson. The word was 'theatre', and mother, having been called from the room, I sat, knowing that the word was somewhere near me in the nursery; and then it came to me that Theatre was painted on the drop-curtain of my toy theatre, and I got up, pulled aside the red velvet tableaux curtains (copied by mother from those at the Theatre Royal in our market town) and remedied the scholastic lapse in a second.

2

To approach that model theatre was fatal, for you promptly became dead to the world. Even father had a pondered facetiousness ready for it and was quite offended, on general principles, that his suggested Greek inscription (which he wrote out meticulously and which looked like 'Hoi-yoi-Oy' to me) was not incorporated into the *décor*: it meant, I believe, 'We aim at the noblest art', which, as far as doing the thing properly and taking things seriously went, we did, but there was an unspoken feeling that if father's kind of art crept in and took charge the theatre would cease to amuse or please at once. Emphatically we evaded hoy-oy-oyings, but, as against this, Marcus took a hand and cut a trap-door with his penknife up which the Demon could be poked, or twitched by cotton from the flies, a device of which I became so enamoured that for months not only the Villain but all unsympathetic characters came up it as well, until I learnt from mother that Irving had never treated himself to such an entry or exit, even in *Faust*.

For that theatre Mell made elaborate transformation scenes, collapsible kitchen tables and handkerchiefs with a large inked handmark for Widow Twankey, a hint she had picked up from Dan Leno, and the ballets were strictly dressed alike, while a matinée of *The Geisha* at the Theatre Royal, Kingsmarket, moved Mell to construct a perfect little veranda of painted *papier mâché* which she covered with single blossoms from a spray of artificial lilac on one of mother's summer hats, to imitate wistaria. An artist friend of ours told us that Mell must have an uncommonly straight eye, as the veranda was to scale to the fraction of an inch – he measured it. The ideal Stock company came from the Addison toyshop: the dolls were four inches long, had pink wadded bodies and limbs, with china heads on to which wigs could easily be fitted. And no doll trod those boards who was not previously made-up, with pink from a virulently-coloured boiled sweet, and face-powder (or failing all else, icing-sugar).

Between lessons, walk, hoops and gossip with cronies in the Park, and later, waiting for the daily arrival of the governess, with a pink nose and a bicycle, came the mid-morning milk and Fairy cakes alone with mother, gossips in which, as with the theatre, time ceased to be, and once was to bring down from above the patient, wondering Miss Abernethy to shepherd me to sums on a slate at a preposterous hour. The Fairy cakes have now, in their pristine glory, gone off the market, although they cling like divorced countesses to the title. But who dies if memory lives?

With father in London at his office, Marcus once more quite suddenly not with us (Winchester) and Mell at the High School, it was I of our family who got the lion's share of the nursery.

It was a good room to loiter in when the action slowed down: one could even enjoy a cold in it or whoop and be sick in it without unfriendly feelings. The furniture was rather battered, the upright piano, poor soul, a horror whose keys badly needed their teeth brushed, and the pictures were bygone supplements of Nelson watching Trafalgar, while a midshipman bound up his own wrist and was chaffed in the process by a senior officer in white knee-breeches, and the middle-distant deck was filled with sailors in Sam Weller suits and varnished pot-hats, and a nice, greedy nineteenth century chromolithograph of an inn parlour and a beaming maidservant in a mob-cap serving a capon to a tableful of huntsmen who grinned from ear to ear, gallantly toasted her in tankards of beer and a spirit that I long believed to be admiration until I became very much older indeed and perceived to be what Mr. Sinclair Lewis dismisses as 'belly smiles'.

On the floor was a large square organ that you turned by a handle and on to which huge perforated records of brown cardboard were placed in the gramophone manner. It was seldom enjoyed: it had a large capacity for alarming which may have been due to the castratedly ecclesiastic sounds that it emitted, or to its repertoire, only one item of which I remember, 'The Lights of London'. Oddly enough, and before I ever saw London, this tune conjured up a vista of a wide bridge aligned with standard lamps that I have since identified with so many of the existent bridges in town.

Another ne'erdoweel toy was a box of stone bricks which traditionally belonged to my brother. These depressed us even to look at: they handled soapily and had a dreary smell of what I now diagnose as provincial side-streets and Nonconformity, and the sheets of models of what you could build from them were enough to put anybody off at any age.

The dolls had an unreliable time of it; I don't know what sort of mother Mell had been but I can answer for my own persistent-ly non-maternal instincts. Far too large to go on the stage, I must have regarded them as would an actor-manager his daughter who refused the theatre as a career, or his son who chose the commer-cial life. I certainly once gave the dolls a Bible reading, but mainly because I had a dressing-gown that buttoned down the front and a cap shaped like a biretta, and fancied myself as a Padre.

Mell and I both wrote as a matter of course – I even finished two novels; to ages up to sixteen this form of endeavour presents no difficulties whatsoever. Mell ran more to historic plays (a line from her *Robin the Outlaw* ran, 'Now let the jerkin ring!'), but she seldom finished anything. She completed a quarter of a Chi-nese musical comedy with an opening chorus of coolie gardeners grouped round rose bushes ('the trees were planted long before we came') which a subsequent study of professional libretti leaves me still considering was cuts above most of the shows then being produced: it would, indeed, be impossible to be worse than some of them.

My novels were descriptive and satiric. I went to the living for my characters, and no love affair could live, or did, in such an angry sea, nor was any engagement able to withstand the gales of chaff in which I conducted it. Even the heroine (Aggie Drum-head) had a face that was merely 'sensible', lost the affections of her 'intended' upon a picnic, and, taking an after-luncheon nap, descended into hell, from whence, amid detailed and adjectival descriptions of troops of fiends, she failed to rise again on the third day. Aggie's comment on this work was, 'Well, there's a cheek!'

3

The use of a pen only became irksome when letters of thanks to godmother, grandmother and such other remote London per-sons as plied me with presents for mother's or duty's sake had to be tackled and which couldn't be covered by verbal thanks to the givers in Addison itself. And that wasn't all. For through the last week of December and the whole of January small double-leaved invitation cards with a festive coloured picture appeared upon my breakfast plate. 'We hope you can come to our Party', said they in print, with the sender's name (more victims to the ink-pot in other nurseries) filled in below, or 'We are giving a New Year Party and are expecting YOU', they said, with another and different picture. Sometimes a sail appeared in the shape of return cards supplied to me in which the mere scrawling of my name at the bottom of the printed thanks and acceptance solved the compositional agony. But one or two houses, quite monstrously closing their eyes to the juvenility of the illustrated invitation, sent stern, adult white squares of printed announcement, to acknowledge which that baffling, treacherous and currishly snapping commodity, the third person singular, had to be resorted to, a medium in which I am not at my best to this day.

CHAPTER VI

I

THE EXPERIENCED party-goer in Addison learnt very soon to know what to expect in the way of entertainment, and whether the seven or nine o'clock sight of Aggie Drumhead sitting among the other nurses in alien halls was likely to prove a welcome one or a fly in the ointment; learnt, too, to remember from year to year if the presents had to be fished for, hunted, competed for, just given you from the tree, dipped for in tubs or put by your place at table.

Some hostesses had 'the touch', others would never learn the secret of successful party-giving in this world.

At the head of the latter category were the Ackworth-Meads, who lived in that enormous pseudo-Gothic mansion in a rather characterless road which connected Addison with the outskirts of Kingsmarket. Here, once deposited in the vast and stone-flagged hall, small children were set upon by clouds of maids and footmen and later heavily escorted into a bogus banqueting-hall, the whimsy of a builder of 1870. And from that moment you were lost – literally, for in that crowd a familiar face was an event. No expense was spared and no pleasure accrued and the arrival of the nurses at the end of the party was bellowed by an auxiliary butler.

'Miss Barbara Morant is called for!' or

'The Misses Field! The Misses Field!'

(It was at the Ackworth-Meads that I once mistook the son of the house for a hired waiter and addressed him, irretrievably, as such.)

Or there was Mrs. Jasperleigh, who was actually Mrs. Jasper Leigh, but considered that this telescoping was More Toney, as she confided to mother whom she adored. A wealthy widow, she possessed one precocious and overhandled daughter of my own age, Thelma, whose unpopularity from Addison to Kingsmarket, yea, down an entire reach of the Thames to Addison's Villa, was an accepted thing and a general act of faith; and over the parties at 'Broadacres', which my mother with an appearance of inadvertence once alluded to as Broadmoor at an At Home, and whether the parties were of birthday, Christmas or Fifth of November, hung an authentic and dependable blight. For if the Ackworth-Mead assemblies remained chronically Institutional, the Jasperleigh gatherings were ungenial and flustered. Over the whole problem of Broadacres we Morants ponder still. For it was, visually, a promising house enough, countrified, though of no interesting age, and even Mrs. Jasperleigh's success in damning its interior with chenille spiders couldn't, we decided, be the determining factor, in that our own drawing-room at Evenfield was by no means devoid of contemporary aesthetic errors. As for the Jasperleigh grounds, any retired gas inspector could singlehanded have made a better job of it than she with all her gardeners. She hadn't what is called 'the Green Finger'. Things simply didn't come up for her, or if they did were formalized out of all beauty, unapproachable, unpickable, unfriendly. Could it be, perhaps, that house or garden was haunted by some elemental? I have long entertained a vague suspicion of a certain shrubbery of Broadacres, but the case is dismissed as Not Proven. And then, too, she had a genius for spoiling her own effects. She stuck a pigeon-cote in the middle of the lawn, and suffered a privet clipped like a giant bee-hive to blot out the daylight from her own ground-floor boudoir. Mother called it The Bunion. And Mrs. Jasperleigh finally developed a passion for garden ornaments, preferably of maundering peasants in stone trousers and terra-cotta skirts, and sometimes sabots.

As for her parties: there again, it may have been the elemental (if any) or the house itself or Thelma or the unhappy hand that operated so persistently in the grounds, but I know that intimates of other nurseries – like ourselves and the Fields – viewed with lacklustre spirit the impending gala as we discussed it in the Park and wondered If Thelma Would Be Awful. For Thelma, at ten, mistook herself for a hostess of forty-five and imitated any lo-cution or mannerism of her mother's that suited her. But if you hit her she became her age at once, and whined, and then in-formed upon you. She occasionally mistook herself also for Ade-line Génée and sometimes for Madame Patti, an opinion that was not shared by dancing or singing mistress, and of all the children of Addison who were least likely ever to be asked to perform in any capacity, Thelma Jasperleigh was the one.

One January party at Broadacres I remember clearly. Mell and I were standing about feeling draughty in our party dresses of Roman satin before we were scooped up by an elder for some laboured gaiety; my arms were bare and the Maltese silk mittens did little to relieve matters and left one's fingertips chilly. I always turned cold if I were bored or worried. I do still. And then the lit-tle Fields came in and the great parquet-floor'd room was cosy at once: for in spite of the Dante readings, the children of dear Mrs. Field were our allies through thick and thin, and loved us and laboured faithfully for us by painting and drawing and needle-work presents—they all embroidered beautifully, it seems to run in that family, and their shyness was never awkward, but only of the goodness of hearts too simple and sincere to parade or know their own value. We called them 'the little Fields', I don't know why, for they were all taller than Mell and I, and even the youngest, Clover, was slightly older than myself, but 'little' remained as a prefix just as the Irmine child became fixed in our consciousness as 'Baby' Irmine until she must have been quite eleven.

It was Daisy Field who sacrificed her pocket-money for two whole weeks to send us sweets when we had chicken-pox: Primrose who escaped to Kingsmarket alone to buy us what we called real grapes, for we discounted the monkey-and-sawdust kind which was all that Addison's greengrocers could produce; and poor little Clover who burst into shameful tears at school when she heard I was worse and ran out of the classroom and hid in a housemaid's cupboard without permission (she the docile of the docile!); and all who pooled the cream of their toys and games – lend or keep, it was all the same to them.

The Fields weren't well off but always looked nice in a velvety Libertyish way, and even cut-down clothes were transformed by the handworked silk flowers with which their frocks were sprayed and garlanded.

Thelma, I remember, was in pink plush – her mother's taste in dress was what you might expect, and it accentuated her sallowness and dark, straight hair. Thelma looked critically at the advancing trio and said to us, 'Here come our little three. How badly that Primrose holds herself'. Mell and I got up steam at once though we said nothing until Thelma remarked, 'Muvver and I can never *imagine* why you and they are such pals'.

'Oh?' muttered Mell, 'Well … we are fond of them.'

'But Mr. Field! Only a music master!'

I don't know if Mell meant to, but it was certainly I who got in first, for I slapped Thelma on the face and cried myself, and missed her cheek and hit her nose, and I'm glad, and it bled a little and I'm glad, and a spot or two spattered on to her pink plush and I'm glad. The little Fields hastened to us and Daisy, the eldest, put her arm round me and said, 'Oh *Ara!*' and mopped my eyes with a handkerchief (with a daisy worked in one corner) that she pulled out of the little yellow velvet bag that hung at her waist.

I suppose there was a scene of some kind and a lot of emotionalism from Thelma and Mrs. Jasperleigh, who excelled at tensions, and how it all ended I forget: but I do remember that a nice elderly man suddenly loomed and looked amused and vanished, and that dear auntie S (Mrs. Stortford) grinned fatly and delightedly at me later on, and nodded and privily made the gesture of nose-punching.

2

The parties at Baby Irmine's were so few and far between that I can only recall one; I have heard since that the Irmines were very badly off, and Baby was in point of years an after-thought, like myself, with a lot of grown-up sisters whom one never seemed to see at all.

Of the Irmine house, 'Holly Lodge', I can only see one room, far too small and rather dark, and full of birdcages and the droppings of their inmates, who frequently were allowed out and said 'EEK', to one from unexpected points like picture-frames, and the veranda which was littered with incredibly paintless chairs.

Auntie S gave good parties because the atmosphere radiated humour and the rooms were full of cats whom she named after coins: there were Penny and Farthing and Tizzy and Stiver, huge comfortable tabbies. But these gatherings were far more mother's and Mell's than my own, owing, again, to the age question and to Evelyn, the daughter of the house, who in my time was always tennis-playing and 'out' and so in a different world, though excellent fun and company if circumstances ever threw her my way. The Stortford garden was, indeed, sacrificed almost completely to net and balls, and the daily gardener, stooping in what was left over for vegetables, received many a crack on his behind from too vigorous a service, and once retaliated in exasperation with a small beetroot, as auntie S, grunting with delighted laughter ('Haigh! haigh! haigh!') related to mother.

The parties given at 'Stamboul' by Mrs. Martin for Janet were memorable for the cakes which that redoubtable Scotswoman (she was a Miss McIntyre) baked herself and which contained so much stout and even brandy that I wonder we weren't all under the table.

Stamboul, over our garden wall by the apple-trees and facing our nursery, was a place of slippery floors and decorative conflict, for whereas Hubert Martin had served in an administrative capacity in India, his wife clung tenaciously to the symbols of Scotland, and the result was Benares brass, pedestal lamps ending in elephants' feet, tigerskin rugs and plaid curtains of hunting McIntyre tartan, a notion which possibly derived from Balmoral, while our games were looked down upon, snarled at and grinned over by various gnashing trophies with horns, whiskers and beards.

Stamboul's interior was never to mean much to us (I think in all our lives we only saw its drawing-, dining- and smoking-room). It was the grounds that were our stamping-ground: vast, and full of seakale under bell-glasses, an enormous fowl-run and marrows on hotbeds with a pleasant stuffy reek, and cucumbers in frames. It was by the rhubarb bed and the seakale pottings that we tended to converge, for there, by propping a small ladder against the wall, hoisting feet over the top and seizing a bough, we were back in our own garden, thus saving a détour down part of the Martin's road and part of the length of our own.

In festivity, Janet was always put into a kilt, silk blouse and machicolated velvet jacket with cut-steel buttons, the whole embellished with a silver-mounted grouse-claw and a gargantuan safety-pin that I long believed to be a pantomime property, and always during a pause between games she was set by her mother to perform a reel or sword-dance. As her talents lay conspicuously in other directions we enjoyed it; also, the swords never ended up in the same place, and once Jan kicked them right into the hall and once (oh heavenly day) one of them struck the screen behind which the ventriloquist was preparing his act a resounding whang that felled screen and performer in one soul-satisfying wreck. He emerged – poor plucky wretch – blowing up his exiguous moustache and saying to Mrs. Martin, 'Quite a come-down! No trouble, no trouble at all. The figure is undamaged'.

The show must go on! And go on it did. And I sometimes wonder where that ageing entertainer is to-day. He would, now, be quite seventy-five, and I picture him in a bed-sitting room in the backwashes of Pimlico (which *smells* of decline, architectural and personal) and ponder upon his fluttered joy if he could but know of the clarity with which I can still see his face and hair and waiter's suit; he the outmoded one, *passé* for drawing-rooms, not good enough for the halls, he who has utterly failed to memorize *my* face – one of a line of well-brushed children who spelt his rent and food, yet, could he but know, that unremarked entity is still, oh enviable! in the movement with much of the future yet before her ...

Ventriloquist, sleep soundly, you have earned it. You have kept with heaven knows what of shift and makeshift and evasion and contrivance and sacrifice your tiny banner of vaudeville flying in winds fair and foul, keeping faith with the great names of your profession.

The figure is undamaged.

Of her own performances, it could have been torment to poor Janet, paired as she would be with Mell when school term re-opened, to know that she had made once more an exhibition of herself. But neither Janet nor Mell thought of the affair in that way I am certain; maternal edicts and even suggestions were carried out as a matter of course. On the other hand, the separation-by-wall alone did not invariably make for intimacy, for were not the Randolphs upon our right hand (by the rockery) and partitioned by a mere fence? And with that family we made no headway at all although the Randolph child came to our larger parties.

I knew their garden pretty well, thanks to the fence and the knotholes in it, or through precarious balancing upon clinkers where the Solomon's Seal sprang up every year, but I never remember playing in it, wherefore I deduce that we and the Randolphs offered each other hospitality strictly *pour la forme*. Little Gladys Randolph was a Christmas tree doll of a child with all her goods in the shop window: her mother was exactly the same doll thirty-five years later and was rumoured, with breath distinctly bated, once to have been upon the stage, a fact that it was expected she had now lived down in that hot-looking house with its calceolaria-lobelia-begonia garden to which the gates of 'Rose Glen' gave access.

The Randolph parties were null affairs in which the iced cake of the tea-table made its ravaged reappearance at supper, a circumstance that I found depressing, for if you were faced with the same cake four hours later you lost all sense of time and couldn't enjoy the fact of still being out of bed at nine o'clock, as the cake still leered at you that it was only four-thirty. No. That unshaded house was never to become familiar to us. Neither was 'Tralee', next us on the left, separated from ourselves by another fence and owning the silver birch behind which the red winter suns rose so engagingly.

Its garden was otherwise entirely given up to pines and old gravel paths, the house to old ladies whom Mell and I called 'the Miss Cocksedgees' and who were seldom glimpsed by ourselves, until that morning when Johnnie Lawnford, the doctor's son (brother to the manure-throwing Chetwyn) and I suddenly got tired of the resources of our own garden and were mysteriously visited by a social urge that sent us calling. The occasion being a formal one, we laid our half-eaten apples upon the gate-post of Tralee and advanced up the gravel drive to that creeper-infested dwelling. Prior to that, I had found a packet of unused At Home cards in a dining-room drawer, and Johnnie and I consulted as to the sentiment to be written upon the couple that we filched. I marked mine 'To Enquire', and Johnnie his 'P.P.C.' We didn't know what the letters stood for but dimly connected them with ceremony and the niceties. And then it came to me that a certain type of call necessitated one or some corners turned down, and in an all-or-nothing ecstasy of politeness I turned down all four corners of my own card – it looked like a small dining-table.

On the way out of Evenfield Johnnie said professionally, 'I wonder if she'll let me look at her tongue? Old people never will'. (By old people he meant and I understood perfectly any person of thirty or over, and I was struck with the truth of the remark. The aged were, now one came to think of it, a mass of reticences: they received with indulgent smiles and a turning of the topic one's suggestions that one should sponge their backs; I had, now Johnnie mentioned it, never achieved the spectacle of an adult tongue fully extended, and even those of Addison's elderly men to whom I had taken a passing fancy had consistently refused to share my bed for company.)

Johnnie added loudly, 'I once just missed seeing a dead person in Dad's surgery, and Dad of course has actually seen a *corpse*'.

The next thing that happened was that we were in the drive of the Misses Cocksedge and the maid, in a goffered cap like a jelly-mould and streamers down to her rump, was opening the front door. Yes, Miss Cocksedge was at home but Miss Clara was out. And the whole of the rest of that warm autumnal morning is a blank.

What *did* we talk about? Did Miss Cocksedge come in from some domestic supervisal? A book? A pre-luncheon nap? Was she astonished, peevish, amused? Did she (could she?) rise or sink to the occasion, remembering the sudden adult accesses to which children even in the middle of play suitable to their age are so unaccountably prone?

And how did *we* come out of it? Not too discreditably, I imagine, for Johnnie was a frank and friendly soul while I by taste and circumstance was much in the company of adults. If it comes to that, I can only set the visit in autumn because of those half-eaten apples and the streams of small crimson creeper with which Tralee was festooned. It seems to flourish in the suburbs.

It never even occurred to me to ask Johnnie, or even to speculate upon, what were his interests and friends. When together we existed vitally: parted, all was a forgetting.

3

The little Fields were intimates from the beginning, just as their mother was one of the half-dozen Addison residents to whom our mother opened her door and her affection. And fate has allowed me to remember a whole tract of the scene of my first visit to 'Cumptons', that red-brick, vaguely Tudor house of theirs which stood on a corner and thus commanded a vista of the endless road up and down which Mell and Janet tramped twice a day to the High School, and a view of a silly little cul-de-sac road that ended in gates which led to the Park, and which even then was aligned with small houses of the type that Dickens would have dismissed as Spoffish.

It was a summer's evening and old Caspar's work was done: that is, it was warm July between tea and my bedtime that mother and I strolled the three-quarters of a mile from Evenfield to Cumptons, and I can see us all on their lawn; mother in a floppy hat swathed with mauve tulle, and the fair head of Mrs. Field as she bent to me, her large-featured face beaming, and the stuffy smell of sun-heated grass and evening primroses closing, the sunset glaring on window-panes and the glimpse of Mr. Field at a lower window reading *The Surrey Comet* in a velvet smoking-jacket and looking remarkably like Beethoven as he did so, an unrehearsed effect, though he was a music master. And running from the kitchen garden came Daisy and Primrose in overalls embroidered by Mrs. Field; Daisy dark-hair'd as her father, Primrose fairer than her mother, and one of them dropped to her knees as she put her arms round my waist and the other said, 'Oh, you darling!'

They spoilt me always, and do still, and I can squarely state that it never did me any harm.

But the third little Field was missing, it appeared, and on mother's enquiry the face of Mrs. Field fell, and she began in that low, shocked voice that we were in time to know so well in social calamity and local scandal or illness, to tell us that 'Poor little Clovy' had been sent to bed for taking a dessert pear from the dining-room dish. And that particular visit ended (my hostesses the shy ones) in games of 'Steps' and 'Statues', at the latter of which undignified pastime we all cheated uproariously and as a matter of course (it is a game that fairly shouts for illegitimate embellishment).

Presently a third smock was visible at an upper window and the tear-sodden face (a swamp! a quagmire!) of the youngest Field looked out at us. The Fields were always heartbroken and stricken at their mild naughtiness and at any temporary loss of favour with their mother as Mell and I were, too, over ours, with the difference that in the Field family loving disgraces were more numerous and of greater variety since so many of them had their roots in financial stress in which a strawberry stain on a best frock became a betrayal of the budget.

Yet it was the Fields who gave the happiest parties, or so we thought. To begin with, we were always made insidiously to feel the guests of honour: my tastes in toys, sweets and games were minutely remembered and catered for, and the gentle chaser 'That's *Ara's* place' to some seated and bright-eyed expectant before the conjuror's paraphernalia was no uncommon thing. Also, at the Fields, one met the cream of one's friends and mother was always invited, and went, because she enjoyed the Cumptons atmosphere as much as we did, and there was always something special for her in the treasure-hunts, to find which she was privily smuggled into another room in case the other mothers should be hurt and offended. One year, her trove was a china castle with bastions and portcullis, hollow inside for the nightlight that would shine through the barred windows. I have it still.

And the food was always wonderful. The Fields had a cook who really was faithful and devoted, a thing that usually only happens in novels, and her richly-iced cakes were as good as the Martins' and took the eye far more, and even if you went to ordinary tea or stray lunches you were offered, on leaving, lemonade that was strong and really cold, or Stowers' lime-juice, and could be sure of a huge, crisply brown fowl on the dining-table, which always was our idea of high wassail.

The Domrémys lived about a quarter of a mile beyond the Fields in a huge bastard building with two square towers and distributed such incredible quantities of presents from a fifteen-foot-high tree in their otherwise gloomy billiard room that guests were positively embarrassed, and lived in luxury all the rest of the year, cheerfully outrunning the constable until he caught up with them and they ultimately went bankrupt, so I heard, and left 'The Towers' for ever.

Or there were the Raymonds who lived in our quiet road, just missing the turnip-field but falling heir to a meadow as frontispiece, who, one Christmas, packed their eleven-year-old son dressed as Santa Claus into a monstrous cotton-wool snowball glittering with that powder called 'Jack Frost', who, at a sign from the ring of children, rose from its inn'ards; a scene – it took place in the hall of 'Meadhurst' – which is fixed in my memory partly for its own sake and partly through the description of us invoking the gift-bringer as retailed by the Raymonds' nurse to Aggie ('An' then they all called out, "Father Christmas, come HUP!"').

And to these houses must be added the generous sprinkling of those who never became intimates, but upon the visiting-list of whom, for this reason or that, Mell and I were fixtures, and I can 'feel back' now the sensation of attractive strangeness that descended upon me during those journeys by hired brougham to localities I couldn't recognize, in a darkness relieved by but a stray lamp-post, and in which I lost my bearings completely, and to this day I don't know how far we drove from home – or how near, and the only familiar thing fined down to the faint smell of the Shetland lace shawl in which I was wrapped.

When the party was at the Raymonds, two gardens off, the affair was simplified to a rush with Aggie on foot lest I catch cold, with a velvet shoe-bag containing my slippers. On cold nights my frocks culminated grotesquely in rubber boots, mother being the first parent to introduce Wellingtons to a startled Addison.

I don't know what general opinion prevailed about those parties, but personally I am still convinced that they were far more fun, infinitely more original than anything offered to children to-day. Mothers probably spent about half the money, but at least they were prepared to take time and thought and didn't lean exclusively upon the hireling and the big shop, and if we had our local failures they were failures of temperament (the Jasperleighs) or the result of mass thinking and production (the Ackworth-Meads). Who but Mrs. Field would have thought of putting an individual iced cake inscribed in pink with its owner's name by every place at table? How many mothers to-day would import, as did auntie S, a real automatic-machine into her drawing-room from which, with supplied pennies, we drew scent, chocolate and coco-nut ice? Who to-day would, as did Mrs. Raymond, invite a ten-year-old Barbara Morant as sole guest to luncheon and let her choose in advance any dishes she liked? (I plumped for roast chicken and cherry pie.) Or give for her daughter, son, and myself a dolls' dinner-party (at *night*! Positively from seven-thirty to nine) at which we sat down at a small table of white enamelled wood and were served with a real miniature jelly and a roast partridge, dished on the dolls' dinner-service. Poor little Bertie Raymond, breathing heavily, carved the bird, once on to the linoleum and once into the fender, until the nurse stopped bathing the baby in another corner of the nursery and very kindly took over while the host's eyes brimmed with mortified tears, but cheered up at dessert and smoked a chocolate cigar … and how enchanting it all was. And going home, I was so uplifted with grandeur that the escort of Aggie was suddenly intolerable to a woman diner-out and I sent her on ahead to walk the fifty yards to our gates.

CHAPTER VII

I

INTO THE PLANNING of our own parties at Evenfield mother threw all she had of liking of the thing for its own sake, of love for Mell and me, affection for the majority of the guests, plus, who knows? a substratum of remorse towards the large number of those present whose ways were not her own and never could be, whether she acknowledged them by the formal call or not.

Our drawing-room was a large one adjoining the billiard room and on the ground floor facing the garden. It was, as I have hinted, by no means devoid of aesthetic error, but then nor were the drawing-rooms of anybody else, except that with some people bad taste goes on for ever despite what current fads may prevail.

Of our decorative scheme, a fair estimate is that, conventions being what they were, it might have been very considerably worse, but that, judged by red-hot stop-press standards, the drawing-room was pretty far gone.

By the large french windows there was for two or three years a 'cosy corner' with a canopy, which contrivance was neither cosy nor a corner, being set at a left-angle to the fireplace. At a considerably earlier period there stood in line with the door an organ, something smaller than those in churches but startlingly large for a private room. My impression of it is that it was here to-day and gone to-morrow and for it I never formed the remotest affection. It was, of all people, Marcus who seemed to use it most. Cuss was never particularly encouraged as a musician but talent will out, and he could play with considerable effectiveness by ear and even better from the score, which has always struck me as being the more remarkable feat, possibly because one always disparages that which one can do oneself, for in time I could play the better by ear, but boggled eternally at the printed note. Ledger lines! As soon would I cope with a cloud of gnats!

The organ was another source of tilt between Cuss and father, who once caught his son playing airs from *The Messenger Boy* upon what father described as 'an ecclesiastic instrument', and Marcus's amusement overrode his exasperation once more, and after that he resorted to the upright Bechstein at the further end of the room. And on many a night when Mell was reading or doing preparation before her bedtime, and mother and father dining out or attending a Shakespeare Reading, I have fallen asleep to *The Greek Slave*, *The Geisha*, *San Toy* and

'Oh, listen to the band!'

of which the first line runs

'Where's the music that is half so sweet?' ...

Where, indeed?

The piano back, suffering the taste of the day that even mother made no fight against, was draped with a black cloth stiffly embroidered in gold thread curlicues enclosing circles of iridescent glass, but at least no photographs in silver frames littered its top.

On more than one occasion I got out of bed and went into the drawing-room to dance to the music. As the years passed, these extempore posturings took form, and gradually entire solos remembered from matinées seen in Kingsmarket became the only desirable things to perform. Sometimes Mell joined in too and we took turns at being the entire chorus and would put the brass fender into the middle of the room for footlights, and on anniversary occasions would throw each other bouquets out of the drawing-room vases.

Mell's age protected her, but I sensed even then that to let these performances extend beyond her and a few capriciously selected cronies – who kept their mouths shut: they probably could also do things which must never come downstairs to the At Home day, and look at poor old Janet – might let me in for something that would wipe all humour and enjoyment from the business. And to a child a grown-up person *is* the public, no more and no less intimidating than fifty or five hundred, a feeling which I've carried over from the nursery all my life, which leaves me completely unable to understand the entertainer's point of view when he denies nervousness on the grounds that his concert was 'only a small affair' or just in a village hall'. But to me, people at small affairs and in village halls remain eternally people, as alarming as a packed audience at the Albert Hall, and my discomfort and shame at playing the piano to Miss Myra Hess or our dear Mrs. Stortford (who is almost tone-deaf) would have been of exactly the same quality and volume, then, as it would be to-day.

It cuts both ways, because I was never less or more nervous at executing *pas seuls* before large Addison audiences than I was to, say, the little Fields. For of course I was found out (my downfall occurred over an imitation of the will-o'-the-wisp's dance in *Bluebell in Fairyland*), and of course I became in dreadful demand at once and the local Ninetta Crummles for years. To explain one's unwillingness was impossible when one didn't know the reason, and this fact was eternally beyond the scope of parental understanding which spends the other half of its time in cautions against 'showing off'.

This, to me, was one of those baffling troubles of which, later on, I was to collect so many samples: the woe to which one isn't officially entitled. For, on the face of it, what more could a child desire? Lovely little sparkling frocks, and the centre of the stage …

I hadn't even the urge to commit the business to paper in some caustic verse or tale in which the oppressors came to humiliating ends. I was probably afraid that *that* pleasure would go overboard as well!

And yet, thanks to stray London shows and the constant source that was the annual Kingsmarket pantomime, I wanted to go on the stage and dance.

My governess misunderstood this best of all. Through the pince-nez which clipped her chilly nose she looked her kind bewilderment as, a little arch and bright, she protested, 'But, you don't *like* dancing, Barbara'. Barbara, hopelessly involved in her mind, stammered out, 'It–it isn't the *same*', and I know now what she meant: that an audience of the public is tolerable because it comes to you fresh and doesn't know, for instance, that you once ate too much Christmas cake and were sick, or stole a Fairy cake out of the dining-room cupboard, or had said you thought the Bible a silly book, and dull, or when. (It was after that morning reading, conducted apparently at complete haphazard by Miss Abernethy, which had landed me with Joshua – if it were he – making the sun stand still. As I didn't know that the sun moved this seemed unremarkable, and, explained, quite pointless, by a governess eager to find wonder in everything and religion in all.)

Father's attitude to my performances would have seemed the last word in inconsistency to anybody but his children, who expected little from him at any time but the incalculable, for it never occurred to him for one second that having turned my feet danceward and to publicity, might turn my mind to the theatre. He enjoyed the entertainments at Parish Room, Town Hall and High School quite unmistakably, and became positively sentimental over me afterwards while the cab waited for our party in the night air and you could hardly get into it for congratulatory friends and kisses from heaven knows whom; but he read the Riot Act over me when I told him I wanted to be in the next Kings-market pantomime. It was one of those homilies that began, 'As soon should I –', and somewhere about the middle, his polished periods became peopled with harlots and whores who, as it were, came in by every comma, except one Scarlet Woman who entered after a full-stop. I thought she sounded immensely attractive, and never for a moment associated the adjective with her face, red with anger as Cook's sometimes became, but with a picturesque gown, square-cut in the neck, with sleeves that wrinkled to her delicate knuckles. (Years later I was to see a poster of Jean Stirling Mackinlay in just such a *robe de style* and the exact colour of my imagining!)

Meanwhile, I continued to Crummles and was the delight of Addison's chief dancing mistress, a neat golden-hair'd and tailor-made person who came down from London once a week, and whom everybody liked, in spite of her hair, because she knew her job, was just, was universally suspected of a strong bias against Thelma Jasperleigh and openly convicted of removing that acidulated aspirant from the front row where she had placed herself to the last row but one, where (in mustard-coloured satin or billiard-green moiré) she could nothing common do, or mean, upon that memorable scene …

For the dancing-classes were weekly 'occasions': the standards weren't exacting but the dress-standard was, and the mothers, including mine, sat in a large semi-circle of chairs to watch and get together and have some delicate scandal or criticism, or exchange warm praise and affection, or, haply, to hope they would 'see' Mrs. Morant at their next Progressive Whist.

'Neat your feet, Nellie!' and (with approbation)

'Nellie! … Nellie!'

'Daisy, spring!'

And Daisy Field, her nice face like an eager terrier, vigorously sprang, or, as I was to find out years later when under the hands of a famous ballet master, executed some *échappés*. Dear Miss Anson didn't know one correct term in dancing, but she got her effects. To her, a *pas de basque* was eternally, 'Rise. Pass', while a *tir-bouchon* was a 'twist' and a *coupé* 'cut and up'. Into what terms she would have translated a *grand jeté en tournant* God only knows. The pirouette was, of course, a 'turn'. Years later I met Miss Anson at Brighton, and pulled her, I am certain, neat leg – for we never saw it above the ankle when she raised her skirt to sketch a demonstration – and after affectionate greetings I told her that George Robey was doing a pirouette at the local Hippodrome, to which Miss Anson interestedly stated that 'some of these comedians are excellent dancers', which floored me on the spot.

'Thelma! where *are* your elbows? What are you thinking of? Pay attention. Watch Nellie.'

'Stand! ... now Barbara is going to show you a new dance. Come along, Barbara,' and (bending to me and sotto voce) 'You're not nervous are you, dear?'

I didn't like it, except in gorgeous, unpredictable flashes, but I don't think I ever let her down.

As for the new dances which I was to 'show', sometimes after only one lesson, I also attended once a week Miss Anson's packed and infinitely more advanced class, which included professional stage children, very curled and overdressed and even rouged, at a town two stations down the line.

At four o'clock, after a march-past that was surely superfluous, we formed into two lines, curtsyed deeply ('*Why* do you curtsy like a Gaiety girl?' my ballet master once exploded at me), dispersed to the changing-room or (the Elect) upstairs to tea with the school Principal and her daughters, or down the road to tea with the Fields, or sometimes, for our sins, to Thelma's nursery, which was characterless and boxlike.

2

The High School wasn't really a High School in our time: its title persisted from a former epoch before Addison became the spread-eagle suburb, part-town, part-village, that it was as we knew it, in which the typically substantial villa nudged a buttercup field, as like as not.

It must have been the family men like my father, originally Londoners and still City-bound, to whom the Waterloo train service and an increasingly fashionable liking for semi-country life and its attendant fresher air, were responsible for the selectiveness which was to creep in and which eventually ended in the old High School packing up and moving to a sulky and defunct-looking mansion standing in its own laurelly grounds in a road near the Stortfords, and gave Madame Fouqué her chance to acquire Mayvale House and run it as a large private school.

We all called her Madame, save in exasperation and affectionate derision, when she became Muddarm, in imitation of the loyally Britannic pronunciation of the mathematics mistress whose French accent could be cut with ease by any one of Scotland Yard's blunt instruments, and who on one wet morning, making the weather excuse for her unpunctuality to prayers, exclaimed, 'Eel ar ploo tootle-a nuit, ay la *boo*, voo savvy, Muddarm! Ay mong bicyclette … !'

Madame was a dear, a caution, a volcano, a waterspout, a kind, unreasonable despot fairy-godmother. She was, in short, a force. Not a sparrow fell to the ground without her and precious few would have dared to attempt the feat in her company.

Four foot ten in her shoes, she resembled an elderly Geisha without Portfolio, although she couldn't have been more than forty-eight when we first met her, with her blue-black hair brushed back to its little coronel. Her command of the English language was, and remained, fluent and incorrect, and her high-necked gowns were in sorrowful colours ranging from manure to mulberry.

Madame is evidently a woman who invites adjectives, a sin that my father would have deplored (giving reasons).

Once a week Madame received in her double-drawing-room, which was plushy and palm'd and slightly gilded and dark and rather suggested the foyer of the Kingsmarket Theatre.

Her two grown-up daughters, in plaid silk blouses, appeared, and sometimes Léonore sang to us (she was star soloist in most of the school plays) and sometimes Irène recited. Irène was quite a good actress, but her choice of recitation was apt to be ambitious and not in keeping with her dramatic and downright character, and rather ran to poems of the romantico-Tennysonio type which, on one occasion, caused mother to murmur to Mrs. Field that Irène must learn to lance a little if she sought to lance a lot, at which, as usual, tears of reproachful merriment poured down Mrs. Field's cheeks.

At these functions, Madame spoke alternate French or incorrect English, her daughters fluent and ambitious English slang with a French accent, and ourselves incorrect French with an English accent. Now I come to think of it, I don't remember ever seeing Madame eat one crumb of anything; she seemed to exist on ipecacuanha lozenges whose aroma she blew into the face of all-comers when, little hand tapping their own to emphasize a point, she put her face into theirs.

'*OCH!* (*lozenge*) she is a darrling gairrl', when referring to a new boarder, or, on the subject of myself becoming a pupil:

'When she has ten years, you shall send her (*lozenge*), *n'est ce pás, Bébé?*' Sometimes as a special favour the cream of the boarders themselves would be skimmed from the linoleum'd and gas-lit dining-room where they munched stacks of bread and butter that Madame, in English-speaking vein, called 'tartans', and very shyly would be dotted about the drawing-room to enjoy her wonderful cakes which she sent for to Rumpelmayer's in St. James's Street. Quite often, with superb favouritism, she would lean over a boarder's plate and twitch its contents off to give to me. 'Bébé likes ze liddle kek wiz glaze.' And quite suddenly her face would change from the lemon of good-nature to the orange of fury at a giggle or a dropped pencil-box in the hall, and she would scutter out to give the culprits hell, upon which Irène or Léonore would say to mother or Mrs. Field, 'I do weesh mother wouldn't do thatt! She is so offal!' or, 'I bet zat is Margairie, she's frrightfully notty but a rripping good sort'.

3

I never became a Mayvale pupil, but my lessons with Miss Abernethy were supplemented by classes at Madame's. Besides the dancing classes there was a weekly gymnasium, with no apparatus except dumb-bells and indian clubs, which occasion somehow always seemed to invite lugubrious weather and wind-tossed shrubs tapping at the windows. I can't remember the feel of *one* sunny gym afternoon! We seemed, in retrospect, to march and double and bend and sway to an eternal thunder shower and prematurely lit lamps!

The gym mistress, Miss Withers, was, like Miss Anson, a visiting one and I don't know where she came from even now, unlike Miss Anson, who confessed to us to a house at Sutton. Miss Withers never for a moment suggested her profession, being spectacled and scholastic looking, precise and spare and agile. Her directions she would call out in a prim, rhythmic sing-song.

'*One* two and sink-the-heels, *one* two and sink-the-heels', or 'Arms *up*wards-stretch-and knees *for*ward bend, *one* two!'

It was, I found, impossible not to make verses about her as one bent and marched. I was the smallest and youngest in the class and she called me 'Trotty'. (*Trotty!* Yet for some reason, I neither resented nor realized it.) On one deathless day she announced to us all when we'd failed to master some figure, 'Now, tired as I am I am going to skip round with you', and this gave me a hymn as well that I called *Tired As I Am.*

> Tired as I am I will skip round with you
> Bright is my voice though my feet are as lead,
> Washed in the blood of the lamb I forgive you
> All the long hours I am kept from my bed.

To which Mell added:

> *And* when it comes to the Great Resurrection
> Secrets of hearts all examined and known,
> I will remember you all with affection
> Tired as I am, while I skip round the Throne.

Back in the Fields' nursery we would all sing it, Daisy and Primrose faithfully imitating our imitations of The Withers Voice, while Clover's large eyes filled with appreciative tears, as her mother's did. Mr. Field heard us at it one day, listened to our explanation, grinned guiltily (for was he not a sidesman of St. Anselm's?), took us all down to the music room and there and then composed a setting for *Tired As I Am* (it was, he told us, in F natural, and included a fugue-like prelude). He exonerated himself completely and in the handsomest way over the whole business on the grounds that so much good music was wasted on trashy words.

I went to Madame herself for French in her study, and did pretty well, as her kindness and generosity were infinite, when she chose. It was a bad afternoon when one wasn't dismissed with at least one present, and her Swiss Dujas chocolates that we called 'mud' in allusion to their consistence were a dream. For a while I was partnered at the lessons by the little Raymond girl (of the dolls' dinnerparty), but the least bad weather affected her, whereas I tramped in my rubber Wellingtons in rain or snow to Mayvale. La *Boo*, vous savvy, Muddarm, never worried me. And then, too, Madame had a stimulating habit of awarding me illegitimate 'prizes', as might a dear animal out of *Alice in Wonderland*, as I alone constituted the class and there were no examinations.

When one was bored or stumped for the third person plural of an irregular verb there was always the garden to watch: large, dotted with monkey-puzzle trees, its turf worn bald in patches by tennis shoes, and a strolling mistress, or groups of released classes talking and exchanging glass pens, and what, to my acclimatized eye, looked fatally like picture postcards of favourite actors and actresses.

For a flurried space I learnt the violin. Mell was always far more adept than I, but at one period it looked as though I was headed towards a new phase of Ninetta Crummledom, what time I could execute simple little solos. The threat of instrumental fame in Addison was mainly due, I think, to my height, which was little taller than two violins, and was happily scotched for ever when my fiddle was stolen at the time we left Evenfield. I hated the lessons and the strings hurt my fingers; you couldn't take liberties with that instrument nor did it offer the smallest scope for error or illegal effects, or even original composition, at which it inexorably croaked its protest, its raucous voice telling one of deficiencies at every turn. Mell approached it without ambition, hope or aim, and quelled the brute through sheer indifference, thus graduating to a place in the St. Anselm's orchestra, where her subordinate but correct scroopings harmed nobody.

And then I began to go to Mr. Field for piano tuition, and when I say that he taught me all I know, that is at once not only a lie and a gross reflection on that true musician, but is an inner truth that wouldn't appeal to the purist. For if he accomplished little with me technically, he did much of secret burrowing into my mind, sorting, translating, illuminating the apparently lightless and unlightable, flying into gusty tempers which never seriously upset me, as he spoke as man to man, sweepingly including my own crassnesses with those of a surprising number of established eminents, both conductors and executants.

My ear, he said, was remarkable, my sense of modulation and rhythm no less so, and my touch instinctively sensitive. But we just couldn't make use of it, or harness it to the donkey-work. He said once that my musical instincts were as old and sure as Handel and my execution barely fledged and below even the small measure of my years.

But over the thorny hedge of staves and crotchets, Arnold Field and I could at least see each other. In patches, such as affairs of phrasing, I sometimes fluked into his esteem; at other times his backhanded reward took strange forms.

'Yes … you played that *exactly* as Adela Verne does, with that exact wrongheadedness. What *neither* of you will see is that this recurrent motif is like a sentence in brackets, a sort of aside, and not a self-contained statement. Here …' and he edged me off the stool. Or (as I battled through a Schubert march):

'Ah! ah! ah! Landon Ronald, Landon Ronald! *One* two three four! Perfect time. Horrible. You aren't beating carpets. Even a march can have swing. Not that Schubert ever ought to 've written that nonsense. Suppose he was unusually hard up, poor soul. It always makes me think of a dustmen's annual outing to Chingford.' And, 'You've got more music in you than my three put together. Even Clover knows what a demisemiquaver is and has no more real idea of the piano than my boot.

'You have things you want to express and can't: most people haven't much to express, and do. If your mother'll let you, read the Lives of the great composers, it may at least help you not to hate their work. (*When* I have time, I shall write the best Biography, by which time you'll have taken up the bassoon.)

'I'm not going to advise you to go off to concerts and hear all the best stuff because to your sort that isn't necessary, except for prigs' parties. You've got all the essentials, already: but I *do* insist that you try and learn the scale of D, for instance, and the meaning of a tied note. Your technique is past praying for, at present, but that *may* come. As it is, you contrive to give a false value to what you can play through your natural gift that you haven't worked for.

'If I ever stooped to your methods of improving upon the work of my betters because I couldn't read a chord and carrying it off with an air I'd probably be a howling success. As it is, I'm the best amateur interpreter of Bach in England, and who thanks me? Half of 'em wouldn't know if I skipped a page. But at least I give 'em the foursquare gospel according to St. Sebastian, and don't fob 'em off with Arnold Field.'

Sometimes, when we were more than usually disgruntled with each other, Mr. Field would refresh himself in unorthodox ways; it took the form of confirming him in the faith of my involuntary musical intelligence; we got a lot of laughs out of it and were so able to send each other away temporarily consoled. It was a game to me, the more fascinating because he took it seriously.

Sitting at his piano (a baby grand, and a lovely, singing Lipp, the best in the world, I think), he would play over here a bar and there a phrase or fragment or two, and ask me what it suggested. 'And think before you say it. Don't try and impress me, or be clever.' And down would come those cushioned hands which looked so misleadingly inept for the shining oblongs of the keys.

I was shy at first, fearing to offend his gods, but that soon went. It was a horrid tune that he played. I considered.

'Um …' Jiggety, babyish, not worth the humming. 'It's rather stupid', I ventured, 'it's about people who don't know much about anything.'

'Good girl.'

'And they've got behinds like our cook.'

He chuckled. 'I shouldn't wonder. It is the dance of the Mädchen from Fürth of *The Mastersingers*. That is Wagner's idea of silly music, and in my opinion he succeeded perilously well … and this?'

'It's green', I said, quite sure of my ground this time. 'Moss, I think, and it smells good.'

'Nice … nice … but I cheated, there. It's a passage for woodwinds, and their chords are *always* green or brown or silver.

Chiefly brown. You can't convey it on the piano. That was the adagio from *The Midsummer Night's Dream* Overture, a very pleasant thing. You get your moss from the wood near Athens.'

Over portions of Bach fugues I was uncertain, beyond the fact that I connected them with decimals and the engine-room of a river steamer into which I once had fearfully peered, and said so. 'It's not exactly music, is it?', I apologized.

'Hark at her! But I know what you mean. The fugue is the exact equivalent of the artists' exercises in perspective and foreshortening. Or if you like, it's a proposition in Euclid, and as exact. It even takes in your steamer's machinery, and your decimals which recur in the same way, and that's why so many people can't stand up to Bach, because they can't perceive anything beyond monotony. All art is one and has basically the same laws. It's fascinating.'

When he alluded to some famous composition in A flat or to 'Number Three' I turned blank at once, but he had but to hum the opening bar and I could usually do the rest, probably adding with surprise, 'Oh, is *that* what it's called?' Every now and then he would play something with chords deliberately but slightly wrong, telling me to stop him when he made his mistakes, and over this test, granted that I had heard the piece before, I scored one hundred per cent of successes though I hadn't one single correct expression with which to justify myself; I sensed the wrong effect at once but could only express it by going to the piano myself and selecting and testing notes until I had made the chord. Here my score was about eighty-five per cent of success and Arnold Field's interest grew with his despairs. As for the time question, that I was never to learn from any printed score or teacher, though with the tempo of a piece once heard I could never go wrong. From astonishment, exasperation and incredulity Mr. Field refuged at last in pity, as though I were deformed – he became, so immense was his rancour at my imbecility, positively sympathetic!

'If I could *only* find out what your difficulty is with notes and time! Why, Primrose knew her notes and made reasonably good shots at ledger lines when she was eight. But then she thinks *The Merry Peasant* a pretty tune, so there you are. (Never have daughters.')

I faltered, 'Miss Abernethy tried to show me, too: she makes me count "Tar-tay" and "taffa-teffé" instead of "One-two" and "three and-four"'.

'Nonsense. Waste of time. It's simply taking away your old problem and giving you a new one. If you can't three-and-four you can't taffy or whatever it is, either. The thing is that you don't know what you're doing or why you're doing it.' He plunged his hands into that velvet smoking-jacket of his. 'Let's go into the garden.' And together we pottered quite happily. The Field's garden wasn't as large as ours, or so various, but over it hung an atmosphere immensely right, as right as poor Mrs. Jasperleigh's would be eternally wrong, and it was warming as the sun to come suddenly round a corner in the summer and see a book of Daisy's face downwards on a seat, and odd to be in the garden without her or her sisters and Mell and to know that they were together in Mayvale classrooms half a mile up the road. Sometimes the pomposity of this thought so overcame me, as it had with Aggie Drumhead after the dolls' dinner-party, that, holding a rhubarb leaf for a sunshade if I thought I was unnoticed (in which case I should have thrown it away at once) I became for swift unnatural seconds a caller at an At Home day with ruched chiffon parasol and mother-of-pearl card-case like Mrs. Domrémy's and once actually enquired of Mr. Field, 'Do you enjoy the growing of these blooms?' Luckily he, stooping over the tieing up of some gladioli, didn't hear. And gradually I found that his preoccupations left me safe to practise these character impersonations, and became by turn a famous composer exhausted with composition and taking his ease in the grounds, or Little Nell to the Grandfather of Mr. Field, who said very ungrandfatherly things when he found slugs or wireworms in the borders, or a musical protégée, penniless and with consumption but of incredible genius, and quite often Evie Green in the first act of *The Country Girl* (that would be the year that mother made me sunbonnets to match all my frocks). The musical comedy was dangerous, because even thinking of sonsy Evie Green set up a train of association which led to the singing of the music and oblivion of Mr. Field and of his overhearing. One day, I was well into 'Hark to the sound of Coo' when he *did* hear, and without even turning round he grunted, 'You seem to have got every nasty effective trick in the bag'.

'She sang it that way', I said, hastily defensive. Hadn't Mell and I come home steeped in it, sulky with concentration in the Waterloo train, out of sympathy with life and Addison and Evenfield and even our family because they didn't move and have their being under sun-steeped apple-boughs by Hawes Craven and solos backed by a rural chorus?

'Glad of it.'

I wondered a little what he meant, but without anxiety, for I sensed that Mr. Field was licensed to be queer just as some people are licensed to sell wines and spirits ... of course I see now what was working in him: relief at my deliberate apeing of a model that cleared me of any meretriciousness which would clash with his assessment of my musical nature.

It may sound singular if I say that with Mr. Field, the expert, connoisseur-bully, the delightful and incalculable guesser, understander and appreciator, I was at my least shy; more, that I once played him a little bit of nonsense of my own composition (carried in my head and ear, I couldn't have written it down for a thousand pounds). The thing itself was inspired by and dedicated to one of auntie S's cats – old Stiver, if I remember, and Mr. Field was unconsciously at the back of whatever form it possessed as a solo: for here was a hint of that 'silly music' of Wagner's peasants in cat-language, a little of its elementary obtuseness, and there an attempt at its sudden movement after bird or rustled-paper-game, and the motif was a somnolent, satisfied phrase as of much milk and a prospective place in the sun, which literally *was* composed by Stiver, for heaven knows I didn't consciously make it: it was that the great striped old dear set up his own atmosphere which came through to me as do the personalities of people.

In playing it to Arnold Field I was banking on his absentmindedness, his reassuring inattentions – even on a crushing snub in his assumption that I was making the usual hash of the work of a real composer. And he didn't fail me: he walked about the room filling a pipe and cursing a mislaid matchbox most of the time, which was emboldening to a performer of my mental process-es. And when I had finished, airy with relief and guilty, with a self-consciousness that drove my hands and nose into some of his Bach albums that I couldn't read three bars of, he said, 'Any more?'

'No.'

'You make it?'

'Yes.'

'Quite pretty. Think you can remember it?'

'Yes – no.' Maladroitly I saw the trap, the possible future of playing in drawing-rooms.

'Any object in view?'

'Mrs. Stortford's cat, Stiver, you know'.

He thought and grinned. 'Ah ... pleased about something. You mean that Mur-ow-wow motif (you hurried that a bit; it's a retrospective thing ... looking back on a good gorge or mice, or something). *Leggiero penseroso*... "Mur-ow-wow –"'

'It's "Purr-*purr*-purr",' I objected.

'Same thing. Don't *peck* at it. *Sostenuto*, that's what you're after, or *andante cantabile* –'

'What's that?'

'Roughly, a singing kettle. Do that bit again.'

Nervous at last, I bungled it handsomely.

'No no no! Here', he edged me off the stool. 'By the way, it's *your* piece, but I don't like that chord. It's too plainspoken. If you want to get your cat effect you've got to convey here and there a hint that its apparent stupidity isn't more than top-dress-ing – get inside the skins of the things and people you're writing about – and the only way you can arrive at that, musically speak-ing, is by making subtle a chord now and then. Now, leave your purrs alone, I like them. But in your fourth bar, when you've stated your theme, give us a surprise, and at the *da capo*, vary it.' As I didn't know what my fourth bar was or where in the Stiver-pic-ture it occurred, we finally had to set the whole thing down on paper, I giggling, he peremptory and businesslike. And if I write the words here, it is not only a piece of self-indulgence as recall-ing a very illuminating morning, but to show how the expert sees a thing, the way the amateur attacks it, and, if it can be conveyed, how our versions varied when translated to the keyboard.

My version:

> I'm Miss-es Stortford's cat
> I'm lying in the sun
> My milk is done:

I'm lying in the sun, and Miss-es Stortford's cat.
> But suddenly my ears
> Perk up, oh what was that?
My broad-striped fur that heaves with purr
> Is lying in the sun.
Was it a rat, and is it worth
The heaving up of all my girth?
> I do not care two straws
> My milk is done,
> With head sunk in my paws
> I'm lying in the sun
My broad-striped fur still heaves with purr, purr...
> purr...
> I'm Miss--es Stortford's cat.

Mr. Field's version:

> I'm Mrs. Stortford's cat, I'm lying,
Lying in the sun, my milk is done.
> I'm lying in the sun, and
> Mrs. Stortford's cat.
But suddenly my ears perk up
> *Oh, what was that?*
> (I'm Mrs. Stortford's cat).
My broad-striped fur that heaves
That heaves with purr
> Is lying in the sun,
> Is lying in the sun.
Was it a rat, and is it worth the heaving up
> Of all my girth?
I do not care two straws, my milk is done,

With head sunk in my paws I'm lying,
    Lying in the sun.
My broad-striped fur still heaves
    With purr ... purr ... purr
I'm Miss-es Stort--ford's
        Cat.

Over our versions I happily forgot my diffidence in argument. Mr. Field, chuckling, said that there was much to recommend both our efforts but that his was the more interesting. And then, going off at a tangent, he opened another door for me when he embarked upon musical phraseology and said what disservice the printed word nearly always did to the composer, and cited Shakespeare's *Orpheus with his lute*, which I knew and had heard from the Shakespeare Readings, and laid down the law that *whatever* the setting used Shakespeare had done his best to ruin every effect they'd made for him. 'Have you ever *seen* it written? It's ghastly, unforgivable stuff.

> Orpheus with his lute made *trees*
> And the mountain tops that *freeze*
> Bow their heads when he did sing –

Lord! And it took Sullivan and German to rescue him! *They* scored it so that it was transformed – that doggerel!

> Orpheus with his lute
> With his lute made trees, made trees
> And the mountain tops that freeze
> Bow their heads when he did sing - - g
> Bow their heads when he did sing ...

and so on ... That's German ... lovely, plastic, swinging stuff, and it's the same with even musical comedy. Most of their song hits are hits because of the orchestration. Take your beastly "Coo" song. Written down, it goes

> Hark to the sound of "Coo", of "Coo", of "Coo"
> Calling to me and you, to me and you,

(It doesn't even scan!). But consider the lyricist: he *made* it with those repeats and shakes.

> Hark to the sound of "Coo - - OO - oo"
> Of "Coo - OO - oo", of Coo,
> Calling to me and you - OO - oo
> To me - EE - ee and you …

Heaven help all musicians. They need it.'

And thanks to that, even now I mentally transform the printed line into possible music. I started from that very lesson, and monstrously turned the Schubert march into a plausible waltz (Mr. Field said that for the first time he very nearly liked it!). And then he said a curiously prophetic thing.

'One day you'll probably do something that'll rather disgrace us both, and make a lot of money out of it.'

CHAPTER VIII

I

In the summer, Addison officially came into its own; officially, because, summer or no, Addison stood upon a singularly depressing reach of the Thames, with an interminable towing-path to the landmark of Addison's Villa, bordered with pollarded willows, alders and all the more riven and unfriendly of trees of the kind which in the catalogues of nursery gardeners get described as 'this prostrate subject', while the flora were represented by bulrushes, goldenrod, and tall, seedy magenta horrors that even marauding childhood rejected.

If you would escape the towing-path and struck off to the right, you first of all fell into an overgrown ditch before achieving the dreary safety of the commonland over which, in autumn, brooded haunted-looking sunsets, while if you turned aside to the left you merely fell into the river. But in spite of all this lowering scenery and greenery the Thames is after all a river, and the river at their doors (and often under them in the winter), it followed that the modish Addisonian sailed it and boated on it in the hot months and even achieved Henley regatta from home moorings.

2

It may have been that we were inlanders – Evenfield was quite a mile from the river – that we never became river-lovers or boat-wise, or what we called bilgeworthy; to this day I am unable to tell which is upstream and which down, and the currents and shallows of our reach, together with the workings and even the purpose of the locks, remain a sealed book to me, explain the lock-principle to me who may. Sometimes I almost think I have grasped the reason why craft must be arbitrarily elevated and pent, or sunk, while parties in them wait like truth at the bottom of a well, and the next moment understanding escapes me – like the time-and-note question! For if the river flows *flat*, why pump it up and down? It isn't as though there were submerged rocks or icebergs or atolls or reefs or Niagara waiting for one, and if –

Oh bother! I've long given up asking for enlightenment in case somebody tells me, and I feel in my bones that the explanation will be tedious.

And then, healthy Mell developed river sickness, poor toad, and invitations were a martyrdom to her until she had to come out with the reason for their refusal, which she called the upper retches of the Thames. One year she hopefully set out with the Fields to celebrate Daisy's birthday with a picnic tea and supper at Sunbury in the punt of a dreadfully rowing and knowledgeable Field uncle, and was so ill at tea that when she began again at supper the uncle said with harassed humour, 'All up? Then we'd better start for home'.

If the river never meant anything much to me, the reason was partly geographic but mainly because mother disliked it (as part, I know now, of Addison), and because I have always been painfully susceptible to atmospheres (those sunsets over the commonland!). Also, the river was to gather about it fewer associations for me than almost any other known inch of the place, and without mental data I am always lost and uncertain.

Father wasn't much of a hand at it, either: I don't remember ever once seeing him in a boat, but I do remember how he put us off the towing-path at family walks by a tendency to apposite quotation, and a brief excursion into the realms of what he called the study of Nature, which made Mell and me hot with vicarious shame.

As for Marcus, he never had time for the river, his life at that period being alternately earmarked for school and seaside lodgings. It was, and such as it was, I who was most on the water in June and July; everybody who knew us was kind and they little guessed what a deadweight they had taken aboard in myself, or that, always interested in people, I went with them far more in hopes of seeing a known face gliding by under a scarlet sunshade, whether its possessor be loved or liked or family joke or prohibited person or detestee than for a share of my hosts' favourite locks or reaches or views or moorings.

River hospitality brought the strangest combinations of people together, with the disregarded individual coming out strong as *an* oarsman, the social aspirant prominent for three months by unsuspected ownership of laid-up dinghy or skiff, while the Addison prominents and leaders got laid up themselves until the gentle autumnal mists and rain should put them squarely back in their right place, the drawing-room, with its Progressive Games, Book Teas and whist. Meanwhile, for me, the afternoon was a success if I could be tied up by, or even glimpse, jolly Evelyn Stortford, who punted competently as became a recognized tennis addict, or if I could subduedly shout to Johnnie Lawnford catching minnows with a butterfly-net in the stern of the doctor's boat. I once came home and swore that I'd seen Miss Dove madly pulling as she whizzed by but Mell said I'd imagined it, and that she'd be in St. Anselm's curtseying at some special service.

Mrs. Markham, on the other hand, was a feature of the river and dashingly could manage with hard ability any type of boat, as seemed fitting in one who was rumoured to smoke cigarettes and to want to read Shakespeare in costume. She owned an electric punt, and in a floral toque and hogskin gauntlets would manoeuvre it skilfully for incredible distances – our Bank manager once deposed that he had seen her at Southend, and although nobody quite believed it, it was felt (*Hamlet* in tights) that it was the sort of thing that Mrs. Markham *would* do. And as every river breeds gossip as it does pike and dace and all the unpalatable fish, there was little Mrs. Oswald, but when your hair is as auburn as hers it becomes a challenge to society to tie up anywhere, and every stone ginger-beer becomes automatically a bottle of champagne, and whether there was ever a grain of truth in the things which were said about her I don't pretend to know; all I am quite sure about is that, to-day, her exploits would probably get her voted the stumer and Grundy of any average bright young people's party! All this, of course, I heard many years later. And if you consider that it was all a storm in a tea-cup, I would remind you that the capacity of a cup for upset is several trillion times greater than the resistive power of the North Sea (or German Ocean). Not that Mrs. Oswald was apparently distressed at the Addisonian *on dit*: I think even if she had been, mother would have kept that side of things from us if for no higher reason than her own engrained contempt for mental vulgarity. All we knew was that Mrs. Oswald invited the knowing adult expression, just as we were aware that Mrs. Markham evoked another type of grin to which, somehow, it was permissible to allude and which could be laughed at and discussed without cautions and shooshings.

Meanwhile, I was in love with our next-door neighbour, Mrs. Randolph, for quite a fortnight (that golden hair!), and was miserably discontented with my own wealth of curly brown thatch and with the whole of my appearance because it didn't remotely resemble hers, a condition that was to descend upon me whenever I admired anybody and that I took about twenty-five years to slough off finally and completely.

And just as Mrs. Randolph was beginning to take a real fancy to me – I went off her, in that instant and painless way that is only possible to children whose devotion has not been seriously involved, and found myself landed with a perfectly unwanted, full-sized lady, who would actually venture to come to her fence and call over it to me, driving me to cover in the thickets of artichokes further down the path.

I committed a poem to her and her garden which thank God I have completely forgotten, except for some nonsense about 'crevices and crags' which rhymed with 'yellow and purple flags', and like nearly all juvenile verse it was insincere, uninteresting and unexpectedly deft. When I ceased to idealize Mrs. Randolph I wrote a comic song about her called 'When Bertie Goes After The Girls', that was one hundred per cent better, being full of authentic stuff! It dealt with a Piccadilly masher who specialized in ornamental (and blonde) girl friends who at last grew so numerous that individual outings with him became impossible unless the ladies walked crocodile – like the girls at Mayvale! (Mrs. Randolph in the last chorus figured at the very end of the queue.) Of this, I remember only isolated lines:

> When Bertie goes after the girls
> Two on his arm and six behind ...

and

> Just like a beautiful necklace,
> He is the diamond clasp, they the pearls,
> Ne'er such a sight was ever seen
> When Bertie goes after the girls.

And I wonder how Mr. Field would have phrased *that*!

For my Piccadilly masher I was indebted to – of all people – my father, partly through his fulminations over current musical comedy and its follies 'if not worse than folly', and to his entrancing hints about a place called The Burlington Arcade which, according to father, lived in some perpetual, disreputable twilight that no gentlewoman could penetrate without danger of something that we were left to invent for ourselves overtaking her, and where, quite incredibly, and surely irrelevantly?, it seemed that Honour Was Bartered: which gave me a vista of rows of people all sitting in an arcade and cheating at arithmetic when they weren't using a Latin crib, until Mell said that if ever you didn't know what father was driving at, it was sure to be men and being kissed by the wrong people, which made everything sane and reasonable in a twinkling.

Meanwhile, I seem to have drifted a long way from our reach of the Thames (as far as Mrs. Markham!).

We once actually gave a picnic ourselves, but our parties, always so successful indoors, were not so in this element, for Mell of course wasn't with us, preferring to nurse her stomach on the bank and meet us on our return to help in those deplorable aftermaths of cushion-toting and hamper-hauling; mother, trying to rise and pass the large bowl of salmon mayonnaise, caught her foot in a stretcher and flung the whole mayonnaise overboard to save herself, and our collapsible horn tumblers kept on telescoping while being filled and lost us quite three-quarters of our shandygaff. And then a steamer laden with trippers in pilot caps and straw hats and a harpist plonking away and pork pies and a 'cold buffet' in the saloon came by, and her wash rocked us until we were all quite maddened and mother said, 'This party is evidently *meant* to be a failure, we'd best not fight it', at which we all foundered in laughter, guests included, and Evelyn Stortford said, 'I like a party where *everything* goes wrong, you know where you are with that sort. It's when only one or two contretemps happen that it's really frightful', and some boy (who might have been Johnnie Lawnford's brother, Chetwyn, or little Jacky Barstowe, or could it possibly have been Trevor Ackworth-Mead?) leant, rapt, over the side and gloated, 'Isn't it *wonderful* to think all that mayonnaise has gone down so far? If I had a landing-net, I do believe I could get some of it up, Mrs. Morant'.

Mrs. Jasperleigh early found out that mother avoided and evaded the Thames, and being much under her influence no less from her devotion than her awareness of the Morant standing in Addison, took it into her head that mother considered river hospitality as socially beneath her, not realizing that mother's dislike of the water was as pure and uncontaminated and self-contained as a siphon of soda. It was enough! Mrs. Jasperleigh and Thelma would shun it too. And she did, giving reasons, and making allusions to possible future yachting holidays at Cannes, which she pronounced as though that resort was a tin of fruit.

But some family or other actually did own a yacht: a small, steam-run, charming affair with glittering brass and hanging wire baskets of pink geraniums, and they once invited me to be of a party and I must have gone because, although I've no recollection of mother being on board, for some reason I see myself with that double sight that *Peter Ibbetson* discovered, wearing a yellow linen smock and silk socks, green sandals and a huge green rush hat, whereas I'd much rather remember where we went and what we had for luncheon and who was there and what they said.

So much for the river as we knew it. On land, all was gas and gaiters. Mrs. Raymond gave haymaking parties for the Addison children friends of her own trio in part of her grounds, and to this we went carrying miniature rakes, and there was, with typical topographic perversity (for it ran parallel with a row of horrid little two-story villas) a quite lovely meadow one stretch away from our turnip field and opposite the Raymonds' house, which in July was studded with buttercups, daisies and marguerites, its hedge festooned with briony. Here, mother and I once (only once?) sank down before luncheon, up to our shoulders in all that green and white and gold.

3

It wasn't, of course, all haymaking and yachts and salmon mayonnaise and garden parties, though I have forgotten to include a jolly and rather squalid annual fair, with the Kingsmarket Military Band, which for two days in July was set down in the Vicarage Field in a cul-de-sac road by the post office in Upper Addison. This function was known as 'The Band-and-Fête', and it may have been for charity. I, mishearing as children do the sense of words, always alluded to it as The Bandon Feet, and it had a stall where with luck you won large, squat brown humbugs. And there was a large merry-go-round which ranked (and still does) for me with the harlequinade as a source of mental uneasiness, possessing as they both seem to me to do an other-worldly element into whose power one may be drawn if one isn't very careful … those assured figures of brass, whose forearms *only* moved, quite dreadfully, and kept time with the whining or stridulous music … the menace that is steam which as evening draws on, glows, as do the names Cumnor and Glamis, with a misty doom … those haunted, haunting and *knowing* hoots that the thing as a class, race, or genus emits from its apex quite (apparently) without reason, but for some excellent and awful motive of its own which we mustn't know….

Before the whole circular contraption with its brass and glass and gilding and secret sub-life I would stand, wondering as I regained the earthly sanity of coco-nut shy or Aunt Sally whether one could get round, lay, or exorcize the merry-go-round best (or at all) in story, verse or music, while Aggie Drumhead faithfully plodded after me. But even now I can't overcome my unease at merry-go-rounds. Is it possibly because their musical repertoire is almost never current, but of an era forgotten or superseded?

Once, we stayed at Bognor. Three large fields away over hedge and cornland was a fair, and in the fair was a merry-go-round whose lurid glow could be seen from our hotel windows, blasts of whose melody were borne to my appalled ears upon the autumnal air. It played in its own desolating fashion, for I really believe it could make *Ta-ra-ra-boum-de-ay* and Sousa's marches things of menace, that most bleak and ghostly and fascinating tune, *Sand Dunes*, which is melancholia incarnate even when helped out with a ballroom and débutantes. I was so overcome that I ran to mother's room, indicated to her the window out of which we both leant. A little was enough. She promptly went to her trunk and taking out a flask of brandy gave us both a drink. After a long silence we both said 'Hell!', and closed the windows!

Mrs. Jasperleigh gave a number of iced At Homes from which mother returned, as she said, faint but pursuing, as she allowed herself, a mild whisky (at three-and-six a bottle) and soda, while I gather that auntie S's affairs involved nothing more strenuous than looking on at tennis sets. It was the riverside residents who came out strongest, with their lawns that sloped to the water, and to these houses that mother, and later Mell, dropped in for an hour or so. I got the betwixt-and-between functions, and of these my completest recollection is of an afternoon fancy-dress garden party given by Mrs. Domrémy to which Mell and I drove in a hired victoria right through Addison, dressed respectively as Veronique and one of the Little Michus.

The drive to The Towers was the best part of it, for it took us from our house right through the main shopping street, past the Board School and down a residential road past innumerable well-known front gates, and in the toyshop I saw a new doll that wasn't there the previous day, and something else unfamiliar shining in rows in a cardboard box, and promised myself an investigation next morning, or on the way home from French with Madame; and the Field's drawing-room was empty but there was a head at Mrs. Field's airy bedroom window which suggested that they were dressing for the party, and further on Mrs. Stortford's gardener was weeding the gravel of the eternally sunless drive, and I actually saw the bun of Miss Abernethy bent over her bicycle as she wheeled it down her side turning where she lived, and wondered what she was going to do when she got indoors ...

Outside Mayvale a string of girls was returning from hockey in the Park shepherded by lean Miss Kirkby (of the Boo and the Ploo), and one of them saw us and her mouth became a delighted O, and she pointed, and they all turned, and Miss Kirkby grew red with the difficulty of simultaneously greeting us and scolding the pointer, and muffed it, and called out to Mell, 'Never let me see you doing that again!' and to the offender, 'How nice you look!'

Thelma made appearance as The Belle of New York, and some young man came along late, as Widow Twankey with a Dan Leno make-up, and we took a shy but easy fancy to each other – for who could fear a pantomime Dame? What drew him to me I don't know: I suppose it was my dress that was copied to the last detail from the theatre posters of the musical comedy. And when the inevitable Thelma danced, Twankey said, 'A Salvation Army Lass doing the cake-walk is *well* worth the price of admission', and to me, 'Why aren't *you* performing? My small brother thinks the earth of your dancing', and because he was a Dame with a low-comedy dot at either end of his mouth it was possible not to lie and say I didn't dance at all, and to conspire with him not to ask anybody to request me to do so, and he kept his word, leaving me to an afternoon without apprehension. He turned out to be a Barstowe, elder or eldest brother of freckled Jacky at whom I threw a stone in the Park because I hated his white felt hat. Jacky had at least two brothers, Mell said, of whom father's 'Ha-Clifford!' of the Royal procession was one.

CHAPTER IX

I

ALL THIS SORT of thing apart, it was our garden which really meant summer to me, and if anybody fears that I am going to enlarge upon it I can assure him that I am going to make strong efforts to refrain, bored to resentment as I have so often been by the exactitudes of novelists and their confounded multi-leaved *Encyclopaedia Britannica* and the uprisings of their *verbum saps*. All I will say (at any rate for the moment) is that we had a chancy mesh hammock tied between two apple-trees that bordered the party wall to Stamboul into which it was difficult to get, out of which more difficult to unpack yourself, but at least it was in the shade, unlike the glaring publicities of Mrs. Jasperleigh's garden furnishings, and that there was a greenhouse in which Stiles seemed to grow nothing but the more repellent cacti and some begonias, yet which smelt quite delicious and stuffy as if the rarest blooms were under cultivation – I can't think how he did it! And in the kitchen garden stood a large stone tank, put in by mother herself, in which toads could be lowered to swim with pathetic human perfection their little breaststroke, and on the sides of which sporadic and unsuccessful efforts at plank see-saw were once made by Mell and myself until I entered the Cavalry for a brief spell, mounted on a huge bath-can of red tin lined with blue.

One could be noisy in the garden though we seldom were: it was large enough to protect on its three sides Cocksedges, Martins and Randolphs. It wasn't in the least picturesque but I loved it, and even Mell, at seventeen, would come through the french window of the drawing-room after dinner to gallop round the asphalt paths in the summer dusk; I would watch her from the bathroom window while being dried by Aggie. (It was in the bathroom that I first put that sooner-or-later question 'How do babies come?' Aggie Drumhead happened to be physiologically 'for it' in my case and her sensible, 'You must ask y' mother', very pleasantly got me nowhere.)

In the mornings the borders fairly *raged* with the smell of alyssum, and we had a passion flower which seemed to oblige every year and which most lovely of things I've never seen since. The lawn was large, blindingly green and probably tiresome for Stiles owing to its crops of daisies and dandelions, but his ploddings back and forth with the mower at least contributed another good smell to the day which drowsily competed with that emitted by the lavender bushes.

Actually it was Stiles and the kitchen garden by the tank that gave me my major contentment, for what more could anyone ask than fruit and vegetable snacks all round one, there for the pulling up or picking off, plus unlimited if disjointed conversation when Stiles was weeding the asparagus trench? Our dialogue progressed well until he got to the middle, then we both closed down until he returned to weed the other side.

'Stiles, don't you think that with toads having faces like ours and proper mouths they could be taught to say things, if parrots can without?'

'Well, Miss Bobbin, if you ask me −' (*he moves off and silence falls for ten minutes*). I stood in a nice, stupid, sun-warmed coma.

'− it may be all for the best'. Stiles had returned. 'If you get mystifyin' them toads there's no sayin' what they mightn't come out with.'

Stiles was an excellent crony. We never played down to each other and he never insulted me by a bogus belief in fairies or Santa Claus although we used both parties for the entertainment and profit they could afford. In this way he could and did tell me long instalments of a story invented by himself about a Frog Fairy while being perfectly aware that neither of us believed in her, and on Christmas mornings he would bring me large sugar frames with a scrap in the centre for the picture 'from Santa Claus', as he told me the shop they came from and when he had bought them. What line he would have taken about Peter Pan I can't imagine, but feel sure that it would have been satisfactory and healing to one's self-respect, and generally speaking one on the chin for whimsicality! I think that he would have asked, as I have so often asked myself, why Mr. and Mrs. Darling didn't go to the Police Station at once, instead of accepting the disappearance of an entire nurseryful overnight.

Stiles specialized in horticultural Malapropisms which I was then too young to appreciate; to him an Antirrhinum was an Anteroom and an Ampelopsis a Hankylopshus, while, flowers apart, we treasure one sentence upon the subject of mosquitoes; 'Ah ... some calls 'em Musketeers but *I* calls 'em Gimlicknoses.' And his principal verb was 'to mystify'. It covered all the ground – literally, just as the house servants employed the word 'fornicate' in several connections but the right one. With them to fornicate or to be fornicating signified alternatively insincere flattery, a state of fluster, a waste of time, and a cook's complaint that the sweep had been fornicating half the morning with the flues was entirely typical. Between the lot of them they have so confused me that I have practically had to eliminate the word from my own vocabulary, not that it ever occupied a prominent place therein, just as in the same way and through a similar abuse of the word on the part of one of my friends who positively ought to know better I have been compelled to jettison 'criterion', unless I put in some uncommonly hard thinking beforehand!

At noon, Stiles retired for refreshment to a potting-shed round a corner, which Cuss and Mell called 'The Alps', why I never asked, taking it for granted that the rather hollow sound of one's footsteps in that dank cul-de-sac made the sound of 'alp-alp'.

On arrival in the morning, Stiles's first house of call and job was to the glory-hole, a window'd dug-out also facing the front gates, where he cleaned knives on a cocoa-coloured board with Goddard's plate-powder and (I believe) polished boots and shoes. The place stank comfortably of knife-powder, and it is a fact that the face of Mr. Goddard on the tin is far more vivid to me to-day than is that of any one of my family, including mother. Stropping, his fat circular face beaming good-humour and his large rump a little protruding for ease, Stiles would turn profile to talk to me like a 'songs at the piano' artist as I lounged by the water-butts at the top of the steps. The butts were ostensibly kept for shampoos, the local water being hard, and smelt of smoke and gnats and tar, and although I can't answer for the water that our hair was ultimately washed in, I do know that the shampoo was a delicious rich yellow cream called 'Egg Julep' which was sold in large round china boxes like potted meat. The process (like mother's absence at church on Christmas Day) seemed to last for aeons, during which one lost all sense of past bread-and-milk or impending bed. Whether Mell, in her time, hated it too I don't know. I must ask her.

If these occasions were a trial to Aggie Drumhead as well she never showed it: patient stolidity was her strongest suit and she would even manage to give in to my wish that I be read to while the involuntary tortures of combing were suffered. With the current issue of *Little Folks* before her on the day-nursery table she would lean, combing, while she read a rather unhappy serial called *Sheila's Secret* (which she pronounced 'Shella', and thus, as with Fornicate and Criterion, put me out for several years to come in the matter of pronunciation). What the secret was I haven't the faintest idea, but one illustration depicted a stormy-looking school-girl who looked ready for anything. I can see her face distinctly to this day, and should have liked to go to La Belle Sauvage and look up old files of the magazine and discover what *was* the matter with the girl.

We never made much use of our treeless lawn except to lie on it and sometimes with rugs and sticks to make tents for enemy-camp games with Janet Martin. Mother preferred the veranda as it wasn't overlooked by the kitchen window, and for a brief while a clock-golf set was laid down, and several matches played with friends who strolled round replete with Sunday roast beef, and, their duty to pleasure accomplished, would sink down by mother under the Japanese honeysuckle to enjoy her tea and her talk. One man I can't place was home from India and couldn't take his tired eyes off the lawn and kept murmuring happily that it was incredible:

Why we never played tennis at Evenfield I now attribute to mother's dislike of all active games and to Mell's satiety with them at Mayvale; between the two of them I got none, and in London was too diffident to learn a game whose standards of performance were becoming higher and higher, and that is one of the good things of life which I've missed completely.

Mell's birthday is in May, and one year it was as hot as July and that meant a veranda tea and sunhats; mother got the spring flowers by an April birthday: poor Cuss and father fell heir to those iron-grey months, January and February, and of all the family it was I who collared the autumn with October and its reds and greens, copper and mauve, with the apple-trees dressed for the occasion and celery available and muffins 'in' at last, roast pork for luncheon, bonfires by the currant bushes, hoar-frost and dahlias – and a resultant capacity for melancholy and nostalgia. You can't have everything.

2

In the late summer before breaking-up, Madame staged two fixtures: a term-end dancing display and a huge fancy-dress fête for a charity which she called Ze Whiff an' Strey. What constitutes a waif I have never discovered as it seemed to me to be more a feature of the narrative-verse of George R. Sims than an actuality, but I suppose there must have been juvenile strays, though it seems unlikely.

It was at this time of year that Madame burgeoned and became what we called cream of Tartar: against her even mother could do little and to quite a large proportion of the pupils and mistresses she was Muddarm until the holidays, for she disposed of the leisure of everyone as a General does his forces ('At tree (*lozenge*) you shall come for rehearse until siffen. Zhere will be no tea, you shall bring some kek in a bàgg'). Into all this I was drawn, and solo dances and special appearances were remorselessly contrived for me, and not soon shall I forget the costume for a ballet of sailors as conceived by Madame, nor the rumoured tension at Mayvale while she debated the relative merits of caps of white satin or blue silk, while the pleated skirts and everything capable of a border were edged with red-white-and-blue ribbon of which the shops still had a plentiful supply left over, I think, from the coronation of King Edward the Seventh.

For the Scottish reels foursome Madame evolved kilts of red sateen pleated all the way round. This brought the tension beyond rumour and almost to our gates, for here Mrs. Martin rose up in the craggy might of her ancestors and fought a battle with Madame Fouqué that did credit to her clan and blood.

March, march, Teesdale and Wensleydale! ...

and not only was Mrs. Martin's blue bonnet over the border but her cap over the windmill as makeweight. Didn't Madame realize that the kilt had an apron and that to pleat the front was unhairt of? And wheer was the sporran, relic of the day when the Scots wore scarce aught else? That settled it! The sporran was suggestive and stiffened Madame's resistance to its inclusion: had not Madame herself banned the Cake-walk at the dancing-class when hinted to of its origins?

It must have been a rousing session, that one at Stamboul, for Madame had actually walked the mile and a half to the Martins to quell rebellion, and what with the decent, Sabbath-keeping outspokenness of Janet's mother and the improper reticences of Madame they should have made a drawn game of it. But Mrs. Martin (née McIntyre) was hampered by her own tradition of hospitality, and, we heard, plied Madame steadily with her rich cakes while in full quarrel (which prolonged it), and although her guest refused to budge one inch in the matter of the kilt, Mrs. Martin withdrew Janet from the foursome, and there was a coldness ... indeed there were several. For during those weeks the social temperature annually fell in varying degrees all over Addison, with mothers maddened by sewing-machines whizzing our garments that, as they put it, would never 'come in for anything' after the display, while the machines and sewing nurses of other parents stood only too idle, their daughters having been quite monstrously passed over.

Sometimes when things looked too black, Léonore and Irène Fouqué, whom everyone liked, stole privily from Mayvale and rushed in different directions about Addison, picking up the pieces, before dropping in, carked with care, to Evenfield and mother's laughter and sympathy.

'But, Mrs. Morant, *what* to do? Mother's being too, too ridiculously insupportable! And it's always the same thing over these expositions. Even poor Miss Anson – a wreck! Mais enfin, it's forgotten for us', from the histrionic Irène.

And Léonore: 'A terrific rrow with Mrs. Culver over Dorotée and her shoes. It's offal. And I know the Culvers haven't a sou to jingle on a tombstone, as I told Maman. But if you say one word she is blessed!'

Of my kimono as originally conceived by Muddarm, all I need say is that my hair was stuck as full of miniature fans as a porcupine with quills, while my obi was tied in front in a large bow – a joke I was *not* allowed to share for many years! but which *gaffe* mother blew to auntie S and Mrs. Field, who laughed until they cried ('So Buggins becomes a harlot at nine years old, but I suppose you can't learn the business too early'). To which sally auntie S responded, shaking, 'Haigh! haigh! haigh! It's *no* use, auntie M, I shan't be able to go near the show now because of exploding.'

The display was held in the Jubilee Hall in a part of Addison which began to become another suburb and that we hardly knew; Madame's plushy drawing-room was not large enough for audience or performers. It was a deplorable hall, bare and comfortless and created, I should think, for Methodist whist-drives or Salvationist testimony. Miss Anson hated it because its acoustics were unfavourable to the hearing of commands, and we never shook down in it because it was to us an annual fatigue made slightly alarming by the sprinkling of those theatrical children imported by Miss Anson for effect, who kept the show waiting while their hair was frizzed by a hairdresser. I, more used to them from my extra tuition in their own classes, was never badly awed, and the creatures were harmless enough, if stagily dressed with a tendency to tulle and semi-concealed artificial flowers about their draperies and to call one Darling in a businesslike way before putting themselves in the front row as a matter of course.

As for the floral Fête, on the strength of the Whiff an' Strey it was crowded affair held in some field which I've never since been able to locate.

3

And then, as when a curtain is lowered, Evenfield, the garden and all our friends were suddenly hidden from sight. The seaside holidays had come round again, Cuss reappeared on the stairs, father ceased to catch the train to Waterloo, and we left in two cabs for the usual places, and left, it seems to me, without a parting word or backward glance.

Barmouth was caddying for father on the links, a miner's cottage facing the mountains that were full of small and unbalanced black bulls and huge mushrooms, terrifying thunderstorms, bannocks and milk for supper, Aggie reading *Kim* on a minute landing, and myself being given a penny by the greengrocer, who liked the look of me, and spending it in a slot-machine at the station featuring photographs of the kind known in certain circles as Art Studies (When Bertie Goes After The Girls, in short!). But the highlight of Barmouth was a beach concert party whom everybody blindly and doggedly called The Niggers, for they neither blacked their British faces nor rattled bones, but were straw-hatted and blazered and could be edifyingly sentimental, especially the pianist, who played the organ in church on Sundays, and owing to the smallness of their platform had to stand up behind his piano to sing a lugubrious ditty whose burden was,

Oh, *lucky* Jim, how I en - vy him!

Jim, if I remember, had by his superior attractions stolen the heart of his bosom friend's, the singer's, fiancée, which accounted for refrain number one, leaving the rejected lover so mourning that when Jim predeceased him refrain number two was accentuated and the gentleman was duly interred

In a churchyard (*pause*) by the sea.

As against this, there was a delightful red-faced comedian with very blue eyes who sang a song about a disarmingly unpunctual fireman and his outmoded equipment, the chorus of which has always, when sometimes I murmur it now, struck me as being quite admirable stuff, for, Editorially speaking, it was snappy, factual, and wasted no time on side-issues or excuses. It was in point of fact hot news!

> I was late. I was late,
> The engine it had rusted and the boiler it had busted.
> I was late,
> And when I came
> They'd started the new buildings
> I was late, late again.

Nor did The Niggers overlook that clean British fun which thrives upon domestic catastrophe and that is first cousin to the lodger and the mother-in-law as a laugh-raiser. Two lines of this *chronique douleureuse* – it happened at night but the nature of it escapes me – ran (*prestissimo*),

> There was Pa, he was half undressed
> Sitting in the gutter with the mangle on his chest …

It comes back to me that the lodger was *not* forgotten, for was there not another song which (unconventionally, surely?) praised him?

> Our lodger's such a *nice* young man
> And a nice young man is he,
> *So* good, *so* kind to all the compan - ee …

And there was a chorus:

> OH, what do you think of Mary?
> Hi, hi! where d'you think she's gone?
> With a dandy coloured coon on a Sunday afternoon
> Hi, hi! *that's* where Mary's gone.

The phrasing (thank you, Mr. Field!) of the singer was 'a dandy-coloured coon' and it was years before I realized that there should have been a vocal comma after 'dandy'; as it was, I, thinking in terms of dandelions, pictured the coon as of their tint – a not bad guess, America containing such a goodly proportion of what they call 'high yellows' in a population that Mr. Sinclair Lewis has described as 'one hundred per cent mongrel!'

Shanklyn was a charming two-storeyed white lodge with an orchard and the landlady's twins for me to play with, and terrific heat, large iridescent shells to be bought in the Chine, and falling in love with that most charming of all pierrots, Mr. Clifford Essex (whose altar was a very crowded one indeed: one was lost behind all those adult backs!).

Bembridge was a ghostly and constant feeling of depression, an avenue, and a sea that came right up to the brambles, also a deserted house on the cliff through the windows of which pictures still hung askew on the peeling walls. Dreadful!

Ramsgate was heatwaves and fish, viscous nougat, French sailors unloading and a stout lighthouse whose beams swept our bedrooms on The Paragon, and huge buoys in rows on the harbour, an all-pervasive smell of hot asphalt, and a pierrot called Uncle Arthur in a little boy's linen sunhat who had my heart for a few weeks but never displaced Mr. Essex.

Tenby was flat scones called Batchcakes, gloomy lodgings, inconvenient bathing and learning to bicycle, with mother rushing after my vanishing machine from which I hadn't learnt to dismount.

Swanage was the whole of a furnished house on the cliff with a shadeless garden and a clientèle of thirsty dogs that pots and pans must be filled for.

Sheringham was unclean farm-house lodgings and mother quoting things about The Garden of Sleep, and exquisite shells for the picking up on a lone, lorn and distant bay that would have suited Emily Bronte down to the ground. Damnable!

We went away a lot, in those years (mother's dislike of Addison?), for not many Easter holidays passed without another exodus, though not always with father and Cuss. A birthday at the sea was a real misfortune that only overtook mother, who incredibly didn't mind, and poor Mell, who did, what with posts arriving late and no further delivery after tea and friends ungettable and presents at the mercy of the local shops and the cake beyond the skill of the baker and no treat procurable, unless you were the kind of person who is satisfied by looking at a field of cowslips or bluebells in a wood and coming home uplifted and purified and, generally speaking, full of emptiness.

Lee, in Devonshire, was a gothic, flint cottage, and mother's first attempt at bread-making that was heavy, heavy, damned heavy, like Jingle's luggage. And in our little churchly parlour I was suddenly free'd of diffidence and reluctance by one of those unpredictable flashes which occasionally allowed me to enjoy the dancing-class, and staged an entire variety act of song and dance for mother and Mell, after which, appalled and deflated, embarrassment gripped me as usual, a condition in which I remained indefinitely.

I tracked down and bought an Easter egg for the Vicar (why?) but ate it myself.

Lee was, finally, an endless cliff walk to Ilfracombe *but* the discovery in a shop in the arcade of a 'hand-painted' post card of Ada Reeve as *San Toy* (which really should have been *Toy San*: what was the librettist thinking of?), and coveting it with deep, determined avidity, and pricing it and finding it was fourpence (fourpence!), but I got it at last, then suddenly lost it, and suspect Marcus to this hour, for he was still a martyr to that lady, whereas I was merely attracted by her tunic and tights.

CHAPTER X

I

GOING AWAY was corner seats and *Comic Cuts* out of which Aggie, low-voiced, would read me the jokes: tunnels that smelt of gunpowder, sulphur and soot, hardboiled eggs that tasted of tunnels, while at every major station glass swing-doors were engraved with the names of Spiers and Pond.

The return journeys are all a blank and the next thing of which one was aware the garden, with globules of dew on the dahlias and a scent of trodden leaves, and finding the trees in full apple, the pears now grown from peg-tops to stewing size, and

Stiles trudging about with a damp sack over his shoulders. One year I gave him a mug with 'J' on it in forget-me-nots, for I had early drawn from him that his name was James and that he lived in Nutts Lane. He assured me that it should have a good place on the mantel next a vawse he won at a Band-and-Fête and (on the other side) a red First Prize card for the best potato entered in the Cottage Garden Class at a flower-show outside Kingsmarket in 1888 before he come to live at Addison or I was born or thought of – a misty reminiscence which left me feeling outside the pale, and incredulous into the bargain; for if *Stiles* was doing things and having fun before I could join in too then everybody else must have been also, and I'd missed something, but over which I can't have dwelt long, for, as in an irrelevant dream-sequence where everything at the time seems ordered and reasonable, there was suddenly at the end of the kitchen garden bordering the road a large fowl-run that wasn't there before, and in it hens smelling richly and sourly and a handsome rooster with auburn feathers the colour of Mrs. Oswald's hair that Stiles referred to as 'that Dung 'ill', and a black hen with a face that immediately recalled aunt Caroline, one of father's sisters, a discovery that I went into the house to announce to mother, who tried to look disapproving and ruined it all by full agreement – she couldn't bear aunt Caroline, who thought and said that my skirts were too short and my necks too low. She lived in what I have since learnt was Onslow Square and gave one luncheons consisting chiefly of massive silver dish-covers and a phalanx of unfriendly, starched maids who seemed to sense the tension-in-law. Her mother, old Mrs. Morant, had tricksily cornered what humour her family possessed and had a tongue which if translated to the theatre could easily have been trimmed into epigrams, but being merely a gentlewoman of the old school she got no laughs at all except from our mother. 'M'mm …' she dismissed aunt Caroline's stricture, 'it takes a good woman to have a really nasty mind, and if a child with uncommonly pretty legs can't show them it's a pity. But Caroline's prudish, you know. She was *born* unmarried, even if she is a widow … I always did think your two *most* satisfactory, Halcyon – Melisande and Babs, I mean, not your limbs, though it's from you they got 'em. The Morants run to bedposts though I kept my ankles until I was nearly seventy.'

And just in the same way that we never even by accident seemed to hit on the same holiday places as our friends, so it never, I think, even occurred to us over hoops in the Park to ask each other what sort of a time we had had. Real life to us was Addison, and the annual departure a whim entirely of the grown-up mind, like paper patterns and no-sweets-before-breakfast, and so glad were we to be home that we fell back on semi-serious quarrels, even with the Fields, and would separate for luncheon with a 'Good-bye, enemy'. And October being my month, and I alive as in no other, as I am to-day, I even contrived a pomp-ous row with the gardener and wrote *him* a note (it began 'My Good Stiles'). Fired by father's feats, I began a Life of a French Countess called Hélène de Gruyère who was a confidante of what monarchs I could remember and put a fact to, including Louis the Fourteenth and Henry the Eighth, whose faces when bested by her tongue became 'infected with collar' – as indeed they probably were. But I soon scrapped her, for wasn't my birth-day coming near, and, better still, the Fifth of November and a large party at Evenfield beginning with tea and a mask beside every plate and progressing to a dusky lawn, with Aggie distrib-uting the smaller fireworks from her bulging apron, and ending with a gargantuan bonfire topped with its Guy? A night that was ravishingly *heilige* and anything but *stille*, what with the distant poppings and ploopings and rockets going up in gardens and backyards all over the neighbourhood, and the sky shimmering and vibrating with lurid glares and glows and percussive flashes. We did the thing properly in Addison, and for days beforehand stuffed dummies, idiotically gazing like paralytics, were wheeled about in handcarts and prams and numbers which would satisfy even those strongholds of Guydom, Lingfield and Lewes.

Over our own, which were sometimes groups of current vil-lains including Kruger and a murderess whose name I've for-gotten, mother and Mell worked for days, so that the midday break from lessons and escape to the garden became more of an urgency than ever.

On the Fifth, people were invited to Evenfield to whom mother wanted to give special treats and pleasure.

Mother, unlike dear Mrs. Field, wasn't temperamentally a Good Worksy person: all her kindness was of amateur status. Mother was no hand at raising the fallen, or Bible readings, young people's clubs, Christian young women or any praiseworthy endeavour which has official notepaper. Her affection for the humble was undiluted by conscientious considerations; it was possible to her to make of those who served her warm and personal and lifelong friends in a real way that many who use the expression as a Christian or snob flourish never truly achieve. Breaches of faith and confidence, all forms of disloyalty, pettiness and dishonesty mental or material were the only barriers. It was a highish standard that she set, but if you think it over, a profound compliment, as it was, *au fond*, a sincere and classless assumption of shared human virtues. Hit or miss: unlike Mrs. Field who, when domestically or philanthropically betrayed by her protégées and finds, forgave them on principle, while mother, on being let down, took it as hardly as she would an unkindness from Mrs. Field herself. A vulnerable mistress for all her outward show, the bad servants traded on that side of her nature and the good respected it and her.

Cooks and houseparlourmaids came and went, and I suppose did all the things which they do to this hour, except that even the worst of them cooked better and all knew at least the rudiments of her job, and through chance and change Aggie remained, though even she had had predecessors, stop-gap young women who, to me, came from the unknown and vanished into the same.

When a kitchen crisis occurred Mrs. Couchman was sent for, and she came, fair-hair'd and beaming, and unpacked her Japanese hamper containing apron and house-shoes as if she had reached her haven and home, though she actually lived in Nutts Lane near Stiles.

'Oh Madam, isn't it lovely to see Miss Barbara's sun-hat hanging up again!' this apparent orphan would murmur, although she had two children who fully shared her feelings about us, and a husband as well. She was of the type which if a friend attempted murder would apologize below-breath, 'Of course it was very wicked, but she looked a perfect picture with the knife in her hand', and was one of the few devoted mothers in the world who could admire the children of other women above her own. With her, Mell and I enjoyed The Divine Right, and as for myself, if I can't pretend that at that period of our lives I felt for her as other than an intermittently pleasant part of the landscape, I see now how deep was her place in my regard.

For with Mrs. Couchman my sense of security was so entire that to her I would give, and so confide, all that I had to offer. To her I could read verse and plays finished or half-written: for her I would dance and sing the last musical comedy I'd seen in Kingsmarket: for her (oh ultimate concession!) I could even play the piano if the drawing-room were empty, and about this social facility I was at times bewildered and unhappy, for wasn't it a disloyalty to my family? And if she was an audience too perfect for the good of any performer, I can honestly say that her uncritical, wrapt attention and laughter did me no harm at all, for while it lasted I was absorbed in the job of entertainment, while she peeled potatoes, her sleeves rolled above comfortable and I am sure comforting arms. Perhaps it was that I instinctively counted upon her unsophistication and its accompanying ignorance of how far short of the model or ideal I was actually falling. I only know that for our dear morning help I danced better than ever I had (save in flashes) for Miss Anson and the watching mothers, played with more freedom and expression than ever I had for Mr. Field. Authorship alone suffered no sea changes. You can't improve or ruin the written word at nine and ten and eleven years old …

To our firework parties the Couchman children, Hope and Connie, were always invited, while their mother, busy with the washing-up, would be fetched by one of us to see the fun; their faces, mother once told me, were absolutely *bored* with excitement and ecstasy, so unutterable was their enjoyment as Stiles moved about in the dark touching off the more expensively alarming of the effects – those which are suggestively marked 'Light the blue touch-paper and then stand aside' (they were run very close in cost and hinted catastrophe by those others labelled 'Tie to an upright post. Not to be held in the hand'). So awed with bliss were the Couchmans (and I) that I only remember once that we all laughed aloud and interminably when mother aimed a 'starlight' at the guy and it lodged in his mouth like a cigarette. She said, 'I couldn't do *that* again if you paid me a hundred pounds', at which Hope and Connie looked at her, the guy, and each other, and suddenly emitted aching squeal after squeal and respectfully hurried away, doubled up, to get over it behind the gooseberry bushes.

It was on the cinder path by the rhubarb that Evelyn Stortford lit a giant Chinese cracker with horrified bravado, shouting for all her twenty-five years, 'I'll do it! I'm a Briton!', and on the other side by the rockery that the manure-throwing Chetwyn Lawnford laid two rockets, lit, and stood on them to 'see if they'll carry me right over the fence'. And for me the party wasn't even over the next morning, for there were deliciously-smelling aftermaths to be found all over the garden: charred rumps of Roman candles, iridescent circles on tree-trunks where Catherine wheels had spun: the bonfire a mass of still warm ash …

And a voice, suddenly and without transition, is declaiming 'Lead me to my chamber!', and it is another evening in the warm and curtained drawing-room, and mother in laced Liberty velvet being armed towards the french windows, as Cleopatra, to a round of applause from the evening-dressed assembly. In flannel dressing-gown, I struck the only unmodish note as I watched and listened for a treat in the abominable Cosy Corner. Cleopatra had been giving somebody a hot time and has threatened to have him 'whipped with wire' (unless I've dreamed that line?), and I must have got out of the room somehow because the next minute I was on insecure skates of shiny yellow wood careering round a railed-off enclosure marked DANGEROUS, and being frantically pursued by old Mr. Martin, Janet's father, and rescued by that bold veteran and brought back to the main pond where the ice was holding, and people even curling.

We had skating every winter under the red sun that smouldered above the silver birch in the 'Miss Cocksedgees'' garden.

And just before we all dug in for the winter, before the yellow fogs descended upon us and the pea-soup came round again, the little hump-backed Italian with a hurdy-gurdy ceased coming round the drive of our house and playing ghostly operatic clichés to us as he hopefully smiled up by the old lilac bush. He always came on Thursdays at the unnatural and eccentric hour of five p.m. when the road was more deathly quiet than ever, and Thursday was dancing-class day, which meant that at the very moment that he wheezed out *Che farò*, or whatever it was, I was always being pulled out of billows of shaded chiffon and received my first impacts with Verdi, Offenbach and Puccini through smothers of that pleasant fabric; and although I never knew his name, that hurdy-gurdyist, again, is a face which is more photographically clear and distinct to me now than many a one I would and should be seeing in my mind's eye.

2

I was sitting reading in the hall one evening and expecting the arrival from the passage of the maid to rattle at the little brass gong which would signal family dinner and my bedtime. Mother and father were talking in the billiard room, and my ear suddenly became aware that something was amiss. It didn't appear to be so much what they were saying which gave me this impression as my intimate familiarity with parental tones that recognized the key in which any discussion was pitched; and if I stopped reading and listened it was partly because I considered that nobody had any conversation with father that couldn't be heard by everybody, but chiefly because, if mother were being worried, I must be ready to spring. Had they mentioned any names I should have gone away, because in my vague code that would have been eavesdropping. But if it all sounded respectable enough, wrapped in a decent cloth of anonymity, my instinct remained wary.

'It could *only* have happened here!' exclaimed mother in her voice of low, sarcastic resignation, which, however, covered so many trivia that one discounted the indictment and waited.

'Oh, Halcy, Halcy … come, come! It might have happened anywhere.'

'It's the lack of common charity that I can't stand. I could have found it easier to forgive if the Addisonians had really meant it and taken concerted action with something to go on, or made a stand against something definite however narrowminded, but not they! It was the result of pure unmitigated idleness and irresponsibility. Petty persecution or a badminton match — it's all one to them.'

'Yes, yes … but, well, she and you – '

'You mean I didn't "call" on her? No. I didn't. Frankly I didn't think she was up to sample, poor wretch. One must draw the line somewhere for the children's sake, and I consider that I've a right to reasonable elimination. But there's a pretty wide gulf between what's happened and not calling! It's the whole atmosphere of the place … suburbia incarnate at its worst – '

Father was sharp and at his 'Oh, nonsense!' I bristled on mother's account. Father was a good man and a generous, and of course terribly clever and knew dates, but he must *not* speak to her in any but a soft and even tone (*andante cantabile*, as it were!).

'– and suburbanness is a state of mind, not where one lives.'

'I see that point'. (Father was being fair and reasonable: he was, after all, a solicitor.)

'Not that it isn't possible to combine the two in one egregious whole', finished mother, sticking to her guns, whatever they were.

'Well … if you really feel that way –'

'Oh I do, my dear. This business has about been my Waterloo.' I knew that expression so didn't make the mistake of confusing it with the station that for me led eternally to Drury Lane, Royal processions and chicken mayonnaise.

'– there's nothing for it but to refrain from renewing the lease. Luckily it has only a year and a bit to run.'

That gave me ajar and stopped any wish for further enlightenment; mother had got what she wanted, whatever that might be, so needed no further protection from me. But I harassed myself over the matter for an eternity – quite two half-nights – and her pokerfaces (I knew them all) though disturbing were soon forgotten; for time went on and nothing happened at all: and therefore nothing would.

CHAPTER XI

I

AND 'A YEAR and a bit' went by and we were leaving Evenfield and Addison and I have no remembrance of grief … not one, unless you can count the only scene that I recall, of saying goodbye to Aggie Drumhead outside the bathroom door. She was crying. I was off to the Fields where mother and I were to spend the last dismantling days, father slept in London at his mother's house in Sloane Street and Mell was taken in by the Stortfords. Mrs. Jasperleigh had emotionally offered to house us all but it was felt that that would be asking a bit too much, and of course Broadacres was still Broad-acres, and Thelma still being Thelma, a decision that suited Mell and me, though I really don't believe that mother was affected by what walls enclosed her last residential hours in the place. Marcus was by that time up at Oxford and so as usual out of everything.

I walked alone to the Fields at a time when I should have been Abernethy'd with lessons in the day-nursery before shopping or paying the tradesmen's books with mother. I suppose I said goodbye to Stiles, but that's gone, too. I'm being at least honest, and not retrospectively attributing to myself sensations that must have been there in view of what I did later, and I do believe that it was. Mell who did what crying there was in our family: Mell who having been uprooted from Addison never expressed even one faint wish to be replanted there, either then or thereafter.

The human heart may be desperately wicked, but it is beyond question cranky!

I see Mr. Field looking down on me in the music room at Cumptons as he said, 'Well, we're going to miss each other in spite of everything, aren't we? If you do anything clever it was I who taught you, but if you're stupid you've never heard of me. Is that a bargain?' He is instantly replaced by Miss Anson, to whom with the downcast head of acute shyness induced by the strange nature of the occasion I present a white kid handbag, and for a briefer moment when I give to Miss Abernethy a muff-chain of a truly shocking design that got itself called Art Nouveau.

The little Fields made us all toilet bags embroidered with circles enclosing daisies, primroses and clover-leaf. Their mother hadn't allowed them to be told the time our train left for Waterloo but sent them off to school as usual. 'It seems so unkind, but it's all for the best', she said, her eyes brimming with tears that this time were not of copious, guilty mirth at mother's quips.

Mrs. Jasperleigh gave us all gold bangles rattling with charms, and declaring that to part at the station would be quite beyond her powers of control, went to bed with hysterics, or so auntie S declared in a letter.

Of the platform scene I've no remembrance at all of the time of day or type of weather as we slid past the row of familiar cottages whose gardens faced the line. But I do recall the enormous cake that Mrs. Martin put on the seat beside Mell: that rather incredibly old Mr. Martin appeared late and capering with haste with an even larger box of chocolates, and that most improbably the elder Ackworth-Mead son whom I'd once mistaken for a hired waiter was seen by me with Mrs. Markham who had four dogs on a lead. (This is ridiculous. They must have arrived separately!)

2

We were going to live in London, and before the new home was ready to be distributed, alarmingly, among relations. Mother bagged old Mrs. Morant for herself and me: father fell heir to his sister, aunt Caroline, and Mell stayed with cousins in Kensington who were of ages up to twenty-three and went out a lot, and could be generally counted upon to cause a cousin from the wilds to forget her origins and make another start, mother said, referring to the move from Addison and its possible marks left upon a daughter of nineteen as though Mell had had an illegitimate baby and was in the fallen woman class until socially reinstated. Actually, Mell would have gone her own way and settled down wherever she went, for unlike me she was more dispassionate in her approaches to life and people, an onlooker who settles back in his fauteuil, whereas my sort is perpetually on and off the stage itself, like a wrought-up producer who only slumps into his stall when things are running smoothly or total despair with the cast has set in.

Marcus's comment from Magdalen was, 'Well, thank heaven we're out of *that* doghole'.

And every night for quite a year I included in my prayers, '– and God bless Evenfield'.

PART TWO

CHAPTER I

I

MELL WAS to be dropped into a new life ready-made for her, mother to settle back into her old world, father to know little change in a life which was largely spent in London in any case, and Marcus, who like all sons lived from his cradle up in acquiescence of mobility in the interests of any career, even became a junior member of father's firm without one single scene that I know of, so hypnotic is family intention.

It was I who had to start all over again, in houses without gardens, gardeners, garden parties or bonfires, with all of magic contained in a bundle from the greengrocer and glasshouse compressed into a punnet, a new school to shake down at and friends to break in from their beginnings: people without context ...

Our bicycles were sold for a song (it must have been a lugubrious one) to the Raymonds because we were unused to traffic, and I at least must never go out alone further than the corner pillar-box because of nobody-explained-what, I to whom a three-mile radius in every direction was as familiar as my mother's face, I to whom every sixth door was available at most times of day. In town, you either called because you were relations or upon calling terms or not at all (no impromptu impulses and half-eaten apples laid on the gatepost). Conversation with shop people went largely by the board as well, for in houses like Granny Morant's the food arrived at the area door via a chain of domestic conference with cook or (wine) the butler, while the park-keepers and chairmen in Kensington Gardens were too numerous and busy to remember one in summer, in winter one didn't want their chairs, and they confined themselves to scolding people off the Round Pond if the ice seemed to be holding. For skating there were Prince's and (roller) Olympia, a sorry exchange that Mell and I soon gave up in contempt, for hadn't we had a clear half-mile of forest-bordered lake in which Charles the Second had fished while Nell Gwyn fixed a red herring to his line, and the Addison ponds on which one was taken round by friends and rescued by Mr. Martin and picked up by Evelyn Stortford when crashingly one fell?

It was things like Prince's which broke the healing skin on that cut which was leaving Evenfield. For of course the cut was healing. I defy anybody of any age not to become one of London's lovers if given what the law calls 'reasonable access' to her.

2

I became one of Louis Hervet's slaves, and for the first time ceased to be a Ninetta Crummles, learnt how little I knew, and really began to dance. On and off, I was under his hands for six years, until I was past eighteen.

Hervet, like Madame Fouqué, was a character and one of the few dynastic ballet masters left in London. Equally master of piano or violin, he may have been a first-rate dancer in his youth, but I think his heart was always with music. And just as Mr. Field could do nothing with me beyond a certain point, just so did I bring to Hervet all my potentialities and defects, and although I went further in the technique of classic ballet than ever I had on Mr. Field's piano with the printed score, so Hervet to his nervous despair could get me no further. I could damnably please, he once fumed: I could dance any current musical comedy actress off the stage (which of course wasn't dancing at all): I could do a travelling arabesque *sur la pointe*, then why the blazes did I let my other leg drop as I moved when it should be extended at waist level? My *entrechats* were like a faulty electric current, twinkling but gone wrong: with me an *entrechat quatre* turned into a dishonest *entrechat trois*.

'Why can't you do four pirouettes?'

'Because I fall down', I answered.

'But good God, when I was studying at the Conservatoire I spent my *time* on the floor!' and,

'Do you need the whole of Kensington Gardens to do *déboullés* in?' I said apologetically that in doing those spins round the room on the half-point I lost all sense of direction.

'I know you do. You'd crash into Buckingham Palace from the courtyard, because you never remember the first principle of all forms of the pirouette which is to turn your head sharply halfright with every spin, or half-left according to your direction. Your *grand jété en tournant* is very pretty, but you don't get that hovering effect of hanging in space that Nijinsky does because you forget *to stiffen your muscles when you're in the air*. There's no secret about it that's his property alone, in spite of the nonsense they talk about him.' For Hervet was at all times as ready to dethrone the established past and present as he was to pull me to pieces in the interests of the dance. Taglioni's arms were too long and she had to learn from her father to cross them over her head to minimize this defect: on the other hand, she practised until nausea set in as her father believed that every day must show some definite improvement, however slight. Pavlova was a perfect machine but would never achieve greatness except with the mob because she danced from the waist down and couldn't make use of her face – a heartless performer ... no warmth. Genée, now, was all warmth but lacked the Grand Manner because of that element of *gaminerie* which made her so delicious. Nijinsky was a third-generation dancer, and these children were reputed to be born with bird-bones – hollow – which gave them their spring and ability to bound to astonishing heights. Nijinsky-could jump a clear four feet into the air with no take-off at all. About the début of Maud Allan who was drawing fashionable, artistic and political London to the Palace Theatre Hervet had least to say. Elongating his already long and mournfully humorous face he pronounced,

'Looking down a well ... pointing up at the moon and falling in a heap on the floor ... Now! *Battements* ...'

Sometimes the world would be too much with him right in the middle of a lesson and he would sit at the piano playing fragments of ballet and murmuring '*Narcisse... Narcisse*'. I learnt to play them all as well – the fragmentary method suited me, too – often without the slightest idea of the ballet or composer I was memorizing and would re-hear it with astonished pleasure in Rimsky-Korsakov and *Schéhérezade, Cleopatra* and *Hungaria*. *Cleopatra* was an appallingly dull affair, but I forgive it all for that motif where the mummy is slowly unwound, and which consists merely of a few repeated bars on four notes, for strings; it seemed to me, and still does, to contain the very spirit of that Egypt I have never seen, but which as a sheer word suggests a sombre ebony thick inlaid with patines of bright gold … Boïto did the same service in his *Mefistofele*, in a passage (for brass) about heaven, which I have never seen either!

Unlike the majority of Hervet's students I didn't expect to become a professional dancer or teacher, and so was free to enjoy him as a human being without pestering myself as to rate of progress or his own quality as an instructor. I found him exasperating and lovable, funny and impersonal. And I liked his classroom (a converted drawing-room) which was high-ceiling'd and hung with prints of famous ballerinas dating back to La Camargo, and full of an atmosphere of the past and Georgian tea-parties, while you had but to look out of his long window to be switched two reigns ahead, and sense the fog, the hansom cab, and in the house opposite a lean silhouette in a dressing-gown smoking a pipe of shag while Doctor Watson sits by the fire being A Little Nettled by This Want Of Confidence …

In the six years to come, I think that Hervet realized that as I had no fish to fry I was to be regarded at once as personal friend and one without status in his rooms, and I do believe that when intermittently I used to drop in for a little *barre* or centre practice if life's action slowed down elsewhere we would put in far more conversation, fulmination and criticism than work. He wasn't to live long after our final drifting apart, and my admiration for his tolerant refusal to belittle English dancers because they weren't Russian remains as bright as ever. He never saw the rise of British ballet, unless you could count the Empire and Alhambra stock company which commonly supported Continental *Assolutas*, and would have taken it matter of factly if he had, paying it the true compliment of satire and constructive criticism, as he did to

Maud Allan, whose ingenuous art was to be killed by plagiarism and a franker era broken to the brassière and the *cache-sexe*, and who was to relapse at last into a very full-dress Mother Superior in Cochran's revival of *The Miracle*; to Genée whom I was to watch through her retirement, Phyllis Bedells through hers, Pavlova slapping Mordkin, severing the partnership and dying, and Nijinsky living on, his mind haunted by the ghost of a rose, his bird-bones soaring no more, a faun resting in the afternoon of his career ...

CHAPTER II

I

IF MY MEMORY of our move into and out of Evenfield is a blank and gaps, every detail of our entrance into our London house is catalogue'd. It was the business of remembrance-of-faces over again, with the principals dim and the auxiliaries unwantedly clear.

It was in spring, our convergence by taxi from the relations' houses to our own, and there were the usual inartistic and improbable contrasts of apple and cherry blossom going on against the background of grey sky and chilly winds, while in the eiderdown'd nights lambs were dropped by perplexed ewes in Kensington Gardens (Oh, what a DAM' fool nature is! If she's a mother, I wonder what bemused dolt ever married the creature).

Father and Cuss of course were and remained out of the worst of the scrum, and father would merely pass down the road by a new and more convenient route to the City, remarking as he did so that whatever Halcy decided he must have an 'adequate' study, a stipulation he would have made, I think, had our new home been a mansion in Park Lane or the sort of Holborn attic in which Chatterton breathed his last. It was mother and Mell who really settled everything, I who just dropped into a bedroom and shared den which sprang up overnight from bare walls and packing-cases.

It was my very first unshared bedroom, and any initial awkwardness or doubts the room and I might have had of each other were swallowed up in my elation and pride. And by the time I was taking sole possession for granted, we had become so mutually accustomed that we could no longer see straight about each other, and didn't try to.

It was a pleasant house in Kensington Gate, a cul-de-sac which gave me a fractionally greater freedom, and the small, oblong garden open to the residents was at least a place where things grew, though nearly everything which children crave to do in open spaces was forbidden in the same disheartening spirit which discouraged street musicians and hawkers at area gates. It was, even for the garden of a London square, quite dreadfully overlooked by the pillar'd houses and more in the nature of a rural gesture than a place where you could laze in deck chairs or secretly build your January snow man. The nurses liked it for that reason, for they had but to put head out of upper window and ejaculate in the extraordinarily elliptic manner of their kind, 'Now then Esmé, what did Nanny say?' to earn their gaoler's wages and save a walk down three flights of stairs. The things that Nanny apparently once said, translated into the language of reason, logic and sanity, boiled down to prohibitions in which shoes must not be scuffed on gravel, hats hung by their elastic on the boughs of trees because of 'the soots', and what seats there were avoided if in white sailor suits 'because you never knew with the pigeons'. Insane to the end, the nurses would thus pass the English language triumphantly through the mangle.

I once mentioned it all to father, for my ear perceived that all was not well, and he, as so often happened, forgetting that I was thirteen and not thirty and an L.L.B., laid down his pen (he was engaged upon a Life of an incredible old party called Madame de Brinvilliers for a pocket series of 'Prominent Poisoners of History' who ate two raw eggs she had ordered while being tortured) and said, 'It must be remembered that the domestic class is in a rather unhappy state of transition: centuries ahead of complete illiteracy, they are at the same time many more centuries behind an even elementary scholarship'. He went on to say that since the industrial revolution of the 'fifties the social hierarchy admitted to no peasant class as it did in France, Italy and other countries of

Europe, but was mistakenly causing a pressure, wholly artificial, of the peasant *in esse* into a state of living, spending and calling (or occupation) which in point of fact it was by no means yet fitted to fill. Moreover –

I unconsciously beat time to these rolling periods with a paper-knife. But we did arrive at the point when father decreed that 'soot' had no plural, a disability it shared with cannon and salmon.

> Soot, cannon and salmon,
> They don't have a plural at all,
> So it won't be a hap'orth of use
> To make it a sorry excuse
> When handing your flitches and gammons
> To hungry-faced beggars who call
> That as there's no plural of salmons
> There ain't any salmon at all.

I hummed and composed, willy-nilly, as I opened the gate of the Square garden, and was pestered by the chorus, with full orchestra on the repeat, for the rest of the afternoon.

2

Now that Aggie Drumhead had left us and gone via a holiday at her home in the country to a post at the sea, as she wrote to mother when asking for a testimonial, I had with much help from mother and Mell to look after myself; there wasn't room for a successor to Aggie, and this lone-wolf state made an impression upon the children who lived near and opposite us, who regarded me as something set apart in that no cautionary head was ever at window calling down obscure nonsense to my intention, and was the reason, I suppose, why a small deputation after much over-shoulder peeping at me and conference straggled up and let the spokesman (a girl, of course) ask, 'I say, are you *very* good?'

'I don't think so', I stammered.

'Oh, I say … thank you. It wasn't that you *looked* it, you know, specially, I mean', the spokesman apologized.

Silly with nervousness I said, 'Father writes books about Courtesans' and a boy of about fourteen assured me that there were *rows* of them in the Tower of London and that Beefeaters carried them with tassels on state occasions. And after that we played our first game together and I became one of them, and in due season the mothers called and all was Second Thursdays and iced coffee in the summer, and bridge or a little, a very little, music in the winter. Progressive Games seemed to have vanished overnight, whist was now in the Lotto class and the Book Tea was no more.

Our house had no name, only a number; there was what London house-agents call a garden, a laurel-bordered square about the size of the kitchen yard at Evenfield with a colour-scheme of black and bice green.

The house was soon lightened with gilt-framed watercolours, glazed chintz and here and there a remembered piece of furniture. Watts was off and Turner still on: *Hope* was relegated to box-rooms but *The Fighting Téméraire* stayed the course.

What prompted mother's choice of Kensington Gate I assumed to be that South Kensington in one direction was full of aunts and Emperor's Gate a bowshot away concealed a great-uncle, a handsome, ferocious old person who sat half under the table at dinner, his shirt-front an inexorable arch in which his beard was buried, and who must have looked quite extraordinarily tipsy until you guessed that he was only bored, for if he came to tea he frequently fell asleep in your face for brief and baffling periods, his shoulder-blades almost on the seat of his chair, his beard pointing to the ceiling.

My own selection of a house would have been, and still is, governed by the conviction as to whether it looked the kind of place outside which friends could assemble for the Derby: if it had the sort of steps down which a wedding or any party could come and look happy, with a conveyed assurance that they hadn't gone out of the life of the house or of mine: whether I could visualize the heads of people I loved or liked at any window from the street, be convinced of the comfort of a pet cat on the plinth of a gate-post, and what sort of setting the house would offer for good-byes after a summer evening at the theatre. Houses, to me, must have their exterior possibilities and amenities; their aura positively mustn't begin and end inside the front door.

There are houses all over London that possess façades which are unmistakably for the sports car and sweaters as others are ear-marked for Daimlers or broughams; others are beyond question for children, nurses and flowered wall-papers: some for lonely note-writing, bewildered great-nieces and butlers: plenty crying out for débutantes and Press photographers – all this quite apart from the old or historic mansion which keeps its own staff of ghosts and visions. It wouldn't, for instance, be fair to sense crinolines in Bruton Street, sedan chairs in Arlington Street, exquisites in St. James's or Caroleans in Pall Mall, because that sensing is wisdom-after-the-event, and cheating.

3

Quite soon I was going to school unattended. Even then I was seldom alone upon the walk, for a few of the Kensington Gate children usually joined me at some point, and for nearly a year I walked down part of Gloucester Road with that youth who had had the mishap about courtesans and Beefeaters: he was a pupil at Gibbs' preparatory school in Sloane Street and his name was Donald. Those in his favour were All Right, those out of it were Wet. He would cascade down his own steps opposite our house and hang about for me to appear. To call for me vocally or in person of course was not to be thought of, and he got round that by loudly addressing a non-committal remark to an imaginary individual.

'It's all right, I've seen to that', or

'No, I shan't be late'.

Mother, chipping an egg as she glanced over the Square, would say, 'There's your gentleman friend, better not keep him waiting'. He learnt Latin, which to me was a stopper to unfettered speech for several days as there seemed no suitable remark in the universe to make about it, and had, I remember, just reached an exercise which stated 'Marcus has a large head and a small mind' that broke the ice because of my brother. I took it home to Cuss and he said he remembered it well and that they'd roasted him about it at Winchester. School itself, besides having a smell of new varnish, was permeated with the odour of scrubbed stone and pipeclay, a blend which seems to lend itself to youthful association and general high jinks, for the hinterlands of theatres smell of it too with the addition of gas, drains and oranges. (Why doesn't some parfumier bottle it and call it *Soirée au Théâtre*? For a shilling, and two sniffs, one could get an entire outing; and I'd like one called *Vaudeville* as well, consisting of more and stronger oranges, peppermint, smoke and beer. Its stopper would be a small glass figure of a red-nosed comedian.)

I liked the feeling of possession given me by my armful of shiny new exercise books, and, shyness and getting lost on the way to classrooms once over, I felt important at having so many doors upstairs and down passages at which to call. I never got into any serious rows at school, but as most mistresses like to be able to tie a label to everybody, I was early given to understand that talkativeness was my worst fault.

School was a prolonged and pleasant phase, where I made no great or lasting friendships, although quite inevitably one makes the mistake of assuming one's love for school-fellows on the grounds of the years one has known them, waking up at twenty-five, thirty – even forty – to the lorn discovery that in point of fact we have nothing whatsoever in common and don't even like each other much and probably never have, though in the holidays we are still Dearest Barbara or Constance on the hotel notepaper!

Because of father it was expected that I should excel above all at history and English composition. Actually, though I rather liked history, mild, unseasoned dish though it was, like a school luncheon, after paternal revelations and purple patches, composition was easily one of my worst subjects, consisting as it did of set essays upon chaste abstractions like Loyalty. Even father said that this literary form 'would tax the resources of an experienced pen', and, smiling grimly, tried to write one himself, and made quite a hash of it too, and if it was ninety per cent neater than my own I swear it was as dull. History's textual references to that ever-simmering pot, the Continent of Europe, were grudging and scrappy and at all times tedious, with the limelight reserved for the British Isles, and geography preferred allusion to exports and volcanoes than to the illuminating hint that climate might conceivably have helped to make Philip of Spain the sensualist that he was, or that an admixture of Spanish and Welsh blood contributed heavily to the fierceness, bigotry and pride of Mary Tudor. But if Spain was admittedly hot in the textbooks it was 'because it grew onions and oranges and grapes, while Mary Tudor sat about in England being merely Bloody, an adjective commendable in the history lesson but inviting expulsion in English composition, and if the Infanta of Castile was allowed to walk on in the procession nobody dreamed of telling us that this title was one day to become The Elephant and Castle, Kennington, thus prisoning the creature in our minds for ever.

Apart from the smell of school and the feeling of ownership of new books, the sensations inseparable from written examinations are my keenest memory. It began with apprehension and a conviction that the classroom and presiding mistress would look different, and somehow alarming and foggy, proceeding to a certainty that the paper of questions would bear no relation to the subject I had been swotting up; all, in short, would be misty and mysterious, time unmarked, and the very thought of returning home to luncheon possible, but highly improbable. Then came the discovery that the classroom and the mistress were perfectly tangible, that the view from a window was visible and even included a passing dog, that most of the questions upon the sheet of abominably blurred typescript were on the whole answerable, even if they were posed in a circuitous and superior manner, and that, above all, every one of the ruses, images, analogies and tricks one had invented at home overnight to assist memory came back without the least difficulty, so that quite unflustered one could even visualize the page on which the fact or date was printed and remember that the battle of Naseby was top right and the Suppression of the Monasteries middle left (Mell must have felt like that about her German turnips and carrots in skirts and trousers!). The ordeal, in short, was an almost equally shocking discovery of normality to one who had braced herself for goblins damned.

CHAPTER III

I

IN QUITE A few years we were to discover that our house for all its pleasant and promising façade was too small for us. London servants were beginning to want a bedroom apiece, and I don't blame them if they were half as unaccommodating to each other as they were to their employers, and in the name of domestic peace the mere family suffered. It meant for all its simple sounding a reshuffle of almost half the existing arrangements above stairs in which the den allotted to Mell and myself had to be given up to Cuss because father wouldn't share *his* study except by invitation, and a transplantation one flight downstairs of poor Mell to what we had hoped would prove to be a guest room in order that the houseparlourmaid might occupy what had been Mell's room at the top of the house. The loss of the den must have been a blow to Mell who was in the thick of what in wealthier families would have been the boudoir age in which fellow débutantes could be tea'd and where scalps and invitations could be compared and past assemblies criticized, and she had to become a drawing-room daughter at those times when Cuss returned with a legal portfolio and the evening paper under his arm. For myself, I didn't care much where I talked, for if drawing-rooms were familiar ground from my earliest years kitchens and bedrooms were no less so, my preparation could be done at the table in my room and all my meals I had long eaten with the family. If she's the right sort, like Mrs. Couchman, and you take her the direct way of being interested in her private life, as good an *après déjeuner* can be spent in the cook's company as in that of old Mr. Justice Farsight of the High Courts, who was a friend of father's and did occasionally grace our table. On the other hand there are inevitably more dull cooks than dull lawyers. But circumstance that could easily have created some arid patches for the lag-behind of a family of adults was seldom allowed for myself. Mother having regained her London life was perfectly prepared to cast it away on my entertainment and didn't go out half as much as she could, or probably, in father's interests, should have. Mell was always placidly ready to keep me company in the evenings, even in the season (she was once twenty minutes late for a theatre through becoming interested in a game of Snakes and Ladders). She went out rather a lot, and said that girls of our sort were really the beginnings of adventuresses as they lived on their wits in the matter of clothes and making two new evening dresses seem like three and a dance frock. Mell could do that sort of thing and has often gone out in the same frock put on back to front and made a perfectly new impression in it, and the things she could do with a hat had to be seen to be believed – here the back-to-front ruse was only the kindergarten of the business! One of her last-minute successes was a large circular ornament set at the side of a brown velvet tricorne she had nothing else for, but felt needed a bit more dash, made of a ginger-nut that she gilded in zig-zags, and once when she had to go to a rather smart wedding and her allowance had run out she made herself a really fascinating buttonhole from a cluster of radishes she carved with a pen-knife, a notion picked up at a fork luncheon given by some woman who had a Swedish cook who was an artist in that line. Mell said that one could get away with effects in London that one couldn't hope to in the suburbs, and nobody, I think, would ever guess that when she sailed into private house or sub-scription dance at the Empress Rooms the gown that covered her had a quarter of an hour before been twitched, reeking, from the sewing-machine. She was the first girl in London to discover and appear in a white *robe de style* of American cloth: it cost six-pence-three-farthings a yard and looked wonderful, like Dresden china, but being completely dense material its action was that of a Turkish bath and had, Mell said, to be reserved for the Stately occasion. When it got smears on it she just sponged it down with soap and water, and when she thought its day was over she made two mats of it for the cat to eat his fish on.

We got a lot of fun out of the attitude to ourselves of some of the relations, particularly aunt Caroline, who sat about waiting for Mell, and later me, to commit solecisms and reveal the clo-ven hoof of Addison, and, always willing to oblige, Mell would sometimes throw her a sop, as she did on that occasion when aunt Caroline over the tea-cups asked her niece if she had yet been to the Academy, and Mell gave her a nervous wriggle and answered, 'Oh yes, it was ever so nice and I thought some of the pictures sweetly pretty'.

But if Mell fulfilled aunt Caroline's lugubrious expectations by not marrying until the comparatively stricken age of twenty-eight it was not through lack, but through amplitude, of opportunity, where other young women in their social alarm were taking the first offer and marrying, as Cuss once said, anything that didn't actually smell, and so condemning themselves to a life of respectable incompatibility and a nullity unimaginable, successful mainly in that they never actually entered the divorce courts. Mell said that the best chance of a happy marriage was to live your normal life not caring twopence if you married or not, until and unless the obviously right person for you turned up. I said, 'But how can you be sure that it *is* the right person for you?' 'You can't', she answered promptly, 'you've got to take a reasonable amount of risk or nobody'd marry at all; even with care the most promising things sometimes go to pot through some detail they've overlooked – like murderers who plan a perfect crime and then get hanged for forgetting to rinse the second tumbler or leaving a Hinde's curler in the cellar.'

If this was depressing, the realism of it suited me. I liked to face facts. Or I thought I did.

2

Occasionally, friends from Addison came to luncheon or tea, and as with the examination papers and the classroom, put my eye out by looking exactly like themselves and being exactly the same. Auntie S came the oftenest but Mrs. Jasperleigh was the most frequent applicant for mother's society, and dear Mrs. Field couldn't make the journey half as often as she would have loved to.

But by that time I was a Londoner, full of school, under the thumb of Hervet, drawn into Kensington Gate games, squabbles and parties, and although I was always pleased to see the familiar faces, I saw them, as it were, in the flat, people with whose context I was out of touch, isolated figures set down in the drawing-room, even a little embarrassing at times as they saw changes in myself inseparable from eleven to the 'teens, which, especially in the case of Mrs. Jasperleigh, were sometimes voiced quite openly and before me, as on that occasion when, loosening her furs, she half closed her eyes, looked ineffable, and said, 'Of course she's turned from a child to a gurl'. Thelma, it seemed, was plunging from one bilious attack into another, so that, as we all said when Mrs. Jasperleigh had left, even Thelma's food found it difficult to agree with her.

I even went down to Addison twice: once to a charity fête where I sold flowers in the itinerant manner in a huge garden I can't place to this day, and to one of their fancy-dress dances given by the Ackworth-Meads, and if it was impersonally Institutional as ever and I recognized hardly anybody, at least I dressed and lunched first with the Fields and went to it with them in a station fly, though every detail is vague, except that Primrose was Cinderella – Cinderella as she probably really was, in golden hair and shyness, where of course the Cinders of pantomime, while seldom shy except when she remembers to register that disability, is advantaged at all points by silken destitution from the pick of the theatrical costumiers at a sum which no doubt covers her entire ball gown.

My own costume, a moth, all grey marabout, silk tights, chiffon wings pastelled by Mell and a close-fitting velvet cap with antenni, had won two First prizes in London, and was, in the true Ackworth-Mead manner, submerged by and outvoted in favour of a boy who appeared as the darkie on the Stowers' Lime Juice advertisements whose portrait on enamelled tin no railway station avoided from Addison to Waterloo. Mother's reception of my failure was, 'Never mind, darling: fifteen you may be, but you *have* kept your looks and figure'.

For the rest, we and our Addison friends saw little of each other. There were school terms to keep, then holidays which would have separated us in any case, and once grown up there were outside interests and livings to earn, or bees in bonnets to be dealt with, while those young women of Mell's age were playing a lot of games which by no means ended at badminton, bridge and tennis, as bit by bit I was to find out.

3

In time, I was to have a tilt with – of all people – Madame Fouqué. She was one of our old entourage who had let us go with regret but with whom no correspondence was exchanged, and I was content it should be so, for surrounded by authority, hedged about with majesty and disorder marks and plush, was she not living and being truer to type and memory than if, like dear auntie S and Mrs. Jasperleigh and one or two of the others, she had burst into our London drawing-room? But that we lived in her memory was tangibly evidenced by a letter to mother which stated in her spidery continental handwriting, that I recognized from sundry 'Bien' and 'Très Bien' which had in red ink decorated my exercise books, that Miss Anson was leaving and that 'notre chère Barbara' should come and conduct the dancing-class (to my delight they were still Thursday fixtures).

The delight was incidental and submerged in a healthy exasperation at Madame's (Muddarm, in short) having approached mother and not myself. I was eighteen! Even to-day I think she was wrong and mother was inclined to agree with me: 'But I suppose she still looks on you as only a kid'. It never occurred to mother (or to me, either, for my life is infuriatingly paved with *ripostes manqués* and *esprits d'escalier*) that if Muddarm regarded me as a child I was not fit to teach my contemporaries. Still simmering, I pondered the suggestion for days. My final refusal was based upon the undeniable fact that I not only had no strictly amateur class routine with which to fill one and a half hours of blameless dance, but that I was now steeped in the realities of the Hervet technique which, slowly and sweatingly, taught you your job while achieving no showy results likely to appeal to Addison mothers.

Deep down, I knew that my reason was an obstacle insuperable, a protective state of mind. It wasn't so much that I had been particularly blissful at the dancing-class. But I guessed that whether I succeeded or failed as Miss Anson's successor the past would be irremediably blurred, for there's no getting over the fact that for better for worse the latest impression has the pull. It can sometimes be a good thing that this is so, and one deliberately exploits it. I have often rushed to buy a frock I didn't want if worried by temporary financial stress, while as for the personal side, I have on many occasions been impelled to the telephone to talk to people I love if the day before they had ever so trivially disappointed me in response, simply because their latest set of remarks – even their inflexions – would quite illogically be for me the true ones. Which points to the fact that some of us need constantly renewed reassurance that all is well and that we are holding the emotional fort. Trilby, I remember, suffered from this malaise, too. The religious-cum-churchly call it lack of faith, and modern complex-hunters a sense of insecurity.

Anyway, the result of my final refusal of Madame Fouqué's offer was a coolness, and of all the well-known Addisonians I think she was the one of whom I saw the least; certainly none of us seemed to drop into Mayvale when prowling old stamping-grounds. But the breach wasn't entirely to lose us Léonore, who, I am pretty sure, would have seen at least a portion of my point of view, though Irène, it afterwards appeared, was losing herself to us in a certain degree by marriage.

Addison was becoming matrimonially minded.

God! how they married! And an unforeseen feature of the business, leading over the next twenty years to sundry complication, vendetta and consequent treading on eggshells and pulverizing of the same by the unwary Londoner, was that they all seemed to be marrying each other.

How many times have I gone down to tea and gossip at Addison, brimming with affection, good-will and, generally speaking, the ringing of old bellses, to return mired to the hocks with the way I had put my foot in it; even mother with some cordial Tally-ho would cut a voluntary now and then. The subsidiary *faux pas* one could commit were and are so endless that a listed attempt is impossible: the principal *gaffes* one could, and still does, commit are very roughly threefold.

One alludes to some man to one old friend, only to discover probably years later through a third party that she had for some considerable period expected to marry him herself and didn't because he became engaged to somebody else who was apt to be yet another friend in common.

Or one's memory, clogged by numbers, resurrected in some familiar drawing-room a detrimental souvenir about another man, which memento, whether correct or fixed to the wrong person, was equally fatal in that he was now the brother-in-law or even husband of the person to whom one was speaking.

Or, secure in one's neutrality, one either spoke with warm affection about somebody who, by marriage, was now in vendetta with the friend addressed, or delicately hinted at a timeless dislike of somebody else who by in-law relationship was now automatically sacrosanct.

Sometimes I, and occasionally mother as well, would return to London hardly knowing whether to groan with futile remorse or cry with laughter at the unwitting stir-up we had given the suburban stew.

4

If this were a story about Jews there would be at the beginning a long family tree to which the reader, dazed with the offspring of uncle Fritzi and attributing them to aunt Naomi when they were actually the fruit of Gertrud and Otto, is invited to refer. As I am one of those to whom genealogical tables mean nothing whatsoever I won't attempt the Addisonian embroglio in that manner, for here we can only hope to survive by the lighter colloquialism. But it came to this:

Irène Fouqué commanded our thanks from the first by marrying right out of the neighbourhood, and somebody that none of us knew; her husband had an estate in the real country and we are on the whole totally unable to remember either his Christian or surname. All that can and does happen about this is that Madame, now a proud landgravine once removed, will sometimes, and apropos nothing, burst into eulogies of one Dique, until by a process of elimination, assisted by the introduction of Irène's name into the sentence, we gather that Dique is not only Richard but her son-in-law, at which the civil, attentive bedazement fades from one's face until next time. Dique is virtue's pattern: he is 'Och! (*lozenge*) a veritable Engliss spor'. He is inferentially the son who might have been expected had Gilbert Frankau married Ethel M. Dell, though whether he beats his relations with a horsewhip is doubtful. And when I think of Dique I picture him as being completely bronzed and strong and absolutely silent, with a jaw that becomes squarer and squarer with integrity and loyalty and breeding and chivalrously suppressed passion: he goes up to bed on horseback and wears pink pearl studs at regimental dinners …

Léonore obliged us even further by not marrying, and becoming second in command at Mayvale, where she was immensely popular with the girls. And there, for the moment, straightforwardness ends.

For Janet Martin married one of the Irmine sons, and Mrs. Randolph's Christmas-tree doll of a daughter married another, so that they became sisters-in-law, though I don't fancy that the mothers were ever on calling terms in the old days, and Mrs. Martin was prevented from openly deploring the match to quite half her world because an Irmine daughter (not 'Baby') married a Domrémy whose sister became engaged to the Ackworth-Mead son whose sister rather incredibly married the elder Raymond boy (who smoked the chocolate cigar).

Evelyn Stortford also did her stuff by wedding a nephew of the dashing Mrs. Markham, and all might have been well, as few of us had ever grasped his existence, but we rather felt that it closed Mrs. Markham to us as a source of facetious reminiscence now that she was officially Evelyn's aunt.

Here comes a breathing space of peace and relative calm. For none of the Fields married (I suspected them of liking their parents too deeply for innovation), so that their home stood for us as one of the few remaining strongholds of neutrality, a clearing-house for speculation, comment, inside information, criticism, laughter and the shaken head and whispered theory (Mrs. Field contributed this in the old way, as was to be expected).

Thus we learnt over scones dripping with butter and sometimes to a fugue of Bach from Mr. Field in the music room, which made our gaping interest in gossip seem more reprehensible and squalid, but didn't stop us, that Miss Dove's devotion to the vicar, her fastings and loneliness, had made her very queer, poor soul, and she took to locking herself into the church all night when the keys were entrusted to her by that verger who drank and to whom Mell and I had composed a carol: that the Irmine-Domrémy marriage was very much resented by the Domrémys, who contributed birth and debts to inferior birth and no money at all, so that Mrs. Field and the girls had themselves set to and made the bride's trousseau ('She had nothing, it was shameful', dear Mrs. Field confessed, low-voiced as ever in catastrophe): that the Ackworth-Mead-Domrémy romance was in point of fact a misunderstanding (here mother and I laughed aloud, and Mrs. Field hesitated and, apologetically, eyes guiltily streaming, joined in too in the well remembered way).

It happened, related Mrs. Field, wiping her eyes, at an evening picnic on the river from which the party had returned late. Further, it was known that the second Domrémy girl (Flossie) had long been much admired by Trevor Ackworth-Mead, but that he had actually come back engaged to her sister, Flora, and it was believed by their friends ('Oh Ara, you are a bad chicky! You always were, weren't you, darling?') that the darkness had caused the mistake. (Here mother joined her shrieks to mine, before we fell to in genuine sympathy over the tragedy —for young Ackworth-Mead was standing by his guns, and it was a nice point as to whether in fairness to his bride and her sister he should not have frankly owned up, but as mother said, gentlemen always pay for it and think nothing of wrecking three lives for the look of the thing.)

Thelma Jasperleigh, for whom her mother postulated the Duke of Norfolk at the highest estimate and a non-Addisonian at the lowest, out of the blue married not only a resident but Chetwyn Lawnford, and we all sat round and said, 'Lor!' at regular intervals. Chetwyn, it seemed, was now a doctor, and would in a few reasonable years take over his father's practice. Meanwhile, the couple would live in a Lodge near the Park gates.

This looked as though Thelma, at a complete loss for ruction-by-intermarriage, she being an only child, might steer into placid waters, and merely take it out in setting the friends and patients of the rival doctors by the ears. But fate, resourceful to the end, suddenly discovered that Johnnie Lawnford was still on the market and not doing his duty by the cradle and the State, and impelled him into the arms of that frail lily, the Raymond child, my stable-companion in the French class, which at one blow gave Thelma the Ackworth-Mead daughter (who had married a Raymond), together with the Domrémys through the Ackworth-Meads and the Ackworth-Meads themselves plus the Raymonds with whom to embroil herself. Indeed, if one could work it out, Thelma must have done the best of anyone in the way of potential rumpus: what she set her hand to she did well, and although we have all long given up trying to work out her relationship to anybody, she certainly succeeded in alienating at least two families, and I believe that even Mrs. Jasperleigh, when out paying calls, frequently had to turn back on recollecting that through her daughter she was not any longer on knocking terms with that particular door. 'And that', said mother to Mell and me, 'is what I rescued all of you from. Can you wonder I hated the place?'

Once when at tea with the Fields and knee-deep in intermarriages and warfares, I said in high irony to Mrs. Field that I supposed that little Jacky Barstowe (he whom I had stoned in the Park because I hated his white felt hat) was now a family man. But it seemed that the Fields had never known the Barstowes, which rather surprised me until I remembered what a sprawling place Addison was. Primrose vaguely recalled that the Barstowes lived in the Martins' road near us, and she rather thought they had left some years ago.

CHAPTER IV

I

I WAS TWENTY when Mell became engaged, and that and the preceding year or so was a period of discovery.

I found that for all my gregariousness, which all our lives had been far more marked in myself than in Mell, the social life was not necessarily sociable and was on the whole not my line of country; that the social path was a lonely following in Mell's wake; that this business of coming out involved a basic insensitiveness to people and surroundings which I just couldn't achieve. The garden party may be a lovesome thing, God wot, but to assemble together in the hope of enjoyment struck me as going about the business in the entirely wrong way – like Mrs. Jasperleigh! My kind of party gets together because it *knows* it is going to enjoy its component parts in tested liking or love.

I missed Mell quite dolefully. For the eight years between us had created a situation in which at seven and fifteen, at eight and sixteen, we hunted together, sometimes even dressed and hatted alike, a thing which becomes abruptly impossible at nine and seventeen, and from then on to my early twenties I had to watch Mell becoming a young woman, losing her until I myself was twenty and over, catching up with her for such a little while before marriage finally broke our alliance. Also, it gradually came over me that Mell, whom we had rather regarded as a casual on-looker, had for all her leisured manner and outlook at least done something with her life by marriage, which was a definite and tangible thing, satisfying the standards of society which in serene and practical vulgarity judged not by the turmoil of the mind or nagging aspiration, but by results.

And I had done nothing.

I found that extraordinarily enough it was I who at the formal function was far more shy than Mell, though I have often watched her groping for the suitable and friendly topic to servants, old women, hawkers and piano tuners – people who never gave me the slightest difficulty because they were individuals being quite obviously themselves. I suppose it was people in the mass who broke me, for they seemed to be being nothing but a noise or something that they put on for the evening, like a white tie. And if I say that I found the conversation of the dance floor was so staggeringly imbecile that it struck me speechless it is in no spirit of priggishness, but simply that my interest in partners as human beings with ideas and offices and prejudices and fears was always ready to be aroused and that it was invariably handed back to me on a salver, the idea apparently being that no girl could sincerely be looking beyond the matter in hand, or alert to anything more cogent than the debatable merits of *Destiny* and *The Passing of Salome* as waltzes. And indeed, from their point of view, I quite see that to be paired off with a young woman who wanted to ask, for instance, if they believed in dragons, or to enquire their opinion upon the possibility of making a parrot sing a ballad right through to piano accompaniment instead of learning only stray bits of it had its unnerving side. Nor I think would they have been pleased had they known that I was liable to sudden cravings to sit by the fire and roast chestnuts and kick off my satin slippers and read, or that I once solaced myself in the middle of a two-step with some popular Filbertian knut by composing a limerick to him.

> This man is an anthropoid ape
> In his gibus and trousers and cape;
> Evolution's a farce
> If its sum is this ass
> From whose arms I soon hope to escape.

('Yes, I *do* so agree about *Gold and Silver*–')

And then a line from Dickens would quite devilishly slide into my head and make me laugh. 'Don't look at *me*, you nasty creature, don't!' And I felt much better for quite ten minutes.

One of the troubles about ball-rooms is their lack of scribbling-paper. Had a bunch of it been laid on every table in sitting-out places and hung on the walls I should have covered most of it during the evening with notions inspired by those present, and, slipping the notes into my bosom as they do in novels, have resembled Melba by the time I left.

But with the old and elderly men I got on well. Their initial incredulity broken down, we would drift together and explode with laughter at each other and the world, and talk our heads off. We knew where we were with each other. They wanted nothing of me or I of them, and our companionship was undeafened by the splutter of all that fish which gets fried by the young with the young at social fixtures or which is fried 'off' for them by matchmaking mothers or elaborately unobtrusive chaperones. No grandfather has ever been the worse for knowing *me*! And whatever anybody might say, and doubtless did, I can honestly state that, to me, one foot in the grave was nearly always better company than two on the drugget. And I think, and hope, that for all the oldsters did for me, in encouragement, advice, kindly chaff – even cautions about detrimentals, I repaid the debt in giving them back a taste for life, and that I moved were it only by a fraction that hollow feeling of neglect which can be the portion of the retired, who having given health and youth and brains and energy to country and family, sits back so often alone with nothing else to offer but himself and his philosophy.

And there it was. Meanwhile, I was already a last year's débutante, for I had refused to emerge from the known territory of my home until nineteen, a year later than the statutory age, guessing that what I found outside it might not suit me, by which time I should be committed. I could dance far too well for an amateur and not quite well enough for professional stardom: I could play the piano too well by ear to receive credit for it, too badly by the score to be an asset, and not at all except for touch and phrasing from the professional point of view. I think I gave the social life, a reasonable trial and probably had quite as much of what aunt Caroline would term 'attention' as Mell, and even one or two proposals which I was quite unable to see as a part of life, but only as an adjunct, like the ball supper. I suspect that I had far more flirtations than Mell, and certainly, knowing them for what they were, sheer susceptibility, I fell in and out of love half a dozen times, which is always more fatal from the worldly point of view than is the conduct of the apparent iceberg who freezes men for just so long and then melts to a mush overnight for one particular man and marries him out of hand.

Finally, I discovered Marcus: found that he was a man and quite a nice one, and not just a brother you passed on the stairs, or saw flinging, school cap in hand, out of the seaside rooms.

2

I had lived on and off in the same houses with him for twenty years. I actually saw him for the first time one night when he opened the front door in Kensington Gate before dinner: a rather good-looking stranger to whom I had a right. And if I say that his face was at last and for ever memorable, it was because I had lost sight of him so long and so frequently that on his returns from school or university he never looked the same twice running.

I don't suppose that Cuss thought anything unusual about me that evening, for all his life he'd seen me through the eyes of his ten years seniority; besides, he'd had Mell to sharpen his teeth on, and may, for all I knew, have simply thought of me as a kind of extension of her. (He told me afterwards that I gave him the nearest approach to a Glad Eye that he'd ever observed in me!) And there the matter ended for weeks save for my awareness of Marcus in the house. Brothers and sisters don't alter towards each other overnight; but there certainly seemed to be an atmosphere of readiness for acquaintance which hadn't been there before, unless it was my own interest misleading me. And in any case the house was beginning to be upside down with preparations for Mell's wedding, a convivial, exhausting and essentially ridiculous bustle, for the displaying of wedding presents is, if you come to think of it, an amazing piece of vulgarity, for who cares or should care if you've been given a fish-slice or not? And if you admit the principle of this ostentatious materialism, why not exhibit lengths of all the wall-papers you propose to use, or a section of the lead piping that has been selected for the drains?

Mother thought it nonsense, Mell thought it nonsense, I thought it nonsense, as we hurried about in overalls, conforming to that nonsense to please the relations who were subscribing to that nonsense to please the Morants. As for hanging intimate, or indeed any, portions of your trousseau over chairs and screens to be handled by female friends and more relations, that struck me as being such crowning nonsense that I asked Mell to refrain, but she said she thought it was 'expected' and that anybody was welcome to her knickers so long as they didn't grub them.

Presents came from Addison. Mrs Jasperleigh contributed a remarkably hideous Belique object which Mell thought must be a cuspidor and I a medieval bed-pan, and that gave us some bad moments in the composition of the letter of thanks, until mother said she thought it could only be for ferns, and that to write that ferns would look quite delightful in it would cover the ground. But Mrs. Jasperleigh's accompanying note was well worth the space taken up by the object, for she said with several underlinings that the first to go was always quite unspeakable and that her heart went out to her dearest Mrs. M as she, too, would have to learn to steel herself to the loss of Thelma.

The night before the wedding was hard to get through.

We had worked ourselves to a standstill, and in idleness the loss of Mell asserted itself, with all its little dreadful details pestering one for inspection, even to the moment when I should watch the car drive away and myself turn back into the house … that Mell in future would fantastically enough only enter as a visitor.

Could such a situation be? Apparently it could, which made one apprehensive of life, and I think that Mell realized what she had done, as she moved about more slowly, looking a little apologetic and bewildered herself. One thing I wouldn't do, and that was to join in the extra-late family session after dinner that night. I went to bed at the usual hour, saying good-night to everybody including Mell in exactly the same manner as on normal occasions.

There was one consolation: I liked my brother-in-law, David Hamish. For months I had watched him, morally walking round him as a sculptor does his group, comforted only in my inherent reliance on Mell's sense and taste and judgment. I think that to have disliked or mistrusted him would have been comparable only to those unthinkable cases of which one reads, wherein a family has to see a beloved relative die for want of proper food or care.

But routine-keeping or no, I got up towards two a.m. and rambled downstairs to the drawing-room, switching on a light and idling past the long tables of wedding presents, and then on impulse rearranging a few. With the Addison gifts I was especially unfair: pushing them into better places, giving the cheaper ones more prominence....

Among the stacks of still unopened letters was one for me. It was apparently written by a minor poet. But the signature was M. Couchman.

My dear Miss Barbara,

It was like you to write and tell us all the wonderful News about dear Miss Melisande, tho' as Connie says, nobody could be good enough for her. He sounds a splendid gentleman and I pray for the happiness of both. You are never far from our thoughts and to hear from you cheers my day, as I can never forget the Old Days.

Miss Barbara when I read your letter and saw you had asked me to come to the wedding, I had to run next door and tell Mr. Stiles and could hardly wait until Connie and Hope came home from work and they thought I was having a game with them. But I shall have to content myself with knowing you asked me and picturing it all as I have my husband bad again with his chest and he doesn't seem to take his Food when I am not their to give it to him. I did not trouble dear Miss Melisande with our troubles but am writing to you instead. How I wish it might be, but on the Day we are putting Miss Melisande's photo she gave us on the table and cutting some flowers from the garden to set near it and Hope is doing a bit of overtime for Mrs. Markham to give us a special supper in honor of The Day and Mr. Stiles will have it with us, so we shall be so grand and proud! I am going to wear the dress that Mrs. Morant once gave me so I shall feel quite The Queen.

With love and respects to my dearest Madam and Miss Melisande in which all join from your affectionate servant,

M. Couchman.

I knew that M stood for Matilda: mother told me so about four years ago when it had first occurred to me to ask....

Her letter didn't make the rest of the night easier to get through and one must be at one's best, for at weddings the daughter of the house is all things to all men, but I guessed that I was going to be suddenly and unsuitably assailed by the urge to cast down my bouquet and have a peep at the Couchman party and their gala-table, and if it were my wedding I should be looking out for people I was fond of all up the aisle, and wondering if their new hats were comfortable and where they'd bought them instead of fixing my eyes on the altar, and I'm perfectly certain that when my car had driven away honeymoon-stationwards I should want to stay behind with the fag-end of the reception and talk it all over and join my husband later, however much I loved him.

3

In church it occurred to me as I glimpsed Addison faces that it seemed my fate to meet them again when my mind was preoccupied and overlaid with distractions. There they were, all looking familiar, saying what you might expect of old and affectionate friends to whom, in my turn, I was being affectionate and adequate and we just didn't get through to each other for one minute Mrs. Jasperleigh came nearest to reality by usurping the traditional privilege of the bride's mother and flooding her pew with tears from the voluntary to Mendelssohn, and for that I was grateful (If Mendelssohn's heirs and assigns could have drawn royalties on all the grafton voile and Matrons' Hats created for his composition they'd all be multi-millionaires by now.) Aunt Caroline also helped me a little by saying, as she sank into a chair in a buffle of mauve ostrich plumes, or whatever that noun of assembly may be, refusing champagne and seeing me fill a glass for myself, that the young didn't need stimulants, to which I answered as I hastily downed my portion that believe me they did, not remembering the probable years of auntery ahead of me in which, deflated, I should have to try to live down that riposte even if in the interim I'd long become a total abstainer.

It was over and Mell had driven away.

One of her last utterances to me as she put on her going away dress was that after she'd recovered from the excitement of being able to buy all the clothes she wanted at highty-tighty shops she would get so bored that she'd be reduced to cutting up the chair-covers for summer frocks.

The going upstairs alone to Mell's empty room spared me nothing – indeed, it rather overdid its harrowing intention by making me completely numb.

Halfway up the staircase I heard Marcus playing the piano in his den; he had had an upright Brinsmead installed some years ago, but didn't seem to use it much. The door was ajar and I stopped a second, partly of pure fatigue, partly of a necessity to distinguish what he was playing. It was a catchy tune I must have heard and even danced to: a one-or two-step, its name, if known, escaped me.

Cuss had removed his morning coat, his silk hat partnered by a bottle of Pilsener gleamed from the piano's top.

'Hullo, that you, Bunt?'

'Just going up to change.'

''Strewth! Well *that's* over.' His tone of a shared martyrdom suggested that he wouldn't actually object to a visitor and I went in, and even sank into the one arm-chair. I said, at random, 'We're feeding out to-night to save the servants.'

'Where?'

'That arty little bunghole in Gloucester Road. It's the nearest. Father's going to The United University.' Women can always adapt themselves to poached eggs on seakale in domestic stress but the male stomach remains proud.

'I shall dine at the Savage.'

'Oh, Cuss, come along too! It'd – you know – take the edge off the situation for us. But if it's just mother and me–'

'Oh … all right.'

I sensed, then, that Marcus could think and feel. And he'd had eight more years of Mell than I. If one came to think of it, they'd had a little life together from which I was shut out for ever, about which I should never completely know in this world.

I asked, embarrassed with gratitude, what he had been playing, and his answer seemed to be involving him in some mental calculation, as though he were playing for time.

'How did it strike you?'

'I liked it, it's hummable without being insipid.'

'You learnt the piano with Field, didn't you?'

'Well', I amended with a guilty grin, 'I had lessons with him. He used to play classic bits and ask me what they suggested. It was fun.'

'Well, what did the thing I was strumming suggest?'

'No, that's not fair, Cuss. You know where you are with people like Beethoven and Handel and Mendelssohn because their compositions were nearly always meant to be about *something*, whether it was woods or plane trees or moonlight; it's just up to you to guess right. And although I always did think that every Movement but the first one was less like moonlight than anything imaginable, I saw the point about the Athens wood and even the plane tree at once. Now what you were playing conveys nothing but modernity and a pretty girl, possibly, and certainly dancing, and I only get *that* because it's in musical-comedy rhythm. If I'm talking nonsense it's the champagne speaking, but if there's anything in what I'm saying then it's me being intelligent:' I stopped, because my ear suddenly remembered some sentence which was composed in exactly that manner, and then it came to me that Mr. Field had said good-bye to me in the music-room in words scored, so to speak, in a similar way. '*If you do anything clever it was I who taught you, but if you do something stupid you've never heard of me.*'

'Cuss, d'you remember the organ at Evenfield?'

'"The ecclesiastical instrument",' he grinned, 'and how father read the Riot Act over me for playing light music on it.'

'I wonder where it is now.'

'Mother sold it to that little secondhand dealer in Lower Addison.'

'Outram? *Did* she? Why didn't I know?' I felt faintly affronted, but the organ had never meant much to any of us so I abandoned it, a chunk of my memory to be set up in the home of somebody else. Cuss said, 'You play by ear?'

'Yes, but not for family or friends.'

'That's comprehensive! I can only really play from the score–' and I never could.'

'Any good at composition?'

'None. I'm never sure enough that when I think for certain that I've made a really original tune it won't turn out after all to be *Old Black Joe*. As for things like *Destiny* and some of *The Geisha* I've composed them so often that I've lost my nerve.'

Marcus really laughed at that, a thing I'd very seldom heard from him. He said, 'I can compose a bit but it's the lyrics that bosh me'.

'Cuss, you wrote that tune, didn't you?'

'What put you on to that?'

'Your face slipped. Well, three cheers for you. I think it's excellent, and I'm practically sure it isn't *The Orchid* or *The Geisha* or even Mendelssohn! Do play it again.' He did, and I liked it as well as at the first hearing – always a test. I told him so and could see he was pleased. 'It's a pity something can't be done with it', I pondered.

'Well, as a matter of fact I am going to show it to a chap at the Savage who does a lot of additional lyrics and stuff for musical shows.'

'What fun men *do* have! Now, women's clubs are all bridge and filleted plaice.'

'Well, the Athenæum's mostly bishops and chandeliers. That's why I joined the Savage, which has a matey atmosphere and no side allowed, which is restful for those who, like myself, haven't anything to be sidey about. At a distance we're all equal in God's sight. Besides, it seldom answers for fathers and sons to belong to the same club. They're apt to meet in the cloakroom.'

'"As soon should I expect a son of mine to spit into the butterdish",' I murmured. Marcus's reminiscent grin was a broad one. 'At over thirty I'm beginning to value father as a London museum piece; the result is that we've never got on better.'

I was sincerely glad, and said so, for now that I was seeing father more clearly as a person rather than as a curiously misfitted addition to our family party I had had my moments of concern for his possible feeling of isolation, and some of these I unloaded on to my brother who, after all, sees father as man to man in the same office every day. But Marcus shook his head. 'He's all right. Absolutely self-contained. I think his generation is extraordinarily complacent; it's our lot that's uncertain of itself.' He began to play again, half speaking the chorus – Cuss, like myself, had no voice worth mentioning.

> They're all after Pott
> They're all after Pott,
> The cutter, the schooner,
> The collier, the yacht …

'What's that? I know it,' I asked drowsily.
'*The Messenger Boy*.'
'Why Pott?'
'It was a skit on the *Captain Kettle* yarns that were coming out at the time in one of the magazines. As a musical comedy it was a fine show. Pott – Kettle, you see.'

'Thanks. I think I can manage that,' I murmured. And so once more, after twelve years, I fell asleep to the sound of Cuss's playing.

CHAPTER V

I

AND AFTER THAT I got the habit of the den and of Marcus's company.

We liked and rather suited each other, it gradually appeared, and even exchanged views and information about Life, with a capital L, and our own lives, with none.

Tired as I was (like Miss Withers at the drill at Madame's!) I couldn't get the sleep I was craving for on the night of Mell's wedding and took it out in writing the rough draft of a lyric suggested by Cuss's dance, tune, whose general shape I remembered distinctly. I called it *Stammering* and the words matched his rather eccentric rhythm, and even got out of bed to dance it to see if it were practicable from every point of view, which it appeared to be. I showed it to Marcus next day; he played it over, I sang it in my no-voice. We pushed the arm-chair aside and danced it together. He said, 'That's the kind of bunk I couldn't write if you paid me. Sing it again', and remarked upon my good dancing, a compliment which I couldn't return. Now that I came to think of it, I never once remember seeing him go off to a dance, and never dreamed of asking him to partner me, relying upon my hostesses to look after me, and if they failed I never went to their houses again. There are limits, and sitting waiting to be chosen by creatures like the youth of my Limerick is unpleasantly like The Dogs' Home. Sometimes I telephoned, or was rung up by, one of my Old Contemptibles, knowing that our evening would be more conversation than waltz, and on several occasions my escort was that Donald who lived opposite us, and who, while my attention was elsewhere, reappeared in my life as a long Second Lieutenant.

Marcus was blown and collapsed into the arm-chair. It was then that I asked him about dances and he said he'd never cared for them. Over the months, he told me that the Law bored him too, and that the Savage was the only real interest of his life, and going to the theatre, and odds and ends of musical composition, and that he'd like digs of his own, and could I see father's face if he were ever able to afford to clear out?

I concealed the pang of premonitory disappointment as I agreed that I could see father's face clearly. One mustn't use personal influence to hamper men. I despise clinging-ivy women. And even had I lent myself to that sort of moral suasion I had no real idea of the extent of my hold over Marcus … I could only hope for the best. Our friendship was young, yet. I'm pretty good, usually, at poker-faces, but must have given something away that time. Luckily, I had what novelists (to father's indignation and contempt) persistently allude to as 'an alibi', when they really mean that they have an alternative reason or excuse for any line of conduct, for Louis Hervet was dead, and that morning I had had a letter from his executor, saying that he had left me the colour print of the dancer, Fanny Elssler, that hung in the classroom and which I had always particularly admired. 'You were one of his best students', wrote Armand Hervet, who was now carrying on the Hervet tradition (he was a nephew, I gather); 'he often said you could have done *anything* if you had cared to.' That meant if I'd worked harder. It was curious, I thought, as I alluded to the letter and print and covertly watched Marcus, that only the material things of life are to be had through effort, but that once you become involved with human relationships your labour goes for nothing, half the time, especially if you are betrayed by your own good feeling.

To the Hervet-Elssler item Marcus found little to say. He had overlooked that tract of my life and probably thought I was out shopping and amusing myself all those years that I was fagging at *barre* and *enchaînements*. Instead (how incredible are families with each other!), he actually told me that one or two of his 'things' had been accepted and even used in various musical productions. This, I suppose, was tit for tat, except that my interest in his feats would have been instantly aroused and hadn't been given the chance to be.

I quite saw how it had all happened. His life with Mell was inevitably over; father's reactions to the theatre, meaning the actresses in them and their germ-carrying potentialities moral and physical, were well known, and I just hadn't occurred to my brother. To tell mother would have involved her in difficulties, for, whatever anybody says, family life has got to hang together somehow, and a tacit plot against the nominal head of the house may make entertaining reading but is seldom amusing in real life, and mother had had her fill of our cantrips with father at the dining-table in the old days.

Cuss, I learnt with delighted and rather hurt incredulity, had done a certain amount of tinkering, devilling and transposing for various more or less established men who wrote additional lyrics for revue and musical comedy. It was quite badly paid, he said, and the chances were against himself ever getting anywhere particular, especially in revue, where numbers were so frequently changed or scrapped overnight – often before production – that the publicity department which did the bus and Tube and other posters were exceedingly chary of naming anybody except the dead certs like the principals, while even the numerous authors were in type so small that it took the eye of faith to perceive them, half the time, and for much the same reasons. Also, the business was largely clique. You were, Marcus stated, either 'in the set' or not. And that again depended upon what clubs you belonged to and whom you could get to know sufficiently well to cocktail, lunch and dine.

This was depressing and fascinating hearing, and like all amateurs I only believed one half of it; I have a great natural affinity for fools' paradises and to me the theatre had been a happy thing: a delirium of excitement ending in Dan Leno, a transition so swift that one second my eye was on the old rocking-horse in the nursery and the next fixed upon the velvet curtains and the footlights; the theatre then became early luncheon in Kensington Gate, running down the steps into a hot afternoon and Marie Studholme in a chiffon hat and fluffy, spangled skirt: it was beauty coming surely into its own and Lily Elsie in *The Merry Widow*: it was talent recognized and everything-in-the-right-niche. And if anybody failed upon the stage it was because they were victims of untypical bad luck or obviously bad actors. And it was my own brother who was hinting of the glue and battens that composed Ruritania, of Diana in difficulty with her landlady, of the Miltons whose tragedy was that they were constitutionally unable to remain mute …

'Are you "in the set", Cuss?'

'I am and I'm not. That's to say that whereas I'm about a thousand miles behind being Paul Rubens or Ivan Caryll or Lionel Monckton I'm now an accepted outsider. I've put in quite nine years at the game. In that time I've had one original number accepted and thrown out at the eleventh hour because the show was too long, four collaborations in duets and solos taken, and roughly seven jobs of bedevilling other men's notions. And that's good going. And even that all came in a bunch when I became an accepted nobody. For years I couldn't place a thing.'

It ended by Marcus surprisingly announcing that he would take my lyric to his man. While I was waiting the result I amused myself by an old game of mine which consisted of attempts to circumvent fate by anticipating all possible outcomes.

The lyric was returned, but with some distinct words of praise and liking from vague but authoritative sources.

I was rather amused, touched a little that Marcus seemed to expect me to mind, solicitous before the probable outcries of this unknown quantity, his sister. I reassured him. 'My dear soul, I've always done that sort of thing. *Stammering* is only unusual for me because it's impersonal. Mell and I were always writing rhymes about people', and I quoted all I could remember, including the *Tired As I Am* hymn. '*And* Mr. Field set it to music.'

'Field? Well! ... Who would have thought the old man to have had so much blood in him.'

'I know. And Mell wrote a bit of a rather decent musical comedy once.' Cuss had missed that. At school, I suppose; but he ransacked me for more souvenirs and we had a talk about the old days that lasted until it was too late to change for dinner and father was not amused.

'She used to play the violin,' Cuss kindly informed me.

'Sausage! of course I know *that*. With a stocking round her eye.'

'I remember. It was pretty awful, wasn't it?'

'Was it? I hated the violin, myself.'

'Well, they told her at Mayvale she'd never be any good at it.'

'*Did* they, Cuss? Did she mind? Who said so? What did mother say? Oh *curse* the gong!'

2

Of course mother and Mell and I had intermittently talked over the Addison days and people, Mell and I because we liked to, mother only occasionally interested, acting more as referee to our statements about individuals or misstatements about the names of their houses. I found it immensely restful – a walnuts and port relaxation, or like reading history in secure knowledge of the outcome – but I had accumulated plenty of surprises in the process. We mostly fell into reminiscence or speculation when father was from home; I think we all felt that his contribution would be too cut and dried to repay hearing.

Mother's well, when she felt like filling our cups, was inexhaustible, or seemed so. It was, for instance, not until I was quite nineteen that I heard that the eldest Irmine son had been frantically in love with golden-haired Mrs. Randolph and had been by his father forbidden to Call. Even I had not been forgotten, for it seemed that Chetwyn Lawnford had actually had a fight with the Raymond boy as to which of them should marry me. Chetwyn! Now, if it had been Johnnie ... but his manure-throwing elder was completely outside my comprehension, and I rummaged memory for a single incident that might put me on the track and could find not one!

It made curious hearing, this item about that stranger-child that was myself, feeling still a backwash of responsibility for her behaviour, wondering what she had said and done in these incredible circumstances: sure, only, for good or ill in what she had not done, for I had married neither combatant!

Mell said Chetwyn often came into the garden at Evenfield and was rather a nuisance to the Cocksedges (though the Martins didn't mind as Janet was with us all, too) on the relief of Mafeking and Ladysmith days, when he found a cornet from somewhere and blew it all over the lawn.

'But Mell, was *I* there?'

'Oh yes, I expect so. You bought a button of Baden-Powell in Kingsmarket on market day because you said he was the prettiest of the officers.'

'I never did!' But I knew Mell was right. She mayn't have been a very good general noticer of trifles, but what she knew she knew in a most comfortingly reliable way.

'Mafeking Night ... what did we do?'

'Nothing,' said mother promptly. 'Father wouldn't take any of us up to town because he said the streets would be too rowdy. And I expect they were. It was kept up for two nights.'

'But didn't any of you do anything?' I persisted, acquiescing in the fact that whatever happened I must have been in bed.

'Oh, I suppose we decorated Evenfield—'

'The Domrémys gave a party', pronounced Mell, 'and I went. They said they'd bought up all the bunting in Addison and had to send to London for more–'

(*'Oh Mell, what fun!'*, I interpolated, for some reason with fervour.)

'– and they had a wonderful spread–'

(*'Trust them for that'* said mother, with a bankrupt look in her eye.)

'– in that bony dining-room of theirs, and I got rather squiffy for the first time.'

'No. The second,' I cut in, 'there was the rum-and-milk morning.'

'Howdya mean?' Mell's oblivion was complete so I had to tell *her*, and felt quite important and in things again. What a bran pie is collective memory! Nobody remembering or forgetting the same details or, having jointly recollected incidents, viewing them from different angles. So might one clutch up a prize or something awful, at any moment. For – I suppose it must have been in the summer – I once said that I wondered what the river and the lock were looking like, and wouldn't it be a lark, and cooling, to be in Mrs. Markham's punt, to which mother inevitably responded 'Heaven forbid!', and said that that walk along the towing-path to Addison's Villa was like one of the cycles of *The Inferno*, and that she could smell the scented rushes still, and it was no use concentrating upon *Alice Through The Looking-Glass* because it didn't lighten th' encircling gloom one bit, and never had, and no wonder poor little Mrs. Oswald had thrown herself into the weir.

'*What?*' I clamoured.

'Yes, poor little wretch.'

'I remember,' said Mell. 'The vicar preached about it, and said the human heart was desperately wicked–'

('Was he *that* kind of vicar?', I asked. 'That's not even original nonsense'.)

'– but that though she'd committed a sin against the Holy Ghost, God had actuated her for His own inscrutable purposes.'

'He would,' said mother, 'he was always a oner for trying to square the circle. *Oh!* how angry he made me! We had our only real row about that.'

'*Did* you?' (So even Mell didn't know everything.)

'Mrs. Oswald ...' I was pondering, 'was she the one who lived in that awful little row of villas by the buttercup field, and had two little fairhaired kids at the dancing-class?'

'No. That was Mrs. Guinness. Mrs. Oswald lived – oh, somewhere. I dunno! – in one of those houses on the way to the river.'

'Riverdeep Road.' But Mell's prompting seemed to me to be more topographic than personal.

'Why did she throw herself in the weir?'

It was mother who answered. 'Gossip.'

'Oh, *that* woman ... with red hair.'

'Yes.'

'What did they say?'

'Can't you imagine it? She was supposed to vamp various husbands, and of course she was attractive, in that frightfully second-rate way. There was never anything serious against her except her appearance, which made everything she did suspect to some of the Addisonians of the kind who were just her sort. I was always rather sorry for her, but she was genuinely unpresentable; one just couldn't ask people to meet her. What made me so sick was that these people didn't even realize that aspect of her – too semi-demi themselves! – but just took it out in general snigger and taboo.'

So that was the meaning of the disturbing discussion I had overheard in the hall at Evenfield that evening when the question of a lease arose. I also suddenly remembered the book I was reading: *Down The Snow Stairs*, by Alice Corkran. I have it still. And it was the unknown Mrs. Oswald who had lost me my home.

The role of Gummidge is seldom a sympathetic one, yet even Dickens hinted at a grief in the past of that abysmal old party at only the results of which does he invite our derision, and whereas the statement 'My neuralgia is troubling me today' will always command respect, nothing is to be hoped for the announcement, 'I am suffering from a return of my nostalgia'.

Mother was saying, 'Still, that business gave me the courage to persuade father to up-sticks and away'. She added, 'It was the Stortford's gardener who found her, auntie S told me.'

I was confused by all the things that people had been doing and knowing at the time of the Oswald affair, yet my own movements were as eternally hidden from me as were those of the chief figures in my life, and it gave me a disembodied feeling as though I didn't belong anywhere in the past or the present.

I said at random that I didn't remember the Stortford's gardener. Mell responded, 'You wouldn't, you were too small to be there much. He was the one who said that tennis was only fit for fiends to play, when somebody hit him with the ball'.

'He was the world's worst gardener', amplified mother, 'so the Stortfords told me, and used to sell their fruit. Not that there was much. Old Stiles could be quite maddening, but he never took anything.'

(So Stiles wasn't a fairy-storyteller and giver of sugar pictures; but just an honest gardener. And the vicar was a bromide and not an affectionate beneficence with beautiful manners.)

Mell, on the whole, was an excellent guide to Addison; authoritative as a nurse she would decide for me, 'Yes, you *do* remember', or, 'No, you wouldn't know them, they were rather before your time', and 'Oh no. A *horrid* kid. You're mixing her up with so-and-so'. It was one of the reasons that made me miss her when she married: a source of supply removed to places like Hounslow and Salisbury where, as a soldier's wife, she must trek at insufficient notice, and, as she said, feeling like a very superior camp follower at whom the regiment was probably grinning behind its hand.

Mother was, of course, commonly sound on facts, but I had to be ever on the alert to decide how much of opinion was tinged by retrospective distaste; Marcus was gappy and scrappy, although his denunciations and dislikes of Addison and Evenfield were as vivid as mother's and far more violent, influenced as they were by his ructions with father. With even my own memories I was dissatisfied in the light of the items which were so constantly cast to me. Had I, in point of fact, appreciated everything to the full at the time? Enjoyed myself gratefully enough? If so, how had I forgotten, say, the Mafeking bits, or Chetwyn with his cornet?

CHAPTER VI

I

WE WENT DOWN to Addison several times over long periods; it was still a journey taking most of the afternoon. Two calls were almost impossible to fit in comfortably and owing to all this we never even saw Evenfield for many years, though within, to me, tantalizing reach of the house.

We had news of it – the Fields were actually acquainted with the tenants, but 'Oh, Mrs. M, darling, it will *never* be the same to us', one of them would cry over an opulent tea in their unchanged William Morris drawing-room.

I was shy with them. They were so tall, so tall! Young women, looming over me who never seemed to grow, they were still embroidered and artistic and soft as I stood about the room in what people were electing to wear in London. It made me brittle and nervous and superficial for what seemed like ages, until the day when I realized for good that during those years our only mutual understanding as individuals was hardy-perennial love, and that we hardly knew each other. Whether this also struck them I don't know. It would be more like them to see us through the haze of the past, and their unreasoning confidence in us may also have included a belief as unquestioned in their comprehension of all we really were.

2

On the afternoon that I went to see Evenfield and nothing and nobody else I went alone. And once in Addison I was so excited that I almost ran all the way.

Addison was looking so like itself that I felt nothing in particular as I steamed along, though I received one surprise, which only shows how unobservant children can be – unless it is visual selectiveness governed by routine. The railway hotel, of elaborate early Victorian stucco, was still called The Duke of Albany; I never went inside it in the old days and was never likely to now, which was as it should be. I noticed with incredulity and pleasure that the fence bordering its garden was in exactly the same state of disrepair as it used to be in our time. What I had failed to take in was that the rather neglected garden itself was large, matured, and full of ancient trees (I was to discover that Addison is in Domesday Book, and that innumerable unnoticed gardens of unknown residents were tracts of primeval forest).

A hitherto unperceived wing of The Duke of Albany was of earlier date than the main building – early Georgian, at a guess – and extended the length of the garden, and pleased me with its long windows that reached to the very turf, and suggested an Assembly room for the quality, spreading satin, and the sipping of frothed chocolate. Since then, I have several times been seized with a faint and insane idea of taking a room in the hotel, becoming known to that garden, and sitting for do-nothing hours looking out upon the Victorian scene in front which took in the Lawnford's wall and our remarkably hideous Jubilee fountain, which consists of a trough containing a cone decorated with a stone soup-plate enclosing a bas-relief of our late dear Queen. And if I have deprived myself of the pleasure of the uncertain shades in the Albany garden, it is because one must conform to the Addison pattern. No innovations … it kept its secrets and memories then, and so must to the end. Addison might be going to be confusing enough without superimpositions.

But outside the station still waited the musty flys and victorias – not a taxi in sight! Every horse drooping inside his nosebag as I remembered him. The station was the same, too, but looking very much at a loose end, as stations do in the middle of summer afternoons.

The only change in our road was that the letter-box in a wall was now a pillar-box on the path, and I smacked it for its presumption, for was there one single extra house there since our day? No. Therefore more letters couldn't be being posted. I looked at the bricked-up wall, and thought how many hundreds of letters to relations, 'The Stores' and Leicester Square for my dancing frocks and shoes had gone through it in the past, to say nothing of that box of glacé fruit shot in fury through the slit by Cuss, that winter night!

And then came a hot blast of scarlet brick, geraniums and red-hot pokers, and I was passing Rose Glen, the Randolphs' house. I neither knew nor cared if they had left or not, for their railings were beginning to become our grey fence, and then I was outside Evenfield and leaning over the gate which was the same choc-olate-colour, and if anyone came out into the drive and looked civil and offended I meant to turn on my social taps and tell him that I used to swing on it.

But there wasn't one head at any window. The occupants, or their predecessors?, had cut down our almond tree (which was cheek, and philistine) and I couldn't find the lilac bush; the pane of glass I'd broken in the glory-hole had been replaced and the tradesmen's door was closed, so I couldn't see the monstrous dustbin. On the other hand, I gave them full marks for having relatively decent curtains at the dining-room windows. Ours were of beads, yellow and blue, like a Margate tea-shop, and if you wanted to say anything to anybody in a hurry as he left you were bound to be hit on the cheek by about twelve strands. But I missed the rose-trees whose circular plots were apparently filled in: they had never looked particularly pretty, but on frosty morn-ings it was to them that mother and I went with a steaming slop-bowl of toast and water for the birds, and they just supported half coco-nuts for the tits.

In those years I never dreamed of ringing the bell, declaring myself, adducing the Fields as reference or asking for an imagi-nary person in order to get a good look at the hall. It was enough that Evenfield was there and looking exactly the same – even the knocker had been allowed to remain. Just to knock and run away would have given me much material, for the timbre of that horseshoe of brass would awake its own set of associations, and I should see more clearly that cauliflower fur cape of mother's (had it one button or two?), re-smell the veil of dotted net which covered incredibly her face, re-feel the coldness of her cheek chilled by the fog of London, and remember more of the fairings without which she seldom returned.

I moved away to the fence bordering the kitchen garden. Under the door in it through the dog days of July I had poked cinder parcels attractively wrapped for the fooling of whomsoever might pass – one had to wait interminably sometimes, and would, still. What a quiet road it was! Like an avenue which has lost the courage of its convictions at the last moment. I climbed the fence, and there, empty but still standing, was the fowl-run and a squint-eye'd view of one end of the artichoke bed. A good view of the kitchen garden from that fence was never possible, although I had forgotten the reason for it, which was a remarkably meaningless privet bush. I wondered how many generations of our artichokes had made soup for the house since our occupation. I felt like the last person left on earth, and wanted my tea; the fact that boundless opportunity was all round me prevented my taking it – a richness of choice! I tried to calculate what Evenfield and I would have been doing on such a day and time and time of year. Tea on the veranda, perhaps, with mother? Or out at a garden party? If I loitered behind a lime-tree should I see us coming back from it? See what mother was wearing and if, judged by the present fashions, she looked ridiculous and like a revival of some *passé* comedy?

And I went back to the shops and had a horrid, pretentious tea at the successors to Peach's, and smoked, and thought 'Lor!' and 'Well …', and was quite glad to be getting back to London, its stir and ostentatious air of boundless opportunity.

3

'See anyone we know?' asked mother, at dinner.

'Didn't try to. I just did Evenfield.'

'I suppose it was looking exactly the same.' Mother's tone was humorously resigned.

'Exactly the same.'

'Where did you have tea?'

'Peach's, only the shop's quite different now, and I forget the name of it. Foul cakes, all buttery cream. Winter has gone too, but they've kept the shop absolutely as it used to be and it's still a baker's.'

'He made very bad bread. Papery and doughy,' said mother; 'I only kept him on for the kitchen and general emergency.'

'Then where did our loaves come from?'

'Oh, a van came from Kingsmarket, I expect. They had a very decent place at the foot of the bridge where I got most of our party cakes.'

I remembered. (So Winter, my familiar shop, wasn't an excitement, and glass bottles of sweets and Jingoist cakes iced with the name of Buller and French, but just a bad baker.)

'Not', said mother, 'that Peach was very much better, though I liked old Miss Peach, so ordered what I could from them. But not soon shall I forget the ineffable mess Peach made over one of Mell's birthday cakes.'

'I remember.' Mell and I said it together, this time. Although it was only mid-May there was a heat wave and we had celebrated, panting in sun hats, in the garden. It was Mell's sixteenth birthday, and mother, with the vaulting ambition carried over from Gunter and Buszard, had ordered a cake with a sugar rose-tree on it, the tree to sport sixteen roses. When the thing came home, it resembled a brown nightlight on a footstool, for Peach, out of his depth from the start, had contrived merely the stump of a tree, but faithful unto death had fixed sixteen sugar buds to it. But in spite of that, Peach's to me would always be luxury and opulent chocolates after the dentist, which was mother's lovable but singular manner of appeasing my ordeal, and Easter eggs lozenged with colour and tied with silk ribbon, special friends to tea and a smell of good things. And I still stick to it that Peach's was a rather nice confectioners and looked as period as Fortnum and Mason, until both shops most unwisely scrapped their arched entrance and windows of William and Mary green in favour of straight plate glass that any shop could rise to.

Why do they *do* it? When will old-established firms realize that for every uneven step they level, for every pillar and arch they improve away, curve and bow they align: for every black canister marked *Macaroons* that they replace with doiley and cake-tongs, and every dimly-gilt scrollwork of name or trade sign which they abolish in favour of Neon lights, they lose and for ever innumerable customers? The customer is always right, but the past is always wrong. Mother herself thought it a pity and said so, and this was praise that I clung to.

CHAPTER VII

I

AFTER MELL'S MARRIAGE the next few years seem to have been lived all round father's illness. He had in the interests of professional punctilio neglected a cold which, from never seeming to leave him, settled on his lungs. Even then, when faced with a definite ultimatum of the Either-Or nature, he fought against the upheaval involved by a foreign cure. All he would at first tolerate was prolonged summer holidays during which mother and I took it in turns to hold the fort in Kensington Gate and try with what intelligence we could to comprehend his legal cases and the subjects of his current biography. I never crammed so much history in my life! But at least my turns at housekeeping threw Marcus and me more than ever into each other's society.

Sometimes we would go to look up Mell and her husband at Hounslow or Shorncliffe, or wherever the vagaries of army life set her down, and I think that Cuss and I were both glad to be home again. Mell had her own interests-by-marriage which cut off brother and sister at the source, and that may have been a good thing for I can't guess how she would have taken the change-over of Marcus from herself to me. And by this time our joint memories were all at sixes and sevens, and allusions of any date made by one of us must inevitably leave the third party out in the cold; even *contes* of Addison upon which Mell, from her immunity, pounced avidly, excluded Marcus, who quite straightforwardly wanted to forget the place and that he had ever lived there.

It made me feel immature and lonely. For to be the sole member of a family to stand out for even an old affection means mental isolation, and the others were so invulnerable in their various ways! I envied, even while I deplored. My feeling for our old home became at once an escape and a burden. Also I was missing mother, and full of unhappy guilt that I wasn't doing the same by father; futilely remorseful for the love I'd never quite been able to give him and of pity for the fact that he didn't even know it. Yet when Mell's husband's regiment was ordered to India it seemed to be about my last straw. Even Grannie Morant lapsed with age into her own generation once more by falling into the mechanical habit of wondering to me why I wasn't getting married. When I knew her better we had baited each other very companionably in the past, if father wasn't there; before him, we both recognized that appearances must be kept up.

When first the old dame began to tell me that I ought to be thinking of marriage I stymied her completely by just asking 'Why?' This is a question that her generation doesn't expect and for it has prepared no answer, its mind being a woolly mass of assumptions none of which has been clearly thought out. She once did assemble the wits to tell me that I wanted children, and I told her quite truthfully and in that tone of voice which in a man is sometimes accompanied by the screwing of a monocle into the eye that if I had closed with some of the offers I'd had, I should by this time be nicely stocked with infancy unblessed by the church, and that she'd have been the first to round on me for it; and she laughed and had some sherry and said there was at least one thing about me: that I had inherited the Morant sense of humour. Actually, the Morants have a sense of wit, like father, but mother's side have a feeling for humour, which is not the same thing.

Poor Grannie Morant, having discovered me in the family heap, rather hankered to adopt or annex me, aunt Caroline having been no good to her in any way. 'How she came to be a daughter of mine –' she would sometimes say with regretful self-complacency. 'Well, nobody knows if *you* don't, old dear. Perhaps he had his hat on at the time, like the man in the story.' And of course that rude and ancient jape passed right over my grandmother's head as so often happens with the changing tempo in chaff of one epoch and another. She could cope with the tortuous advances upon verbal felicity of Oscar Wilde, nobody more so, but the quickfire of a Robey must eternally catch her napping. She was always too proud to ask for enlightenment – which could be a mercy – and covered it by ringing bells for servants or fluking into successful rebuke on general principles.

But if I gave as good as I got over the question of my own future it was partly automatic bluff, and while I was perfectly sincere in wishing to remain as I was, without disturbing innovation (like the Fields), her sort of attitude does undermine one. Nor could I mentally laugh her off. Too suggestible to outside opinion, I suppose. I wanted happiness quite consciously but it must be on my own terms, and my grandmother's downright, outdated pronouncements succeeded up to a point in deepening my sense of insecurity. And having done this for me, plus having become a small part of my life, Grannie Morant was failing, with mother and father away and no-upset-by-doctor's orders, and Mell was already on the way to India.

It was Cuss, helped subordinately by myself, who made all the funeral arrangements, and there again I had to readjust myself to the novel idea of Marcus as head of the house. Even aunt Caroline deferred to him during that period.

I think I was conscientious for the good of our home; I had unexpectedly little trouble with the servants as I came fresh to handling them and, unlike mother, was not already committed and involved by knowing too much about them and to a certain standard of indulgence. Nearer their age on the whole than she was, I expected and usually received a nearer approach to fair play and consideration. Mother had long given up except in extreme and flagrant instances thinking that she had any rights as an employer. I didn't, and didn't intend to. If domestically let down I was hurt, indignant, disgusted and aggrieved, and showed it, and it seemed to cut the ground from under the maids' feet. I began to see to what an extent they try it on with mistresses where a little honest-to-God emotion on your part pulled them up in a jiffy or reduced them to sulky amendment of ways. The art, it appeared, was to get your scene in first. It jolted them into astonished realization that you are a human being and not an insensate aloofness, one part oppressor and three-parts gull.

But it could be and was occasionally wearing.

Also, I had my own difficulties. For the boy across the way (he of the verbal contretemps with courtesans, who had long become an even longer soldier) had, it seemed, decided to marry me, and I hadn't realized, in spite, or perhaps because of, my wide assorted reading how curiously hard it is to refuse a perfectly nice and decent man gracefully, kindly and plausibly. For such glib and facile dissectors of human relationships, novelists are amazingly crass: and just as nearly all of them will make it perfectly easy for lovers to spend week-ends with each other without one word said about their families, servants or the total hold-up of the weekend shopping or the cats to feed, so they are apt to be blind to the embarrassment caused by inflicting profound disappointment upon the rejected suitor. If writers deal with this set-back they express it in terms of theatric despair or total rebound, whereas in real life you have to stand at the window and watch an individual who is also a well liked friend crawling home as forlorn as a child through your action, tongue and point of view. Proposals, in short, have their social side which must be dealt with as competently and are as inescapable as in the paraphernalia of the tea-table; enormous issues are involved in surroundings not of heroic size and far-reaching results must be groped to through clipped colloquialisms.

And so I refused Donald, and so felt guilty and inadequate apologetic and unhappy. I believe that at one point I fell back upon that cliché of hoping that we remain friends, but after all, aren't all clichés what they are because in constant use, and in constant us because they express what we mean? I *did* hope to remain his friend and it seemed unfair to me that I should not merely because of all inequality in emotion between us. But for once, Donald, of hurt disappointment, lost temper and manners and almost shouted at me that he didn't want to be friends with, but to marry me, which sounded more like a threat than a compliment, for if friendship in to be ruled out in favour of a state of tension which must have it peak and then decline, what was there left for either of us? We had insufficient shared memories to fill the gap, and although I knew that my decision was right for me, it distressed me and brought me to the point when I felt that every move I made was liable to be mistaken one, and filled me with longing for something familiar and known and kind.

But Marcus was out so much in the evenings after his work.

2

During this time I was taking my mind off things by writing a lot of verse and even lyrics; as usual, most of it was satiric. I was as a matter of fact drifting into a habit of thinking in terms of possible song titles ever since Cuss and I composed *Stammering*, and it is a regrettable truth that on returning from my grandmother's funeral, sheer reaction and regret for the old lady gave me one of the most effective lyrics I ever wrote, for which Cuss unknowingly supplied a title by telling me, when I lamented that in church I was totally unable to feel anything, that death ceremonies took people in the strangest ways, and that he had heard of a woman who, when burying the husband to whom she was devoted, saw a pall-bearer trip over the webbing at the graveside, and was overcome with hopeless and unstoppable mirth.

I went upstairs and wrote *Everybody Kept on Laughing*. I even composed the music for it which Marcus scored. Actually, it composed itself; it was one of those sudden notions of which one gets a full-length view from the beginning, and no doubts at all. It was a laughing song in which the entire orchestra joined in vocally on the penultimate line. The chorus ran:

> Everybody kept on laughing
> Till I thought they'd never stop:
> They boo'd the great tragedian,
> They cheered the great comedian,
> He was such a one for chaffing
> That he got them on the hop
> With a *Ha* ha ha ha ha ha ha,
> Ha-ha *ha* ha ha ha ha-ha ha-ha

Everybody kept on laughing
Till I thought that they would drop.

And on that, the production side, as I saw it, showed a small stage-within-a-stage upon which, while the chorus ran its course, appeared a typical black-clad tragedian with raven locks whom half the chorus boo'd while the remainder kept up the melody and who in dumb-show orated, only to give despairing place to a carrot-wigged red-nosed singer who, in dumb-show, sang his comic song while half the chorus cheered and laughed and the remainder and orchestra joined in the laughter.

Cuss was immensely on the spot over his share in it, and scored the final *da capo* choruses in a lower key before reverting to the original which, he explained, not only gave contrast and a sense of climax, but got the full value out of any chorus whose voices happened to be in the middle and not the top register, a professional point which would never have occurred to me but which I learnt and saw was intensely right. Also the theatric psychology of that change of key interested me for its own sake.

Having temporarily written myself out, I had an uncontrollable urge to see and have a word with Evenfield again, and went to Addison for the afternoon.

3

I had made up my mind that in no way would I trade upon the situation and constitute myself a drag upon Marcus's freedom. He would, I think, have stayed at home with me on many nights when I myself had no engagement and was feeling depressed, but I valued him by now too much to be ranked as a duty, and the life and aims he was pursuing were older than our friendship by far.

As things turned out, it was to Cuss that I owed a number of jaunts and a sight of a world hitherto closed yet somehow instinctively familiar. And what a world it was! I enjoyed it enormously but couldn't live with it. It is no small thing to be at a party where the room is full of men and women handpicked for their looks or talent or both, and I found that the only possible way to weather the ordeal was to arrive in the simplest dress I had, no jewellery, and, as one of father's Restoration biographies had it, 'the head worn plain'. Even charm needs contrast and I supplied it, and Cuss said it was clever of me. Having achieved this silverpoint effect one could let go on one's manner, and I did to the best of my wits and adaptability, and as far as it is ever possible to the outsider, I succeeded, on the principle that if you sit about looking like a distinctly *rusé* edition of Emily Brontë and then smash the effect by a catchword or gag, you bludgeon the company into curiosity and interest.

And what a company! Never in my life had I seen the pleasantest insincerity brought to a higher pitch, or dreamed that such a percentage of words in one lorn sentence could be only conveyed if in manuscript by italics. That actors were infinitely samaritan in trouble I could well believe and had always accepted as an axiom, but unless you could go about placarded 'In Extremis' I guessed that the stage world had its other aspects. I had one authentic surprise; had thought that the theatre stars and satellites were remote and chilling but that if ever you got past this you were in with them for good, only to discover that the reverse was the case, and that once vouched for by even such frail reeds as my brother, they were immediately and confusingly accessible to chaff, even unto discussion of abstractions and the outline of world events; but that should you even ghostlily hint at a business deal, their geniality, while abating no whit, privately went bad on you, and you were actually out in the street again. They were, in short, magnificent encouragers so long as somebody else could be found to whom to pass on you and all your works. Their readiness to read scenes, plays, lyrics and sketches was generous and flattering, immediate and optimistic, until you took them at their word, when all was evasion and excuse and procrastination, and I began to see Marcus's difficulties, man though he was, and to be sorry for them with the real sympathy that comes with one ounce of experience. But having no fish to fry, I could and did relish them all with gusto, nor can I ever forget the famous serio-comedienne with whom I actually exchanged five sentences who announced, 'Well, I *do* know the right knives and forks to use so nobody can call me illiterate':

or the three-hundred-pounds-a-week low comedian who exclaimed quite violently, 'No, I will *not* send my son to Oxford!':
nor did I fail to crepitate with inner amusement at that army of
stage men, comedians and others, whose fancy it was to speak fa-
cetiously and to mutual laughter in exaggerated imitation of the
cockney accents they were born with. And how over-whelming
was their tact to the small fry! You could tread on it, smell it,
feel it, and in this all-brothers-together mood the social air was
thick as a Witney blanket – and indeed I think that some of them
sincerely felt quite one-third of it. And how elaborate was their
solicitude, did one walk with them: what skipping manœuvres
were undertaken to occupy the fatal, dangerous place nearest the
pavement's edge: what apology-preceded hands under one's elbow at crossings, and sweepings off of homburg hats in lifts, and
pluckings off of one glove to shake one by the hand! Should they
propose to telephone to you, they Gave You A Tinkle, and they
never left but Must Be Toddling, saying as they did so Bye-Bye.

And how unmistakably amusing and alert they were, whether
in praise or fulmination, with a sort of transatlantic verve all their
own and which made for the time the men and women of one's
own world seem dense and stuffed.

CHAPTER VIII

I

ONCE AGAIN I stood outside the gates of Evenfield on a summer
afternoon.

The turnip field opposite was, I had heard, now the playing ground of some club but at least assured the quiet of the
house. As I looked about me my general sensations were the same
as upon former visits but overlaid with nagging worries I had
brought with me from London. Father was, so mother wrote,
'losing ground, I'm afraid, quite obviously', and had been ordered
to Switzerland, and no nonsense about it. And mother would
go with him. Whether to keep on our Kensington Gate house
was a question that would depend upon father's progress and the

expense of his treatment ('one of those places', wrote mother, as ever recklessly gallant in reverse, 'where the miserable invalids cough in open-air beds and costly draughts from the Scheidegg and the Friedegg and the Dorfegg and the Badegg. I *wish* you could come out to us, darling, but fear you'd be bored stiff and I suppose someone ought to be at K. G. to look after poor old Cuss and the servants, and you've managed quite wonderfully, bless you. N.B. – Florence is *always* enraging about her supper and you were quite right not to let her have the ragôut to finish. Get her things like kippers and sardines, it's all they really expect, but I surmise they were trying it on a bit with you. Give Cuss my love and I'm longing to hear his and your new "work". How funny you should have both discovered you can do that sort of thing, but you were a quite amazingly musical baby and would oblige any passer-by from your pram with any comic song they asked for. Cuss used to play quite a lot at one time…').

I looked again at the front of Evenfield. So, down this back-water a pram had bowled with me in it, singing like Ophelia snatches of old songs (very old ones, by now!), and I wondered what they could have been. That baby, I felt, was still living some-where, self-contained and not a day older, and I was only a dim relation, full-grown and full of stale perplexities.

My desire to get inside Evenfield was now a growth: it was preposterous that of all the Addison houses re-entered over all these years and years my old home remained socially closed to me.

Climb the kitchen-garden fence? It was too high. Always had been. Besides, the successor of old Stiles might be hoeing or weeding, not that I couldn't hide from him in the artichoke bed as I had from poor Mrs. Randolph!

With dismayed self-admiration I found that I was through the gates and walking up the drive.

I rang the bell, though I didn't quite dare use mother's knock-er, it would sound too peremptory and businesslike, and I had no business. A maid opened the door and I was too occupied with incoherently trying to make out a plausible case for myself and hoping I looked respectable to be able to see the hall properly.

Also it was on the cards that my feet might take me off again in mid-sentence.

I faltered that I had once lived here for eleven years and would the lady of the house, I had stupidly forgotten her name but understood she knew the Fields, very old friends of mine, allow me to see over it? A few minutes only… happened to be passing …

The maid listened, dubious and uninterested with a face that by now my more practised eye recognized as domestic resentment at any slight extra-routine work. She went into the dining-room (why the dining-room?: the drawing-room was on the left of the hall), and murmurings (they *had* repapered the hall and I must say it was an improvement) gave way to the emergence of the mistress. Her name it appeared was Mrs. Willis.

A dragon I might have coped with, a frosty eye sympathized with, mistrustful cross-examination I could even have welcomed. But she was cordial. How dreadfully so I was to discover as she showed me into our dining-room and entered quite shockingly into my feelings, flaying me with outraged embarrassment at every word as she crashed into what she assumed were my emotions with assurances that she could understand them perfectly. Our progress developed into a monologue interleaved with pungent mental ripostes from myself. For at the supreme test of sympathy she broke down.

She showed me over Evenfield herself. She was at my elbow, or ahead and demonstrating, in every room.

'And this, of course, is the bathroom.' (*How could it be anything else, you crass old beast?*)

Hadn't I stood on the w.c. lid a hundred times to watch Mell cantering in the garden at dusk? Wasn't it on the rim of this bath that night after night I had deployed a flotilla of china and celluloid birds and fish which, when, Aggie Drumhead pulled out the plug, were raced to the bath's end? Or wasn't it? Perhaps this was a new bath which knew me not. I asked Mrs. Willis, very lightly and as if in self-derision at my sentiment, but she said it was the same, as, old fashioned though it was (*cheek!*) her husband who had arthritis found it more convenient than the up-to-date kind to get in and out of. I noted that all the incandescents and gas-globes had been superseded by electric light but decided that this was allowable.

'This, I expect, would have been your nursery?'

'No, the spare room.' I hoped that my voice wasn't stony. (*Why should you 'expect'?*)

At the door of mother's bedroom (thank heaven it was shut) I gave up, glancing at my wrist-watch with overdone exclamation at the hour and my non-existent appointment for tea. 'It's been more than kind of you' (*you unmitigated Chesterfield sofa of damnable stuffed obtuseness!*), 'I've always rather wanted to see the house again' (*you unforgivable monster of imperceptive and blasted insensitiveness: you blind halfwitted poopjack!*).

'Not at all. I expect you find it very strange to see strangers in your old home.'

'Well… perhaps, a little' (*Damn you, you hellish old bromide. And don't say strange and strangers in the same sentence*). As we were suspended in mutual inanity at the front door a spaniel scuttered through the hall and she stooped to rumple his ears. (*You'd better send him away. Father would never have a dog at Evenfield. Their barking bothered him when he was writing.*)

2

I hurried away, turning at random into the Martins' road to cool off on their gate. It would be kind to me for the sake of old times and I had never known it intimately, our entrances to Janet's house being largely over the garden wall. Good friends, there was a soothingly platonic element in my feeling for Stamboul, which was looking exactly as usual and as large, its gilt weathercock at rest in the sunlight.

I had been inside Evenfield for roughly twenty minutes; in that time I had seen exactly six rooms, having avoided mother's and leaving the whole top floor and kitchen quarters unvisited. Only 'seen' was not the word. For on combing my memory I discovered that circumstances had rendered me practically blind to what rooms I had been shown, like the nervous deafness which actors know and dread when they dry up and literally can't take a prompt. The dining-room now a morning-room, the billiard-room where now the Willises dined, and even the draw-ing-room meant nothing whatsoever. The day nursery was, if I remembered, a bedroom, and all had been repapered, had dif-ferent furniture, putting one's associative eye out at every turn. That, given a chance, I could have overcome: common reason showed me that it was inevitable. It was kind Mrs. Willis (*devil burn her*) who had made the whole twenty minutes null and void, the impact of her presence, her atmosphere at every door, so that all my perceptions were atrophied, all my memories overlaid and blurred. Would it last? Or would the polish return with time? Had she robbed me temporarily or for ever? Even the closed book that Evenfield had been, the ultimate belief in refuge, come chance come change anywhere else in Addison, was now taken from me. For the first time I should look back on it without confidence.

I loitered from Stamboul and prowled the row of houses op-posite searching for familiar doors, and couldn't find one and got into a mild panic until I deduced that the builders had been at work and that those houses which once were detached were now partnered by others. It spoilt the effect and looked suburban and I hadn't noticed it all this time because this was one of the roads leading to Kings-market that I'd never had time to explore. Nobody we had cared for very much had lived there. But I could still resent innovation.

The door facing me opened and a man came down the gravel path. I sheered off in confusion and made some vague apology as I caught his eye.

'Excuse me, are you lost? Can I direct you? Miss Ambrose is in, if you wanted –'

(*Miss Ambrose?*) I said 'Oh, thanks very much. No. I was only looking about. I used to live in Addison'. Here our polite glanc-es became hopelessly entangled. His face was faintly familiar, or rather as if a stranger had contrived to suggest somebody whom I did know. As a face I liked it: he had a legal lip, slight crows-feet and a clever eye, all of which now came into action as he said, 'I thought I couldn't be mistaken. You're Barbara Morant, and we knew each other'.

'Ohhh … are you – Trevor Ackworth-Mead?'

'Not in the least. I used to live in that house.' He indicated the gate outside which we had met.

'Then you're a small boy in a white felt hat with a nurse called Phillips, and I stoned you because I hated it,' I ventured, not realizing that the man looking at me must be all of ten years my senior.

'Try again. That was my brother John.'

'You mean Jacky?'

'Jacky … how he'd hate you for that!'

'Then, you're – why, you're "Ha-Clifford".'

'I'm Clifford, but why Ha?'

'Father … Royal processions … Queen Alexandra or somebody … and we lunched in his office.'

'Yes, and you–had a cart-wheel muslin hat.'

'Look here … who do we know?'

'Practically everybody, at a guess.'

'How heavenly!'

'Not at all. I remember you as a Little Michu at some party in pink. We talked most of the afternoon.'

'No! You *weren't* Widow Twankey–a dear! at the Domrémy's?'

'I was, and a dull afternoon it was except for you.'

'Was – er – your mother friends with Mrs. Jasperleigh?' I couldn't remember Mrs. Barstowe, or whether she came to our house, or was dead at the time, and I can't now.

'Oh, we *knew* them.'

'Ha!'

He smiled, too. '*Not* the happy hand with parties. And, of course, the child, Thelma …'

'Yes. Ah …' We both laughed then. So we'd cleared *that* space round us, and Jasperleigh discussion was safe. But I had to remind myself that Clifford Barstowe was an Addisonian and probably committed by taste or family to one faction or another. He probed,

'But you left Addison?'

'Ages ago. And you?'

'We cleared out about two years after the War.'

'All of you?'

'John's in the Air Force, my mother died in twenty. We moved to Hampstead when we left Addison. I've chambers in Fountain Court now.'

'Are you in the law?'

'Barrister.' (So I was right about that legal lip.) 'I was duty-visiting my old aunt, she took over our house when we left, heaven knows why.' The implied criticism of Addison made me refuge in saying that I didn't think we knew Miss Ambrose.

'You wouldn't. She was long after your time,' he answered (so like Mell!), authoritatively chaperoning my memory in a way that warmed my heart.

'Can't we have some tea somewhere? Or,' he suddenly looked harassed, 'you aren't married and settled here, by any chance?'

'No. Like you, down from London on a prowl. Look here: do we say "Mr. Barstowe" or what? There must come a point when one can't go on you-ing people –'. He nodded abruptly. 'I know what you mean. This antick leaping into Christian names is quite alien to my generation and even to yours. It has a suburban smack.' He was talking like a barrister now, which amused me. 'But in our case surnames would be ridiculous.' So, here was a new friend for me, ready-made because he was an old one, a singularly pleasant state of affairs.

We went to tea at Peach's and talked our heads off. At one point I asked, quite easily, 'But Clifford, how well do we know each other? I can't remember.' To my infinite surprise he understood at once, without damping me.

'Never very well. John came to some of your parties and I was sometimes asked in for clock-golf, and I suppose our mothers called and then there were, as you say, the Royal processions. But in a place like this it's so easy to be on terms without intimacy. Children meeting at school, and so on, and parents having to know others for their sake. Actually, John was too young for you and I too old. But your nurse brought you to tea with us once.'

'*Did* she?'

'I came into the schoolroom and you suddenly called me "Master Barstowe". I must have been quite seventeen then, and we had a stuffed carp in a glass case and you said it was just like the vicar.'

'*Well!* …' .

'I thought what an extraordinarily intelligent child you were. It *was* like the vicar intoning; he intoned so flat that he had to go to Field for lessons in pitch.'

'*What!*'

'So the organist – what's his name –'

'Rammedge –'

'– told my father.'

'You don't know the Fields?'

'Only of them. Field was entirely wasted on Addison, even what's his name –'

'*Rammedge! –*'

'– thought so.'

I thought, and blurted, 'Whom do you know well? It's going to be rather eggshelly and Agagish if I have to skirmish round everyone in Addison with you, and they've married so, and you wouldn't believe how angry it seems to make them.'

'I ought to, I've been in the Divorce Courts often enough.'

'That's different, that's a clean smash. But Addison embroglios trickle on and on, and you never know when you've put your foot in it and it has to be explained how and why. Oh, it can be very funny, but I don't want to fall foul of you … I'm safe, so you can say what you like, but what about your – your commitments?'

'None, I think. I'm a Londoner too, you know.'

'John?'

Clifford smiled. 'Also quite neutral, by this time. He was at school and technical college and all that and didn't have much time to become involved, though there was a time when I was rather anxious about him. He grew very good-looking at about twenty –'

'Impossible!' I exclaimed, forgetting that freckled, square-faced Jacky Barstowe was Clifford's brother. Clifford shook. 'We're beginning early! But he did, and he had one or two very narrow squeaks with some of the local maidens, like Ackworth-Mead. *He* made a mess of things, poor chap, and such a good fellow, too.' I nodded. 'We're in on that: no tact needed.'

I found that Clifford Barstowe's Addisonian pattern was not the same as ours; but over many of the old crusteds, like Mrs. Markham, we could halt and swap anecdote, and grin, and I think our reluctance to leave Peach's was mutual; we certainly stood outside the shop looking about us like trippers.

He said, 'What a terrible place Addison is! Like an unfinished Main Street township: you almost expect to see open prairie down every side turning, and like the Middle West it's veneer'd with sophistication and minus the mellowness of a market town or the rurality of a village, except in the badness of its shops. It never changes and yet its additions are damnable and the architect ought to be gaoled for a criminal assault against nature; for, essentially, the place has its points, it's well-placed and surprisingly full of really delightful period houses and gardens.'

'Like the Albany.'

'Yes.'

Well... it was all true, and my eye had seen and my reason known it. But as you don't abandon a loved face that has been pitted with smallpox, there's no real reason why you should turn faithless upon a locality. I had left my youth in the place, and there it was.

3

I hankered to go to Aggie Drumhead and stay with her at her cottage in the country. We had always kept in touch, remembered each other at birthdays and Christmas, while every Easter she sent me the first spring flowers from her little garden with renewed hopes that I would one day come to her.

And at last I went, leaving London in the interval between mother's bringing home of father to unpack and repack and start for Switzerland. I allowed myself only one week, during which I arranged as far as one ever can with servants for the comfort of Cuss who would, he said, dine a lot at the Savage, and men, take them all round, are more mentally concrete than we are and not very susceptible to atmospheres and emptiness and departure or nocturnal apprehension.

Aggie was what I needed; knowing me inside out, she would still remain basically uncritical. I was fixed in her mind as an affection, part of the life of her young womanhood, and the changes seen in me would be all superficial and (I hoped) for the better. Also, Steeped in Addison, deflated about Evenfield and full of my meeting with Clifford Barstowe, I wanted to ransack her memory. For the first time I should see Aggie's home that was hitherto an address in roundhand on ruled paper, might touch those roots from which came ill-used boxes through the post full of violets, primroses and sometimes snowdrops, knowing at last a village which I had guy'd on paper in the nursery when perpetrating my novel about the imagined home life of the Drumheads ('Well, there's a cheek!'), examine her collection of souvenirs, Evenfield snapshots taken on the lawn by me, countless things mother and I had given and forgotten, so that I should feel I had roots in Aggie's soil, should not come as one so often and so dreadfully does without my shadow to a new place that must be broken in and learned.

She didn't fail me. Most nurses are hoarders, and her small, low rooms, comforting in themselves and full of stout dog and good sonsy cat with eyes of ginger-beer green, and a sooty-kettle perpetually ready for tea, were touched in so many nooks and crannies with our things, our presents, and an anecdote for all, were it only a bare sentence. Aggie did all her own work and wouldn't hear of my helping, treating me like porcelain when I felt more like a kitchen basin, telling me to go and see the village, outlining walks and landmarks that should not be missed, asking me each morning over brown eggs if I had slept well, which I seldom had; it is mostly in fiction that the weary Londoner sinks into dreamless nine-hour sleep. Actually, the country with its weight of quiet must be trained for as the mountain climber does by walks of increasing length, or the dancer by limbering up. But it was authentic country, not a compromise like Addison, and it didn't like me much because it saw through me, rejecting me as a possible lover or even admirer as it guessed my affections were pledged elsewhere and that until I had had my fling and seen the error of my ways we should never come to terms.

I liked my little walks, loved the village shops (so like the old row in Kingsmarket!), and I bought boiled sweets from glass bottles until Aggie cried out.

I liked coming back to her best and rediscovering her: hearing her calling a trough a troaf and the lichen on trees litchen, chaffing her once more about the way she ate oranges, sticking a lump of sugar into a hole in the rind and *slooping*, shooting the pips away with genteel *th'ps*. Mell and I always called it Thepping when Aggie got really started. She had changed wonderfully little in the twenty-one years since our parting.

In the lamp-lit evenings while the sky turned green and then a really magnificent cobalt, Aggie and I (still eating and drinking though supper was over: I do like a house where unscheduled snacks are always inviting you, even if you don't want them!) talked over old times; she brought out photographs, clippings from *The Surrey Comet* of entertainments at which I had danced, the family album that once I had avidly coveted and even a programme of the Kings-market theatre ('Y'mother let Beatrice and me go to the pantomine together and I sh'll never forget how it snowed', said Aggie, thereby presenting me with a brand-new vision with which to decorate the Martin's road, of cook and nurse struggling down it through the iron-grey air of nineteen-hundred-and-two).

'Oh Aggie, what were we doing in the nursery?' I asked, insanely.

'How should I know, my dear one?'

'Did you like Beatrice?' Somehow, that side of things, the Evenfield staff alliances or strifes, had never occurred to me before.

'She was a very nice woman, y'mother liked her, too.'

'Did we have any bad duds besides Amy?' Amy, I knew from mother, had stolen the wine and had an affair with the butcher's assistant. Slooping and thepping, Aggie dubiously exhumed one, Lotty, who stole a brooch of Mell's and wore it shamelessly upon her bosom on her afternoons out, and a couple of friends who engaged as cook and houseparlourmaid and fought all over the kitchen and then right outside in the back yard.

'What fun', I said, 'how nice and full-blooded and eight-een-ninetyish! I don't believe maids have the enterprise, now; they just take it out in petty pilfering and complaints and demands and not knowing their job. D'you remember the Barstowes?'

'Oh yes. Jacky had a nurse I didn't seem to get on with. Very independent in her manner and didn't speak to a person properly, not what I call properly.'

'And Mr. Clifford?'

'He'd be the elder brother, he was more of an age with Miss Mell, but he admired you. The nurse said he said you was the prettiest child in Addison.' So I told her about our meeting and – I hadn't meant to – about seeing Evenfield plus Mrs. Willis. You can more or less think aloud to people who have been your nurse; even their tracts of non-comprehension are restful and you on your part leave them plenty of grist to grind slowly and comfortably in their minds through the long winter evenings.

'What good times they were!' I finished.

('*What a terrible place Addison is!*')

I'd half hoped that Aggie would support Clifford Barstowe's denunciation, and Cuss's and mother's dislike and Mell's indifference, and rescue me from my own state of mind. But Aggie said, 'They was. I was very happy there. And do you hear from Miss Daisy and Miss Clover? I always thought they were the nicest of y' friends.' And never later than ten, Aggie would cease to yawn squarely and enormously (like an Edward Lear drawing) and apologizing the while, and say, 'I'll call in Bouncer and then if y' ready for Bedfordsheer –' Once as we creaked, still talking, upstairs, she said, 'It's funny how ready you are for bed these days, you used t' be a Turk when I come down f' you in the drawin' room'.

'Yes, I remember. There was so much going on and one didn't want to miss anything … Aggie, wouldn't it be fun to live at Evenfield again!' Aggie's smile, lit by the candle that she held, was a thought dubious. 'I daresay you'd find changes, and, of course … being used t' London b' now …'

4

Two days before I was due to return to Kensington Gate I was strolling back down Aggie's lane to midday dinner. She was leaning over her low flint wall ploddingly looking about her and had a telegram in her hand at sight of which my inside turned over, as forecasts of Mell's boat being sunk, cook having walked out on Cuss and father collapsing on the journey home assailed me.

'Better return everybody kept on laughing
going into new show rehearsing now Marcus'

For one liverish second Aggie's cottage tilted sideways. When it became normal I told her, mistaking her relief at the absence of calamity for pleasure. She said, 'Well I never, you was always a one for writing pieces. Would you be ready f'r dinner because it's ready f' you', and preceded me up the hollyhock border.

I heard later that what we had eaten included one of my favourite dishes, Irish stew, but all my appreciation was concentrated in one spot, though there came one second when I do seem to remember seeing a huge and golden bread-and-butter pudding which I imagine I ate. I went upstairs afterwards and sat on the honeycomb quilt in the bedroom which smelt of syringa and plaster with a dash of the dog, Bouncer, and a faint whiff of Irish stew, and considered Fame in all its branches, known or imagined. I thought with fervent and sincere vulgarity of money, not that I had ever been allowed to lack it, but enough is so emphatically not as good as a feast, and it would be pleasant and preposterous to be in the class which can buy silk stockings by the dozen pairs at one blow; I thought philanthropically of how wonderful it would be to pay the Swiss bills for father's cure: of building on that lean-to extra bedroom for Hope Couchman, a place of her own having once been revealed to me with many exclamation marks and in strict play in a long Christmas letter as her dream now that she and Connie were women grown, devoted though the sisters were: and of how I should enjoy giving Mr. Field a thumping cheque for the Salzburg Festival and heaping pretty dresses on the girls. I thought in vengeful sort of how it would fulfil me to swank to Broadacres and Mrs. Jasperleigh, and then to Thelma's Lodge in a car twice the size of hers (if she had one) and of how she would respect me for it and how I should despise her for that and enjoy doing so! And I thought, in the cosmic manner of causes to be supported and heartened, of animals and the elderly and lonely to be assuaged with comfort and security and attention. And I had a sharp bout with my lower nature in respect of packing and leaving Aggie at once; the disappointment of staying on would probably be good for me … prevent swelled head. And beneath all that I knew, because I'd often thought about it, how unforgivable it is to disappoint people, and that one must remember that one's own peak-time of happiness or prosperity doesn't commonly coincide with theirs. Aggie might have planned my dinners, with their surprises, for the whole week, and on the principle that most of us have at least once in our lives been the supreme interest and stimulant to somebody else, she might even be counting what days I had left with her: might, who knows? be keeping some trump card up her sleeve that through my desertion would remain unplayed for both our lives.

They were rehearsing my and Cuss's song, were they?

Let 'em! Publish and be damned, as Mell had tipsily exclaimed to Aggie on that rum-and-milk morning at Evenfield. None of which considerations prevented my consuming impatience for my very first rehearsal.

CHAPTER IX

I

CUSS, AS WE dined alone, was in a state of sober pleasure – almost fatherly to me! I praised him for his cleverness in working off our song and he said that once every so often that kind of thing did happen and was so dead easy that you were left at a complete loss and began smelling rats everywhere until the curtain had actually risen, and sometimes for several days after it had. The whole thing, related Cuss, had been accomplished in that typical manner at once breathtaking and lackadaisical which could be such an integral part of theatric business.

He had dined with A, and afterwards gone with him to his flat, where later B, assistant to the great C, had rung up, making mingled complaint and enquiry as to the lack of a six-to-eight-minute production number for The Guvnor's new show as D had turned in a thing C didn't like. Upon which A told B that Morant had just played him what promised to be a winner, and B, catching at straws, came round to the flat and heard it, and was moved to such profound agreement and appreciation that he actually muttered that there might be something in it, and, annexing the manuscript sheet, said he would talk to C in the morning, or, failing him, to his producer, E.

'And there you have it', said Marcus. 'If I hadn't been at the club that night, or A hadn't blown in and B hadn't telephoned, or had, and we hadn't gone to the flat … if and if and if … that's the way things get done and don't you forget it. And for this one schemes and swots nine years when it might have happened in the first week of the first one. But of course I'm clashed glad you're in on this. It's beginner's luck, and don't forget that either. Oh … there's one thing: they're rather keen on your idea for the final chorus – tragedian, comedian, and all the rest of it. They'll probably rename it "The Laughing Song" and get someone to jam in extra verses without a with-your-leave, but that'll be letting you down lightly. I've seen only the *idea* of a lyric and music retained, just enough to dish the author without doing him any good.'

'Don't damp me too much.'

'One couldn't, in this game! Only don't expect too much, and don't take *anything* too seriously. You are rather that way, you know.' (So Cuss had noticed?) 'Oh, and by the way, Barstowe rang up. I told him you'd be back this evening and he'll ring again.'

'He's such a nice chap, Cuss.'

'Yes. One never knew him very well; father and he used to go up on the same train to Waterloo when Barstowe was studying law.' So there was another picture for me, of father top-hatted and umbrella'd, leaving for the City and being Ha-Clifford on our platform through the fog-signals of December that I could hear from my bed and the wilting heat of summer when the chocolate went blue on you in the automatic machine.

2

To watch anything your brain and hand have evolved in the quiet and indulgence of your own house being translated, pruned, subedited, adjusted and adapted for that huge house, the theatre, where every effect must be 'more so' and magnified three times to secure normal vision, is an education. It can be an education in dismays, disgust and disillusion, or in appreciation and admiration according to your nature, perception and producer.

Those to whom I was introduced were immensely kind and *affairé*, and absentminded and unimpressed and fulsome with me, and when they got started upon *Everybody Kept On Laughing* I might have been one of the cleaners for all the court I attracted, with the difference that experienced theatre cleaners are essential and authors aren't, there are too many of them.

I had sensed instinctively when writing it that 'Everybody', as our number was known by behind the scenes, must have pace and movement and exact timing, but to watch exact timing being arrived at is an anxious and fascinating and laborious affair. It necessitates, in brief, that on the second your last word is sung, the last bit of 'business' worked, your entire chorus (unless the finale is a tableau) must be cleared off the stage, which is to say that if, when the orchestra stops, even one chorus girl is seen to be still vanishing into the wings though all that remains of her is one ankle, the effect is ragged, under-rehearsed and spoilt. Absolute smoothness for eye and ear is essential, and the incidental obstacles to an effect I had lazily watched in other theatres a hundred times and taken for granted gave me a wholesome respect for producers that I have never lost.

To me quite unexpectedly, the *ha-ha-ha's* of the laughing lines gave the producer trouble; half-sung and half-laughed he pronounced the effect patchy and muddled: rhythmically laughed by the chorus in unison he swore was artificial and unoriginal and perfectly flat and a little bloody. Painfully and eventually it was threshed out and tried out and finally confirmed that the chorus should only laugh in rhythm on the first line and disintegrate into laughter on the second: that on the repeat, the conductor should be allowed a fractional pause in which to join in, and be followed by the whole orchestra who would cease to play but be privily timed by the first violin who would signal them to resume. This exact calculation took about a day on and off to get smooth.

As against this, the little scene-within-a-scene was astonishingly effective and quite beautifully timed from the first; the tragedian didn't make the mistake of over-acting, but looked gloomy and futile and unappreciated, and the low comedian replacing him seemed to have every music-hall trick at his fingers' ends, so that even I who had knocked up the song and Marcus who had scored it and knew every minim by its Christian name were surprised into giggles. And I may as well say that I have watched that number night after night from all parts of the house and seen the audience whether stalled or shawled gradually warming from chuckles to genuine roars of amusement, so contagious is laughter to the mass mind if it is well done. I think it was that touch in which the orchestra gave it up and joined in too that finished off the audience.

The show ran for seven months and netted me a nice little sum. It was nothing approaching what I had headily expected, and, consulting Cuss as to selling the number outright in case it was suddenly withdrawn or the show a failure, he reminded me that at present I was in no position to make terms or enemies and that a royalty system was always safer in theory, as the show might not only run but side-lines must always be safeguarded.

Meanwhile I sat about waiting to be famous and singularly little happened. We'd had an excellent Press in only one of which critiques was my name mentioned and in two Marcus's, on the programmes we figured in an unappetizing miscellany of names in minute type at the end of all the interesting data, and on the first night it looked as though everybody in the theatre, including the cat, the commissionaire and the firemen, would receive a curtain call but ourselves. Not one soul approached me with offers of much gold for the loan of the song even to sing in his bath, although I was interviewed for a women's paper which alluded to me as 'the composer' which gave us some happy and caustic moments. I was making weekly an amount which, while not perhaps in the grandiloquent income class, was overwhelming pocket money and didn't spend it wildly because it might cease to be at a week's notice, like the cook. The excitement died down, I found my greatest stimulus in taking friends to see the show. On the last night The Guvnor himself said to me, 'Don't forget us, and give me the first option on your next number, I can always use the best', which Cuss declared was not only wholly untrue because he didn't, half the time, but was encouragement for which most people would give their eyes.

3

During the seven months' run of that show normal life reasserted itself, alternated only with the light and shade of my friendship with Clifford and father's increasing weakness as reported by mother from Switzerland. I was maddened to go out to her, but her answers, don't, don't, don't, were lovingly final, carrying me back to nursery days in which, looking beyond veto, one sensed trustfully that one was being wisely protected from alarm or upset. Marcus girded at his own inability to stand by her but he had the business to keep warm: father was worrying a lot about it and it wasn't only the fret of invalidism, he'd always been inclined that way. And he was writing a Life of Anne Boleyn which struck me as quite immensely pathetic in the circumstances. My one consolation was that mother had heard our laughing song and was greatly taken with it, and wrote that she often caught herself humming it in the Swiss hotel, and that a chambermaid liked it too and begged to know what it was, and mother's struggles to translate it into even Ollendorf French tickled Cuss and me tremendously.

> Tout le monde est ri-ri-riant
> Jusqu' j' pense qu'ils cessent jamais,
> À bas le grand tragedien!
> Et vive le bon comedien!
> Encore! et Bis! les gens sont criant

À ce blagueur vif et gai,
Avec Ha ha ha ha ha ha ha
Et puis Ha ha ha-ha ha ha ha-ha
Tout le monde est ri–ri–riant
Jusqu'j' pense qu'ils succombaient!

Father, she reported, was inclined to be 'more than a little concerned and sniffy' at our connection with the theatre, and this Cuss and I found heartening: it was a flash of the patriarchal spirit … a breath of old times … an effort at authority that we were both sincerely glad he had the strength to make. She had kept from father the fact of Cuss's years-old association with the lighter stage ('It isn't always best to tell them everything', wrote mother as though she was father's child as well: 'What an uncommonly decent sort she is!', exclaimed Cuss). We had both been distressed during father's brief stay before the journey to Switzerland, and our solicitude for his comfort and wishes, though very genuine, made for self-consciousness, thanks to family reserve. Cuss and I saw ourselves that suddenly to heap attentions upon somebody whom you've spent much of life civilly evading, circumventing and being amused by, gave a hypocritic effect, but we agreed that father didn't appear to see beyond our intentions, which was a relief.

One thing charmed me about our recent success: it just didn't exist for Addison. Our friends there, incapable of a deliberate ignoring, were still faithfully stewing in their own juice, and if told by myself, would be quite magnificently uncomprehending of the relative size of the feat.

There was one exception. I had sent a copy of *Everybody Kept On Laughing* to Mr. Field. His answer was grateful, ungrudgingly affectionate, starkly honest and immutable, which delighted me.

… 'I sensed that one day you'd do something of this sort. It seems to be a very catchy thing and what the public would be apt to enjoy. Marcus has served you well in his scoring, the descending octaves of the laughter-lines are admirable (were they your harmonies or his?). I suppose that this means that you have found your métier and will stick to it … No, I think you are quite safe as to the 'unconscious plagiarism' that you always complained of in your compositions; it was all a part of your sensitiveness and suggestibility that very nearly made you so satisfactory to teach, but of course *could* be highly dangerous, but your song quite emphatically does not smack of either Schubert, Quilter or even Edward German, or of *Ta-ra-ra-Boum-de-ay*, *Pop goes the Weazle* or *The Washington Post*! It is, as far as I know, original, but I am as far as appreciation goes out of my depth, being a bit of a prig and a purist as are so many of our poor submerged brotherhood (which is doubtless why we *are* submerged by worthless butterflies like you), but at least my interest and affection are always at your disposal. I shall hope to be honoured by another lyric soon: shall be a better judge of *serious* toshery – like the younger Strauss and *Gipsy Love*, for instance. But technical toshery is, as I say, rather beyond my scope …'

The day that mother and father left was so unreal and horrible that Cuss quite off his own bat recklessly posted our one-step *Stammering*, to The Guvnor, and I went down to take my mind off, in Addison and asked Clifford to dine with us that night.

Mother and I had stood on the steps while the taxi-driver and Cuss dealt with the luggage, father, wrapped in rugs, waited inside the cab and the servants ghoulishly hovered in the hall, and it wasn't for days afterwards that I remembered even something of what she and I had found to say to each other.

I told her that I was going to Addison and she said, 'You *are* a rum 'un! Well, enjoy yourself and give my love to the Fields'. I muttered because of the publicity and the listening ears, 'Will you hate Switzerland?'

'Oh no. It's full of what Aggie used to call "Pretty Bits".'

'That was about the Chine and the Old Village at Shanklin,' I put in.

'And I shall prowl a lot, and I love mountains.'

'Well, don't overdo it, ducky.'

Mother disclaimed at once as she always did, and no words of mine would stop her, or ever had. She had always been more adventurous than Mell or I and the picnics of childhood were for us apt to degenerate into alarming walking-tours when all we wanted was to digest our tea because of mother's urge to 'see what was round the corner', as though she expected to find a branch of The Home and Colonial on the top of Cader Idris instead of, as I once protested, just more corner. She had let us in for that frightful ordeal at Barmouth – it concerned those odious little black mountain bulls and getting lost and darkness coming on, and I reminded her of that evening as we stood there, and then the taxi was ready and Cuss holding the door, and what were mother's last words to me or mine to her I don't know.

4

I would 'do' the river, this time, follow that lugubrious tow-path towards Addison's Villa which had been the bane of all of us when accompanying father on Sundays. It would doubtless feed my remorse.

To get there involved passing Evenfield, but strictly speaking that wasn't my fault, was it? I had leant on the gate and that was over. Very well, then.

Leaning on the gate I noticed this time that the superior Willis curtains were not visible. Looking about me I found a post driver into the border by the further gate: in white lettering on the board it gave notice that This Desirable Detached Residence, fourteen rooms, bath and usual Offices, garden of three-quarters of an acre was to be Let or Sold. The house-agent was a local firm.

Compelling myself to stick to the programme I seethed along the towpath, and Evenfield did this for me, in putting father and even for the time, mother, clean out of my head. That To Let board at once depressed and allured me; it was a chance in a thousand that you must snatch at and a taunting of you to make good on much otherwise wasted emotion. Here was my old home available and a Morant – the only loyalist – ready and willing, and Evenfield waiting for its Morant.

Emotion I think has its burdensome side: I feel that this is an aspect of things that engaged couples sense; longing, irretrievably pledged to each other, there must come flashes of objective sight in which their mutual compulsion to see it through lies heavily upon them, though bliss be round the comer; intervals in which they view with resentment the loss of dignity to which their transports and jealousies commit them, plus glimpses of the bondage that is being publicly *affichés* to each other, consciousness of the greedily facetious eye of society boring into so frail a thing as their shared idealism. And to lose you must first possess, while failure to possess is unthinkable. It is a vicious circle.

I was to go faithfully through all these phases over Evenfield.

5

But at least I could now see the house alone, and empty of Willis possessions, I was thinking that night as I sat facing Marcus at our dining-table with Clifford on my right. I was tired, and soothed by the company of these nice men of mine who were so fond of me, whom I so valued. I told them about Evenfield and Marcus said, 'Oh my God', very kindly, but I was suddenly acutely aware of Clifford, and found that his glance at me was faintly harassed. I am pretty sure he guessed even then what was in my mind, equally certain that Marcus hadn't the remotest suspicion.

6

I stood once more in the hall of Evenfield alone with the echoes of my own footsteps, my only links with the world the key and my London-bought hand-bag.

The house-agent, roused from doldrums, was delighted to see me and as usual tried to conceal his state. His eulogies of the house would have been entertaining had not all my senses been humming with impatience to be off.

'And why did the Willises leave?' I asked of real curiosity which he characteristically mistook for smelt rats and advance disparagement.

'Mr. Willis was a bit of an invalid', (*shade of my father! How can an invalid be 'a bit' of one?*), 'rheumatic trouble, I understand, and wasn't quite prepared to face another winter.' Actually he corrected himself, 'This is a very healthy part; there are occasional floods of course, but only if you live *by* the river, but Evenfield is exceptionally well-placed. There are sometimes winter and autumn fogs, of course, that is inevitable in the Thames Valley.' (*I thought, if you'd had as many plates of pea-soup as I've eaten in yellow fogs in Addison they'd be enough to float a battleship.*)

His version of my old home was amusing; the drawing-room was Spacious, there was Ample Cupboard space (which hadn't occurred to me), Absolute Quiet (which I knew already), a Handsome billiard room (which it wasn't), Good Larder, scullery and butler's pantry (and I saw once more the butler – mother – washing teacups while I asked her, 'Would you say that I am a strumpet?' I very nearly repeated the query to my eager young house-agent!). Abovestairs were exceptionally Commodious dressing- and staff-rooms (*four, my lad, and one of 'em had no fireplace, and a door'd and dark recess in which for some years family trunks were wedged*). The garden was Well-planned (*by mother, or her predecessor or Mrs. Willis?*). There was a Convenient tank for watering the vegetables (*oh shut up, you ass!*).

I studied the house-agent's office which I think had been a shop, and couldn't quite place it: it was near the Fields' end of Addison and might have been a small greengrocer who left when I was about seven, or that stationer where Mell and I bought picture post-cards of actresses.

It was quite ostentatiously still in the hall, and I was glad. Evenfield was mine for an hour and the question was where to resume our long-interrupted conversation.

The billiard room we'd none of us cared for much, and it now smote me in all its bareness and still smelt vaguely and unaccountably of chalk. The dining-room, only slightly smaller than I'd imagined, was rather civil to me, having seen me and been re-introduced by Mrs. Willis. We were at a loss with each other until I opened the china cupboard, remembering those Fairy cakes of eleven o'clock lunch. The cupboard and I recognized each other instantly, but our sudden meeting made for awkwardness.

I passed through to the kitchen. It had new panes in the window (would or would not that be accounted for by Mrs. Willis, or Cuss's exasperated golfing feats with pears and a walking-stick?). It would be just about *here* that I had danced to Mrs. Couchman … the walls had been distempered blue which was chilly and

Italianate and displeased me, especially when I saw that the grad-
uated line of ovals where our plated dish-covers hung was now
no longer visible.

Damn Mrs. Willis.

What else was there to remember? Somehow, the late owners
were still in the atmosphere. I felt them most strongly in the upper rooms, the floor most familiar.

I went into mother's bedroom with hesitant expectancy. Its
strange, sprigged paper twinkled at me odiously and put my
mind's eye out. I was so fond of the room, so sorry for it because
mother had never cared for it as being of Evenfield and Addison,
alienated a little from it and her by my obstinate affection, for can
a place where you have been disposed on winter afternoons for
a sleep at an unnatural hour preceding a party ever be nothing in
your life but a bedroom?

The night-nursery looked absolutely unrecognizable. It had a
ridiculous flocculent paper of red and gold and a gas-stove mask-
ing the small fireplace. I couldn't strive against them, had never been able to remember what our wall-paper was like in that
room, was so confused by the Willises aura plus emptiness which
carries its own atmosphere that I sat down on the dusty floor
and nearly cried. In every direction my thoughts were jammed:
I couldn't recapture epoch. I thought of Aggie Drumhead plod-
ding about the room (past me, through me!) and could only see
her as I had at her cottage; Mell had slept against the wall facing
me and all I could manage about her was that she was now in
India: mother had come in a hundred times to report dinner parties downstairs – I measured her track with my eye – and all my
brain could produce was that she lived in Kensington Gate and
was now in Switzerland. I knew that until I could sweep away
every physical and psychical trace of alien ownership and recreate
the whole house from cellar to attic as it was in our time I should
never be at peace with myself or Evenfield. I wasn't, in short,
going to be done! If it comes to that, I wasn't able entirely to
lose even myself in the past, as fragmentary thoughts of our cook,
Clifford, my Old Contemptibles, the face of The Guvnor and
the orchestra in full blast with *Everybody Kept on Laughing* briefly

possessed my brain in turn and were chased away. I didn't want them there, and went upstairs to the box-room floor (it was there that I realized that what had been Cuss's room smelt of the Albert Hall, and that meant a tiresome two minutes with *The Messiah*).

It was perhaps going to be a good thing that one wasn't quite able to afford to lease the house and use it for holidays and weekends, my secret ambition. Even if I could there was the question of leaving Cuss, and I didn't see him as being willing to come back! And it was all so impossible at present that I was positively relieved ...

I said good-bye in a provisional manner to the day nursery; it had, as I suspected, evidently been a bedroom: unknown wall-plugs and wires sprouting from the ceiling hinted at electric light, in just that place was once a plaster rosette from which hung the chain of our oil lamp (to this day I don't know why we never had incandescent light in the nurseries as there was in all the lower rooms). But at every turn there were Willis traces battling against me, trying to crowd out my set of personal associations. Sometimes they didn't succeed, as I found on going into the backyard and seeing it looking singularly neat and Institutional – like an Ackworth-Mead party! But I was ready for them! They'd taken away the water-butts, cleared the further corner of my own familiar stinking dustbin. But sometimes they did succeed, as they had over the night-nursery and a shocking matter of bookcase shelving in the drawing-room, and I stood in the middle of the room and thought that time and affection ought to be able to rise above these trifles, that I was being monstrously deprived of my hour with the house by the chattels of others, for having put their confounded shelving in the drawing-room I couldn't remember what was there in our time. Love should positively know its job better than this, I thought, given a willing heart to work with ...

It was in the motor bus going back to Kensington that the phrase *Love, give me more memories* slid into my mind. A waltz-song.

I wrote it that night in twenty minutes, and as with the laughing number the theme presented itself to me on a plate. It was in what Mr. Field would term the serious-toshery manner, with swing and sweep and (I hoped) plenty of scope for the harp, which has always been the making of three-four time, to my mind, and, given favourable lighting, is so singularly beautiful to *look* at from the audience.

For it I was to receive several thousands of pounds which it was never worth, but there seems to be no proportion in these matters. It was composed thanks to three rows of built-in book-case, one gas-fire and two wall-papers that I resented. I was to hear it via the instruments of bandsmen and the whistling of errand boys until, initial elation over, I sickened. All I can plead is that the feeling which brought the thing into being was a very real one, and I suppose that always tells.

Cuss scored it for me.

CHAPTER X

I

I RETURNED HOME to find Cuss fuming. The Guvnor had turned down our luckless *Stammering* which, as I wasn't aware that he'd had it submitted to him, left me unmoved. But Cuss was seriously worried: he said that in his experience there was a rhythm in the success-scale and that once broken it was finished for ever: that to succeed and then be rejected was equivalent to beginning all over again, only much worse.

I'm afraid I was inadequate, that time, for I wanted to go all over the Kensington Gate house and tally up relics of Evenfield. Some of them I could place instantly, a wicker chair in Mell's bedroom that mother used in the drawing-room, our nursery milk-jug that still survived in the kitchen quite incredibly un-chipped through all the years and the removal from Addison, with its frieze of Greek dancers round the base; two chests of drawers, one in my room, another in the bathroom now full of spare curtains, packets of soap-flakes and bottles of ammonia, but once the repository for Aggie's aprons, my dolls' underclothes and a tea-set I never seemed to play with. But a child's interest in and observation of furniture is unreliable; it takes things for granted and I wanted exactitude … I even rushed into Cuss's den where, such was his extraordinary rancour, he was actually immersed in legal papers, to pick his brains about a doubtful washhand-stand in some bedroom, and the revolving book-case in father's study, and the wall upon which that frightful steel engraving of the Flood which now hung in cook's bedroom had hung at Even-field. He was too oppressed to be helpful and I don't think he'd have helped me if he could. It took the form of championing a picture I'd often heard him revile.

'That engraving', he informed me crisply, 'is a proof before letters, and quite valuable.'

'It's a foul thing, but where did it *hang*?'

'What *does* it matter?'

So it ended in a letter to mother who answered that it was on the staircase facing the hat-stand and that the curtains in father's study were the old drawing-room ones from Evenfield, which seemed to me so remarkable that I broke off and ran down to look at them and didn't even recognize them then. But there were (only one missing) still those hand-painted porcelain tea-cups and saucers rimmed with gold that mother used to wash herself. We used them still for afternoon tea every Sunday, and for visitors.

2

During the following year father grew weaker, I had about my first unhappy disagreement with Clifford, and *Love, Give Me More Memories* was scheduled for inclusion in the Guv'nor's new revue and then capriciously transferred to his new musical comedy, which Cuss, a new man at this turn of our fortunes, said was a step up.

But I was concerned about father, infinitely more anxious about mother, and the thought that Evenfield might be let – be-trayed – over my head was always at the back of my mind.

Mother had a new worry herself: finance. The cure was an expensive misnomer, she had no idea of the date of her own return (her way of putting father's chance of survival) and so no idea as to whether to dispose of the lease of our London house,

which was in any case now a bit too big for us. Another uproot-
ing appearing inevitable, it made me cling closer to my hopes of
acquiring the dear and the known …

Yet she was in her enforced inaction full of interest, immensely
cheered by my waltz-song. Cuss made her a copy and she played
it on the hotel piano ('… a *beast!* but the visitors and tatting hags
and Cook's brigade took to it at once, so if your Guvnor doesn't
look slippy it'll be a dead letter before it's produced in England!'.
She went on, 'The words: you say they're too sentimental, but
I don't agree. There's a kind of genuineness at the back of 'em
which is *entirely* missing in the slop-songs that usually get sung
and I *do* trust doesn't point to some "overtakement" going on in
your life, poor pet …').

Well, if she could keep a still tongue about her harassments so
could I about my little bit of nonsense.

3

But at least in all the uncertainty of our future one thing was
clear and established, the instant success of the waltz-song, and it
was entrusted to the one musical comedy actress whose work I
thoroughly liked and who is one of the few singers I know who
doesn't make unbecoming faces, or emit that tiresome bleating
quality like the Vox Humana of an organ, on high notes, and she
saw at once that the waltz mustn't be ranted and over-stressed
and marked and paused on and, generally speaking, torn to tat-
ters, but, within the boundaries of its rhythm, given out as simply
and selflessly as a bird sings, and the combination of her rather
childish head, her artless fluting voice and extremely hardboiled
knowledge of how and when and where to suppress her training
was irresistible. Incidentally, she had her natural side off the stage
as well, and once told me that on first and last nights if she had
to make a speech she always smeared her gums and teeth with
glycerine 'because when I'm nervous my lips stick to my teeth
and I can't smile properly unless I start licking myself like a cat'.

If I was to find myself of some little consequence at rehearsals:
if the producer came at last to ask me if I were satisfied or had
any suggestions: if even the Guvnor once shouldered through

the darkened stalls to ask me if I liked the limes, I was also to discover that successful song-writing can be one of the most infallible ways of remaining anonymous that there is. Had that waltz number been a play or a book I should have been known in a week. Actually, though it sold as sheet music in its thousands, was included in most dance programmes, sung by professionals and amateurs all over the country, rendered on seaside piers, recorded for the gramophone and even broadcast, it is a literal truth that not five persons in a thousand assimilated the rider to the title, which was Barbara Morant. Ask anybody you like, to-day, who wrote, for instance, *Tipperary*, *Home Sweet Home*, *The Lost Chord*, *The Rosary*, or even *Just a Song at Twilight* and *The Maid of the Mountains*, and you will see what I mean. But I got my golden harp and plenty of it, and I got my shade of limelight (which was a most haunting silvery-lilac) and, as the comedian put it, to descend from the sublime to the gorblimey, cheques that made me open my eyes. I gave Cuss forty per cent, which he said was too much as the basic melody was mine as well as the words.

Mell sent me a cable on the first night. 'I shall remember you all with affection tired as I am while I skip round the throne what fun damn India wish could be listening love Mell.' Cuss calculated that it couldn't have cost her less than three pounds four shillings counting the address. Days after the show had settled down to its run came a letter from Mr. Field.

'... that's what I call *real* toshery and most tuneful, and it isn't Handel or even Gounod! My warm congratulations on your having entered the door of music by the tradesman's entrance. The girls hum it till I could strangle them. We all thank you for the tickets, the family is writing to you now. When are you coming to see us slowpokes on our eyot?'

4

I suppose I was rather tipsy with money; I took taxis without realizing I was in them when a twopenny bus would have got me to my destination almost as quickly: I bought shoes that cost five guineas and food for Cuss and myself from Fortnum and Mason (one Devonshire Pie costing thirty shillings was so crammed with perishable goodness that it grew a beard and whiskers in the larder before we had got through a quarter of it). I even braved a frock from Worth, and paid for it in alarm and embarrassment at the business of fitting and showroom and my totally inept armoury of knowledgeable comment. I beat down this withering memory by sending mother a money order that would settle her hotel bills for three months ahead and arranged, with much advice, for six pedigree fowls and a cockerel to be delivered to Aggie, and had an amusing morning choosing patent luxury furniture for the chicks they might hatch. I scurried about Addison rounding up a builder for the Couchman lean-to bedroom, and sent the foreman in with a note to Hope saying he was a present from me and enclosing her money for the midday lunches of the men, and tips when the work should be finished. I drove up to Cumptons and swept off everybody at home (Mrs. Field, Clover and their old nurse) to Brighton and luncheon at a nice dreadful café because I thought Esther would be alarmed by the Metropole, and shopped half the afternoon instead of sniffing ozone to fill the car with boxes of chocolate, sports coats, and heaven knows what for them, and because Clover was torn between a brown and a green suede hat bought them both while Mrs. Field grew more protestant and rebukeful every ten minutes in her low voice so familiar to me in confidence and related catastrophe. But undoubtedly tipsy though I was with fairy-godmothering I wasn't a complete fool; quite apart from the homilies of Cuss I have a strong streak of caution in me and was banking more than I spent.

In the hall of Cumptons I got Mrs. Field to myself for a minute while Clover and Esther staggered with dress and confectioners' boxes into the drawing-room. 'Let me have my fling, it won't last', I apologized, for the worst of lavish giving is that the recipient isn't being heady and blinded too, but under the humdrum burden of unrepayable obligation; anybody can buy things, but the Fields have *made* me their presents, cutting into leisure and pleasure and reading, tennis and walks.

'Oh Ara! We've never had such things! I don't know what the others will say when they get in this evening … and to remember

Esther and dear old Cookie …' I was, as ever before her affection, tongue-tied. It may be more blessèd to give than to receive but it's far more interesting: I was spending hey-presto cash for work that wasn't intrinsically worth the rewards or proportionate to the labour involved.

CHAPTER XI

I

IT must have been on a Saturday that the telegram came, for Cuss was with me at luncheon. He glanced at it and when Florence left the room said as he slit the envelope, 'This'll be about father. I suppose he's gone'.

I said, 'Oh … poor old father'. But we were wrong.

Mother had met with an accident while on a walk. A guide had recovered her dead body two days later. The sender of the telegram was writing.

2

It must have been some considerable time later that Cuss and I spoke to each other, for we were in the drawing-room, the lamplighter was going his rounds and Florence drawing the curtains. What we had done in the interim I haven't the faintest idea.

When the servant left us alone we sat there, victims of family reserve, eyeing each other as warily as ever we had in the early days of our friendship. Cuss said, 'You know, I shall have to go out there. There'll be bills to settle and the funeral to see to and endless red tape to cope with'. He thought, and burst out, 'I wish to God I knew a bit more French, or German'. I laughed at that; it wasn't a pretty sound and he looked apprehensive for a second, and then, as nothing appeared to be going to happen, he said, 'I do admire the way you're taking this'.

'May we stick to business, please, Cuss? Lots of it, and dull, you know?' He bit his thumb and nodded, but I don't think he really understood.

It was typical that the effect of this news upon father occurred to neither of us at the time.

3

As we dined, Cuss said, 'They'll have to be told, I'll do it', and I heard his voice outside in the hall and strained my ears, for all I was longing not to overhear. ('Florence, we've just had some pretty dreadful news' – and then her shocked sibillating.)

'And that's that', he remarked, 'it'll keep 'em busy and happy for the rest of their time here.' They were like that, I assented. Afterwards, we sat together talking; every hour counted and I was thankful for the respite from solitude and bed. Cuss drew up a table to the fire and made notes of all we must do.

'There's Mell, you must cable her first thing to-morrow, Bunt. And phone the relations.'

'They – won't come and see me, will they?' I stammered. He looked harassed. 'Tell 'em you're seeing nobody.'

It was perhaps then that I began to realize that for the future I could decide things for myself. Mother would have let them all in, trampling over her lest she give offence; it was only to the social life that she closed her doors.

'Gimme some more whisky and have some yourself.'

'I shall be tight.'

'Do you good. My God, I wish *I* were … now, look here, the thing is this: what are we going to do with you?'

It was the first time I had ever heard that question. Mother would have known, and done it … she'd have begun by seeing me into bed and giving me a hot bottle, and now I was free to stay up all night … I had to shove my hands under a sofa cushion in case Cuss saw them.

'We shall have to get rid of the house and you'd better give the servants notice. You can't hang on here alone and I don't know yet how we stand financially, with father's expenses going on.' He thought and drummed the table. 'You wouldn't care to go out to Mell in India, I suppose?' I just shook my head. 'Besides, she'll be home on leave in a year or less', I reminded him.

'So ... um ...', and Cuss began to draw staves and musical notes on the scribbling block. 'You wouldn't – care to come to Switzerland with me?'

'Couldn't, my dear.' Mother had never had the slightest feeling for graves, far less than I, therefore she would not be there for me. Some day, perhaps ... I had one instinct alone, to go back to Evenfield where she was most likely to be recovered: it was a necessity, now, against a whim. You can't say things like that to anybody, but the bald scheme I put before my brother then and there as he stared and considered, looking responsible. And to my infinite surprise and relief he thought it on the whole the best plan as I should have friends within hail; he didn't waste time damning house or neighbourhood.

'And you, Cuss?'

'Well, I've always wanted a place of my own, you know. I suppose one oughtn't to say so –'

'I know, don't apologize, it's quite natural.'

'Well, thanks. I could shake down with you, Bunt, but after a certain age the parental-roof business becomes slightly ridiculous – not that there's any of that to fear any more, poor chap ... look here, I shall be abroad indefinitely, old thing. If you get into any sort of a hat, send for Clifford.'

'Yes.'

'Or if there's any business about Evenfield you can't cope with – it's the deuce that Evenfield's not on the phone –'

'It is, now.'

'Oh? Good. We're all right for money, that's one blessing – there's such a lot to see to one doesn't know where to *begin* ... get Florence to call me at seven and bring my trunk down; I shall have to be out first thing rounding up my passport and going to Cook's ... and phone the office that they must carry on. We'd better be making a move, it must be getting late.'

The clock's hands pointed to five. For a second, Cuss's hand was on my arm. 'Well, sleep if you can.'

'And you.'

4

And a week later the letters began to arrive and the enquiries, the terrible sympathy and loving offers of help and hospitality.

Would I go to Cumptons? Of course I must stay at Broadacres, make it my home if I liked, and Mrs. Jasperleigh felt that in a sense her life was over, but I was past even astonishment. Thelma's letter at any other time might have surprised me: it was perfectly normal and adequate, whereas at all times it was difficult to remember she was a woman with a life of her own. It was, I think, the first sight of her handwriting I'd ever had.

The Stortfords were arranging for a memorial service at St. Anselm's, but auntie S advised me not to come down for it: 'your mother would so hate you to be upset'. That nearly snapped me. Janet Martin wrote affectionately from an address in Hampshire that conveyed nothing to me at all and only deepened the confusion: she outlined her own life of rural activity and chicken farming with her Irmine husband. Mrs. Couchman wrote:

'… We can't believe it my dearest Miss Barbara, yet I sometimes think She is lying where she would wish to, she was always one for the hills and the mountains and the beautiful flowers will be All round her in The Spring and I like to think that Help comes from the hills as we are told … I can't bring myself to pass Evenfield and go round another way when out … We are all going to the Service. I hope you will not think it presuming …'

Madame Fouqué practically ordered me to stay at Mayvale:

'You are no longer young girl but it is not convenable for that you shall live alone, your Mother would not wish it. Later when the Affaires have arranged you shall return yourself to your brother.'

Léonore was italicized and explosive with emotion, and what had possessed 'the darling' to venture out unguided?

Evelyn Stortford, it seemed, wrote very much as she spoke:

'… Mother told me: I missed it in *The Telegraph* and we don't take *The Times*. Oh Ara, how too frightful … it seems only yesterday that Mrs. M was on the river with us …'

The address, near Kingsmarket, was unfamiliar.

And it all meant nothing at all: nothing would, until Cuss wrote, and Mell, and I dreaded their letters as much as I craved for them.

Clifford telephoned every day, it was a routine support I learnt to depend upon. It was to Clifford that Cuss sent the second wire asking him to tell me in person that father was gone. And later came the letter:

'… I saw mother, my dear, and she was looking wonderfully like herself (I'm not lying to ease things, it's true). She'd left the hotel, they told me, to try a new hike she'd heard some people talking of – it wasn't a real climb, of course, but, I gather, no place for the novice, and she got into difficulties … it wasn't a long drop, but the light was beginning to go, and she never had much eye for detail, as you know, when she was set on a thing. It used to give Mell some bad moments, in the old days … it was a spinal injury and the Doc says she couldn't have suffered, and that if she had lived she'd have been paralysed. So let's thank the powers that be for what we can. He said these cases are mostly numbed from the moment of impact –'

I broke off there because I had to. At the back of my mind, mercifully overworked, had, with a crowd of others, lain the thought of her alone and conscious and cold – not frightened (one was never afraid of that where she was concerned), but cold, wanting her comforts, a hot drink, her eiderdown. She hated the cold so.

Oh, my God.

'… I'm giving a fiver to the chambermaid on mother's floor; she's been extraordinarily decent and seemed really fond of her, and is doing all her packing up. I'm letting the manager have all father's clothes, rugs, and so on. He's been decent, too.

'About father: they'd had to tell him before I got round to the Sanatorium. I had a long jaw with his Doc and he said it was Impossible to keep it from him as they couldn't know when or if one of us was arriving to take over. He said the shock accelerated matters to a man in father's state, though it was only a matter of time in any case, which we practically knew already. Actually, he did linger on a day. What I feel quite frankly is that as things are it's the best thing that could have happened. I'm giving the Doc father's signet ring and gold links, he's really a surprisingly nice old fellow, and knows his job, as Germans do … all mother's things are being forwarded as soon as possible.

'The cemetery here is really lovely, there's an informality about it that our beastly British cold storages seem to lack, in my experience. Mother's plot is —'

I folded up the letter, at that point. Later, perhaps … It was Mell who, saying nothing, said most:

'… I'm not going to write about it, my dear, until *much* later. You know I'd give anything to be with you and help, and can't, and there it is. I'm not going to suggest your coming out to us here because I know you won't, and I don't think I would, either. I expect you're sick to the soul of answering difficult letters as it is, and aren't they awful to *write*? I never could rise to a really good one; somehow all one's sympathy and feeling evaporated the moment one put pen to paper.

'How incredible you should hanker for Addison! I don't believe you'll like it, you know, so many of the old gang have left *and* you may have servant difficulties, but won't the Fields be thrilled! Tell me everything when you have a moment. I'm afraid you and Cuss are absolutely wallowing in work … of course Ken Gate will have to go. It was a nice house and I liked it … I'm at the moment conducting a row with one of the regimental cats. "It was like this", as one of the Evenfield cooks used to say when she'd smashed something. (N.B. Have just remembered her name was Carrie, and mother loathed her …)'

5

The house was put into the agent's hands: the lease hadn't much longer to run — rather under three years, but none of us wanted it, a fact of which it became very soon aware, as houses do. Some of the furniture was sold, some aunt Caroline housed for Marcus; the old Evenfield stuff, furniture, pictures, curtains and china, went to a warehouse the Fields told me of, in King-smarket.

I was glad of the dusty, tiring work, of sweating and a whisky and soda. As I sorted and packed, there was suddenly a sensation of lack, and I had to stop and find out about it. It was that from now onwards there was nobody to tell me I looked tired and must stop. I had absolute freedom, and it is one of the most horrible sensations I know.

6

When I had cleared up in Kensington Gate I went to and from Addison to keep appointments with plasterers and paper-hangers and all that platoon of labour which stands between nearly everybody and his new home.

Old friends were helpful, ecstatic, curious, exclamatory, and it didn't get through to me for one moment, and wouldn't until the fuss was over and I myself settled in Evenfield with mother.

Meanwhile, Evenfield was standing there being just a house filled with packing-cases and the front door perpetually open.

And then Clifford had his turn with me.

I had found it singularly difficult to discuss my plan with him ever since his harassed glance that night he dined with us, though the reasons at work behind it weren't clear. Doubts from the family were understandable: they knew me and Evenfield inside out, but Clifford Barstowe, a comparative stranger, would surely?, be robust and tangible and objective, and from the kindest of motives put a logical finger unerringly upon the flaws in my defence, as he must have done a dozen times in Court. How mistaken I was I discovered on the afternoon that he and I first went to Addison to interview the house-agent.

What I now wanted was to buy Evenfield and this I hadn't dared tell anybody but Clifford who wouldn't beat me down with solicitudes and apprehensions, and I had my first surprise when he negatived the idea outright. I gave in, a little deflated and sulky, before his experienced arguments as to possible difficulty of re-sale, size of house in these days of small families, cost of repairs, and so on, and he was obviously relieved but still, I sensed, dissatisfied. He said quite unexpectedly, 'I wonder if Addison will understand your affairs being handled by an – um – outsider. Of course, I am also an old resident, which may make for righteousness, but still –'.

We had turned in at the Park gates. It was early autumn, my time of year, when there are chestnuts to grind out of their green burrs with your heel and the smell of wood smoke drifting from where the men were burning dead leaves and bracken, and clashes like a distant medieval battle which was the stags having at each other, clattering away as mechanically antagonistic as ever, bless them, while the does followed on pointed feet and nudged and dunted us for opened nuts that their wet, tender noses might avoid pricks.

Out of the blue Clifford said, 'I *wish* you weren't set on this idea'. Coming from him it was a bad shock to my hopeful state of mind, and I could find nothing to say. I think I was afraid that he would come out with something else and increase the burden. He looked away down the avenue as he added, 'I'd thought of something so very different for you – for us'.

Of course I knew what he meant and of course I'd guessed it for some time; even poker faces and reserve aren't sufficient guards to the suggestible and between the mutually sympathetic.

'I thought perhaps that might be it, my dear.'

He looked at me, then. 'But if you think that my own personal feelings are standing in the way of approval of your taking this house you're wrong, believe me. It's more than that. I want your happiness. I hope I rate it above my own, but one never knows. What's actively worrying me is that you appear to be illusioned. Oh, I'm not attacking Addison, it's probably no worse than similar places and lots better than some. But I've made quite a study of you, you know, and I'm afraid I see what may happen to you if you go back to live alone at Evenfield.'

I literally dared not say a thing.

'Two things may happen, rather: you will either see Addison and Evenfield as they really are, suburban and a little dull, and be badly disappointed, or you'll continue to be blinded, and that house'll be so chockful of ghosts of the past that you'll be miserable.'.

7

When Evenfield was ready to the final tintack and saucer, and the London house, save for my bed, bare as a bone, I went from room to room, the switches snapping loudly in that emptiness, and unexpectedly found myself succumbing to sentiment.

So I was, after all, one of those clinging-ivys I'd always tried to avoid being? For I saw that although the pulls and claims of the Kensington house were infinitely feebler than those of my old home they were unmistakably in the same class ... I even wondered why I didn't mind leaving this house more. Hadn't mother eaten here, rested there? Wasn't there still the mark on a panel where she had once tried to beat out a smouldering kettleholder that caught fire at teatime? And in Mell's room a splash of ink on the wall-paper from her fountain pen? And all the notable things of life had happened here: growing up and long skirts, first flirtation and proposal, dances and the beginnings of selectiveness and criticism, finding Cuss and coming round to father. And yet the sum-total was and remained a newspaper against a picture-book.

And then it occurred to me that from this house my entire family had left me.

PART THREE

CHAPTER I

I

I WAS IN my station fly: it smelt as of old, of mustiness, battered straps and damp hay, and those free-and-easy breaths of it that I was at leisure to take suddenly presented me with another whiff: of Maltese silk mittens and shawl. ('*I wonder if there'll be ices, Mell?*'), and I remembered for the first time since childhood a party treat, oranges quartered and filled with stiff red and yellow jelly, delicious after heating games.

This was beginning my adventure in style ...

I would go to bed early after a dinner cooked by my servants: I would have breakfast in bed and if they didn't like it they could go: I would listen to the great-great-grandbirds of those mother and I had fed with warm sopped toast – surely they'd sing better for that background of ancestral good living! And if they woke me too early I would unpoetically shout Shut UP! at them with none to hear; I'm no Elizabeth in her German garden.

And then I planned my first day in Addison.

There was too much, a plethora of choice: the garden to go over in detail, luncheon to order in the kitchen of which I was mistress ... or should I be high-handed and old-world and summon Cook into the dining-room, like Grannie Morant? But mother used to tour the larder every day; I knew that because, now in full spate of Evenfield memory, I recalled that all our cooks used to keep wedges of suet in the flour tub, and the coolness of rummaging it, and that we'd had a huge stone filter with a tap, from which nobody ever seemed to drink; and there was a thing called a Thermogene, a vast, cottage-loaf-shaped siphon covered with wire netting, into which metallic bullets were inserted, the result quite often being fresh seltzer water.

I peered out of the fly. It was creaking past the Randolphs' red-hot house. It had turned in at our drive.

2

I used the knocker as mother did, her signal to me that it was she and none other returned from London to me waiting in the hall or lurking on the landing.

It was a mistake; had given me for an instant a sense of dual personality. *Which of us was this knocking? Why was that child outside the front door?*

The houseparlourmaid opened to me, conventionally smiling. I said, 'Ah, Mabel' ('Ha-Clifford', in short!), and found the ejaculation, as father no doubt had done, a most useful one, combining as it did non-committal geniality with absolute meaninglessness.

There were flowers in the hall, from the Fields with a loving message of welcome, a bunch of dahlias from the Couchmans hoping I wouldn't take them amiss, and full of the lean-to bedroom and of how Hope didn't know if she was on her head or heels with delight and would soon be too grand to speak to the family, but of course that was only my joke, dear Miss Barbara, and the men were so good and the foreman so kind and always with a Joke that sets us up for the day, and it was such an interest to Mr. Couchman and they wheeled his chair out into the garden every fine morning so that he could see the men at work as it made A Change, and yesterday they give him some tobacco ...

There was a telegram. 'My wishes for your happiness when settled in will come if invited Clifford.'

3

I have never understood those people who are slaves to immediate unpacking: I want to enjoy the moment of arrival and unless one's trunk contains something indispensable I wish to forget it indefinitely. Unfortunately, leisure, even liberty, is an art you must learn, and Evenfield, I thought, must teach me as I fought down my automatic impulse to throw back the lid and grovel. As it was, between arrival and dinner the telephone rang three times. I had retained this Willis trace, for if moving with the times means a telephone I suppose we equally moved with them when incandescent finally superseded those flounced standard lamps in the drawing-room; besides, there were Cuss and the theatre with whom to keep in touch, and London friends, perhaps.

The first call was from Broadacres and Mrs. Jasperleigh, very home-sweet-home and heart-bowed-down and even a little tearful as her voice meandered up and down the sociable scale of welcome, and of course I must lunch with her next day as I should feel (*vibrato*) quite lost all alone, and of course I warmly declined (*allegretto vivace*) and of course nobody but Mrs. Jasperleigh could conceivably have entertained such a notion for a moment and I must write to Mell and tell her. And just as I was enjoying it all and hoping for more material for the family, even for Clifford, who in a punctilious and well-bred manner saw the point about the Jasperleighs almost as well as we did, as his half-finished sentences and unwilling smiles betrayed, Mrs. Jasperleigh smote me down in my very hall.

She supposed I'd heard from Thelma. I hadn't.

'Well, I'm not surprised. You've known her all your life. But she's so utterly different, dear … changed person.' (If Thelma's being awful there's no change, but I merely said 'Oh?' with sympathetic interest and devouring curiosity.) 'Of course, it was a disastrous marriage –'

'Would you *quite* say that?' I temporized, with my ears on stalks.

'She could have married anybody –'

(Bosh!).

'– one or two men – county, title, money – quite wild about her – wouldn't look at 'em' (Rats!) 'and then – a country doctor! Of course Chetwyn adaws her …'

'Well, that's something, anyway.'

'Of course,' added poor Mrs. Jasperleigh, 'she's a marvellous hostess … friend of mine – very high up in the I.C.S. – says the *perfect* manager, and her house, well, you must see it, that's all! See it. Very big noise in the War Office and his wife dined there not long ago and he said to me afterwards, "Mrs. Jasperleigh, this – is – *the* – perfect house".' I supposed as I breathed civilly into the receiver that that meant six chromium operating tables and chairs from Tottenham Court Road and one witch-ball full of daisies and lilies made of fish-bones and collar studs. 'But reelly, darling, I don't know what to do. When she comes to see me it's like a visitor … and when one's bin so close … of course I adaw Broadacres … got everything as I want it and people are always saying to me: "Mrs. Jasperleigh, this is a *home* as well as a beauty-spot". But I get so lonely sometimes I think I'll get right out. In any case, there's nobody to *know* any more, your dear mother always felt that …'

I answered rather austerely that we'd never found that difficulty, rather the contrary, if anything, and managed to ring off quite soon afterwards. I was sincerely sorry for Mrs. Jasperleigh and meant in my own time to size up her daughter, but didn't propose to go on collywobbling at the telephone indefinitely. It would be odd if one became sympathetically fond of her, a factor one hadn't reckoned with …

The next call came from dear auntie S, to whom I retailed Mrs. Jasperleigh's dictum while her delighted 'Haigh! haigh! haighs!' of appreciation once more and so pleasantly assailed my ears. 'Now I really feel a Morant is back', she said (*Let's get baby's chair into the nursery and then it'll begin to look like home*). She added that she hated to think of my solitary struggles to get settled in, and on impulse I reminded her of her decision about my chair when we all first arrived at Evenfield, and although she haigh'd again with relish she'd forgotten it completely, which gave me a small pang, even if she remembered a lot of titbits that I fell upon. Here was a mine I would quarry at leisure … one's elders are so beautifully sure of their facts.

Had she, I asked, beginning minor excavations at once, got the same gardener?

'Which one?'

It was well over twenty years ago, of course … one must remember.

'The one,' I said, 'who was hit on the behind by tennis balls and found Mrs. Oswald in the weir.'

'Oh, *Pegler*. No, my dear, he left before Evelyn married. We've had two since then, rat them! Who are you having for the garden?'

'Old Stiles if I can find him. The Couchmans will put me on to him.'

'My child! he'll be over seventy by now! Think again.'

'Well ... um ... when do gardens stop being able to look after themselves and want a gardener?'

'All the time! Who did the former tenants employ?'

'I dunno, and I'm sure I should hate him.'

'Well, shall I speak to my Sims?'

(Of course, if he came steeped in the Stortford earth there must be virtue in him.) 'You are a dear, but I'd rather try for Stiles first –'.

'And what about provisions? You remember the shops your mother used to deal with, I suppose?'

'Whadyermean! Remember them!'

'Haigh! haigh! haigh!'

(Actually, I found that I wasn't entirely correct, and that I didn't know and never had known where we used to get, for instance, such miscellanea as brooms, dusters, garden hose, notepaper and eggs, essentials which had never occurred to me in London, when going over old times.) Often in the following days I rang up auntie S to act referee to my uncertainty: it was our leading grocer, Comfort, from whom mother got the eggs, of course? And auntie S: 'Lord no, never! She and I went to that dairy much higher up. We used to meet there every Monday when she paid the book. She always said Comfort sold Election eggs.'

'Then I'll go to the Dairy too: and where did she get so-and-so and so-and-so?' And quite suddenly, auntie S went dead on me and didn't remember, or never knew – like myself, after all, like myself ... and it seemed to me so important to be right on detail, that, only so, could I successfully reconstruct the old life.

The third call was a male voice which told me (too truly) that I wouldn't know it and turned out to be, of all people, Johnnie Lawnford. I had last heard his voice when I was eleven. It was, he said, good to hear me, and, 'You know my wife, of course?'

'That depends upon whom you married,' I replied, secure in our old association.

'Well – hang it!' That sounded like the ghost of the beginnings of offence and I did some quick thinking and more or less fluked into a correct pairing of him off; but it was, I knew, bad timing, theatrically speaking, and I doubt if a woman would have passed it. 'Of *course* I know! That was my silly jape. It was Estelle Raymond and she and I had French with Madame when she wasn't having colds.'

'She's got one at this moment –'

'Hurray! You know what I mean: it sounds like old times.'

'My respected ma-in-law kept her in cotton-wool, I always said so.'

'Never in my hearing, Johnnie! My dear, are you a stockbroker in checks and a golf handicap, or an Army man silent and bronzed, or a gentle giant with a trowel who forgets to weed and writes sonnets in the summerhouse?'

'I'm head cashier in a Kingsmarket bank.'

'Lor … I wish I could cash cheques with you, but I'm sealed unto our old one.'

'When are you coming to see us? Estelle would have 'phoned but for her cold.'

'Fearfully soon. Where do you live?'

'We've got part of the Domrémy's old house. It's flats now.'

'*No!* What a pity! I don't suppose I mean that, either, politely speaking, but it was a fine house of its kind.'

'Much too big. It sank old Dommy.'

'Anything would have done that. Remember their parties and the stream of presents?'

'No.' (Did or did not the Lawnford-Domrémy mothers 'call'?). 'Oh, by the way, haven't we got to congratulate you on a tune or something you wrote?'

'D'you mean *Love, Give Me More Memories*, or *Everybody Kept on Laughing*?'

'Never heard of that one. No, the other. Lord, how they plug it! You must have made a fortune. I said to Estelle only last night if they play that thing once more I shall switch off the wireless.'

'How heavenly and tactless and Addison of you!'

He was instantly and unnervingly overcome with confusion and involved, insincere apologies.

4

What with the impact of arrival and all these dear people I was, after all, unable to enjoy my first dinner as mistress of Evenfield; emotionally, it was Aggie and her Irish stew all over again.

And I don't know to this hour if Mabel waited well and now never shall, since that will eternally depend upon my memory alone. She was London-engaged and so no doubt would be leaving me very shortly! The cook I secured from Kingsmarket via an advertisement in *The Surrey Comet*, for which paper I had given an advance standing order to the station bookstall, though not quite prepared to give up my *Daily Telegraph*. I felt so certain that our papers came from the platform in the old days that I had asked nobody about it, could remember isolated scurryings to it over the bridge if *Little Folks* was late ...

My initial disappointment at not getting local servants was soon overcome by the consideration that, if I had, my position would prevent me from drawing them out on the subject of Addison and people; the kitchen, in short, was no longer a place in which one danced solos or begged for toffee ingredients, but a room in which inexorably adult dialogues took place, and I must remember that.

That evening, at the back of all my congestion of excitement, I was remotely nagged by the telephone calls, and as I cracked walnuts and enjoyed port (I failed to continue to: had been unable to get our brand in Addison, and after the songs were produced we did go rather gorgeous, better even than father's old-slow-and-sure) I pondered the Lawnford exchange.

He'd misunderstood me so *basically*; I had left as a result a heaven-really-only-knows-what impression. Was I now rated as a Jasperleigh snob? If so, that label would stick with him and, less adhesively, with his circle, when all I'd longed for was that he should love and laugh at Addisonianism with me. Yet Johnnie was ever so slightly up in arms in defence of Addison. But I loved it at least as well as he did. Then why can't he take it as I do?

5

I couldn't stop to rest after dinner before I toured the house, and opening door after door forgot the outside world as the results of my infinite labour and searching filled my eye.

It had been a work ranging from the tedious to the farcical, like an overlong rehearsal, and comprising something of the hazards and responsibility of the antiquary, the curio-hunter, the period costumier and the staved castellan. For I had determined that no lapse of anybody's memory or of mine should be marked off as dead loss except in the last resort, when plausible invention would take its place. There were deliberate exceptions; the billiard-table which I failed to replace, being wholly unable to master a game which looked despondently boring, anyhow, though woe betide the person who omitted to allude to the room as the billiard room. It was now my lounge, leather arm-chair'd and what somebody once described as a man's den without the pipe-racks and disorder. All I saw was that it was comfortable, and in the drawing-room there was no replica of that ornate organ or the deplorable 'cosy corner'; this, I felt, was going too far. The wall-paper, on the other hand, was an example of research: Mell said that it had been a cream satin-stripe with a dado of moss rosebuds, and I got an approximate imitation from our Kensington builder who exhumed sufficient pieces from a limbo of what Potash and Perlmutter would term 'the stickers', pretty mementoes of a more sentimental day. The piano I had hired from Kingsmarket was an upright though I hankered for a baby grand, and on its lid I heaped old scores of *The Greek Slave*, *The Circus Girl*, *San Toy* and *The Geisha* (the assembling of these tuneful relics took me two whole afternoons in Charing Cross Road and they cost an amount which astonished me. One shopman offered me two dozen copies of *San Toy* and asked if I were 'taking out the show', and I wished I'd had a circular feather boa to twitch at him, or a chiffon dustpan hat to nod roguishly; instead, I shook my shingle with regret, and anyway it took Marie Studholme and Gabrielle Ray to carry off those effects!).

Nor in the drawing-room could I quite tolerate that heavy embroidered drape over the piano's back, its absence must rank with the telephone and the electric light as an innovation, but I had the white wicker arm-chair that mother used at Evenfield and into which in Kensington Gate Mell had so often after matinée or dance creakingly cast herself in her bedroom, and here it was once more, by the brass firescreen … The huge curtains over the french windows leading into the garden through which Mell and I had burst as dragons and rainbow fairies were back in place: by electric light they looked more than a little shabby against the inevitable newness. The gilt-framed Turners I so heartily disliked were re-hung and on the hall staircase there was The Flood, facing a nice dreadful hat-rack which I bought in a secondhand shop in Fulham Road: it had, said the salesman, once been hired by a manager for a tour of *Candida*, which I could well believe.

I think the day-nursery gave me more trouble than any other room. Of all the old wall-papers, that was the one I remembered most vividly, and the one most difficult to match, with its pink apple boughs and pastelle blue ground; and then the question of what to do with the room presented itself; it must be a playroom, yet even I saw that at over thirty you can't go back to dolls, their house, and a rocking-horse … Evenfield wasn't to be a museum-piece, but a home. I got over the question by filling it with copies of all the books that we did read and that I could collect from dealers, Alcotts, Meades, Sharps, Wetheralls, and by having tables covered with paint-boxes, pencils and drawing-blocks for the caricatures I still perpetrated, and Patience cards, Snakes and Ladders, which I enjoy, plus a quantity of jigsaw puzzles – excellent for diverting the mind from anger or worry if you haven't a temperature to start with. I even put a *barre* along one wall to practise my dancing by and limber up and was always being surprised by how little I'd forgotten, whenever the mood took me to do *pliés* and *battements* to the gramophone.

But in every room I entered my memory and that of my family, scrappily augmented by old friends (the Fields came out very strong over certain items) had served me better than I knew, and it wasn't so much a case of Love, give me more memories, as a dizzying, cumulative collision with the past ... Even the nursery milk-jug was back in the landing cupboard.

I went to bed in the night-nursery. At not too much after ten o'clock the servants creaked upstairs as well.

It was astonishingly quiet. Strain my ears as I might there was nothing in house or garden to hear.

CHAPTER II

I

After all, I didn't have my first breakfast in bed, my impatience to see the rooms in morning light was too raging. It ended by Mabel's entrance with the tray and my eating and drinking all over the place – a sausage in the spare room, tea in the day-nursery, toast and marmalade in mother's room. Officially that was to remain a bedroom, but no guest, I determined, should ever occupy it ... I believe I even began an apple by the french windows downstairs as I looked at the garden in my pyjamas (how could it be in my pyjamas? Quite, quite. I said that on purpose, because at the moment of writing I was being sorry about father and wanted an imaginary syntaxical set-to with him). The garden was doing me proud so *that* was all right, and I went upstairs again.

The day-nursery was, as always, pleasant (why couldn't I hire Miss Abernethy to sit in it at two-and-six an hour? What is a schoolroom without a governess? Or Aggie at the same terms, to sew in her grey stuff skirt and buckram belt? It was really preposterous that from breakfast to lunch time I should be free of that room, with nobody to spring at me with dates and kings and sums, or catch me as I dodged and hold materials against me for pinning).

This morning I was going to play at being grown-up and do my shopping with a basket; I hadn't arranged to meet Mrs. Field or auntie S or anybody at the shops for that wasn't playing fair; the essence of the thing was that they should occur, take their chance, and nothing forced. To-day I needn't tour the larder because I had stocked it to repletion in advance, and even as I went back to my room the boy was bringing the bread – to my delight in the old way, assorted loaves in a huge basket for cook to choose from, a lavish gesture which pleased me for its own sake! The boy was whistling *Love, Give Me More Memories*, flat, and omitting two grace-notes. I leant out of the window.

'Hi! It's, "tra-la la-la la twiddley-um–te tar", not "Tra la *lar* la-la *lar* lar-lar lah"', I shouted and sang.

The boy looked offended. 'I ought t' know that b' now, 'way it's played all over', he said.

'You ought, but you don't, and I ought to know. I wrote it.'

'Go on?' goggled the boy, bafflingly, and disappeared into the back yard. So now I was probably the local notability or the village idiot who must be humoured, as well as a possible Jasperleigh snob. Not bad going for the inside of two days, but I *cannot* bear incorrect whistling or humming for which, as there are no printed notes, there can be no excuse.

2

That morning, I was glanced at, paused at, incredulously recognized, as you decipher a difficult handwriting, by residents with whom I was in much the same mental state; served as a stranger in shops whose appearance was mainly as unaltered and unalterable as the pyramids (those shops which had displaced the ones I knew I was prepared for by my intermittent Addison prowlings from London, but to enter Comfort's ungreeted by anybody was a minor shock). Nor, that first morning, did I meet one intimate. The high-water mark was reached when I myself glanced at, paused and incredulously recognized our 'Lucilla', Miss Dove. There she was, once you had identified her, unmistakable, in her quenched hat and bright porcelain smile which heaven knows how many times she had unsuccessfully played upon the vicar. Speak to her? I restrained myself. Even one word might precipitate a social avalanche for which I might not be prepared. Evenfield must of course be Godfearing but not if I could help it churchy! Passing on, it occurred to me that we'd never known her, that she was a familiar only as a family joke.

The bank, where I cashed an unnecessary cheque to see if the place was smelling the same, was highly satisfactory; it had the old floor of stone mosaic and its smell I can still only indicate as being of cash, or rather what that word suggests when you read it, gently metallic and a little smoky. Metal shovels, perhaps?

In the toyshop window sat a cobbler mending a boot. This outrage had been perpetrated while my back was turned: the toys had certainly been there up to two years ago.

That afternoon, after a luncheon of some of our old standbys including liquid chocolate with sponge fingers, I found that the time of year precluded a hammock under the apple-trees, and lay on the drawing-room sofa. After a while, my London ear began to cock, waiting for the telephone to ring.

3

The reactions of my first callers were amusing and a little disturbing, if you allowed them to be.

Mrs. Jasperleigh was dramatic. 'But – Evenfield over again! My dear, a shock! Identical! Might never have gone! How – can – you – bear – it? I should be in tears. Floods!'

Auntie S came, saw, squeezed my arm and chuckled, 'Ara, how dear and dreadful of you! What *would* Mrs. M say? How did you do it? *How* Evelyn will chortle! And the "cosy corner" you couldn't stomach! Haigh! haigh! haigh! But we can go one better: I've still got a painted tambourine *and* a stool like almond hardbake that no dealer will take away even for nothing, so we just make pets of them. I call it all quite heavenly. Your mother always said we both ought to keep a boarding-house for decayed cats in Cliftonville.'

Mrs. Field, her susceptible eyes alternately filling with tears of mirth and sorrow, said low-voiced, 'Oh chicky! ... it does bring back the old days so, and what good times we had here. Your parties were always successful, you dear! ... and that hat-rack! Well of course I can't pretend I like it, but I've seen it so often with your dear father's tophat hanging on it ('It was Candida's young man's, last', I interpolated), and I remember your mother once made a dummy and hung it among the hats and coats when your father was entertaining the Church Lads' Brigade', and Mrs. Field's eyes filled with guilty amusement. Then, taking in the wicker chair, 'I've seen her sitting there so often, bless her …'

I received one entirely self-contained tribute, from old eyes which, unhampered by the past, saw the drawing-room as *a* room.

Miss Ambrose called with card-case and kid gloves and was shown in to me. Clifford's aunt and I had never become more than acquaintances, I had no time on my visits to Addison, but she had been very kind about the offer of stray meals when I was moving in. Now she looked about her with obvious pleasure, apologizing for discourtesy. 'But you have made it so charming, so unlike the modern drawing-room, it's a rest to the eye. I must confess when my nephew told me that so young a woman had taken Evenfield I was – well –'

'I know. China satyrs heads on the wall and a red ceiling.'

'Well, something of the sort, perhaps, but this is what I call really delightful. Indeed it reminds me (you'll laugh) a little of our own drawing-room when I was a girl, though I fear we crowded furniture sadly. You have avoided that. Nothing heavy, yet all in such taste … this is what I call A Lady's Room.' I did laugh, then, as a vision of washable tiling, grubby basins, penny-in-the-slot machine and a nameless stench whisked before my eyes.

4

On Sunday, I went to occupy my sitting at St. Anselm's, and discovered that I meant nothing to the verger: it wasn't drink on his part; this man was new, at least to me, so I could only suppose that Sheppard had scoffed his Scotch by night once too often, poor old soul, and, as I knelt, made a mental note to write and let Mell know.

I'd been, after all, unable to locate our old seats, guessed that I hadn't been exact when I realized I was too close to that banner of the star-encircled angel and too far from another familiar whose needlework feet tiptoe'd a writhing dragon in crimson silk … and it might or might not have been this miscalculation which caused me to fail to locate so many churchgoing regulars: or was it that they were unrecognizably aged, or dead? Or had the new vicar driven away the faithful? I was prepared for the new vicar, had heard for some years that ours had accepted a London living, but was faintly worried by the present one for all that; even the Fields had preferred St. Michael's, in the old days. But as the tenant of Evenfield it would have been amusing and warming to bow … I think I would have actually inclined to Miss Dove had she been there, but I suddenly remembered that "Lucilla" was now by rumour in the borderline class, and a change of vicar doubtless meant a change of heart, and heaven knew before what alien altar she was now curtsying. Was it my duty to find her, draw her out, lay at her feet my contribution of anecdote and memory of our ex-minister? No, dammit! I couldn't! Poor Lucilla must ever remain fixed in time as a family joke … and my set of *contes* mightn't be her mark at all, for what solace to the emotionally wracked to know that her earthly god had once offered to kiss both me and my sister, even if we were only children, or that, that little matter adjusted, he had then had a set-to with my mother about Mrs. Oswald? (*Her* opinion against His!).

At the south door I loitered, expectant. Two people spoke to me. One, a woman, had a vaguely familiar face to which I was cordial: she asked me to come and see her and hoped she might call on me and I said yes to everything, and regarded her exit of dithering pleasure with indulgence. She was probably thinking that to get *Love, Give Me More Memories* in person into her house would be meat upon which to dine out for months to come.

The other, an old and kindly man, neat and withered, left me at a complete loss until he introduced himself, and even then he was only a known name to me, but I clutched at it eagerly as I tried to associate it with one single incident in this world.

'I expect you don't remember me,' added Mr. Grimstone. (*Grimstone?*). And then a ray of light was vouchsafed me, thanks to mother. 'Jordan water from the Holy Land,' I said promptly, 'and the silver crucifix for St. Anselm's.' He looked slightly taken aback but elected for amusement. 'Is that all? Now, where do I live? You haven't the faintest idea. D'you remember a house by the river called The Moorings?'

'Oh, but *yes!*' This was too bad, and a blow to my pride, because I *did* know the name and now he'd think I was the usual thickhead who'd left Addison and didn't give a damn. I wavered unhappily until he said, 'You even came to see us, once, with your pretty mother ... and I suppose you've forgotten my yacht as well. You were my little hostess –'

'So it was yours! I'd always wondered. You see, one or two other people had launches, and mother couldn't remember. I had a cartwheel green hat and green sandals –'

'No doubt, no doubt', (one for me, this time!).

'I do so hope I wasn't a little beast,' I submitted, making a possibly called-for apology overdue by about twenty-three years.

'You were most excellent company.'

'Well, thank goodness for that!'

'And I shall always remember how you went for some child at a party and made her nose bleed.'

'Thelma! So you were there!'

'I'm her godfather –'

'*No?*' (*This looked like possible rocks ahead.*)

'– but beyond that I really see very little of the Jasperleighs (*ah!*) and never could quite fathom why I was selected for that honour.' (*I could, you nice old innocent. You're well-off and childless and influential and a gentleman.*) 'Now do tell me what brings you down to St. Anselm's once more?'

'I've leased Evenfield again.'

'Indeed!'

I told him a little of what I felt about it and wondered whether one confided in a Grimstone, but knew just enough to rate him as one of a background of respectables, besides, I liked him for his own sake, and it ended by our replacing each other on our visiting-lists, 'though I fear I have little to offer, these days; my yacht is given up and I'm getting old and since my wife died I have been out of touch with life in general ... but tea on the lawn is still pleasant...'

Walking home to my luncheon of roast beef and apple tart – I loathe apple tart but felt that its smell and taste would bring round the dining-room to a deepened awareness of former Morant sabbaths, I suddenly realized with a start which made me cut the pastry crooked that the fulsome woman who had asked me to call on her must have been an Addisonian detrimental, one of mother's Lord-Have-Mercy-On-Us horde, though her name had gone completely. Well … I could always be Not At Home if she turned out impossible, and I had to applaud a persistence, a magnificent pachydermatude which for a lifetime had waited, pounced, and gate-crashed Evenfield at last!

It was fun to be lunching in the dining-room: my first flurry of rediscovery over I savoured every minute there, sat at the head of the table – father's place for the look of the thing before the servants, but hankered for my old side position on mother's right. From where I now sat she'd be facing me …

As there was nobody to talk to, I began our old game of pretending that father was somebody else, and as this was my inaugural Sunday luncheon, I allotted him Lord Chesterfield, and passed him sugar and cream. Courtesy without subservience …

5

The days were closing in. Already a mist hung over the lawn and turnip field, and any night now, I supposed, through novels I had read which were all agreed upon the subject, I might expect to see the dahlias 'blackened' overnight with frost, an affliction I don't ever remember to have observed in our own or those of anybody else. It was probably going to be time for me to call in Stiles to do autumnal things.

My thirty-fourth birthday was drawing near, a dreadful age, neither fish, fowl nor herring. I must have a party or betray Evenfield for ever, but what would either of us think of a grown-up affair? We weren't used to it, the house and I, only to nice mothers of many children dotted about the drawing-room … and I didn't know one child in Addison. The offspring of my contemporaries must all be too old by now.

I sat by the nursery fire and considered. Evelyn Stortford (as I should probably continue to call her) had a son I'd never met: the Randolph child who I seem to remember had had two children, sex unknown, had moved on somewhere else, and an Ack-worth-Mead daughter who (didn't Mrs. Field tell me?) contributed one son to her husband, the Raymond boy, and goodness knew where she was by now. If Thelma had had a child I felt in my bones I'd have disliked it, and the rest of our circle didn't seem to have 'obliged', except poor Janet Martin, whose baby had died outright.

There must be children to know?

I thought of Mayvale and the dancing-class. On the following Thursday I was dressing carefully for it.

6

I supposed as I went along that mile and a half to Mayvale that I ought to have called upon Madame Fouqué. But I should have to go in by the front door; no more skirtings of the house and pushing open of that back-door into the shrubbery and entry by the ante-room to where the classes were held, for I was now a grown-up, I must remember.

It was Léonore, stooped to the gilt sandals of some favourite pupil, who looked up, shrieked and sprang at me. 'Oh, Barbara, but too wonderful! Have you seen mother? I think she is giving Miss Vansittart a dressing-up in the saloon.' I happily hoped that Mud-darm was being 'offal'. 'But why haven't you looked us up before?'

'I was settling in.'

'That passes me! How you *can* envisage being without Mrs. Morant and Melisande … and, my dear, you're *exactly* the same! Oh how I wish Irène was here! But she is so wound up in Dick and her family –'

'Oh Léonore, how is everything! I *had* to see the dancing-class again! Who's the star turn now?'

'A *marvellous* child – not so sweet as you, but Miss Lamare is stunning with children, oh but infinitely better than Miss Anson!' I was in the great classroom, seeing again the plaster casts which were dotted about on shelves when the drawing-mistress had left the arena, wondering whether Mell had struggled in her time with the plums or that Michelangelo hand of David, examining the parquet floor my own feet had polished so often

… and then there was a stir and Madame Fouqué made entry looking not one day older, and it was in choler that I re-met her. 'Miz Fancy Tart iz tou bàad!' she exclaimed, when her brown eye assimilated my presence.

She took me over like a warder from a constable, had much to say, tappingly upon my arm, but I sensed a change, a lack of the old cordiality, the authentic warmth which broke through her ancient rages and decrees absolute. Of course, we *had* had a difference, but that was sixteen years ago, just a fact without feeling, to me, but perhaps in Addison they clung more to vendetta? I was bright and brittle (like mother?) and suitably deferential when it suited me, but for some reason I wasn't going down with Muddarm in any capacity, whether as pupil, friend or Londoner. She seemed to me defensive (like Johnnie Lawnford?), on the alert to discover snobbisms or vanity or something, the injustice of which I felt without being able to counter it … little digs at me … or was I enlarging everything in my anxiety to slide back into my old place in her regard?

'You are ver' smart.' (Compliment or censure?)

'You are *réussi*, I hear.' (Politeness or indifference?)

'We hav' a wonderful mistress now, a t'ousand time supérieure to Miz Ansonn. You shall see.' (Information or snub?)

'Our bes' dancer is a daurrling.' (Implicit detraction?) I saw. They put me among the watchful semicircle of parents and guardians, Madame at my side, as it were 'producing' my attentiveness like the maddening friend who has seen the play before and intends you to realize that fact with his superfluous pointers.

It didn't take me five minutes to realize that the new dancing mistress was a compromise; well ahead of Miss Anson technically she was far behind Hervet, and instilling mere smatterings of the right stuff without the effective and effortless little flourishes which make amateurs pleasing to an amateur public; as a result the pupils didn't appear to me to be either useful or ornamental performers. The Marvellous child was slightly below the junior standards of the London classrooms and her marvel, I supposed, consisted in a lot of *pointe* work for which she was as yet too young by quite three years, and I foresaw early bunions as I fulsomely agreed with every pronouncement of Madame's and the exclamations of the semicircle. After that I devoted the time to mental selection of children for my birthday party.

Madame had rustled away, and a voice next my chair asked me, 'Which of the little girls is yours, I wonder?'

I had one grin that afternoon during the ten minutes devoted to ballroom dancing when the pianist thumped out *Love, Give Me More Memories*, and nobody even glanced at me.

One two three, *one* two three … poor Mr. Field! *Perfect time. Horrible. You're not beating carpets.*

Madame sent for me to come up to tea in the drawing-room. Healthily incensed I made my excuses and left. I wanted Evenfield, to find it unchanged, even were its present familiarity largely due to my own efforts.

Léonore would have been affectionate and eager and possibly understanding, but one must remember that she was Madame's daughter and partner, and committed to loyalty.

In the drawing-room Clifford was waiting for me and I stumbled over the carpet as I hurried to him. 'Oh Clifford, I *am* so glad to see you!'

'I didn't like to come, before.' (But he didn't look too happy at my welcome, or had I imagined that, as well?)

'And I didn't like to ask you. Addison's a far cry from the Courts.'

'Long Vacation. We've still three days to go to Michaelmas Term.' He made no comment on the house; it may be that he'd forgotten what it used to look like, but he seemed to confine his topics to London and Cuss and old Miss Ambrose, with whom he said I had made a hit. She wasn't from my point of view an Addisonian, but there are times when any approval is better than none.

7

He stayed to dinner and I think Mabel was sulky, and afterwards we walked in the garden which was delicious with tobacco plant and damp earth and celery. I took his arm, which, it occurred to me later, he hadn't seemed to like, much, but I kept my arm in his because I liked him so very well, and because if he was being tightlaced and Addisonian it was quite heavenly of him and for me, or thinking that extra care must be observed towards an unprotected female, or just cautious (the Law Courts), which would have been even better! The real reason escaped me handsomely at the time, and with a whiff of a late-flowering rose I received a sensation that I was walking with father again, father being Not Amused about some cantrip of ours.

'Clifford, I want a birthday party.'

'Ah ...'

'I want a kids' party like our old ones, and I find I don't know any.' He was rather a long time answering that.

'Mightn't it perhaps be a better idea to have a party only for grown-ups?'

'People I know, you mean?'

'That too. But –'

Somehow, I didn't want to ask him to finish his sentence; he got round it by saying, 'Strange children would hardly be a pleasure to you, would they?'

When he had left me to take the last train to Waterloo I went back to the warm, bright drawing-room and tried to read, and couldn't. My mind wanted and intended to go over birthdays of the past.

There was the year that we had the Rainbow party, with all the girls (by request) as fairies and all the boys as knights, elves, gnomes, or goblins; in one corner of the room (I turned my head to it) was a cave, terrific in painted cardboard and pot-plants, with Mell a sequinned monster at its entrance. The prize game was to rescue myself as the Rainbow Princess, and a password must be guessed, the winner to receive a sword, shield and stout sack of golden sovereigns made of chocolate, the losers to receive awards for reasons unspecified. And the year I, as Queen, in a serrated crown and mantle of red velvet, chose my King for the tea-table, being instructed beforehand which boys to refuse and which one to accept, and I forgot and turned down the lot! Or the year that Mell and Janet Martin as witches presided over a wonderful well down which wishes must be cast on twists of paper, when I, as Undine, emerged with the desired present in hand – an effect that cost mother weeks of research for data from the other mothers …

The curtains were hanging very still in the September night. I became alarmed by them at last, waiting as I used to do for them to part upon I knew not what, and turned off the lights and went to bed. Later (too late, probably) the servants creakingly followed me.

CHAPTER III

I

ONCE I HAD a caller who made me laugh aloud. The bell rang, the knocker was knocked, and Mabel ushered in – Cuss! Cuss blindingly smart, who stripped his lavender kid gloves (they *were* lavender, and kid), placed his silk hat upon the floor and draped his gloves across it, bowed, shook hands with me, twitched the knees of his trousers, contemplated his spats and sat down circumspectly.

'Cuss, you fool!'

'A whiff of the old days. I had to comb Burlington Arcade for the props.'

'Oh Cuss, you *blazing* ass and how I like you! How's the Savage?'

'Hush, my dear, we talk about the Royal Academy first. This fellow, Dicksee –'

'No. That's in the Season!'

'Then let's have tea and plenty of it. D'you keep a good table? God's teeth! what a room!'

2

I went to see Stiles. The garden was beginning to sag and look tipsy and was too large anyway for my amateur tieings (when is a rose sucker that must be clipped a shoot that mustn't? And why will the garden-minded allude to things being 'cut back' when they mean cut down? You can't cut an upright backwards).

But I had gathered my apples happily and with wet ankles, rain-drops down my spine and heaven knows what falling on to my hair. The green cookers were still going and growing strong but I missed our russet tree (damn the Willises? or had it failed or died?). My pleasure was unabated by reason of the fact that I could no longer rise to eating the raw green fruit and that I detest all forms of apple, cooked.

Stiles was at home in his four-room cottage hear the Couch-mans, in Nutts Lane. I think, I'm afraid, I recognized him first, yet he was more than a little changed, stouter, and his sturdy autumn tints gone rusty like the October leaves I have seen him sweep so often. Once he had taken in who I was, he came to a semblance of his old self with nothing essentially dimmed but the physical, as is the way of gardeners, who are apt to remain authoritative and dauntless to the end, whether in humble or ducal service. I reminded him of the Frog Fairy stories, begged his memory about those sugar-framed Christmas pictures, and he was non-committal, even if he chuckled. I asked him in my rôle of householder to come to me to work at Evenfield, and here I found longwinded definiteness: he might look in every so often but now his knees and back forbade regular or heavy work. If he heard tell of a likely man –

But I didn't want a man however likely. I wanted Stiles and so did the garden.

On his crowded mantelpiece was a mug, with its 'J' initial of forget-me-nots, but I had forgotten it, and it took Stiles to remind me of that seaside souvenir presented how many autumns ago? by myself. And going home, that seemed to me subtly wrong; if I was to lose Stiles, the break should have been final and no senti-mental traces … it was my first visit to his home in all the years, and that too was out of step. Stiles came to us, not we to Stiles, and at such a time of day, and I'd upset that by my visit … Now, for my life, I should see him, save for brief and telescopic peeps at him bent over our celery trenches, as an old man past his work. It would have to be auntie S's Sims, and that would further tend to weaken the garden's hold on me. For I found that there wasn't so much to do in it as I'd imagined, except for paid experts: saw it sometimes as Just a large-ish garden that I knew in which I wasn't able to be lost to the world, discovered that to pull a radish and eat it on the spot was pleasant but just evaded fascination, especially when an impulse which had nothing to do with the business drove me to the tap to wash the earth off first.

3

Returning from my shopping one morning I passed a woman talking to a young man at the wheel of a battered four-seater.

'Ara!'

My response was only a fraction short of simultaneous.

'Evelyn!'

It may have been that the car and the young man (or old boy) put my eye out, for really Evelyn Stortford, whom I am not going to attempt to allude to as Mrs. Ivor, was looking very like a larger version of herself or a younger edition of auntie S (she had, which you won't for one second recollect, and it takes me some time to, married the unknown nephew of the dashing Mrs. Markham, but her voice and teeth and laugh were warmingly Stortford).

'What fun to meet you! Phil and I have just come from mother's. He's eighteen, can you believe it? Oy! Phil! Come and see Barbara Morant.' He came at once, his face lightening, and wasn't Fair-Isle and sandalled and superior but friendly in frousty pullover, and probably like his father plus the Stortford geniality. 'Mother told me you'd come back to Addison,' he said, 'we can't think why.' I liked that 'we' of implicit adoption as I answered, 'Because I'm spongey and probably a fool. What are you doing in my shops? You won't get much because either I've bought it already or they're out of it, which means they never stocked it anyway.'

'They must seem pretty one-horse after London,' he suggested.

'They're themselves and much as I remember them.' But I must admit that they were tiresome, becoming second-rate-standardized, and slowed up housekeeping unless one telephoned to Kingsmarket. Of course mother had dealt considerably with Harrods, and I now began to see why; and I suddenly remembered that she used one morning a week to 'put out the stores' from that Flemish cupboard in the hall, delving, weighing tea and sugar for half an hour in the dining-room impeded by myself as I thrust my arms into the stone jars, and that the cupboard was now in the drawing-room, full of old photographs and dust-sheets.

Evelyn told me that she lived two miles outside Kingsmarket where her husband was engineering consultant to a large aircraft works. 'And it's quite ridiculous you've never met him, Ara. He's quite kind and I think you'll like him. I had my eye on Harold Barstowe – d'you remember Clifford and Jacky? – for about a year after you left, and we used to sneak off and have tea in Kingsmarket and play badminton in the Parish Room, and then I met Stanley (yes, it's the world's most frightful name, I just call him Ivor) at whist at Mrs. Markham's one night and the thing was done.'

'*Lor!*'

'I know! I know! I often wonder who I'd've married if we'd left Addison when you did: I mean, I *do* see that we're rather like haystacks that catch fire because they're too tightly packed. Poor Harold was killed in the war.' I was to discover that Evelyn's outspokenness, if quite dismaying, was at all times as ready to be directed against herself and all that was hers.

'Well, if it comes to that, Chetwyn fought the Raymond boy about me, once,' I contributed.

'I know! And Mrs. Raymond was fearfully shocked. She told mother, and mother said she'd said that no normal boy of that age thought about little girls in that way.'

'Which one?'

'Ha ha ha! *That* one.' She turned to her son. 'Oh Phil, what you've missed!'

'I dunno. I think it all sounds pretty far gone.'

'And – Mrs. Markham?' I asked with caution, but I needn't have worried, for Evelyn's face broke once more into bright grins.

'Very like herself but we all think a bit dotty, don't we, Phil?'

'Oh I should say, definitely.'

'D'you remember the floral toques? She wears 'em still.'

'And is she still at – I never could remember the name of her house?'

'Oh no, she moved to Aylesbury *years* ago.'

'Why, i' gad's name?'

'She has relations there: Mr. Markham died and I think she was rather bored and Ivor lived with her for a bit and when we married she cleared right out.'

'I' m sorry.'

'Why, Ara?'

'Oh, you know … one more jape gone.'

We had talked for twenty minutes. Evelyn said she was ravening to see lots of me but we agreed that the distance she now lived made a big difference except, perhaps, in the summer. She'd never learnt to drive the car and I sympathized for both of us; to be unenterprising about machinery and repairs seems to afflict women of her generation and even a little those of my own. And there was so much to say! If auntie S was a quarry, Evelyn promised to be a diamond mine, and already October was upon us with its darkening, anti-social evenings … it reminded me of my birthday party and I mentioned it and Evelyn said she'd come were it in a wheelbarrow, and 'Phil' (or did I imagine it?) looked alert. I apologized that it would probably consist of nothing but veterans (remembering not to say grown-ups by an eleventh split second), but he brushed that aside. 'I say! Might I really come? I'm quite good with curate's aids and I can help them into their dolmans and pelerines afterwards.'

'Well, thanks a lot! And while you're on the job you can ease me into my carpet slippers.'

'Carpet slippers!' he raked my feet. 'You must spend a fortune on your shoes.' Evelyn was eager. 'May he really come? He'd love it. *Really*. He's been on at me for ages to get to know you and is frightfully set up when they play your waltz at dances. I say, Ara, you *have* got on! You're the only girl in Addison who's ever done anything interesting.'

Back in the dining-room at Evenfield I savoured that meeting with my luncheon. It had been jolly indeed to meet Evelyn again after all this time, but as with Stiles, quite wrong that she should be motoring away from Addison to a husband instead of going home to luncheon at the Stortfords prior to an afternoon of tennis. It confused me ... and 'Phil'. Such a dear soul, but quite out of the picture. Would nobody stand still in time? Of all the people I could think of it seemed to be only myself who was unchanged, untouched, willing and available, a lonely sensation. And then, as a small bonus, the dining-room presented me with a totally forgotten item, about father this time: father in contempt and sarcasm at Nonconformist hymns, and his quotation of one line (or was it an exasperated parody?) in a brisk and irreverent quicktime:

God be with us all as we *walk* along the Path!

and of how I misheard it as 'Glory be to Saul', until Mell exhumed it quite seventeen years later! And then I remembered that father sugared his soup, a Scottish trick. He said it improved the flavour. And having remembered that, I tried it myself and found he had said a true thing and did it ever after! (It is especially excellent with thick pea soup.) And after luncheon I think I wondered for only a little while what to do with the afternoon, settled in the drawing-room and sketched out two lyrics. They came along rather well and teatime was upon me in a flash.

4

My birthday party was immensely enjoyable of its kind, although it didn't seem to begin until the afternoon when my guests arrived. Cuss came down for it, sanely clothed this time! and was rather at a loss before Stortfords, Fields and the rest, which I hadn't bargained for until I realized how much less well he knew them than I. The party was a small one. I didn't want to leave out Mrs. Jasperleigh as she was one of the regulars in the old days, but asking her would have involved having Thelma as well; I wanted Léonore but wasn't prepared for a backhander from Muddarm and it ended by filling gaps with others I liked but who, as birthday people, were all wrong for the occasion; these included nice old Mr. Grimstone who sat on the sofa, kind and gratified, and Mr. Field whom I persuaded hard as musically sympathetic to Cuss. The party balanced pretty well, but Clifford had pleaded the Courts as an excuse … he had sent me a ring which once belonged to Mrs. Siddons, and a note that ought to have made most women happy for the day, but which, once I had grasped the situation, only had the effect of filling me with those remorses that I had gone through over Donald, if, this time, a thousandfold more acutely. 'Wear this at least for your birthday … whatever happens, you need never fear that I shall be tiresome to you …'

Well, my very dear Clifford, I'm sure I don't know if I'm what is called 'worthy' of you, but at least I was quite certain that I didn't want that kind of commitment yet. I must first have my fill of Evenfield …

I think my tea-table, traditionally in the dining-room, would almost have done credit to mother, except the centrepiece: my birthday cake I had ordered in Kingsmarket, which wasn't in the same street with her whimsies. One year, my cake had been a maypole made of a stout, ribbon-bound sugarstick, the rim encircled with little dancing girls of coloured sugar each holding her streamer – heaven knows where she got them and anyway one seldom takes as much thought for and by oneself. And then – at midday on the very morning came a boy with a box, and it was a cake made by the Fields' cook, larger than mine, showered with silver brights and candles and comfits and crystallized cherries and I could have hugged it. I had a cake! (My own purchase, with a gesture wholly injudicious, I sent into the kitchen.) 'From all four and Cookie, with fondest love to dear Ara. We couldn't let you be without one!'

I wanted silly games, but would everybody enjoy them except to please me? I just didn't know, after all these years … Meanwhile it looked as though Cuss was succeeding in propelling Mr. Field to my piano; that probably meant Bach, and I curdled. My esteem for that composer is unabated but strictly long-distance, and Bach! at Evenfield, on a Morant birthday! And Cuss won, damn and blast him, but I needn't have feared, for with a semi-sardonic glance at me, Arnold Field sat down and played my waltz song, and so beautifully! with rich embellishments and variations of his own, and I sat in a corner with my eyes filling with ridiculous and quite unaccountable tears no noble fugue could have evoked, and didn't know why.

Philip Ivor said to me, 'I say, will you sing it?'

'I can't, my dear. No voice.'

'Then the other thing.'

'Ask my brother.' And he did, and Marcus with an apologetic look at Mr. Field played, and well, *Everybody Kept on Laughing*. Emboldened by Cuss, we sang it together and Mr. Grimstone beat time thoughtfully and said that that was what he *called* a tune, while auntie S haigh-haigh'd appreciation.

Evelyn was the last to leave me: her son seemed to be persuading her to stay, and finally she said that go she must or walk four miles on her flat feet, and he had to give in.

As I was seeing them off a van drew up at the gate, and I looked at it expectantly; an unlooked-for present would indeed be a good ending to the day – Mell's had arrived days too soon and Aggie's flowers were already drooping in the warm drawing-room.

It was a large box, taking two men to carry it, and then I saw initials on the lid as it was brought into the hall. It was mother's trunk from Switzerland.

I told the men to take it to her bedroom, and when they had left I went upstairs and locked the door.

5

I began to look for a flat for Cuss, and dawdled about London feeling lost. But I went to Harrods for things I didn't really want just to be able to tell the assistants to send the stuff to Evenfield. Mother must sometimes have done that, too, and I tried hard to be bored and matter of fact, as she must have been. The Kensington Gate house I avoided: I was afraid that, let or empty, it might make some pathetic gesture towards me as I passed it, loitering.

I had no idea of the sort of home that Cuss wanted, and he was vague, beyond the fact that it must be a flat. Men aren't homemakers, they just use their rooms; it's their great strength and weakness. Flats have their strong points, they are labour-saving and easy to leave and, take them all round, more burglar-proof than is the house, large or small, but as homes flats silence and fail to convince: I think you have to be violently twentieth-century really to settle down in them and of the mentality which on sighting a caller rattles the cocktail-shaker as a Salvationist her tambourine in testimony to good-will. At the same time, there certainly was one roomy flat that suggested possibilities apart from utilitarianism, in The Boltons, very quiet, an old house converted, its point to me being that it was near that detached and now abandoned house standing back in its walled garden where once Jenny Lind made her home. I liked to think of her returning down that bygone backwater in a brougham from the lights and shouts and *bravas* of the Opera, depositing bouquets in the hall, treading those now un-whitened steps and probably enjoying a glass of Guinness prior to unlacing her stays! Her influence might help Cuss with his lyrics and how handsomely she would despise them! I said so to Clifford with whom I frequently lunched, meeting him on the steps of the Law Courts, and Clifford assented that atmosphere counted for much and that the Law, being a notoriously leisured process, had annexed all the best and drowsiest bits of old London where time was not, and took me down a narrow alley through a door studded with square nails and, turning left, we were in an enchanted courtyard, its rose-brick sound asleep, its stillness only broken by the swift passing of stray Clerks and Associates upon the flagstones. 'Atmosphere with quiet *and* comfort,' he suggested suavely, and pointed to a row of Queen Anne windows. 'Those are my Chambers.'

'Oh, Clifford! Bardell *v.* Pickwick! It's heavenly. One can't conceive profaning that with revue lyrics.'

'Why not? The greater includes the less.' His smile was sardonic.

'Beast. And Rudesby.'

'I'm serious. The centuries must learn to shake down together. There is a powdering closet, I keep my papers in it, and a cupboard where I found an eighteenth-century wigstand when I moved in.'

'It's too much!'

'It's bribery and corruption, if not undue influence,' he answered sadly.

6

There were now no flowers in the hall to welcome my returns from London, for I was an Addison resident, and although that was as it should be I did sometimes feel that Evenfield no less than myself was thinking, 'Well, you've done it, this time!' And sometimes, on those November nights as I hurried home from the station past the capriciously-spaced Victorian lampposts which lighted a portion of your way and left you plunged in darkness for the rest, I would ring the bell, and on Mabel's admitting me, would lose sight of my own personality: in that instant of time I was mother in a sealskin cape, alert for me in a muslin pinafore.

As I settled into the house I also found that the dining- and billiard room were most aware of my father's death, most able to make me feel that I was not the real householder. I suppose it was that with those two rooms he was chiefly associated in my mind. The house's feeling for mother, I thought, was of regret for one with whom it had never succeeded in being on terms deeper than business, and that, accepting this, it had let her go in an adult way that I myself couldn't achieve. In that respect if in no other, Evenfield kept me a child still, out of the conferences of grown-ups ...

CHAPTER IV

I

IT WAS THE time of drawn curtains, fireworks, muffins, celery, performances in the Parish Room, and evening parties.

Death sometimes demands that you be untrue to your real self no less than to the deceased, and I must be decorous and mourn in convention's manner, not my own or mother's, to satisfy the sticklers who expect twelve months black shading thence

to mauve, and no nonsense about it. And if on the night of the
Fifth I stole into the garden to listen, see and haply smell the
smoke and gunpowder of others, at least I went unseen, though
not alone, for many people were round me in the dark.

'*I'm not afraid! I'm a Briton!*'

The Couchman children crouched, squealing, by the gooseberry bushes.

'*We've still got three more of the Jack-in-the-boxes, M'm.*' Aggie,
her apron bunched with fireworks.

I began on that chill, still night to feel suffocated and went
back into the drawing-room. After dinner I played *The Messenger Boy, San Toy* and *The Geisha* until I couldn't bear that either,
and stopped. I'd probably shocked the servants beyond remedy.
Who cares?

2

I went calling. There had been no time before and now I had
all the time.

I began, suppressing a desire to climb over the wall, with
Stamboul, to find, as I had expected, that the house without Janet
was largely meaningless. Her father and mother were wonderfully like themselves still though Mr. Martin was certainly deaf,
which made my souvenistic enquiries sound more than usually
worthless. He had always seemed an old man to me in spite of
his spare agility. About Janet's in-laws I dared not ask owing to an
inability to remember which was the eldest Irmine who had fall-
en so heavily for, though I am sure never with, that gold-hair'd
charmer, Mrs. Randolph.

I went home reasonably satisfied with my afternoon, for
Stamboul had never meant much to us and it was allowable that
it still should not … and one thing I had extracted from the visit – two, indeed: for, talking over the old days, Mr. Martin, of all
people, turned up trumps and told me that we had left Addison
in the spring, and when I spoke to him about the friends on
the platform he contradicted me most hearteningly about young
Ackworth-Mead having arrived with Mrs. Markham, a combination which even then had seemed improbable. He was there but

had arrived with a Domrémy son whom I didn't even remember. 'Young Domrémy had a great admiration for your father. I mind that the three of them would come heere for chess,' Mrs. Martin told me, 'but I nivir could thole *his* father, the puir feckless fule. It was freely take this, and freely take that, an' in the end the creditors freely took *him*.' Mr. and Mrs. Randolph had left Addison five years ago and I weathered that with phlegm; theirs was a null abode, blaze as it might with red-hot brick and flowers, and had meant for me disappointing parties. I asked Mrs. Martin if Janet ever saw Gladys, the Christmas tree doll Randolph child, her sister-in-law, and Mrs. Martin said Nivir, and knitted a sock the colour of Aberdeen granite.

Greatly daring, for I think we never knew them, I turned in next door to Tralee, one afternoon, to investigate 'the Miss Cocksedgees', as one day I shall inevitably call them before the wrong audience. The door was opened by a woman who might have been a nurse and I stood there explaining myself. When I had done, she told me reprovingly that Miss Cocksedge had died eleven years ago and that Miss Clara was very feeble now. This was a set-back, as I couldn't remember which of the old sisters Johnnie Lawnford and I had called upon, and had hoped as it were to identify the remains and even to glean from the memory of age, always of greater clarity about things past than with the contemporary scene, some inkling, however small, of what we had talked about, but I wasn't invited in, and that, I told myself, was reasonable as I left the house festooned with its stripped creepers. It was a horrid house, architecturally almost the twin of Evenfield, which I hadn't realized before.

With a distinct effort I made a toilette and went to see the Johnnie Lawnfords, as they were locally and abominably termed. Here, I guessed in advance, I should be straightforwardly bored, for if Johnnie had grown up to be no use to me his wife never had been, my link with her had at no period consisted of much more than the shared French verb in Madame Fouqué's study once a week plus glimpses of her among the crowd at her own parties, and if Johnnie did take me on all over again that would probably be all wrong, too! For Estelle (née Raymond), though sticking firmly to the colds of her childhood, might prove to be any kind of young woman.

She was. Also still pale and delicate and amiable and unredy, and the tea-party seemed to resolve itself into a grisly sort of tennis match − I the ball − in which she struck me repeatedly to Johnnie who attempted to return me to her. Conversationally we clung to Mayvale, Kingsmarket and Johnnie's bank there with an unhappy excursion (the *amende honorable*) into the realms of compliment about my musical composition which in sheer nervous sympathy for them I belittled even below its merits. And it was during that call that I dropped the best brick I was ever to let fall, a man-sized one and heavy, for, inveigled in spite of myself into discussion of what friends in common we did possess and honestly thinking the Lawnfords *hors concours* in that direction, I alluded to the Fields' sweetness in making the elder Irmine girl's trousseau, and there was a vacuum … (You will not remember any more than I did that the Irmine daughter was now related to my hostess through that Ackworth-Mead who had married my hostess's elder brother.) Johnnie said quite disagreeably, 'The Fields evidently don't believe in hiding their light under any blooming bushel'. After that I left as soon as decency permitted. The whole afternoon was also confusing through the Lawnfords' house being now a portion of what had once been the Domrémys', and that whereas in the old days I had never seen the top floors, that afternoon I saw nothing else, being debarred the rooms I did dimly remember through their occupancy by another flatful of tenants. The façade alone was faithful, with its stucco towers that gave the house its name, and it was through those gates that mother and Mell must have passed quite often, to dinner or dance, or (all three of us) to those inordinate Christmas parties.

I came home irritated and depressed, damned Addison, the Lawn-fords and Irmines and myself and felt slightly better, even amused, as a Londoner, until I remembered that I was now an Addison resident.

But there were still prospects: I even had Miss Abernethy on my list. One's governess would remember much; pleasant or unflattering, it was all one to my present mood.

The telephone rang and it was Evelyn's son, Phil, wanting to drive over after dinner; Evelyn would certainly be just what I wanted; I was delighted and asked when to expect him and his mother, but the tiresome youth hemmed something incoherent and I gathered was arriving alone. Well, I'd give him as good a time as possible, for her sake. I must have, for he stayed until eleven-thirty.

3

In between my social rounds the detrimental came to tea. She arrived at the unprincipled hour of four and her name was Miss Spicer, which meant nothing to me whatsoever. She was eager and a little subservient and had teeth, but as she was of the type which has an ailing mother needing Burgundy on straitened means I did my best for her; I've never been good at permissible frostiness, which is an art, like the *mot juste*, and enjoy scallywags with the best if they're amusing, consciously or otherwise, or pathetic, or frustrated, or what an author friend of father's once termed 'anything bookable'.

But the Spicer (how was it I had come to recognize her outside St. Anselm's? Was she the result of juvenile trespass to forbidden doors?) saved me a great deal of brainwork, for she informed me that my mother was such a sweet little woman, that she and her family always thought of me as a little Queen and called me Queenie if I'd pardon *her*, that I should prefer the new vicar to our old one, that she was a Cub Mistress of the local Scouts and that it seemed ever so strange, if I knew what she meant, to think of a gurl like me living alone at dear old Evenfield. In an unobtrusive way her eyes were taking in great gorging mouthsful of the drawing-room furnishings.

I let her carry on as I smoked and watched her, wondering if she were the local cat, mischief-maker, lavender-spinster-who-had-buried-a-soldier-lover, undiscovered-heroine-under-outdated-hat or one of those unexpecteds who, esteemed by all, die with a gallery of pornographic post cards locked in her chest of drawers. But unlike the rest of the Addisonians, she was thoroughly prepared to ask me questions – too many – about my songs; we even skirted the fees I was paid for them, about which aspect she was most persistent. She was also pressing that I return her 'little visit' but I scotched that, making my compositions an excuse for retirement. She did leave, it last, attempting to the end to run me into a corner and commit myself to dates.

I never wanted to see this bore again.

I would like to go to her house and find out if it and her family conveyed anything to me at all.

I don't quite know why, but I mentally presented the whole episode to mother on a plate, without comment.

4

My excuses to the Spicer were partly true: I was intermittent-ly tallying with new songs, regarding them at first as a stopgap, gradually working longer at them and oftener.

I discovered that I had a bent for comic songs, and in those weeks, when the garden was frost-bound and the house so qui-et with not even a visiting night moth to thud softly about the lamps, or darting bat whose entry (into my hair, of all the termini in the drawing-room) to fear, I wrote *Well, it's Something to Know You Can Buy Them, They All Get an Answer from Me, I Began as I Meant to Go On, I Can Get it Much Cheaper Than That* and *You'd Never Think I was a Lady.* They were what I called 'build-up' num-bers in which the verses from innocuousness grew progressively more blue, if your mind elected to take them that way. I sold two outright to a well-known low comedian (only six months ago I heard one of them still going strong in a suburban music-hall, and couldn't listen properly for seeing the Evenfield wall-paper and a Turner which caught my eye every time I glanced up while I was in the throes of scansion and snap). Nor had London interests forgotten me and I was rung up by the Guvnor himself about a new lyric for his next show, spoke to him in the hall, (he would have been about forty-five at the time I was standing there with Mell, waiting to take the train to Waterloo and Drury Lane).

These London calls fretted me for some time. I didn't want them. They were out of the picture. I grew to accept them, be-come interested in them, expectant, harassed if they didn't man-

ifest, bored with the drawing-room as is a man with a too ex-
igeante wife. The room's argument was that I had dressed it up
in costume and it wanted to be noticed: my riposte was that I'd
given it the best, knew exactly what it looked like, was perfectly
satisfied but didn't want to be disturbed now as I had a bit of
business to think out. No, nothing that would interest you I'm
afraid, my dear ...

> But you always said you *wanted* to sit with me.
> I did and I do. I *am* sitting with you!
> Oh of course, if it's going to be a duty –
> Oh damn it, woman, be quiet!

When he left for Switzerland, Cuss had put me in touch with
his Savage Club friend, telling me he would see to the business
end of our musical affairs and handle all scripts not directly sent
to the Guvnor.

Sometimes, things which I realized to be definite disappoint-
ments were announced over the line and then I would flounce
back into the drawing-room or run up to the nursery and either have another falling-out with the rooms or a penitent, affectionate reconciliation with my gratitude and assurance of love
thrown in.

They were a loyal, unchanging refuge from an unkind world.

Having admitted that, what were we all going to do next?

They didn't know; they'd done their part and the rest was my
affair. But I wouldn't go up to London lest I become engulfed.

I went calling again.

5

When Major and Mrs. Abernethy died and their sons and
daughters married or set up careers elsewhere, my Miss Abernethy
moved to a small new house, one of a row, in a part of Addison I
didn't seem to know. It was evidently built by that architect who
now apparently had tracts of the whole place in his pocket and
whose idea of home creation consisted of two-storeyed houselets
covered with pebbles, mean windows that opened on iron rods,
exposed half-inch beams of chocolate and a name-plate swung

on chains over the built-in porch. These houses inevitably attract families whose ideas upon curtains begin and end at blue casement cloth, and at 'Ickleton' lived Miss Abernethy, who had been reared in a home of twenty rooms and a sun-lounge. Marriage capriciously had passed her by, as she was, Mell told me, exactly like every one of her sisters.

I wondered as I pressed her nasty little bell, which went off in my ear instead of the hinterlands of the house, what awaited me. Would she be scholastic and bright, unrecognizable with years, or pink-nosed with sentiment? But when we met, I rapidly reconstructed her face and passed it, perceiving that this was my governess who had merely had a few alterations made upon her face rather than a stranger masquerading unsuccessfully as Miss Abernethy: I also realized that she couldn't even now be much over fifty-four. Her own look of doubt and enquiry gave place quite reasonably soon to astonished welcome. She had answered my ring herself.

She had done her best with the sitting-room: it was Botticelli'd and della Robbia'd and her curtains were burnt umber satin. The isolated pieces of good furniture in that cramped space were refreshing but incongruous.

I quite soon found that either my hostess wasn't my governess or that my governess wasn't Miss Abernethy. She was shy. Of me. And obviously. This was so dreadfully wrong that I began to be brittle (like mother) and to sling my remarks all over the place of sheer dismay. She found me harmless, in time, and becoming more herself told me that I must miss my father and mother, that so many people had left Addison, that it had changed for the worse and that I should not care for the present vicar as I did for our old one and that her work for The League of Nations took much of her time, and then, of course, her little house –

I could match her there, and did, have never found domestic conversation dull, and suddenly Miss Abernethy became herself, showing me for the first time that she was not something you dodged or scamped and didn't think of as quite human and hated to touch, but is a rather likeable woman who, as only gentlepeople do, spoke of her poverty quite openly. 'And even now, with the taxes what they are, I sometimes dread the future a little.'

I left, pressing her sincerely, warmly, and rashly to drop in whenever she liked, full of new respect, even of the stirrings of affection, for her, while a portion of my brain hoped that The League of Nations wouldn't allow of her coming too often. I was remorseful that I couldn't ask after a single one of her sisters, but I'd long forgotten, if I ever knew, the name of one of them. Later, it occurred to me that beyond a few general enquiries Miss Abernethy had had nothing to say about any of *us*. It was a novel experience, possibly pointing to the fact that I was just the child she taught in an Addison family, the beginnings of her eye to the future that was to secure her an Ickleton in which to end her days.

I wonder what mother paid her?

6

Tradition did not fail me and the ice held, that winter, while morning mist hung on the lawn and the red sun loomed through the silver birch in the garden of Miss (Clara) Cocksedge.

As skating was an exercise I hoped that my joining in would not be accounted unto me for heartlessness at family bereavement and went joyfully off to my Carolean canal bordered with its stark chestnut trees with my new and expensive skates clashing in my hand. Astonished, I found, as I trust others have done before me, that the little knowledge had turned into a dangerous thing and that the old knack I counted upon had almost entirely left me. That came of moving to London I thought, exasperated, as I shaved falling for the third time in ten minutes; it wasn't until the end of the afternoon under a yellow sky that I got my balance back and a certain measure of confidence. I came home and spent most of the evening telephoning prospects. Evelyn said she'd adore to skate with me and so would Phil until he went up to Oxford, that she hadn't done it for ages and had never really been good and had put on weight and was terrified of falling ('You must remember I'm nearly fifty, Ara!'), Daisy Field ('Didn't I remember, Ara darling?') had weak ankles and had never been allowed on the ice, Clover and Primrose hadn't any skates and could anyway only come with me on Saturdays because of their work, Léonore thought it too far away but recommended several possible skaters none of whom I knew, Johnnie Lawnford I was displeased with and he, too, would be only available at weekends, Estelle would be fearful of catching cold and the doughty Mr. Martin was eighty or over. Illogically and unjustly I dismissed the lot of them as stick-in-the-muds.

In my bedroom, it suddenly came back to me that Mell used to christen some of the Abemethys from an Edward Lear story, 'Violet, Slingsby, Guy and Lionel'.

I thought, 'Mell, who *was* Miss Spicer?'

But there was no Mell plaiting her hair into a door-knocker by the window dressing-table.

The gong sounded for my dinner.

7

It was when I was returning one fine, chill evening from the ice that I thought it would be pleasant to look up the younger Ackworth-Meads who, as we were never on intimate terms, came low upon my list. Their immense house being nearer Kingsmarket than Addison was conveniently close to my skating stretch; whatever they proved to be like they would give me warmth and a good tea, and if they didn't like my outfit, which was brief and furred, I didn't seem to mind in the least.

It was dusk, pricked by the globe lights on their gate-posts, as I reached the house, a line of cars with a plentiful sprinkling of station flys was jerkily processing round that huge drive to the front doors; through the panes of a cab that halted abreast of me a child's face peered, upon its well-brushed hair twinkled a sequin star.

It was one of the Ackworth-Mead parties! So, Trevor and his wife were keeping up the tradition …

I stood back under a concealing rhododendron bush. I simultaneously wanted to be invited inside and lost in the crowd of other children and was thankful that as a woman this boring and Institutional function could be mine no more. As the small star-topped fairy passed me I thought, 'My poor child, you little know the time you're in for. But *I* could tell you!'

Edging off, I knew that I was possessively envious of those pierrettes and fairies, yet I knew they must grow up and away.

Miss Barbara Morant is called for!

The Misses Field! The Misses Field!

Highflown homilies aren't in my line, and I prefer to remember that I fell into the drawing-room at Evenfield and snapped up an incredible quantity of hot buttered toast.

CHAPTER V

I

I SPENT Christmas Night with the Fields, had allowed my vague and high-falutin plans and faint apprehensions to be swept aside and hardly knew whether I was relieved or disappointed. Glad as I was to be with them, my mind was burrowing up to the last minute for a precedent. Did one leave Evenfield on Christmas Day? Had we ever?

I filled up time with a later breakfast, church, and personal calls with some presents – a pretty country custom I have read of so often and which doesn't seem to be observed in real life: certainly in London your friends on receiving your present on the right and proper day feel that they are last-moment duties belatedly remembered and no gift which does not arrive a week in advance is taken seriously, so perverse are the times in which we live.

By nightfall I was listless, almost regretful that I hadn't closed with Mrs. Jasperleigh's offer of luncheon and tea at Broadacres, yet I experienced a pang on leaving a darkened drawing-room and shutting the front door upon myself. But, had our old Christmases been such a success once the exciting morning was over? Hadn't the doldrums set in after midday dinner? Hadn't father been irascible and more than usually sensitive to my own shrieks of joy and tears of satiety? And mustn't it all have been quite extraordinarily wearing for mother, especially with Cuss at home, damning the whole place as a dog-hole? And why had I suddenly got to have this aspect of things forced upon me, and to-night of all nights?

2

But the light and warmth of Cumptons was waiting for me, calculable, unchanged affection from a family united in numbers as they were in thought. They had altered, of course, but never having lost touch with them I was ready for that: Mrs. Field's fair, springing hair was grey, Arnold Field nearly white (and most becoming, as I told him), and once one had grudgingly assimilated and accepted the height and maturity of the girls there was nothing left to look for or fear …

Removing my wraps in a bedroom I had slept in I managed to convey to Mrs. Field that I hoped nobody would feel it necessary to be sympathetic with me on mother's account or give me special treatment of manner, or by abating so much as one giggle or paper game, and she answered, 'Oh chicky, that's so like her! No, I promise we shall all be just ourselves'. And they were, bless them, and Mr. Field chaffed me with a sub-acid edge on his words about my songs, for which I blessed *him*, but it sometimes seemed to me that the girls, particularly Clover, were making me feel, even for that house where we were always made to feel it, slightly too much the guest of honour, that they listened to my lightest nonsense a shade too fervently as to an oracle deigning to be facetious: it was a mere impression, but it certainly put me apart from them while it lasted, made me in some curious way older than any of them, responsible if not too happily for my own actions instead of, as once, comfortably, irresponsibly merged in my own family.

We sat in the music-room after dinner and talked, and I unloaded everything I had accumulated, of like and dislike and discovery, and asked copious questions about things and people.

'And oh, Ara, *have* you decorated the nursery at Evenfield with paper chains? You and Mell always used to and you did love it so.' I had, and said so, and asked about their own, but they had stopped all that long ago. 'We're getting staid and dull, Ara, and you must cheer us all up.'

'Oh Ara, *do* you remember when a chain fell down on Aggie and Mrs. Morant said she looked like a York ham? She used to imitate Aggie beautifully. And the vicar! "The kingdom of heaven ish like a little grain of mushtard sheed"–'

'Obstinate fellow *he* was,' Mr. Field informed his pipe. 'What d'you think of the new one?'

'I'm told that I shall like and dislike him much more; apart from that he just seems like so much cubic clergyman, to me. I'm willing to oblige, either way. Do I know a Miss Spicer, by any chance? I'm asking because I invited her to tea, but *who is she*?' Mrs. Field began to weep with amusement, and nobody knew, and we all laughed. It was Daisy who said, 'It's funny how *utterly* unlike Mrs. M you are in some ways, Ara. She told us that she used to go round corners and be late for lunch to avoid meeting people.'

'She had to live here,' I pointed out.

'Anyway, they all adored her,' championed Primrose. 'I expect your Miss Spicer did, too.'

'And I'm just a hangover, and in disgrace in several directions;' I answered, 'except with Mr. Grimstone, and in a little while I shall feel my position *that* keen and go and live in sin with him.'

'Your mother liked the Grimstones,' said Mrs. Field.

'Isn't that a good thing! Otherwise, the whole place is being like a large bran pie.'

'Mrs. Grimstone was a dear woman but suffered so terribly at the last.' This, in the old days, was so often the coda to Mrs. Field's dossiers that while intrinsically sympathetic I nearly exploded, and it came back to me that mother once actually *had*, when Mrs. Field, concluding a eulogy of some stainless soul, added, 'She was a great influence for good in Addison but used to get such terrible screaming fits.' Regrettable are the things from which one derives comfort, for this preposterous souvenir seemed to be a connection with mother – a Greetings telegram! – and an assurance that I in my turn was a Morant of Addison. I told them of the Ackworth-Mead party and Arnold Field remarked that the young Ackworth-Meads were too grand to call on 'the likes of us', a comment softened for me by his wife who said that the old people had been so generous to Addison charities and that she hoped I would call on their son and his wife.

'I will, I will! But remind me first who Trevor married. I've dropped enough bricks lately to build a line of workmen's dwellings.' We flung ourselves upon the Jasperleighs and I reminded the girls of that fancy-dress party and of Thelma as The Belle of New York, and the Siddons ring on my finger reminded me of Clifford as Widow Twankey and I told them a lot about him, and Mrs. Field was tenderly interested, tentatively, tactfully romantic (which unnerved me) and the girls contributed nothing at all, as they quietly admired the ring.

I asked about their own work and Clover said that she had given up her former job and was now assistant designer to a Kingsmarket firm of children's outfitters and bicycled in every day; Primrose was secretary to a doctor I didn't know in Addison itself. 'I think he works her too hard, but it's nice for her to live at home,' her mother said. Daisy had no paid occupation. 'We couldn't lose them all,' Mrs. Field murmured fondly, 'it's lovely to have her here.'

3

One of the few authentic surprises that Addison life was to give me came from Thelma Lawnford (and this time I shall expect you to remember that she had married the manure-throwing Chetwyn). For although I never became really fond of her, as was right and proper, I was to develop a certain wry-mouthed enjoyment of her society.

You may not enjoy being electrocuted but you are forced to pay attention to the shock, and Thelma was in a way a live wire: it happened to be in the wrong way, but the current was at least switched on. I had been to see her several times – I had to, or become embroiled in the Lord knows what, and discovered a sharp-tongued mondaine with no *monde* to belong to, who ran her eye over my outfit and furs and said as she kissed the air nearest both my jawbones that there was no mistaking Bradley.

'Mistaking it for what, Thelma? If you mean my cape, it came from Barker's.'

'My dear girl, you're not serious?'

'"My dear girl", I am.'

She drooped her eyelids and became what I understand the Victorian kitchen condemned as Lah-di-dah, and indeed it is an admirable epithet which should never have fallen into disuse.

'Johnnie says you're making a jolly good thing out of music.'

'Thelma, I haven't seen you for quite five years, must we talk about money?'

That stung her. 'And talking of Johnnie, what on earth have you been saying, Ara? He and Estelle don't seem to exactly rave over you. Of course I told them you were nice, really, when one's got past your manner.'

'My dear, shut up. And show me the house. Mrs. Jasperleigh says it's perfect.'

'Oh, mother!' droned Thelma. 'She thinks so because she insisted on running the whole thing, you know her way.'

I did, and cautiously grinned. 'She wanted nothing but Storey stuff –'

'And of course you were out for Mulvane,' I stated, inventing a firm on the spot.

'Well – what do you think!'

I began to see daylight in the midst of my enjoyment at pulling her leg, realized that never would Addison contain two adult Jasperleighs, that one of them must clear out, that the mother wouldn't and the daughter couldn't, married as she was to a local doctor, that Thelma was taking it all out in disparagement of a perfectly good if conventional home while her mother defensively extolled it, and what a pity it all was. How much a pity I saw later when Chetwyn came in from his rounds, and Thelma, unable to express herself in *décor*, made her marital authority unmistakable and ordered him about like a butler. He seemed to be the makings of a nice man, this old acquaintance of mine, though it was difficult to see him through her dust. He was quiet, and disposed to sit by me and talk over old times. When he left us, Thelma put down her cup and laughed mirthlessly.

'Chet seems quite gone on you. Were you one of his girls in the old days, I can't remember?'

I put down my piece of cake and rose. 'Well, good-bye Thelma, I must be getting on, I've one or two other people to see.'

She knew. The morbid and over-sensitive at least react quickly to atmospherics. 'Don't go, Ara, I was only joking.'

'I think I should have thought more of you if you'd meant it. It would have at least shown some human feeling.'

'Well – I'm sorry.' Her eyes filled but failed to move me: tears were ever a Jasperleigh resource. I sat down. 'No bones broken.'

'Oh I know I'm hateful, but it's all so hateful here. I ought to be in London.'

'Then why did you let yourself in for a life in Addison?'

'I thought I could make something of Chet but he's perfectly contented here. I ask you!'

'It's his home and the competition in town is awful, you'd never have such a nice house, there.'

'Why not? Mother would shell out.'

'Can you see any man liking that position?'

'Well … we've had a lot of rows about it already.'

'Thelma, do forgive me, but why with all your chances did you marry him?'

'It was mother, of course. If she'd let men and me alone more there were one or two things that might have come to something, so I made up my mind I'd have someone I'd chosen by myself.' Husband or upholstery, it was all the same to Thelma, but I couldn't help a sneaking sympathy. She gave a brief laugh. 'Luckily Chet was always gone on me. I say, it's funny to be talking like this when we never did make a go of it, isn't it?'

'Pretend we're two new acquaintances,' I suggested, 'and see how we get on; it would be rather fun if we began to like each other.' She laughed at that, and even did touch my jawbone, this time, but this was the child whose nose I had punched for reasons as valid to-day as they were at eleven years old. I think the right woman could have re-made her, with time; husbands are no good, they throw away their aces out of chivalry or throw in their hand altogether, and that's the finish, and a doctor may enjoy being fee'd for ministering to vapours on his rounds but doesn't want to meet them unprofitably in his home.

The telephone rang twice while we finished tea and it was impossible not to hear Mrs. Lawnford's voice, off hand and brusque, as she dealt with her husband's messages. 'Well, you should've rung up before. You know what his surgery hours are, they haven't changed that I know of.' She lounged back and we stood looking out at that well-known view of the Park gates and Keeper's Lodge.

'It's so boring I could pass out. And one can't go up to London all the time.'

'Why don't you get something to do, Thelma?'

'Such as?'

'Well, isn't there anything going on here any more? What price the Dramatic Society?'

'It's all run by the Ackworth-Meads and they make an unholy mess of it. I've often told them how it could be improved.'

'Isn't there a Badminton Club?'

'Oh, my dear girl! And have to meet the Bertie Finnises and the Buckles and those awful Ramsdens? Why, the Finnises are the tinned fish people in Kingsmarket.'

'The poor no use to you, I suppose?'

'Oh, I don't mind going to see the clean ones. It doesn't do one any harm to be seen doing that as you don't have to have them to the house, but I'm not going to become one of the parish tabbies, it's a pretty good confession of failure.'

'Thelma, nobody ever denied that Addison's full of stumers – you should have heard mother on the subject! – but you can always avoid 'em, as she did. There are others, you know. There are the Stortfords –'

'A hundred and fifty!'

'Dears, and fun: then there's Evelyn –'

'I can't stand that sarcastic devil and she's as indiscreet as they're made. You'd better be careful.'

'Unfortunately the same things amuse us. Well, the Fields?'

'Oh Lord! a family of earnest females!'

'Our oldest friends.'

'Sorry, but what can one *do* with 'em?'

'Talk to them. They'll answer. Get to know them, you've had twenty-five years to do it in.'

'Can you wonder your mother cleared out of the place?'

I looked her in the eye. She knew. 'No. I no longer wonder, if I ever did.' She avoided my eye as she mumbled, 'Well, there you are then'.

'No, I'm not. Get this clear. Mother never left Addison because it wasn't Park Lane or what you would call smart, or because somebody's furs didn't come from the right shop or somebody else tinned sardines or the shops weren't Fortnum and Mason –'

'Then what's your idea in coming back here? Want to run the place?'

'I'm just audience. No cards up the sleeve.'

'And I suppose the next thing'll be everybody'll be rushing to offer you Addison on a plate, as they used to.'

'Thelma, you are so unhappy, aren't you?'

She was sobbing, now. 'You needn't be afraid, Thelma.'

But it didn't quite end there, for Chetwyn developed a habit of stopping at my gate on his way home for the talks I would have welcomed and I had to scotch all that, which hurt us both. Even over sherry and firelight he never got within a mile of criticism of his wife, but she wouldn't believe it, and I saw that from now on our only approved exchanges must be via a bed of sickness. Disappointed men are always difficult to handle in any case, and apt to say and do damaging things they only half mean, and if I was to be clutched to illegitimate bosoms I was quite determined that I should least enjoy the process. It was, I often thought when Chetwyn had left me, a pity that one licensed bosom wasn't available, for I would have liked to cast myself upon Clifford's much and often, there was nothing drifting or amorphous about *him*. On the other hand men who love you are very all-or-nothing and women don't always want a pistol at their head, but notice and soothing. And panting a little, flattened a little more, I still hadn't finished with Addison.

4

By this time I had rather thrown up the sponge about social contacts, and waited in the vast Ackworth-Mead drawing-room not caring who came in or what, having arrived, it looked like, said or thought. Only to find that Trevor and his Domrémy wife, whom I have never known well, whose faces I had long forgotten, were the kind of actual, pleasant people you encounter in any London house and that we were free to make a fresh start with each other with no sentimental cans tied to the tail.

If it were true that Trevor had married the wrong sister by mistake on that river picnic you would never have guessed it, for which I applauded him: they seemed to suit each other remarkably well, but then, they'd been married for many years now. We three were to become friends, and I felt that I had passed the test when Trevor, on my alluding to Thelma, screwed his monocle, and tapping a bulldog on the head as we lounged in the morning-room one spring day, said, 'Ah, poor girl, I never could stand her, myself.'

I rewarded him. 'Trevor, do you know that I once mistook you for a waiter at one of your parties?'

'What? Oh good, distinctly good. 'Smatter of fact the chaps the parents hired were better turned out. The Pater used to have economy-waves sometimes, and once, my God, bought me a dinner jacket in Kingsmarket.' His Domrémy wife chimed in. 'My father never suffered that way. He just went bust.'

'Yes, yes. I call that definitely thorough,' assented Trevor, pounding the bulldog.

And they have two quite nice children to whom I am now auntie Babs, so that I have, after all, my roots in the local soil whatever happens.

5

An event which should also have made me happy was that Hope Couchman got married to that foreman who oversaw the erection of the lean-to bedroom I had given her. But I felt a dangerous matchmaker, darting in to alter lives, and although the marriage has been an exceptionally happy one a selfish portion of me regrets a change for which I am almost entirely responsible in the partial disintegration of a family from the group to which I was and wanted to remain accustomed, on which my mind's eye could rest at will. But there it was. And although Hope and her husband live in Addison and even near Nutts Lane, she had moved on.

I went to the wedding, and back in the Couchman cottage and by urgent request, proposed the health of the bride, ruddy and shining in the dress and hat which were my present to her, and we were even herded out into the alley for a wedding group by a local photographer (which hung in his window for four months and scorched me with shame whenever I passed it). But home at Evenfield I banged my beautiful pearl gloves together and one of them split.

'Damn the creatures! It's as though the people in a family album suddenly got up and walked out of their mounts.'

6

And harassment came from a quarter where I had counted upon security. Whether it was a large or small concern depends upon the point of view; most women of my age (I must learn to put it that way and try to feel it as well) would have laughed it off, but as each case is considered by me on its merits regardless of age I have never been successful at generalized flippancy. I had known it in a way almost ever since I met Phil Ivor, but any real feeling behind it had been obscured for me in my gladness to be back at Evenfield and gratification at being accepted and actually liked by the younger generation, a circumstance which, again, could be traceable to my musical successes.

He had dined with me one warm night of early May and was his companionable self, chaffing me, putting me right, and being very fluent and positive and incoherent about everything until challenged, when he went to pieces as they always do, and making elaborate jokes which left me guessing and being at all times difficult to hear, as they always are at that age, until Mabel brought in coffee and left us. And from that moment he became a very shy young man instead of a very fearless old boy, and was subdued and deferent and long-leggedly agile with doors and more difficult to hear than ever, and generally speaking would not let the winds of heaven visit my face too roughly. But as it had only just finished being April I wore a fur which he adjusted – rather often and most uncomfortably, poor child, and when at the third attempt I felt that knobby wrist of his taking its time on the job and a bit more, I understood, pitied the mental conflict that must have preceded his daring in putting his arm through mine. A milestone passed! The first hurdle leaped! And I thought of another arm in mine, a thicker one without qualms (which hadn't seemed to like the proximity!) on another night out here among my rose-trees, and it wasn't Clifford being affronted at an unprotected female being forthcoming but Clifford meticulous lest he become it himself. And how well he would have forthcome! with what instinctive smoothness and acrid touches all his own – like a Chopin Impromptu … and here I was in the scented dusk with a Polka Mazurka. And the unhappy mass of incoherences whose saner components were Phil Ivor stopped with a jolt and said more inaudibly than ever, 'I do love you, you know.' Of course I was pleased and sorry and flattered and amused as any decent woman is at these moments, but that hurdle leapt without damage, my amusement was wiped out as Phil began to have a great deal to say that misgave me. It amounted to the fact that Addison and Kingsmarket, his home and college and father and mother and everything that was his, had sufficed him until I came on the scene, that because of me and all I suggested he now perceived his feminine contemporaries to be inadequate, limited, suburban, off-colour, what you will. And he was glad he'd seen it in time, and it was all rather frightful, wasn't it? when one had got to live in a place …

And he asked me to kiss him and I did, as his mother might have, and felt elderly and responsible and uncertain and probably a bad influence as well out there in the garden where I had always been the youngest, where I had meant to be so happy.

CHAPTER VI

I

I GAVE A PARTY a few weeks later, and I made it a Book Tea for the sake of old times. My guests would probably want the bridge I had never learnt to play – let 'em!, or come to me to ask how one played my game, and I didn't care. Except for Primrose and Clover Field who were unable to come because of their work (that was wrong: Fields just aren't unable to come to Morant parties) I invited everybody I knew including Miss Abernethy and dear old Miss Ambrose (who, bless her démodé soul, crept in on that warm afternoon swathed in a woollen scarf and white with the heat as *If Winter Comes*), and I filled the drawing-room with an overflowing into the billiard room; there was tea on the veranda and lawn and a Kingsmarket band whose conductor I exhorted not to play any of my lyrics.

To my surprise the party was a success: as Thelma put it, 'These things are so ancient I suppose they've come round again and everybody'll be Book Tea-ing soon.'

It was when the majority of the guests had dispersed up and down the road and only a residue of intimates remained that I realized that a crowd is protective, stifling perception by sheer weight of numbers. For, looking round at all these faces familiar to me from my earliest years, I suddenly ceased to be able to merge myself in them or to take my old place in their lives and regard; as in those first weeks in Kensington Gate when they came to London to look us up, I saw them once more as just people in the flat, and could find no margin of sentiment anywhere that could save them for me. I felt in that moment an absolute rancour against the lot of them for the stresses and emotions which they had caused me, that some glamour which was an aura about them all had gone completely, that we were in the last resort simply a handful of women in a suburban drawing-room – I really believe that their age was the only thing I didn't lay up against them! And it was all quite extraordinarily painful. And when they had gone

I sat in the nursery and played an abstracted game of Snakes and Ladders with plenty of cheating, and cried a little.

2

I went next day after tea to see the Fields, being rather badly in need of general consolation, and only Daisy was in to welcome me. But this was no London visit with one eye on the clock: I now had all the time there was for Fields or anybody else in Addison. Yet Daisy said the others would be disappointed at missing me, and suddenly, 'You know, I can't believe you're back here, Ara. Every time you get up to leave I think you're going back to town with Mrs. M ...', and then very soberly, 'You don't look a bit well, darling, mother's very worried about you. We hate to think of you all alone at Evenfield.'

I found myself at the window, looking out at the Cumptons fence and some singularly repellent semi-detached houses opposite which my eye had always known and my mind never.

'But – one never is alone, Daisy.'

'You mean? ... do you ever see your mother?'

'No, my dear.'

She was picking at the peacock-blue ball-fringe of the mantelpiece.

'Would you like to?'

'I don't know, Daisy. She'd know what one could stand –'

'Yes, wouldn't she! But you always make me feel you could face anything.'

At least I was definite about that. 'No. Too breakable. There was something about her that was –', I couldn't select the word, and stopped, for 'tempered' sounded affected, '– flexible, unbeatable, perhaps. Your mother has it too, I think, that quality. Our lot is still on the grope and goes to pieces before things like reality. Perhaps they kept us young too long? Were too fond of us? D'you know what I mean?' But I was startled by the fervour of her agreement. 'I've so often felt that about *us*. Ara, when mother and father go I literally don't know what'll happen to me. I can't see any future apart from them. And I can't make up my mind whether you did the best thing in coming back here. I even hoped for your sake at the time that you'd only lease Evenfield for the holidays, as you first planned to.' I seemed to be sitting at the piano, this time, and even playing a few bars. 'Daisy, I've just discovered that the opening chorus of *The Mikado* is practically The Athanasian Creed. Listen:

Who-so-ever would be sav-éd

(*We are gentlemen of Japan*):

but her shocked appreciation wasn't as instant as usual. She smiled at me, but went on, 'I've always advised Primrose and Clover to get work as far away as possible. It's so important to change the atmosphere, but every job is so jolly specialized, now'.

I looked at Daisy, seeing no longer the eldest of 'the little Fields', but a woman with opinions, hinting at things from which I shrank.

3

It bothered me for days, and I took it to Evelyn, into whose house I could now enter without qualms, Phil being up at Oxford again. Cumptons had been my rock of ages and rocks must have no vulnerable surfaces. Evelyn would be normal and direct and emollient – she knew the Fields.

'Daisy wasn't for one second complaining, Evelyn, and of course it *is* important to change atmospheres, as she says, but in the old days one never used to think about things like that. One just lived and enjoyed everything.'

'Yes, but I don't think they ever had the good times you and Mell did. There never was much money in music –'

'But dammit, Evelyn, money isn't everything – I don't want to sound like a novelette and I shall be saying that Love Is All next, but money *isn't*.'

'It matters an awful lot in a place like Addison, Ara; why even here in Kingsmarket I'm feeling better for the change already.' We both laughed, and she went on, 'I don't think the Fields ever really got over the business about Clover.'

'*What?*'

'Didn't you know, Ara? But how incredible! But of course it was long after you left.'

I waited.

'Didn't mother ever tell you or Mrs. M about it? That's like mother. And the Fields never said a word to you? Well, I *am* blowed. But that's like them, too. Clover – well, d'you remember the Irmine boy, Richard, the one they called Rikky?'

'Not in the least.'

'No, I suppose you were always too young, he'd be my age now, or over. Well he had a frightful crush on Mrs. Randolph – d'you remember *her*?'

'Pull yourself together, Evelyn!'

'Oh, of course she lived next door to you –'

'– golden hair and rumoured to have been on the stage.'

'*That's* it. But of course she never was. Well, Rikky Irmine was practically engaged to Clover Field, anyway she wore a ring, I used to meet them at dances and badminton, and she was frightfully in love with him. He was a pal of the Barstowes, by the way.'

I had to listen. If Clifford had been involved in this, or even his brother, John … *he grew very good-looking* … and something about John having a narrow squeak with one of the local maidens … If a Barstowe had hurt a Field …

But Evelyn was saying things, and my ear told me that all was well – for me.

'– and then Rikky quite suddenly got bowled over by Mrs. Randolph, we never could make out why as he'd lived three hundred yards from her all his life, but it was one of those overtakements that do happen when people are all bottled up together and she was very pretty in that sort of way and knew how to make the most of herself as young girls never do, and dressed well and so on, though your mother did call her "The Chiffonier" –'

'And he chucked Clover?'

'No, he wasn't all *that* cad, he must have just made it impossible for her to go on with it (I'm not sure that's not worse). We all saw it, I mean it was *too* obvious (mother gave Rikky hell, by the way; she could do things like that, you know)'. I didn't, but I stared at Evelyn as I muttered 'Good for her'.

'I'm so glad that poor old Phil fell into your hands, Ara. He's absolutely *crippled* with infatuation, and when he's got over you he'll probably have a real affair with a shopgirl and then simmer down until he marries.'

4

And after this, and all that summer, I found I could no longer see anything or anybody clearly, objectively, even retrospectively; I felt alone and fixed in a time of my own which had no past, present or future. I was no longer a real resident, was too committed and versed to be a visitor, that which I had thought familiar was overlaid by facts hurled at me too late for sane assimilation. I even lost my critical bearings, saw Thelma Lawnford at one moment as a discontented matrimonial cheat, at the next as a pitiful woman with a genuine case against her spoilt life, Chetwyn as a trojan of quiet loyal endurance and decency and as a henpecked weakling, Johnnie Lawnford as a suburban bounder and a harmless nonentity to whom I'd been tactless, Evelyn as reassuring friend and prize example of indiscretion, myself as a very damned specimen of unreasonableness, subtly defrauded, yet suffering a grief to which I was not officially entitled.

I saw Addison as a growing tentacle of Outer London, a bus-route full of flavourless, ordinary people whom circumstances had happened to make me know and as a large village with a meadow studded with buttercups, ringed about with laughter and event and love, the most significant place on earth.

5

And then Evenfield started upon me and it chose its moment well, counting upon our lifelong knowledge of each other in its choice of tactics and playing upon my weakest spots – or, I sometimes hoped, the house was so sorry that it used deprecatory arguments to show me it realized inability to keep my pace and satisfy me. It even ceased to be a refuge, for upon my returns to it from shopping or skating and tea-parties I could no longer count upon my own feelings; on one day I saw it as just a large and meaningless house in which I happened to live, and on the next as my devoted home, incredibly minus mother cutting out a gilt cardboard crown in the day-nursery, Mell charging round the asphalt paths, Aggie doggedly removing soaked copies of *Little Folks* that I had left overnight in the hammock, and even father debating with me by the billiard-room fire the merits of Christmas cards bought that morning in Kingsmarket. He had his moments ...

Surely when mother made her own returns to Evenfield the whole house sprang to light and life? For me, the light goes up only when I press the switch ...

I thought of stripping the place of all reminiscent furnishings, and actually did dismantle and redecorate the dining-room, which promptly became nothing at all but a room for which I was now solely responsible, and only deepened my conviction of personal inadequacy, so that I began to believe that even Mrs. Jasperleigh or the unknown Miss Spicer would have filled the stage better than I, have dominated the drawing-room, mastered the garden and quelled the kitchen to more purpose.

Evenfield and I had a hard time with each other through that hot summer when the dust lay on the lime-trees and the lawn turned brown no matter where Sims moved the sprinkler. For every room I settled or ate in had something to say, and it took the disconcerting form of unerring presentation to my memory of innumerable small items calculated to put me out of conceit with my old home (the dining-room was particularly adept at this). I would sit at table, relieved to be back in comparative coolness, anxious to be happy there, and was insidiously assailed by a row between Cuss and father, an irate man mismanaging a sulky boy, unwisely tactless from exasperation, while mother looked harassed, *and for the first time feeling that row*, as shell-shock will strike years later; a moment (had it happened? Was this subconscious memory stored by a Barbara Morant newly promoted to family luncheon, or merely Evenfield urging me, edging me out?) when mother exclaimed that she could *not* stand this sort of thing and for heaven's sake let's have peace at meal-times ... Mell dismally crying over her German by candlelight ... mother taken ill at tea one winter evening and having to give up and go to bed, gasping that it was 'these accursed river fogs' and that 'the place' never had agreed with her, and of my inarticulate fury at anyone just letting her go upstairs while father merely said that her chest was never her strongest point, and of the empty misery the house became until she was down once more: of old Doctor Lawnford refusing to let me into her room and of my kicking him on the shins and screaming so that I woke mother from her needed sleep.

The nursery, telescoping time, made me aware of the long tracts of doldrums in which I sat there becalmed playing Solitaire where once Mell had faced me across the table and drawn pages of dragons for my entertainment, and of finding tea-time with Aggie presiding a boring business of bread and butter and distaste for Mell's avidity over jam after her school luncheons (*Drink in a Bournemouth cup*, in fact!). And wasn't the hall much too narrow for the size of the house and now permeated for ever with my knowledge of suicide in the weir?

I really do believe that the spare-room came best out of the business: it knew I had never cared for it, bore no malice, and had nothing with which to flail me beyond innocuous reminiscence of a gas fire that stifled one and the room's occupancy by a few duty-visitors including the inevitable aunt Caroline. But were my nursery guests always welcomed graciously by an Ara who hated to see her toys handled by other children, and mustn't they sometimes have gone home thinking she was a little beast, thinking it to this day when recalling those times as men and women, not too late for me to put it right, perhaps, but eternally too late in the room where I had been a little beast, where the impression of little-beastliness was photographed upon the air for ever? ... Wasn't I standing on the very strip of floor whose right to practise Indian clubs and dancing steps upon Mell and I disputed so endlessly and even unto blows ... and what was it that had left the garden for ever, so that while looking exactly the same it was all entirely different and lacking in incident, and walking in it one was now never oblivious of time and business and the outside world?

In the house I went from room to room, thinking at one minute 'You win!', in the next 'This has been my fault, not yours'. I found a certain amount of completely insensitive en-joyment in what local doings there were, fêtes, garden-parties, and so on, and had the Ackworth-Mead children much with me in the garden, and felt fifty when we were together and fifteen when they were gone.

I only once came partially to life and vulnerability when poor Couchman died. Dispassionately considered, his release from years of invalidism and monotony and the tax he must have known himself to be upon the family energy and purse was the best thing that could have happened, a matter of time in any case – he was seventy-four, they told me. But in the Couchman cottage, and looking down at my first dead face (to my surprise without shock or physical distress) the practical issues receded while Mrs. Couchman smoothed his hair as though he merely slept and said, 'He is with the dear Saviour'. She was so sure, in faith as in love to me and mine, while I put my flowers by her husband's side and considered what he had stood for in my life: a call with mother armed with tobacco, and sweets for Hope and Connie, the sight of him gardening in his little plot and the tell-tale fleck of colour even then upon his cheekbones, a little-known man who was to be my first sight of death, and I was glad, and told them so, that it was of the family of our oldest friends.

CHAPTER VII

I

I PASSED Chetwyn Lawnford one morning: he was out on his rounds but pulled up the car and stated without preamble, 'You're not looking too grand'. I responded as one does that I was all right and he drove on with a wave. But he slowed again by the Bank and signalled me. 'Are you seeing too many people or not enough?' I didn't know, but was unprepared there on the pave-ment to present him with my rather recent dreads of being alone and my even stronger apathies towards remedying that condition.

Back in my quiet road I came to the conclusion that I shunned the idea of having friends too much with me lest at that very moment my familiars might choose to come back. One must be ready and available, and mother always hated tea-parties … increasingly, like a forgotten name on the tip of one's tongue, they were at the back of my mind, on the verge of manifestation, mother and Mell, father and Aggie, so that I was never my own man. And once my eyes played me a strange trick. I was coming back the rather long walk from luncheon with the Ackworth-Meads, and even the fences of gardens in my road seemed sagging with the heat, yet on reaching the gates of Evenfield, the drive and lawn lay under a powdering of snow through which some crocuses were thrusting, as they used to. And as I quite torpidly became aware of this, the whole illusion slid aside and there was the grassplot dry as a bone under the August sun and the paint blistering on the porch.

It worried me a bit, but increased my expectancy. If things like that could happen. …

I began to stay in house and garden more than ever. This being the case, it was tiresome how chronically tired one was. I thought at last that lack of exercise might after all be what ailed me, and with an effort I went upstairs and put on my old ballet skirts and turned on the gramophone.

It occurred to me as I went through *grands* and *petits battements*, *pliés* and the centre practice of *arabesques* and *développés*, with a lack of verve that would have roused Hervet to his most caustic flights of sarcasm, that not once had a soul in Addison approached me for a solo item at any of the entertainments in the Parish Room, yet I could, and knew it, still dance them off the programme if I chose. I had to stop work and think it out, and was thankful for the rest.

Presumably, the Ackworth-Meads who ran the Dramatic Society didn't realize, or had forgotten, that I was among other things a dancer. But Madame Fouqué and Léonore, who still, through Mayvale, contributed so heavily to local exhibition? I could only suppose that now I literally never occurred to them. As an Old Girl I was older history: Old Girls could be anything, including grandmothers, but no longer in the lists. Or was it a hangover of resentment on Madame's part that I had flouted her offer of occupying Miss Anson's shoes? And I supposed that Addison looked upon me as a householder, who engaged cooks.

The Addison children: was I already in that remote category which was Mummy's-friend-who-comes-to-tea? Had I at nine, ten and eleven regarded the thirties as the shelf and decrepitude? I couldn't remember.

A daurrling child. That was Madame, on the latest Ninetta Crummles at Mayvale. And between the lot of them, it seemed, I was to dance no more.

2

The gong rang for luncheon, and at the top of the stairs, where once I had slid upon my stomach down the broad banisters, raced by Mell on an iron tea-tray, I discovered that I couldn't even walk down: neither will nor muscles responded when I tried.

I hung on to the banisters, hot with the first fear I had ever known, managed to say something about being late, and the stairs went on slanting dangerously to the foot of my own bed, where for some reason Mell stood looking across at me.

3

She said, '*One* two, and-sink-the-heels', and handed me not beef tea but a brandy and soda, and took one herself.

'*Mell?*'

'My dear old thing, what *have* you bin a'doin' of?'

I was instantly, hotly alarmed; perhaps after all she was crocuses and snow in August?

'Have I –? Am I –?'

'You're all right; here's Chetwyn', and she produced him as one old friend does with another, to my content, and he had a drink too and we all looked at each other and were cheerful.

'Nerves and badly run-down. Well, Mell, I must push off, now. I like your booze. Miss, here, keeps a good cellar. I'll be along again soonish.' Apprehension stirred in me once more, and he answered obliquely, 'Nothing, I think, that Mell can't cope with, now. I merely do the jug and bottle department', and to Mell,

'Keep her warm, and quiet if you can. She's rather a Wiry Sal, you know'.

'I know. Good-bye. Nice to see you again.'

4

Mell and her husband were home on eight months' leave, and I worried a little about the necessity for having this unfamiliar brother-in-law at Evenfield, but Mell waved all that aside, stated that she had parked him at his Club and that he quite agreed with her that I came first, that Cuss would take him about and that he and she could district-visit each other easily any time by bus.

Over the weeks that I was still under the eye of the doctor Mell and I covered immense tracts of ground. I asked her hopefully if I had begun to be suburban and she said not in the least, and asked had she started to be bungaloid and like Mrs. Reiver? I answered not as far as I could see, and she remarked that modern station cats weren't half as bad as they seem to have been in Kipling's time, and that their worst failing was a mental provincialism which left Addison at the post.

She told me that it was Mabel who had got into touch with her via Cuss when I had to be put to bed, two weeks ago. Mell was then expected at aunt Caroline's for a few nights before going into an hotel and deciding her own next move, if any. 'Mabel seems to have done all the right things,' said Mell.

'What happened?' I enquired as levelly as might be.

'Oh, you didn't come to lunch and she couldn't think what was up, so she came upstairs at last because the cook was getting riled, and found you –'

'What –?'

'On the nursery landing, in what Mabel calls bally skirts.'

'A faint?' I hated that possibility, had never done so before, and if once one started *that* –.

'I don't think so. Chetwyn seems to think it was more nerves and debility. Has anyone been worrying you, by the way?'

I shook my head, and it ended in that real talk which sooner or later was inevitable.

'I only wish it *had* been anything definite, Mell, like people being catty or slanderous, or edging one out of things; they were perfectly nice. But they don't seem to be doing their stuff in the way they used to: there are no scandals or suicides or anybody wanting to play Hamlet in tights, or being grinned over in Addison. A good many of them are still there, but they've turned into just people one once knew getting older.'

'Couldn't you have attacked 'em all over again on that basis?'

'I suppose I thought I was, but what I wanted was for them all to be the same.'

'No can do, I'm afraid, old dear. After all, they've got a right to go on from being family jokes and "the little Fields", just as you did.'

'I didn't! I was always the same, inside.'

'How would you expect her to like it if someone came back to Addison counting upon finding you as you used to be, even if you were grown up, and then discovering that you're really a Londoner-by-interest, have lived and made a name there and published waltzes that are on piano organs? D'you think that however much you got Evenfield back to the state it was when you left it it'd hoodwink anyone for a moment? They'd know at once that internally you'd moved on, however much you sat on a cosy corner and hung painted tambourines on the wall and The Flood on the staircase. Your only hope of enjoying the Addison crew is by walking with them, not pulling 'em back to you.'

'But then it's dull!'

'Aha! Then you must leave Addison. Indeed, you're going to.'

'No.'

'Yes. My dear, we're all agreed on that, Cuss and Chetwyn and Clifford Barstowe, it seems. It's a question of cutting your losses. If you stick on here, you may become meaningless, too, without getting any satisfaction out of the place, either. Mother kept on top gear by hating the place.'

And having said that, Mell cantered several times round the garden paths in the autumn twilight. I think, now, that she knew I was looking on from the spare-room window into which they had put me because of its better gas fire. And one wet afternoon we roasted chestnuts on the nursery bars; we even went into Kingsmarket and bought skipping-ropes ('I've got rather a bust now', said Mell, 'so perhaps they'll think it's to amuse the children I haven't got'), and with many a caution from her as to how we should both hate it, ran through all the exercises we could remember from Miss Anson's classes. I gave up first, saying, 'But I never did like skipping, so that doesn't count'.

'It's not bad', panted Mell hoarsely, her smart shingle flapping, 'but I can't do doubles again, yet.'

5

She went calling and pleased everyone, I think. Back at home we agreed that we liked Mrs. Jasperleigh, 'and if we were staying on here I'd positively get to know her,' said Mell.

It was so right, so utterly strange, to see Mell coming up and downstairs, sitting in drawing-room, loafing in garden, combing her hair at some oval swing-glass that I had pertinaciously haunted the London shops to reproduce … Most of the time I saw her as a married woman guest in my house, an Anglo-Indian being indulgent of my arrangements; but sometimes in rare flashes she fitted in, and was Mell, living at Evenfield, and then I didn't know whether I was most happy or unhappy. And Cuss came down several times; he even stayed a week-end, of sheer concern, as he told me months later, and I had him put in his old box-room quarters.

Mell had very gently and kindly approached me about mother's locked room, putting the question on housewifely grounds of airing and dusting and the state it must be in – Mabel had told her of the trunk from Switzerland, but I had my way there, and Mell, nonplussed, dropped the subject.

Cuss refused to look up anybody in Addison, but went for a Sunday prowl and came home with a splendid collection of confirmed hates and forgotten grievances and stridulous contempts which did far more to restore me than my tonic. Cuss, too, was faithful unto death in his own way … He even passed a certain tree in our road and something familiar about its boles reminded him that it was by that tree one morning that, accompanying father on a Sunday walk, they had met one of the curates, who innocently blew the gaff on Cuss by asking him how he had enjoyed the Gaiety show the previous Saturday afternoon, they having by the most malignant coincidence occupied adjacent seats in the pit; and then hell's lid flew off and all, said Cuss, was Old Testament and Cursed Be The Man, and He Who Liveth Or Maketh *A Lie* –. And that, as I told him, was exactly what didn't happen any longer in Addison; if people wanted to go to the Gaiety they went to it – only it was usually The Old Vic and tea at Lyons afterwards.

6

They worked over me with affectionate solicitude, that week-end, I don't know whether wisely or not, for in his straightforward desire to earn his keep and entertain me, Cuss would play to us in the evenings from the old musical comedy scores on my Kingsmarket piano, and in bed I would go to sleep to

> *By the light of the sleepy canal*

and

> *Under the deodar, lit by the evening star…*

Once he played a favourite of mother's, the Goldfish song from *The Geisha*, and in that moment I was back at home and all as it used to be, and leaving Evenfield incredible and impossible, and I'd fight them all to stay, so I remained with my own.

I got up, driven by impulse, and cautiously lest they hear me and be sensible and prohibitory, unlocked the door of mother's room and opened her trunk.

The clothes meant little: I had forgotten most of them and the rest she had bought after our parting. It was such trifles as a box of her face powder – *Peau d'espagne*, whose scent returned to me so immediately, that brought her with it, and there was the puff she had used, perhaps, before setting out on that walk … and I despaired entirely in her room, chilly and unaired and soft with dust.

> *For a ladies' maid must learn a bit*

played Cuss in the drawing-room below.

There was the manuscript copy of *Everybody Kept on Laughing*, her writing-case that Mell and I had clubbed together to buy for her birthday from Cecil Roy in Gloucester Road, and inside its compartments what I had forgotten to expect – her unposted letters on flimsy hotel notepaper, and I fell on them greedily, eavesdropping though it might be. They were so like her! And I could at least make Mrs. Field happy by giving her hers, and I envied every one of the addressees as the sheets were tucked back into their envelopes. The fourth letter began, 'Bless you, darling'. It was unfinished. And it was for me.

I read it so ravenously that I took in not one sentence, and locking door and trunk again went with it back to bed. The middle part of it had caught my eye for I saw the word 'Addison'.

'… I sometimes feel that if you ever got the chance you'd actually enjoy going back to Evenfield. You did love the awful old place so! heaven knows why, but you were always the easiest kid to please I ever met and a penny toy made you happy for the day, for which I liked you! And if when I hand in m' cheques you ever should go back I should quite understand, though I'm afraid these things don't work twice. I've sometimes hankered, and especially in Addison, for my old digs with Grandpa and Granny, and I daresay if it'd been possible I should have gone back to 'em, because I've a great notion of letting people *feel* their own mistakes. If one prevents 'em they only go on yearning – like Miss Dove over the vicar! Poor wretch. It's much better to have your head and be disappointed, then you're quit of the business. If I'd gone back to Portman Square I should have had many a facer, I warrant: new (and better) faces at balls, entertainment tapering off because of servant troubles and taxation, and so on. I had the cream of it, and I think you'd find you had, too … I used to sit mumchance in the drawing-room at Evenfield waiting for the blue mould to blossom on me. I could weather much, but nothing ever seemed to *happen*…'

So that was settled, and now I could go.

CHAPTER VIII

I

AND FOUR MONTHS later I was out of it all, sitting writing at my top window in The Boltons and getting the whole thing off my chest. The window faces a little garden like a Beardsley illustration in an old *Yellow Book* and has a stone cupid whose nose has long been blurred by rain and seasons from Grecian to snub.

And I stick my pen behind my ear and wonder what they are all doing at this moment in Addison, and sometimes a very faint sense of glamour comes over me.

Had it been worth while? I don't know. I have had what I wanted, done what I meant to do, and how many people can say as much?

I left Evenfield fully furnished with three years of lease still to run. I couldn't even then face the idea of letting it.

For months I couldn't feel or see clearly about the house: I have experienced it under too many conditions. And this, I think, is the worst of my losses, that every impression is now superimposed on another, that they will not lay themselves out neatly and in sequence, so that for one instant of time I am in mother's room tieing my first bow, resting before a party, and without transition Mrs. Willis is saying (in an empty night-nursery where I sit forlorn upon the floor with the house agent's key), 'I expect you find it very strange to see strangers in your old home'.

And, suppose I went back for the holidays, there is now another intruder to face – myself, in every room and deflated mood, waited upon by a long-departed Mabel, in the garden being calf-loved by a young man who has reached the stage of the platonic-facetious letter, and who, at time of writing, is heading towards a fix with a shopgirl in Cornmarket Street about which he tells me. Phil Ivor, at Oxford.

I shall always love the Fields, Evelyn, the Stortfords, appreciate Madame Fouqué, like the old Martins, be cautious with Thelma and cordial to Miss Abernethy. But, save for my warm liking for old Mr. Grimstone, wasn't this precisely the state of affairs when first we all left Addison?

Well, well! I had to laugh. And I *still* don't know who Miss Spicer is, and nor do Aggie, Mell or Cuss!

2

Mell likes Clifford, and that is good: she even recognized him when he first came to see us in Cuss's flat, which lent a kind of blessing to the affair and surprised me a lot, I can't think why.

3

Mell at dinner one night said that she felt less well in the hills than she expected to, after Quetta, and I asked the reason.

'Too high up, I suppose. Liver. It was something in the air', and I had to leave the table in case I forgot it, and by bedtime had roughed out a new lyric, *It was something in the air that made her do it*, a Beatrice Lillie number, I think, sung with dispassionate understatement and almost no punctuation. I could see her mouth uptwisted at one side …

I discussed it with Cuss at breakfast and telephoned it to the Guvnor, who was out, and I happily damned him, and the telephone rang and it was aunt Caroline wanting to come to tea, upon which I made a previous engagement with Clifford and meant to spend the evening after the Court rose in an atmosphere of wig-stands, Queen Anne brick and plane trees.

My heart suffers little pangs of pity for Evenfield, waiting patiently to be the whim of the next human. There are some of my dresses hanging up in one of the wardrobes.

THE END

FURROWED MIDDLEBROW

Made in the USA
Las Vegas, NV
13 July 2024